WITHOUT A CITY WALL

Richard Godwin is demoralised by his racketty
and successful career in London. Determined
to isolate himself in order to attempt to discover
a style of life in which he can believe, he goes to
a remote village in Cumberland. His arrival
coincides with the birth of an illegitimate child
to Janice Beattie, herself thus thwarted in no
less ambitious an effort to impose her will on
her existence.

It is between these two young people that the
story's chief action is concerned: their passion,
delight, desperation; the tragedies they cause
and the conflicts they arouse for all those who
come in contact with them, while the place itself
– the fells and industrial coastline of
Cumberland – imposes its own conditions and
perspectives.

WITHOUT A CITY WALL won the John
Llewelyn Rhys award in 1968.

Without a City Wall

Melvyn Bragg

CORONET BOOKS
Hodder and Stoughton

FOR MY GRANDFATHER
HERBERT IRVING BRAGG

Copyright © 1968 by Melvyn Bragg

First published in Great Britain 1968 by
Martin Secker & Warburg Limited

Coronet edition 1978

Printed and bound in Great Britain for
Hodder and Stoughton Paperbacks, a
division of Hodder and Stoughton Ltd.,
Mill Road, Dunton Green, Sevenoaks,
Kent (Editorial Office: 47 Bedford
Square, London, WC1 3DP) by
C. Nicholls & Company Ltd,
The Philips Park Press, Manchester

ISBN 0 340 22318 9

CONTENTS

PART I

THE LAND OF COCKAIGNE

"The Land of Cockaigne is the name of an imaginary country, a medieval Utopia where life was a round of luxurious idleness. In Cockaigne the rivers were of wine, the houses were built of cake and barley sugar, the streets were paved with pastry and the shops supplied goods for nothing. Roast geese and fowls wandered about inviting people to eat them, and buttered larks fell from the sky like manna." *Encyc. Britt.*

CHAPTER ONE

His legs gobbled up the placid country road, his eyes foraged all around it greedily, spotting loot in the quite ordinary ditches and hedges and fields, even his arms were swinging too energetically, seeming to plunder the air, grabbing handfuls of light before they could be darkened and lost in the evening.

He had arrived in the village of Crossbridge only a few hours ago and though he thought he had imprinted it on his mind that solitary morning some time back, he could now remember little of the lie of the place. He was not helped by the dusk which crept up from the ground, black mist shiftlessly changing such markers as he had thought to recall. Yet this uncertainty was part of his exhilaration; freedom seemed to begin with such an absence of exact direction.

He came to a crossroads, but the names on the tipsily slanted signpost were of no help to him. Tugging at it first to test its stability, he shinned up the cold trunk and immediately sighted the fell path he wanted to be on. It would be enough for him merely to return to the spot where, a few months ago, his decision had been conceived; to sprinkle a little superstition on the reasoning which had finally brought him here; simply to remember that tranquil morning when confusion had seen clarity in isolation. He dropped down and set off, striding along the road as if he owned the ground he walked on. Or rather, as if he could have owned it, but preferred to be without the bindings of possession, his movements proclaiming instead that superior overlordship which comes from newly sprung confidence.

A tractor came towards him and the man driving it nodded a "good evening". Just managing to stop himself from shouting out his reply, he nodded back, equally cautiously, and stopped to watch the broad span of the tractor trundle up to the crossroads. The engine's throb swirled into the unconcerned silence as he strained his ears to catch its last pulse. Then the silence rolled back on to him until all that remained was the soft push of his breath and a few chirps from those birds piping out the warm summer evening.

Richard Godwin was twenty-four. He was exhausted but pleasant-looking, perhaps even slightly handsome in that his face reflected the fashionable ideal of the moment in its slim cheeks, regular features, nothing too prominent, neither nose, eyes nor mouth in itself particularly striking. It was probably the cut of his hair, expertly razored so as to appear long while yet consisting of a great number of short tufts smoothly running into each other, probably that which could make some people think, for a moment, that he might be handsome. Otherwise his face was unremarkable except when he became enthusiastic; then his mouth would appear to be a little too large and loose. In height and weight he was exactly as he had been on the last occasion when those confessions had been demanded of him, at school, seven years ago. Average. His clothes were precisely contemporary, a brown suit with frail pockets patched on, made of a corduroy which had long lost its relationship to that material of the same name which until lately, in Crossbridge, would have lasted a working man for half a lifetime.

In his attitude there was an undetermined vigour which might loosen to scattered reminders of unkept promise or could, equally, forge itself into determination. At this moment his determination was set, though a little self-mocking. He tried to combat this self-detraction, however; for over the last few years it had grown into a leech, like a malignant deformity of Hieronymus Bosch, for ever sucking away his purpose, and he had to break free from it.

He reached the place – an old bench donated to the parish long since by a vicar whose favourite resting-place this had been – and banged himself on to it, feeling immediately the damp wood clamming his trousers to his skin, settled by the clear definition this gave to his body.

Now he was still and he looked below him at the village picked out by three lights. Above, the sky, where a gauze of gentle summer cloud hid the moon and carefully absorbed the embers of daylight. Behind him, Knockmirton Fell, massed into a solid, black cone.

At this spot on a chance trip to Cumberland he had looked down at Crossbridge and felt an impulse of understanding which – however shallow or even false in his interpretation of it – had constantly risen to the top of his mind as an alternative in that last cycle of metropolitan confusion. An alternative, then a hope, finally the only way.

He sat and concentrated as hard as he could, forcing himself to believe that he could change the way in which he lived his life, find a style which would not be clogged with self-disgust or self-regard, nor be dissipated in nervous, nerveless stupidities. He concentrated, but there was no symbol to aid him; disgust at the past was his only spur. Soon he jumped up and set off down the road. Such a pause was as near as he could come to a dedication. It had to be enough.

His skin was licked by the tang of cool air which rolled down the fell. He felt warm and tireless. The cloud moved gracefully over the tree-tops and there were no sounds to outbid the crunch of his thin shoes on the path.

CHAPTER TWO

"Have you got a light?"

Richard started, nervously. The voice came out of a tree. Remaining on the road he stared at the spot, unwilling to give himself away until it became essential.

"Have you got a light, mister?"

Preceded by a chalky cigarette, a figure which turned into an old mackintoshed woman stepped out from behind the tree and, on unsteady feet, dipped across the grass verge and on to the road itself where she stood, twiddling the cigarette between her lips.

"Yes. Of course. Here."

The match scraped loudly against the striking-pad and, as soon as it was alight, went out. In that brief moment, Richard saw a face as strained and hollow as he thought it possible to be. The skin stretched tightly across the wide brow and swept down from the cheek-bones so fiercely that it seemed that one prick of a pin would crack it open all over. The nose was large and there, too, on its bridge, the white skin was lashed across the bone which threatened to break through. But all this, though distressing, was nothing compared with the eyes and hair; for the woman's eyes were so large that they seemed to extend the breadth of the face, and even at that quick glance Richard noticed a hysterical bewilderment touched with an invitation so disturbingly unbalanced that it was unbearable; as if she had been once so shocked that she could only incite more assaults as a result of it. The hair was as unkempt as a specially dishevelled wig, grey coarse tags of hair skewed in all directions.

11

He struck another match, holding it low so as to protect himself by not looking at that face, and also to save her the embarrassment he felt such disfigurement must bring to a woman. Then he noticed that the mackintosh covered a fur of grotesque tattiness under which was the dull satiny bodice of a frock fashionable decades ago among rather rich, smart women.

She sucked and spluttered over the cigarette, coughed out the first draw, jolting him backwards with the violence of her retching – for it developed into that, as if she were permanently susceptible to it and needed only the slightest touch to set her off – and then stuck the thing in a corner of her red smeared lips, letting it hang there, unattended.

"I've missed that bus again!" she said. "He saw me on the road here, he knows me well enough by now, but he wouldn't wait up at the top. The sod!"

Richard saw those eyes swivelling before him in the dark, and wished himself back on his way.

"I'm scared of walking on my own," she went on, "everybody knows that. It bangs my nerves about and that upsets my system. Anybody would be scared in a place like this."

The appeal was direct, and what made it the more urgent was the tone in which it was delivered; a flattened play on one or two notes only, but in that flatness such vicious bitterness as threatened all who did not comply with dangerous malice.

"I'll walk you home."

"How do you know I'm going home?"

"I don't know. Sorry. I mean, I'll walk with you – where ever you want."

"Walk with me, eh? Walk out with me? With *me*! My young man! Oh! Oh!"

The laugh shot through the cigarette, knocking off the ash and spurting into Richard's face so that he flinched.

"Walk out with *me*! That's good. That's good!"

Still laughing, though now it had turned in on her and shook her several layers of clothing, gurgling in her chest and twitching that tight skin, she waddled up the road.

She walked quickly and Richard soon found that it took him all his time to keep up with her.

"It's three miles," she said. "That bloody rotten bus goes right up to the bloody rotten place." And that was all she said for the next few minutes.

Now the moon came out for a few moments, shining through

12

the haze of cloud as if coldly melting it. The woman walked slightly ahead of him, the moonlight biting into her hair and emphasising its briary messiness. Occasionally Richard would glimpse the profile and the pallid skin flushed by the light to such an anaemic puttiness as made it spectral. She walked with scarcely a sound, and when he looked down at her feet he saw soft bedroom slippers, decorated with woolly pompoms which nodded noiselessly as the soles padded over the damp road, now shimmering faintly.

He fell into step and tried to construct a life around the old woman's presence. All he could think up was a lurid collection of clichés but they kept him busy enough for the next mile or so.

"We turn off here. This is where it gets dark. They should be made to bring the lights along this bit."

The road they had been walking along was a main road in country terms; that on to which they now turned was much less impressive. On the main road, two or three vans and cars had rocked past them, claiming the middle of the road and swinging round the corners certain of being unchallenged, but here there were no such diversions. This road led through two or three hamlets to a village once the possessor of a country seat, now the supporter of a shrub and seed business on the old estate; the road was bordered by woods and, even when there was a break in them, the rise of the road prevented the long view of any illuminated landmark. You might catch the shimmer of light above one or other of the industrial towns down on the coast, but soon it would be gone and was of no help.

Here, Richard was as glad of the old woman's company as she had declared herself to be of his. He could see nothing before him and the crawling of the slight wind along the dry summer leaves trickled up his back, seeming to lift each pore and look inside it, daring it.

"It's just down this hill, over the next and then round the corner. It's next to nowhere. It is nowhere. And I'm stuck in it."

"Don't you like living here?" Richard's question began before her sentence ended, glad to block out the silence.

"Like it? *Like* it? Who would like living in nowhere? There's nothing here for a woman. I used to live in a town, you know. I wasn't born into it, but I lived in it all right. Wakefield. Do you know it? There was some life there, I can tell you. Always plenty to do. Here! Here, there's nothing. Do you think I would be stuck here if I could get away from it, a woman like me?" She

13

stopped, and, out of the dark, her eyes swivelled on and around his face. "Well?"

"I suppose not."

"You suppose not! Huh." Suddenly, she grinned at him, and the black hole revealed by her mouth joined up with the eyes so that the face seemed held together only by a few tight cords of white thong. "You're a young man," she said. "They don't care." She took a step towards him and Richard was wiped by a quick sweat in fear of what her coquettish manner might demand. "Young men don't care about anything much, do they?" She had attempted to murmur, but the words were only harsh, and, as soon as they were completed, the grin destroyed the face again and her breath shot across to his nostrils.

"I suppose not."

"You're doing a lot of supposing tonight. Are you my young man or aren't you? Come on! Are you or aren't you?"

She flung open both her mackintosh and the fur, pinning her hands on the large hip-bones which swung out her long dress like an umbrella.

"Ha!" She took another pace forward, slapping him with the exclamation. "Ha!" He backed away. "Ha! Ha! Ha!" His heels caught the verge and he stumbled and then fell. Immediately, she was up to him.

"You been drinking? Come on! Out with it! I don't mind young men drinking but I've got to be told."

"No. I slipped. I'm sorry." Backing away, he pressed his palms to the wet grass and jumped up, inordinately relieved to find that he was still taller than she was.

"Sorry!" she shouted. "Sorry! Sorry! Sorry! I thought it would come to that. You're all the bloody rotten same! You're all sorry. Don't you think a woman's sorry? Don't you think a woman like me has the right to be sorry?"

She raised her arm, then dropped it, refolded her coat and walked on. Richard let her go but, as her steps drew away, he thought that it would be cowardice to abandon her; if the impulse to accompany her in the first instance came from a residual gallantry which satisfied the donor as much as the recipient, this display of oddness had put her in another category altogether, that of people you must help, no matter what, because of their weakness; he ran after her.

"I thought you were dead," she said, mildly, and continued in the same unperturbed tone, "my Edwin put me here to keep me

14

out of the way because he's ashamed, you know. He knows I need his money. He said it was the only cottage he could find but that's a lie for a start. And he doesn't understand, you know. This living in the country, I can't stand it. There's nothing doing. You know," this time her voice did lower to a true whisper, "I think it could drive you cuckoo if you didn't watch yourself. Cuckoo. I've told *my Edwin* and he won't listen. But I mean it. Cuckoo!"

They walked over the next hill and round a corner, crossing a bridge from beneath which came the drone of fast water tunnelled, and Richard's mind skittered over the possibilities of what he ought to do, how he could help as he knew so little about her, putting himself in the position of the stronger partly to assuage his bewilderment, for it was he who was the more vulnerable in this particular company.

"Here we are then."

Richard picked out a cottage a few yards back from the road; it stood alone and looked as if it had been built by accident and at once forgotten.

"Do you want yourself a cup of tea?"

"No, thank you very much. I'd better be getting back."

"Suit yourself. They call this place Asby. Suit yourself."

She went up the path and stood ratching in her handbag for the key, while Richard waited, wanting to see her in, to put the full stop to this paragraph. Lights came on and without a wave she banged the door and loudly slammed home two bolts. He turned to go, but had not proceeded far when he heard her shout out at him and saw her jutting out of the bedroom window, still mackintoshed, her hair, with the back lighting, now a smooth stack of dark furze.

"Thank you for the walk!" she shouted. "And don't think I won't tell that bloody rotten bus driver when I see him again because I will! Thank you, kind sir."

That was all.

Before the bridge, Richard stumbled about so much that he ended up with his face in a hedge. Rounding it cautiously he walked on, finding that, with the old woman gone, the pitch night gave him no guide. His movement began to match his sense of direction, and for a few hundred yards he wandered blindly. At this time, still off balance from that encounter, the ogres of childhood and vivid Sunday-newspaper storytelling swarmed into his mind, and within seconds of leaving the bridge he was seeing long knives, robbers, beggars, wild drunken labourers, monsters, and

15

because of his physical puerility – he could not walk straight at all – there was nothing he could do to stop these clamouring inflammations.

At last he came to the brow of the first hill and saw, in the distance, but still at a recognisable point, thus reassuring him of the continuity of the road, the single light which marked the junction with what was called the main road; and beside that light there were, he knew, some cottages, even a sub-post-office. While looking back, he could see the old woman's house, ablaze with lights. He paused, set himself firmly in the middle of the road, and set out briskly, hoping, rightly, that the speed of his walk would keep him more or less in a straight line. After a few paces, both the markers disappeared from sight, but he was well enough launched.

He had forgotten such darkness. Forgotten the fears which can breed in a quiet country road. Forgotten such a low-bristling rub of silence, forgotten the moon, the cloud and the smack of open scented night air, forgotten that old lonely people needed to be taken home, that he could feel threatened so sickeningly by another's mere attitude, forgotten the details which made apparent simplicity so unyielding.

The force of the strangeness of it all made him careless. He began to think of what he wanted to suppress – the reasons for his sickening of life in London.

Such had been the strain of those last months that he could hardly remember his life during his first few years in that city. That earlier time now seemed a loose shuffle of sepia-coloured cards. The ordered power of the centre, quiet Georgian squares white-painted, brown benches in the parks and the thin foam from a jet in the sky. A steady flickering of newness, each thing to be plucked. The streets and meeting-places commanded, it seemed, by his generation, the pavements supporting an endless parade of advertisements for themselves, dinky junk shops, kinky boutiques, the uncarpeted acres of echoing museum. Pubs he would know for one drink only, conversations of elaborate early-morning intimacy with people never seen again, the bistro, the football ground, theatres, cafés, caverns, skin after skin peeling away. And throughout, the flats: flats which he shared, flats for parties, flats for refuge, other people's empty flats for affairs, his own flat, flats handed on, swopped, discovered, until all the vast centre of London was two rooms, sep. kitchen and w.c., for ever on the move.

Had he been able to accept his enjoyment of this, it would have been fine. But he could not. There was an ease about it which made him nervous – though why he could not explain; instead of action, there seemed mere movement, adventure was reduced to competition, intrigue took the place of combat, satisfaction of effort – by these and similar abbreviations he tried to describe his unrest and so contain it. He began to have a new respect for people who had stood outside it all and, by themselves alone, built a life; people he had thought to abandon for ever as heroes in his adolescence – like Shelley or T. E. Lawrence; and yet the word 'hero' was insubstantial.

Perhaps there really is something in the belief that a man loses his virtue by being touched. And in London Richard felt himself mauled. By choice, with pleasure, from habit of course – but mauled, so that he could no longer distinguish; his mind was now full of burnished images; another jolt and they were tarnished. In newspapers, on television, and in his own day, he stared at destruction one moment, triumph the next, despair–elation, grandeur–gutter, horror–laughter, extremes ceaselessly shuttling across his mind until, it seemed, he reflected all of them equally indifferently, equally passionately.

He came to think of his life as worth nothing, a waste. That it should be worth anything was difficult to prove; yet the belief that it should resurrected itself and he found no anchorage for it in his flotsam spawnings. Nor did it seem relevant to think of waste as he threw away a paper carton and bought yet another fashionable shirt. Yet the sense of it was there and he clung to it.

But it was swept away.

To what was within him he had finally abandoned himself, trying either to find expiation through the fullness of his greed or to let himself be mangled in it. The latter had happened. He had been drawn into a vortex of his own making, confused images drumming on to his mind like hail.

His work in London. The pink bow on a parcel of superfluities. The tax on returns, not on subscription, the main chance not the best way, the quick shot. Women in London. More. Married. Young. Too old. More. A deceitful confusion which had somehow seemed glamorous. Money in London. More. Essential. Pick it up wherever, crawl for it, insomnia for it, lick. Taxis swinging on to the pavement at five in the morning, dance to the tom-toms in the cellars of the ravemen, trade-men, carbon monoxide fumes from the earth lining the atmosphere so that in

17

ten to thirty years, man, the temperature will rise five degrees and there will be floods. Ah, no. "The English have no working class," the Swedish girl said, "it is a servant class they have. I have lived in your East End." Come into the ... Pugwash conference – including seven Nobel Prize winners – calls for an end to arms race, biological warfare build-up, warns of disastrous consequences merely through having these malignant weapons, votes for change, breaks up, its members go back to work, the slave-saviours. Noise, Noise, Noise – will we go deaf. God willing, please?

Coherence. Those outside the clamour, outside consideration. The fear as a tube train bolted out of its tunnel, and he on the platform, swaying forward to kiss between the open rails, deep and enticing. Sweat-broken startled waking middle of the night, a pin of death stabbing his chest, the long breath while he remembered who he was and then the cigarette while he considered whether he was going crazy, or heartburn, footfall of a coronary – "In the Prime of Life it can happen to YOU! – ARE YOU INSURED?" – no, count backwards – eight, seven, six, five, four, he's a good thing you dropped –

He stopped on the road, the country road, the quiet road. No! His neck was beginning to tick with pain as it had done in London, his skull was beckoned by a gap of fear which would not close – and he was still, in some part, sorry to have left it. No!

He held himself very tensely. Then, allowing himself to feel his muscles relax, he grew calm. That was the last time he would voluntarily invoke that poison as he must now call it. He had thought that he would go mad during those last few months – and through nothing but the rottenness of his life.

He was so preoccupied with himself that he did not notice the bustle going on around the row of three cottages which stood quite near his own. Had he been in the least aware, he could not have failed to be curious over the cars and lights and excitement at such a place at such a time of night, but he passed it by and went the twenty or so yards down the track to his own place. Inside, he did not allow himself a pause but made straight for bed.

He would sleep. That would wash away the infection and perhaps strengthen his resolution. Sleep. A faint buzz came from the neighbouring cottages, but that only emphasised the quiet around. Rich and even silence. He sank towards it. He had come, he had made a start, he had done as he intended.

CHAPTER THREE

Edwin sat in the front room of his cottage, the light out, the fire so banked with slack that it scarcely lit up its own smoke, the curtains open and the door ajar. He did not wish to interfere in what was happening two doors away, but could not do other than strain to catch every sound which came along the short path to his own door. He had pulled up a chair to the fender and his feet rested on it, his elbows on his knees, his hands clutching his chin. The face was clearly related to that of the woman whom Richard had encountered, but what in her had been disturbing was in Edwin ugly. The white skin ached on the large bones, the nose was spotted by pimples and hard red lumps as if it could endure the strain no longer, the eyes were so sunken that the brows above them did not dominate the face, making a powerful line which decisively pointed out authority, rather they hung, slackly, with the wispy hairs on them straggling untidily. Similarly his body, it was thin without the balance of slimness, the shoulders and arms contorted with tight muscle, humpy, unattractive. Only in the hands, perhaps, and in the expression on the eyes themselves could any clue be seen of the force he was capable of. For, at the end of a twisted cord of wrist, each hand dangled like a weight. And in his eyes was not the arrogance of a Titan or any monstrous expression of conceited power, but a bleak determination, so subdued at some times that it appeared no different from melancholy, yet at other times so hard that little, it promised, could deter it. Although three years younger than Richard, the clumsy-looking, ugly-looking man could have been his father in everything about him but his aspect which, at this moment, was flooded with such despair, such torrents of misery as needed a young man's strength to feel.

He sat there, in his best suit, breathing in the fumes from the coal fire and sincerely wishing himself dead. Only by presenting to himself constantly the alternative of oblivion could he bear his present state. For the woman he loved entirely, one who did not care more for him than she did for any acquaintance met on a street corner, was giving birth to a baby, not his, and for the last few minutes he had heard her screams. The more he heard her suffer, the more solidly he sat, until now he seemed petrified in the gloom of his cottage, no more breathing than the huge sideboard, only the bare white of his cheeks and his knuckles indicating any trace of a living man.

At long long last he heard the winded cry of a new child. He rushed to the door, flinging it open, catching it just before it hit the wall so that there should be no sudden noise to scare her. Now he could hear the sound more clearly, and around it the patter of voices busy and relieved. He stepped out on to the path, trembling. There was nothing he wanted to do but go and see, at least ask about her. The cries, the voices, the wind as he stood on the path and looked at the blocks of light coming from her cottage – he could not go. There was no reason, would be no objection; he had been a neighbour for five years, it was he who had brought in the relief doctor when the local practitioner had been found to be ill, he would be welcome – but he could not go. Janice would not want to see a man who felt as he did after the solitary birth of that child, it would not help her. But he had to do something. He could not shout out, he could not ride off and thrash himself into forgetful exhaustion – he could do nothing to take him away from this place where he must stay and wait for someone to bring him the news that all was well. All had to be well.

So he retreated to his own cottage and turned on the light, leaving the door open as his sign. In the small room, three paces and he was across it, he collected himself and brought out the bottle of whisky. This he had procured in the afternoon in case Janice's father, Wif, should drop in on him and need a drink. He poured out half a cupful and went across to the mirror with it. He raised it before his face; his face, he could hardly bear to look at it, ugly, "uglier than sin" his mother had said.

The middle cottage was occupied by Mrs. Jackson who felt no scruples about her place that night. It was in the middle of things. For her, the event combined all the rights and drama of womanhood with all the spice and mystery of scandal. And then there was the doctor's car! Driven right up to her front door! It was with exquisite refinement that she wiggled her way past it, her swagger portraying clearly that Cross Cottages had come of age with such a car just standing around as if it belonged there.

It was she who missed Edwin – she could bear to miss nothing – and so came, after her minuet around the bumpers, to haul him in.

"Well, what are you doing moping here by yourself?" she demanded, bounding into his room. "You must come and see them."

"Is Janice all right?

"Oh, Janice is fine. Why shouldn't she be? I mean, she had the pain for a few hours, but there's many a woman had worse, believe me. And when it came – out it popped like a puppy. She's broader than you think down there, you know."

Edwin winced and locked his hands together. He had made up his mind that Mrs. Jackson's information must serve – even though she was the last messenger he would have chosen – and so that was that; he must not offend her. "But she's all right? As well as can be expected?"

"Oh she's stronger than she looks is Janice. I've always said that. Not just now – the same when she was a little girl – take no notice of her tiredness, I said to Agnes. And to Wif because I speak my mind. I'm not saying the lass is deceitful, but there's people think – "

"So she didn't – she wasn't hurt."

"Hurt? Who gets hurt nowadays? Not that it isn't difficult. Nothing's easy in this world. He's stitching her now."

"What? What did you say?"

"Nothing to worry about. Good God, lad, you look frightened out of your mind. Have some more of that whisky I can see you've got yourself behind that chair leg. It's nothing, you know. Our Belle had one of those Caesareans. She still carries her scar with her."

Edwin did pour himself some more whisky, without offering any to Mrs. Jackson – who was widely known as a teetotaller on account of her husband being such a heavy drinker – but nevertheless she was offended not to be asked.

"Come on then," she said. "Roll up and see the side-show!"

She giggled. Edwin shook his head and rubbed the cup between his hands. Mrs. Jackson regarded him slyly, and then her face sparkled with understanding. "Oh, I see. Yes. It must be very upsetting for you. Mind you, it's your own fault. I've said it often enough. You should be more pushing. All women need a push and Janice more than most." Then faintly appreciating that her remarks might appear tactless, she rushed to make amends.

"Never mind. There's more than one fish in the sea. You're bound to find somebody someday. A fine young man like you."

Edwin stared at her, for the first time, coldly, and Mrs. Jackson

21

shrank back, clearly afraid, and equally clearly the more afraid, because he was an ugly man. "All right. I'll get back and tell them you don't want to bother. I understand, Edwin, and I'll try to put your point of view over."

"Please, Mrs. Jackson! Please tell them that I wish to leave them in peace on a night like this. No more. They have a right to be on their own."

Now Mrs. Jackson was offended at the implied criticism of her own interference and, as she stepped outside, her jaw snapped its anger.

"You haven't even asked me what she had."

"What did she have?" he whispered, dutifully, miserably.

"A lovely little girl." She leaned through the door frame, daring to glare at him now his head was averted. "And I'll tell you something else. Whoever it was that gave it to her must have been a good-looking fella because that baby's looks don't just come from one side."

With that neighbourly confidence, she was gone, and Edwin's head sank to his knees as he groaned at the desecration of what, for him, had been the sacred act of Janice giving birth.

Janice lay back on the pillows in the bedroom – her parents'; her own had not been big enough – which was ripe with the glowing effect the birth had had on all but her; its warm paper, the low pitch of the bulb, the embalmed relief made another womb of it. Yet, at the centre of this the new mother, her flush already faded, lay stiffly, edging herself away, detaching herself from all she had caused. The doctor and midwife had gone, Mrs. Jackson had left, her father was downstairs for what seemed the first time for weeks there was no bustle, no busyness. The baby, in a cot beside the bed, was quivering with that first real wakefulness that follows the crying; over it, rocking the cot so gently that it scarcely stirred, stood Agnes, Janice's mother.

It was at this moment, Janice felt, that she had to claim her independence. She had been consistent from the beginning, but here, at this time, she could be conclusive. She had thought of nothing else but this statement of her position since the baby had finally left her and she shut her eyes to forget the blood and shouting of that terrible moment.

"What's he like, that man who's taken Old Mr. Rigg's cottage?" she began, speaking quietly, but precisely, in control.

"Oh. I don't know. I haven't seen him. Your dad has. Says he's

22

a young fella." Agnes replied without taking her eyes away from the baby, afraid of her daughter's calculated obliviousness towards the child; that manner which had shaken Agnes throughout the pregnancy, and which she had hoped the birth might alter, was as set as ever.

"I wonder why anybody should choose to come and live *here*. Anybody young."

Janice saw that her mother was in that mood of hers which waited for all to pass because to cope with it would be too disturbing. It was not hardness in Agnes, though it resembled it, but a certain obstinate shyness and unhappiness which preferred to ignore what it could only admit in tears. Janice looked down the bed at her hands, white on the white fold of sheet, still glistening faintly, limp and yet longing for something to agitate them, occasionally the fingers lifting to drum silently on the sheet. Her hands had not suffered – but they were about all that hadn't.

In the lapse of speaking, the baby fell asleep and Agnes bent low over it, as if searching for any distress in the face which she could breathe away.

"I don't want it, mother," said Janice, rigidly. "I don't want anything to do with it."

"You're just tired," Agnes replied, without looking over to her, "a lot of women feel like that. Don't ... say ... that." She brought herself upright and whispered to the baby, "You're a lovely little girl, aren't you? Yes. Yes you are. A lovely little baby."

"I'm quite – I know what I'm saying. I'm not delirious or anything. I didn't want it before and I don't want it now."

"Listen to your mother," Agnes said to the baby, "isn't she a funny one? Won't she feel sorry in the morning? Won't she?"

"And I don't want to feed it," Janice persisted, wearily, edging the corner of her bottom lip between her teeth, tugging it. "I don't want any more to do with it than I can help. I don't feel anything for it, mother. I know you can't understand that, but it's true. You persuaded me out of having an abortion – well ..." She paused, recognising the pain her mothre was feeling but hardening the more to ignore it, as she had to do because this *had* to be the time when such points were made definitively. "Well, now that it's here, you can have it. Like you said you would. You said that. You did!"

Agnes was trembling and she feared to turn to her daughter because she knew that she could only cry, and that would help no one; she had to let her have her say and try to comprehend. It was Janice who began to sob.

"You hate me, I know you do. But you don't know how it happened. I can't tell you how it happened. I can't! Oh, you might understand then, but I can't. You hate me! But I don't want it. I don't! I don't!"

She pulled the sheets over her face which shook with the violence of her tears. Sobbing herself now, Agnes went across and sat on the edge of the bed, tentatively stroking her daughter's hand, almost absent-mindedly doing so, afraid equally of accepting, rejecting or understanding what Janice was saying.

"I can't say anything to you," she whispered, eventually. "There's nothing I can say. That little baby hasn't harmed anybody. That's an innocent person. I don't see how you can think about it that way. But I don't hate you. You mustn't say that to your own mother. I couldn't hate you, whatever you did."

"I'm sorry. I'm sorry." Janice's voice, muffled through the sheets, came to the older woman with such a toll of despair that she had to stuff her fist into her own mouth to block the noise of crying which it provoked. "I wish I'd never been born. I do. I wish that. Oh, I wish that."

"Ssssh! Rest yourself. Ssssh!"

Agnes rocked her hand on Janice's shoulder, as gently as she had rocked the cradle.

Downstairs, Wif, Agnes's husband, heard it all and did not know what to make of it. There should have been nothing but joy in him, but that bubble had been burst by fear for both their futures; his child's, and hers.

He went outside and stood away from the front of the house, at the edge of the light-shadow made by the windows; staring into the shifting summer dark, he rolled himself a cigarette. Edwin's lights were still on and he made as if to go to the younger man's, and then changed his mind. Edwin's feelings about Janice were no secret to anyone. He would have enough to cope with.

So he went into his shed. Still in the vice was the piece of wood he had been planing when Agnes had called him to get Edwin to fetch the doctor. He rubbed his thumb over the glossy rim of the wood and then took up the plane and pushed the blade along the clear grain.

Edwin was waiting until all was settled. He had not budged

when the doctor drove away, nor when Mrs. Jackson clattered her way back for the last time. The whisky was all drunk and he started on some bottles of beer he'd had in the house for months. The drink appeared to have little effect on him, stiffening rather than slackening his look and bearing, but making no noticeably effective difference. The yellow flames began to leap through the dust, flicking up the chimney like gaudy trout up a weir. The bulb of the light made the only other sound in the room, and Edwin resented even that low murmur as he sat and listened.

At two o'clock, Agnes called Wif away from his shed and Edwin heard his name mentioned, overwhelmed that they could think of him at such a time, and grateful once more for their discretion, for they did not come to disturb him. They knew that he would have come had he wanted to. He had not. They respected his solitude.

He gave them an hour to settle down, hearing the fluttering cries of the baby, the fast swish of a car away on the main road, the rasping of the grass as some cows moved across it, his low fire. Then he stirred.

There was a large sideboard which he lifted away from the wall, pulling out the length of skirting-board behind it and from there taking his cash-box. By undertaking all manner of extra work, he had managed to save £420, and that while being apprenticed and supporting his mother. It was to have served as a deposit on the house which Janice and himself would live in – it was the substance of his dream of her.

The box was shiny black inside and the smeared bundles of notes, curling away from their glossy reflection, huddled inconsequently inside the tin. Bundles of ten. On the inside lid of the box, a chart, neatly drawn, recording the dates on which the hoard had reached £50, £100, £200 and so on. He scooped up the money in his hand and looked at it as it lay there. The fire was now a thick ash fur and the notes would incite the flames – but he could not; the longer he held them above the grate, the more stupid did such a gesture appear. He put the money back; deciding not even to use it for the present he must make to the baby.

In his wallet were five one-pound notes and one of ten shillings. The five pounds he put into an envelope and, after sealing it, wrote a few words on the front. He washed his hands and face and tidied himself up and then, as quietly as he could, went out of his door and along to hers. The light was on up in the bedroom and for a few moments he stood gazing at it. And the man who had given her that child was not known to him, there was no name talked off, he had never appeared here, nor would he. He slipped the envelope through the letter-box and hurried back to his own place.

It was Agnes who found it, some minutes later as she came down to boil the milk for the baby's feed. For some time she looked at it, knowing that her attention would be more grateful than that of her daughter's, wondering yet again at the patience of the man, the way in which he served his love.

The inscription read:

To Janice,
for your little girl.
All Best Wishes,
Edwin Cass.

CHAPTER FOUR

Richard had already woken up several times and then gone back to sleep with a delicious taste of sloth slithering down his body from his mouth to his thighs. The sleep was so ripe that he enjoyed breaking it, the soft bubble burst and his long breath sealed it again. It was as if a cushion of heather were being gently pressed against his face, and he nuzzled it, his skin, his eyes, his slow opening thoughts all smothering themselves into it, as a dolphin slowly lifts itself from the sea only to plunge into it yet again. It was like a first sleep. In it the past receded in stately order, brushed of that irritating powder with which it always threatens to ignite the present; and the future, which used to pounce into his morning mind like the newspaper shooting through the letter-box, remained insubstantial, willingly formless, a thin coil of smoke playing its scent around his face with no disruptive crackle and jump of fire. He bathed and swooned and rolled in this sleep, feeling that its poppied exhilaration was the first step on the way to his ambition.

The sun came in brightly through the thin curtains, splicing the moted dusk of the room with intersecting rays and beams of copper and gold, making a languorously moving globe of that small room, a burnished cage which swung before his cloyed eyes to the sounds of birds in the steady spinning of the land around.

26

It was after midday when he got up and the sinuous feebleness of putty fingers on clothes splashed him with yet more pleasure. He went outside and breathed in the air clear as ringing crystal, shuddering delightedly at the bite of cold in his warm lungs. Then he pottered around making his breakfast and after it sat back with a cigarette, a cup of coffee, and the transistor murmuring behind him.

A peremptory knock at the door which in two or three seconds became insistent rent the loosened cloud of day-dreams.

"Sorry to interfere," said Mrs. Jackson, all teeth, "but the Co-op van's here. He won't be back till Monday. I held him up for you."

She displayed the vehicle as if she had produced it out of the ground. The driver gave Richard a good morning.

"That's very kind of you – but I brought a lot of stuff with me. I think I've got enough."

"Are you sure now? You needn't worry about milk and eggs – you can get those from Mrs. Law. But what about meat? And sausages? It's a good sausage t'Co-op makes – mind you, it's nothing like Len Turner's at Cockermouth and it can't compare with Miss Ferguson's, but you'd have to go to Egremont for that – but it's a good sausage. *You* won't have tasted anything like it before."

Refusal was thus made both ungenerous and unadventurous. He went up the two steps and into the van-shop where the driver took out the thick brown sausage and weighed out a generous pound.

"Twist it for him, Mr. Porter," the lady said, "he won't know how to do that."

The sausage resembled a thick rope squatting heavily on the white plate of the scales. Mr. Porter dangled it before him and twisted it into portions, threading each segment through the other until the whole was bunched like a brown artichoke. Encouraged, Richard bought a packet of tea, a few fancy cakes and two jars of home-made marmalade – this latter purchase despite Mrs. Jackson's hissing assurances that she herself had some in her larder, better than the Co-op's, which she would be only too pleased to have off her hands. She accompanied him back into the house.

"I see you've taken over most of Mr. Rigg's furniture. He made it himself, you know, some of it. Very handy. Good at finishing. Mind you, he got very peculiar at the end. Not that *I* ever saw anything wrong with it, but he did FUNNY THINGS. You know

27

what I mean? Not nasty. He was a gentleman in his own way. Always wore a tie and a starched collar. But FUNNY. Well, put that stuff down."

Richard squeezed past her and tumbled the provisions on to the table.

"Who was it you got to clean the place up, if you don't mind my asking, do you?"

"Of course not. The agent got someone for me. I believe she came for three or four days."

"She did. She had very little to say for herself. Came from Cockermouth on one of those scooters. I don't like women on those things, they're not built for women, particularly women as fully built as she was. Well now. Next time you want anybody, look locally. Now then. Have you got all you want? Just say the word."

"Yes, I have. Thank you very much."

Preliminaries over, Mrs. Jackson came down to it, and within very few minutes discovered that he had rented the cottage for one pound ten a week – too much she said – bought the furniture for fifty – about right – that his present intention was to live there for about a year, that he came from London where he'd worked on a magazine, was unmarried, had no plans to convert the place – much as she tried to explain to him the value of such an act – that he was an only child of parents both dead, father killed in the war – twenty-seven went from Crossbridge alone, she told him, you wouldn't believe it of a little spot like this, twenty-seven, that was both wars, mind you – that he had been brought up by his grandfather in a small town and was a big reader. As the interrogation proceeded, Richard sensed that he was giving, once for all, answers to questions which would be raised throughout the village and he guessed that with Mrs. Jackson the information was in good hands. No one need be curious again.

To these excavated facts his neighbour was to add the following impressions – though such they would never be called, personal opinion being, in her estimation, at least as concrete as accurate knowledge, and certainly more reliable; that he had some money, not much, but some, tucked away somewhere, was a bit soft, easily led, good-mannered, pleasant, lazy, needed filling out, and would probably not last much more than a fortnight.

"What made you pick Crossbridge, then?" she concluded.

"I came through it one day – just after Christmas. It reminded me of where I was brought up – in Derbyshire I liked it."

28

"There'll be nothing for you to do here. All the young ones clear out – and they're right." She paused. "Well, I can't be kept back. I've work to do, if you haven't; that's a joke."

He smiled in acquiescent recognition and went out of the door with her. She hesitated, hovering with a worried look, afraid that perhaps she had missed something. While searching for this, she filled in with a reciprocating dollop of information.

"I suppose you noticed the carry-on last night."

"No. Should I have done?"

"Well, you might have noticed the car! I don't mean Edwin's old bone-shaker; the doctor's car. Have you got a car?"

"No. Was someone ill?"

"In a way, Janice Beattie – yon end cottage – she had a baby."

"Oh," Richard replied, but seeing that more was expected, "good," he added.

"Good? I wouldn't say it was good. Good's the last word I would give it." Wearily the old woman turned to him. "I suppose I'd better tell you so that you get the story right. Somebody else's bound to bring it up – then it'll be nothing but a load of gossip. You see, Janice's baby hasn't got a father. Well, it must have one somewhere but nobody knows who. Because she went to College – a year last September it'll be – aye, our Janice went to College – she'd never carry a shopping-bag for longer than ten seconds without saying that her arm was breaking – but she got herself to college all right. It happened there. And nobody knows *how* it happened," Mrs. Jackson concluded crossly, "at least, nobody lets on."

"I see. Poor girl."

The woman was about to give him a reply which would have blasted the roots of his sympathy, but then she remembered that he was merely an acquaintance, not yet a proper neighbour, one whose exact weight was as yet unproved; and so she desisted. She contented herself with what she considered an oblique reproof. "Poor baby is what I'd say! Her own mother has to feed it, you know, Agnes. Our Janice won't. I found that out right away. Too much of an effort, I suppose. Well, I'll be off."

Off she plodded with pendulous steps, which swung her body in slow motion. An old countrywoman on a summer-rutted cart-track, her head sat back on its neck, pecking the sky for titbits and gossip. He could not help but like her.

But the dreamy cobwebs of his fancy-free first afternoon had been well and truly ripped down. He set off immediately for a

29

walk deciding to go once more up that fell, this time to the top of it and come down on its other side.

Crossbridge, as said, was a village. From the fell-side you could see it all laid out. It lay in a triangle, each point of which was about half a mile from the other. One apex was formed by Cross Cottages, Richard's cottage, Mr. Law's farm, and a pub, the cottages coming off the road by a cart-track which led through the fields to the fell-dyke road now beneath him as he stood half-way up the height. Also near enough this cluster to be part of it were the Women's Institute, the school, now derelict, the smithy, now abandoned, and one or two free-standing houses. The northern apex was centred on the church, a small late-eighteenth-century construction built on to the miniature chapel from the fifteenth century which had once belonged to Crossbridge Hall and was still connected to it by a tunnel. The Hall itself was now a rich farm and beside it were a short row of council houses, the vicarage, two more roadside farms and a small Forestry Commission depot. The third part of the triangle was that point at which Richard had left the main road when setting back the old woman. It was simply a snaky line of houses, one of which served as a sub-post-office and grocery store. Between these three centres were a few farms, one or two newly built bungalows, another pub and an occasional clump of cottages, some abandoned.

The village, seen from the fell, was at the end of a slow rising plain which began at the sea. There, about six or seven miles away, was the Solway Firth, beyond it the fortress-range of Scottish hills in Galloway. On the Cumberland coast were the mining towns. Whitehaven, Workington, Flimby, Sidwick, Maryport, and behind them a short trailing off to dependent villages. Iron ore had been mined in this area for years, and though most of the pits were closed, their works, and the inevitable rush of minute houses thrown up to man them, were still littered around, rising out of open fields like the remains of an old volcanic eruption. Crossbridge itself had had four iron-ore pits – all small, all soon worked – and the quality of the ore mined there had been higher than that found anywhere else in England. They were clearly visible among the farms and one, Brow Works, had on it a castellated ruin that stood as a sombre landmark for miles around.

All this evidence of mining, from the coast right back to the fell, was now but the shabbiest reminder of the industrial revolution. The coal mines were at present closing down as quickly as the iron-ore mines had done a quarter of a century before. The district had never been a rich or prosperous province of the new world plundered so spiritedly by the mineral magnates, rather the small afterthought, the result of a compulsive looking for the power beneath the surface. The Cumberland coalfield and iron-ore mines had not been particularly rich to run, or never for very long, with nothing like the apparently indestructible solidity of South Wales, Yorkshire or Lancashire mining districts – and now the gutted workings lay over the fields like an old skin, crinkling, splitting, worn, wrinkled, useless. Slag heaps were the church steeples, a sole hooter the bell for matins, shaft-tops the pyres, the fire from the chimneys of the Workington Steel Works flamed over the last rites. And everywhere everything was being undermined by the weevil of decay which riddled the cheap buildings. One tidal wave, one big wind rolling back down the fells, one shudder of the earth, and the whole of that squatting progeny would be wiped away. The greedy rape would be swallowed up.

Though these outcrops dominated the surface of things towards the coast – with little platoons of cottages standing on guard here, there, and everywhere in the middle of nowhere – it was not too difficult to forget them, for the more you looked down at the landscape, the more the farms and their hedged fields seemed to demand rightful attention as the staple, the flesh, the truer character of the area. Some of the farmers had filled in the pits on their land and grass grew on the mound. The land was not as rich as that further north on the Solway plain, but still it was fat and the Friesians tugged at long sweet grass from March to October. Farming was doing well. At Crossbridge Hall a new milking parlour had just been built which would accommodate over three hundred beasts. Tractors moved across the fields, large lorries clanged down the road like fire engines with their cans of milk, big cars stood at the doors, mudguards splattered, wealth showing itself in a carelessness unaccustomed to the area until recently. So as Richard looked further, the mines which had once terrorised the land seemed less and less important, and the lush fields, the firm lanes, the gates and barns and byres came through the rubble and overwhelmed it.

As he stood higher up Knockmirton Fell, way above that parson's seat which in daylight looked ramshackle, even unsafe, yet another aspect was unfolded. For here it seemed that the lowland beneath was nothing but the shrinking away from the massive hills, the feeble train, the necessary but totally unimpressive link

31

which was unfortunately needed to connect the whale-backed fells to the sea. Here, as he looked around him, the fells took the area to themselves. Part of the Caledonian range which stretched at one time from Scandinavia to the Atlantic Ocean, they were supposed to be the oldest mountain range in the world. They were bare. Limestone, slate, granite and Ordovician rock. Scree would scale down a steep side here, there you could see a gash of brown rocks, a legendary wound long cauterised; a tumble of rocks marked some fall years ago, cairns pointed at the sky on the tops, dry walls clung to the hillsides in regular order, bared veins of slate – the whole feeling was of bareness, ageless existence. Celts might have been there, Romans, Norsemen, Saxons, French English, Scots; traces of none remained save the unyielding lines of a few earthworks seen from the air; it was a place which insisted that any life would be brushed away, fluff; any change would merely alter for a while, all impulses would shrink to ironic inconsequence.

On this height, the farmlands, the mining towns seemed so transitory as to make anyone wonder who considered them in relation to those hills. Such stillness. Richard stood under the blue sky; only the scrambling of a few black-faced sheep, only a far-carried throb of a tractor, only the single throat of a hovering lark, rare and welcome intrusions, ripples on this still ocean, gratefully invoking a more human activity than the fells would countenance.

It was mid-afternoon now, and the sliver of sea that was the Solway Firth flashed like a polished sabre, a loose haze shuffled off the hold of the coast towns, the thinnest of veils rose from the farmlands and on the fell top it was clear. Now he stood on the very apex of Knockmirton and felt himself so distend with the sweet cold air and the quiet that his body grew and spread and particles drifted away on their own to wrap themselves in individual pleasure.

Strange. As if he had never thought or existed before. However romantic or debasedly pantheistic the realisation might be, it was there. He was as clean as the slate. All that he had done was of no account. That which he had tugged and torn and finally run away from, was of no consequence now. Only the actual moment, his shoes buried in the heather, his body chilled yet excited by the air, only that filled his mind. The landscape rolled down from him to the sea and its abiding activity so tranquil rolled away his fratching anxieties.

Like the men who had built those stone walls, who left their stock free within them on the mountainside, attempting neither to gouge the land nor to milk it, wary of what they were up against, cautious but not afraid, so Richard thought that he could lay his plans across the empty range his days now seemed before him. He would get up in the late morning and then walk; in the late afternoon he would eat and afterwards write – do one or two articles, perhaps begin the book he had been vaguely commissioned to write, no rush, perhaps do some song-writing again – then he would go out for a drink and afterwards he would read. He would not make firm reading lists, he would not make a tight schedule, he would keep the day open to its own suggestions but have a simple plan ready to carry him through. He had earned twelve hundred pounds clear from a draft film script and that would let him out of wage-earning for a year or so.

Let the externals take shape. Let his actions gain a strong pattern from them. Let the balance between his mind and his body, between tension and laziness, be established. Let him learn that time could trickle through his fingers like the sand through glass, that food could be necessary as well as welcome, that solitariness was not the panic of mismanagement or the retreat before complexity, but a hopeful opportunity for self-justification.

Out of these externals would, he believed, grow a style. The way of life would merely be the beginning. In time, a self-controlled rhythm would encourage him to that self-respect which had utterly vanished. He would see what his life, not meant, not was worth, but see what his life could be; see an order on which he could build his attendance.

The prospect made him enthusiastic and he walked up Middle Fell and along Blake, all the time accompanied only by the tops of other fells, rising and falling, sweeping on to high plateaux or parting to reveal a long slide of valley. He walked until it was dusk and came back to his cottage tired out.

CHAPTER FIVE

So Richard spent the next few days, sleeping late, fathoming that oblivion as if it were a deep lake in which he could so immerse himself as to rub over and clean every part of him (picnicking indoors or out, walking for hours, not yet beginning even the easy course he had set himself, setting aside, for the moment, the pursuit of a style in the act of enjoyment.

For he loved Crossbridge. It was, he knew, grossly sentimental to love so entirely and with such ignorance, but there it was, and perhaps, he thought, only such a total affection could possibly harden to understanding. He loved the cottages and the spaces between them, the curiosity and the greetings of people in cars, vans, tractors, the walk of the women along the road, a man seen scything the banks of a hedge, a trailer jamming against the gate as it unsuccessfully attempted to back into a field, the kitchen in the top pub with its cool fire even in July, the cheerful face of the woman at the post-office, the children with their gadgeted bicycles who swooped around him and as suddenly left, and all in the lap of those fells rising solemnly behind the village.

Nor was it full of odd night-walkers – as that first evening had suggested to him – nor yet empty of all enterprise, as Mrs. Jackson had implied. Many young people had left, as they had done for the last two or three hundred years, before that even– Goldsmith's Deserted Village could be seen at times in every century for a thousand years – but some remained. In fact with the new work around, the silk works, the atomic power station, newer mobile industries, more than ever before found it easier to travel from Crossbridge itself to work that satisfied them. And the bigger farms were once more building up labour forces approaching the size of those hired in the old days, the new intensive work needing men just as the previous extensive work had done. Not that Crossbridge was thriving. It was nothing like as populated as it had been in the days of the iron-ore mines, nor yet before that in the time of the commonly large holdings of farm labourers; while the woman in the post-office had already told Richard that there were fewer and fewer Crossbridge-born and hardly any she could give *details* about. Wif was one of the few who carried in his head names of people, places, dates and fires, incidents, facts of craft, accurate memories of tastes, habits, dress, speech, pastimes; and yet, though Wif's knowledge seemed somehow more substantial, relating, as it did, to time past, Edwin's observations and way of life were just as likely to become in their turn solidly sanctified by change. Though the stuff of the traditions might be altering, the character to create them was not.

About a week after his arrival, the end of the fine spell having left him indoors all day – he had spent the time in luxurious preparation for voluntary effort, the classifying of books, the arrangement of pads and pen, the re-settling of his house – Richard took advantage of a break in the downpour to visit the church. The road stank with fresh wetness and he had it to himself the whole way there.

From the outside, the church was lichened, shining after the rain, built of that slate-coloured stone quarried in the area, standing on top of a hillock made of graves, slightly forlorn.

The interior, however, was beautifully warm and clean. Whereas Richard had expected the walls to be grimy, they were spick white, the pews gleamed, the hassocks looked as if they had been beaten out that afternoon, there were fresh flowers on the altar beyond the polished rail, the bookstall was neatly kept and not at all pathetic as they usually are, the fifteenth-century font was neatly cordoned by a purple rope. There was a single nave leading to the chancel steps which had marked the west wall of the old chapel. The whole was unburdened by any architectural masterpiece – though it was certainly one of the most pleasingly proportioned village churches that Richard had ever entered – and its effect was one of warmth and use. The pulpit, with the glittering brass eagle on its prow, stood in easy relation to the congregation, and the bell-rope hung straight behind the font.

Agnes came out from the vestry, saw Richard and went towards him. Aproned, with dust-gloves on, still hatted, she had been cleaning out the church as she did once a week. They had seen enough of each other over the past few days to feel themselves companionable – that impulse being secured now by their meeting in such a situation – and soon Agnes was telling him about the church, the vicar, the order of service, showing him the visitors' book and inviting his surprise that people from Australia and Canada had been in only a few days before, encouraging him to sign it himself.

With the knowledge of her circumstances as delivered to him by Mrs. Jackson, Richard felt shy before her. It was as if he had some hold on her which could embarrass her completely should he reveal it. For one ludicrous moment he thought it better that he *should* reveal it and follow this by telling her that it did not matter. He sweated at his coarseness as the moment passed. For Agnes's poise acted on him as a tutelary example. She was a smallish woman, slim, grey frail hair, a fine nose and eyes, small hands, stout shoes. It was her skin which impressed him most. About her eyes and the corners of her mouth, it was wrinkled –

35

but so faintly as to mark decency rather than age – otherwise it was as fine and smooth as linen, coloured by tints and strokes which could have come from the freshest apples; as if lace had printed dabs so delicate that they brushed scarcely touching, touched without impairing. And as he was shy with her, so she with him, a cheerful formality of speech and manner not quite hiding, indeed pointing, the gap between acquaintanceship and friendship, the latter being what she was evidently more suited to.

He complimented her – feeling a fool, as *his* formality, the natural reaction to hers, lacked all grace and so took shape in pomposity – on the church. She thanked him, "Have you noticed the new carpet?", pointed to the long roll of red carpet which went from the south door to the chancel steps. It was of sensible material and yet chosen with such awareness of the church's due that it seemed ceremonial, its brightness darkened and enriched by the light which came through the windows. "We needed a carpet for a long time." Richard nodded and Agnes, sensing and pitying his inarticulate interest, continued with more embellishment than she would normally have allowed in talking of it. "But we'd just bought new surplices for the boys – there are only three of them, you know – and the committee's funds were out. So I got two sacks of coal from Mr. Scott – I was going to pay for them myself but he *gave* them – I thought I'd have something useful as a prize – and we made twenty pounds from the raffle. I did it myself – no credit to me, of course. I wanted it to be a surprise so I didn't tell anybody *exactly* what it was for. Anyway, I got it and made it up and it was down for Easter Sunday." Feeling that in her confidence she had somehow slipped into boasting, Agnes blushed and pointed to a small carpet, not much bigger than a mat, which lay by the font. "Mrs. Fryer collected for that. Nine pounds that thing cost! And the poor woman had to put an extra ten shillings in herself."

She looked at her watch and hurried to change and be off. The work had to be done between the four-hour feeds and that left little time for chatter. Richard walked back with her, holding her carrier bag on the church steps as she buttoned up her coat, fastening it to the neck despite the sticky heat now beginning to gather on the ground as the clouds moved off and the sun came through. Later, Richard was to learn that this was only one of the free jobs that Agnes did around the village; she cleaned out the Women's Institute, delivered Meals on Wheels every Thursday

36

morning, went to the local cottage hospital to serve tea to the out-
patients, sat on the church committee, the carnival committee
and the Old Folks Outing committee besides being the inevitable
"Mrs. Beattie'll do that" when anything came up. Yet all was
done without any moral complacency. She grumbled from time
to time – saying that she was the only one daft enough to do all
these things, she laughed at her own constant occupation, calling
herself Mrs. Mop; she enjoyed it, it got her out and about, just as
her annual turn at the Christmas Show allowed her to sing and
clown around to her own and everyone else's satisfaction. It was
this contrast between the meek, almost retiring, certainly fragile
appearance she had, and the steady way in which she pursued
activity and enjoyment, that Richard loved, would come to
worship. She was a good woman, soon he thought of her as the
best woman, the truest, he had ever known; and yet she could be
boisterous in a way which forced a totally different appreciation
of her character. Propriety, restraint, self-containment, precision
– all of which normally lead to a certain dryness, or, at most, a
soft-voiced savouring of the world – were, in her case, the spring-
boards to laughter, relish and bustling grace.

She came from a large family – one of the youngest of ten – and
had wanted as large a family for herself. But after the birth of
Janice she could have no more children.

They walked up the road, Richard awkwardly bending down
towards her as she spoke, Agnes pointing out where the bonfires
used to be – she had corked her face one night and scared everyone out of their wits; where the men had stood to be hired – Wif
had stood there once, the first time she had seen him, and been
offended when she had gone up and said "How much?"; the pub
called The Pit, "There's a lot of stories about that place," she
said. "Potters used to come and set up behind it for weeks.
They'd use the hall and put on entertainments every night –
dunking apples, the greasy pole, all sorts of games, you know.
And they had the most beautiful crockery you ever saw. We
never managed to get any – they asked a good price for those
days – but there's many a house round here where you'll find
potters' plates on the sideboard. They decorated them themselves
you know. Yes. All hand-painted. And the caravans! I've never
seen anything so beautiful in all my life! They still had horses of
course – this is a good bit before the war. But those caravans.
Greens – and reds and yellows – such decoration and always a
lovely finish. I could look at them for hours. I used to say to Wif

37

that if ever I ran away, it wouldn't be for another man but for one of those caravans!"

She talked on about the potters. There, in a grey coat, green hat, a slight figure – it was as if a silver birch suddenly bore tropical fruit. In his interest he overlooked the fact that he might be patronising; and later, when he thought of it, he was glad he had overlooked it.

They turned on to the track which led to the cottages and walked towards the fells, now gleaming under the large yellow sun.

"It was kind of you to see Mrs. Cass home the other night," said Agnes, shyly. "Yes. Everything gets around in this place. Billy Munn had seen you on the road!" She hesitated. "You've seen Edwin, haven't you? Yes. He has this end cottage. He's done everything he could for her. But she won't come and live with him. He supports her, but she calls him worse than muck some times. I don't want to say anything against her because I think that she's not very well. In the head. But she refuses treatment. I just tell you this because she might have said things against Edwin and it would be awful if you believed them. No son could have done more for his mother – and especially when – never mind. I just thought I'd tell you. Edwin's a good man."

She left him and he went into the kitchen for his tea thinking "a good man, a good man". When she had said it of Edwin, he had wished that it could be said of him. The words had pricked his childhood landscape, when to be good was the best you could be. And even though his idea of a good man had been diluted and twisted – now it was the man who achieved himself in whatever fashion, now it was said of someone who did a good turn, now of someone who avoided the vulgar or obvious, mostly it was said as a sarcastic dig – yet when, as then, it was clearly said, it drew on more of him, resounded more lingeringly in his mind than any other phrase. The world became ordered once more, a simple moral form, an acceptable hierarchy, and yet without the fear that must attend a hierarchy of power, or the deceit which always attends a hierarchy of birth or the injustice which attends a hierarchy of money or merit – with warmth only, and the dignity which came from the assumption that in any circumstances a man can act well – and that is enough.

But why the need for a hierarchy? Service, Patriotism, Heroism, Honour, Duty – all the big hierarchical words which had once stirred him, he had seen peeled of their capitals. Ambition, Magnificence, Greatness, which had raised columns to other piles

38

of hierarchy, they, too, were tattered. Many words had gone – and many he still wished good riddance to – all except "Goodness". And if what it evoked in him was to do with the past rather than the present, with retrogression rather than progress, with evasion rather than confrontation, then he was prepared to accept these accusations. For that one word alone, its meaning and its history, stood intact among the debris, and if a man's life lay in becoming – as Richard believed – in aspiring, in moving towards, then some gradation and so hierarchy was needed to give that movement legitimacy. "A good man": to be that would be something.

What thing? The whole impulse was doomed by an unacceptable yearning for simplicity. So he argued against himself. He ought to be enjoying multiplicity and complication! The kaleidoscope of contemporaneity: scholarships, capital, television, and other entangling advantages never given to Agnes; wadded weeklies, motorology, psychology, phenomenology, pop, porn, pot – all that inrush of *lumpen*-information which had suddenly stormed the cosy lighted kitchen that had been his childhood and adolescence, when ignorance knew innocence and bad was black and the map was imperial red. How could there be "good" in the crossbeams of grey light – and so on?

Perhaps there could not. But perhaps, also, goodness was not such a simple element. Perhaps, knowing more about Agnes, he would discover that her disadvantages were just as complicating as his advantages. And the fact was that his own compound of complexity had become intolerable. He was prepared to be told that it was weakness which had catapulted him from London; but he was not prepared to believe it. He believed he had run towards, not away from, something. He had come through choice.

He did not agree with the idea that understanding stops action, but he realised that inactivity would make it difficult to mark a change in himself. He had put himself in a static situation. The first thing to do was to discover its boundaries.

He went outside. The chatter from before the three cottages lifted over the hedge and settled around him. All the cottages had big gardens and Richard had heard the men talking in them on one or two evenings, enjoyed the lapping of their words but never, until now, been inclined to join them. He went up the lane, hesitant before such a self-sufficient order, looking on until Wif beckoned him across. They took him into their company with due allowances but without strain. Edwin was there, determinedly training his garden as if he were entering it for a race, and Mr. Jackson – a docile man, shoulders, knees and neck hourly expecting the yoke, docile relief inhabiting every other feature, thankful that he was, for that moment, unharnessed.

"I was saying that my wife had told me that there's a Swedish woman in a caravan over at Asby, and my wife was saying that this woman thinks nothing of lying around with nothing on, thinks nothing of it." Mr. Jackson spoke very quietly.

"That's what they do in Sweden, Jack," Wif replied, smiling. "You go to Sweden and you've got to leave your clothes at t'customs sheds."

"That right? Eh? Dear me. I'm glad I wasn't born one. They must have queer thick skins."

"They toughen themselves up by rolling in t'snow all winter. Then they hit themselves wid birch branches, in t'summer."

"That right? Eh? I tell you. You wouldn't catch me at it. And the way they talk! Mrs. Jackson says it's just like English – backwards."

"That's exactly what it is, Jack."

Mr. Jackson could be let out on an even longer rope before he felt the tug of the tease. It was as if the constant information passed on to him by his wife had shaped his mind to a funnel of credulousness, the sieve having been corroded or, more exactly, burst, by the pressure of gossip.

Later, Richard took to coming there most evenings, helping with the rough work, not doing a great deal, coming increasingly into Wif's company, being brought a cup of tea by Agnes – then, immediately, another by Mrs. Jackson *with* a cake – by this regular engagement quelling any restlessness or at least averting it. Almost to his own surprise, he began his routine, wrote an article a week, sent off two of them to the magazine he had worked for, had them accepted. In the late evenings, he would read, listen to his records or sit at the small upright piano, plonking his two-fingered way through songs, toying with the idea of writing pop tunes again as he had once, not very successfully, done.

It seemed to him that all things became subdued to his will. He forgot the awe in which he had held the fells and saw them only as more and more delightful, intoxicated by their proximity, feeling that he commanded them. Agnes became ever more firmly seen as an ideal as he watched her come and go about the village and the cottages.

He grew stronger and his face lost its strain. He would wash in

40

the barrel of cold water outside the house in the morning and be exhilarated at the numbing splash which stiffened his cheeks, then set them shivering. His body shook off the lazy gristle which had curdled on it in London.

Sometimes in the evenings he would see Janice at the upstairs window. She had had a set back a few days after the birth – not serious, but she was confined to bed. She would move away as soon as she saw his glance. The sun would slant low across the window frame, touching the thick yellow of her hair until it glowed like the barley itself in that sunset. Then it would disappear.

One day he had walked away from the fells and come to a very small tarn, on land almost flat, a miserable inconsequent overspill, it seemed, from those lakes and waters confined by the hills. A man was fishing, standing on the grassy bank in long black waders, a flat upright figure against the flat cross-barred clouds in the sky. Richard had watched him and grown hardly conscious of time, as he did now, and was surprised to hear the man talking to him and see him come so close. "Yes," the man was saying, "it was a nasty business. They saw his Mini-Cooper over beside that gate – somebody noticed it two days running. Well, they had to have the frogmen out. This place is too deep to drag. Surprising that, isn't it? And they found him with a stone round his neck. He had a good job, everything. The papers said it was about a woman he was going to marry. He must have been upset about something."

At the time, because of the flat manner of its telling, Richard had not attached himself to the story. But when he first saw Janice – immediately he thought that she must be the woman. He became convinced of it, and then, as irrationally, disturbed at this conviction. And even when the most guarded and yet exhaustive enquiries revealed that the young man was from another district altogether, that Janice had been at College at the time, that – as far as he could discover – it would have been impossible, he was not entirely relieved.

CHAPTER SIX

Wif was about half a mile ahead of him on the fell-dyke road. For a few minutes, Richard made no attempt to catch him up, assuming, correctly, that Wif wished to be on his own. At one point, when Wif disappeared over the brow of a hill, Richard thought of returning home so that his inevitable intrusion – they must both be headed for Ennerdale Show – would not interfere with the old man's day. But he had told Mrs. Jackson where he was going, she would have dispatched the information to all with whom she was concerned, and his failure to see Wif would be meat for curiosity. Besides which he wanted to go to the Show.

Wif walked with his shoulders dipped into the space before him and the yellow bait-tin bounced lightly on the small of his back. His hair was tufted thick and unclipped, black and grey like a badger; his cheeks were red, and tiny blue veins scattered a maze of patterns beneath them; his nose was large, sagging slightly over a wide and careful mouth. He wore a white open-necked shirt, gaping on a fiercely red neck, an old jacket, serviceable trousers and thick black boots, tightly laced. He had been born in Crossbridge and though, in his younger days, he had spent many years away from it, doing farm-work, he carried that village in his head. Now he had a pit-top job at a limestone quarry in a nearby village. He kept up his interest in farming and outdoor work by doing odd jobs around the place at weekends and in the evenings.

When Richard himself came to the top of that hill, he saw that Wif was waiting for him and ran to meet him. Usually, Wif was courteously careful to speak to Richard without using dialect. To-day, however, perhaps because the Show was more his affair than his companion's, he allowed himself its accent and, occasionally, vocabulary.

"Dis thou know," said Wif, as they went on, "this is t'first time aa've been til an agricultural show for eleven, no, twelve years. Aye! Yen time, aa would a walked many a mile to catch one. We'd be up be three – and off – when a'd me day spare, thou knows. And I had this day as to-day is to come because of that extra shift aa put in last day of me holidays see, so aa thowt, reet,

42

we'll save that up, an' if Agnes didn't want owt dun – we'll away."

Richard immediately felt uncomfortable that all his days were "spare". And yet . . . a rush of arguments sprouted up to justify his situation, so many that he laughed aloud. He had not realised his defences were in such good order.

"You can laugh," said Wif, grinning back at him, "but that's what we used to do. Mind you, they *were* shows in those days. And when aa was hired at Major Langley's – before t'war – right up in t'middle of nowhere he lives, on t'Scotch border – well he was a good horseman you know. And we would take them all round t'spot, you know. He had two – Bess and Gilded – and we had some fun. We would set off for some spots about midnight, you know. Travel in wid t'horses. Been to Bristol and back in those horse-boxes and you would start dressing them the minute you got there. Mind, I preferred dressing a Clydesdale meself. Now that *is* a horse. I could make t'hair round those horses' hooves as fine as any woman's. Ay. And we'd plait their tails, eight strands, maybe put some flowers in among it – and that brass had to dazzle. There was a fella at Brampton – Newall, his name was, and dis thou know . . ."

They walked on past that abandoned pit which from the fell looked like a ruined castle – even from close up to it, it had a freakish dignity, somehow borrowing from old castles the associations it threw off of lyrical labour and relentless substantiality – and paused on the brow of a hill from which they could look at the sea and at Ennerdale Water. It was a grey sky, bringing out the slate in the hills, spreading an uneasy strain over the place, threatening the land with unwanted rain, and anyone who weakened with melancholy. There were few sounds. It was as if all preferred to ignore this unseasonable interruption of a good summer.

The Show field was about two miles west of the lake, behind Ennerdale village, a small patch of white tents among fields resisting the grey day with perspiring greenness. They walked towards it, past one or two new bungalows, and an equal number of abandoned cottages, down the long-winding road that dramatically shifted the perspective of the view with every few yards dropped.

Wif never mentioned Janice. He did talk of Agnes. "They don't know what to make of her in t'village, you know," he said. "She doesn't come from round here, but my God, she livens them up! There was last year when we were supposed to have those children's sports and the Sports Committee was out of funds. In fact it was skint. Billy Munn's brother-in-law had run away with the proceeds of the annual dance and nobody could say anything, see, it being Billy Munn. Anyway – you know, there are a lot of kids around here who have nothing. I mean they wear shoes and they're fed but that's about it. Have you met Pat Gregory? Well he's got ten – it's why he's on the dole, to be honest, because the family allowance with his dole is more than he could ever earn as a working man - there's a lot like that, you know, and they poach and labour a bit on the side. Better off. Anyway, these Children's Sports. No funds. Comes September. No posters. Enter Billy Munn – no Sports, he says. Well now, you know what, Agnes did? She went all about – herself – walking mind you, and it was nasty, snow, with a tin box I made up for her – I put a slit in it for the coins and a hole for the notes, you know, like they have – she visited every last farm and cottage in Crossbridge Parish and made sixty-two pounds fourteen and two – Billy Munn made it up to sixty-three. On her own! And there were them that blamed her, you know. There was one farmer argued that she was begging. Begging, she said, I'm just getting a bit of a subsidy like you fellows take from us tax-payers every week of the year without a blush! That fettled him. And Greta Hetherington refused to talk to her – said it was "unseemly" for someone on the Church Council to go round with a box any time except Christmas. Well, Agnes went down to see her, she did, and she just told her that if she needed Christmas to do a good turn she was in a bad way. Told her! Mind you, she never forced anybody. Just stated her case. And a good case it was!"

Now they were through the small village – not a soul on the streets – over the bridge, past the Fox and Hounds and up to the Show field. There were cars and vans scattered along the roadside all the way along to it and three policemen purposefully walking up and down, two of them wearing white covers on their forearms. Entrance fee was three shillings and they were in.

The Show field was on the first rise of a fell and hills surveyed the gathering from three sides. Now the clouds were distending and here and there parting to let through that cold blue which had been the sky for the last few weeks. Soon the sun chased away all the sailing-barges of grey and there were nothing but skimpy remainders, whitely tossed about in the wind like tatters of muslin.

44

It was not a big show but Wif took Richard around it in detail. They had come just in time for the Grand Parade of the Beasts, which had been judged all through the morning. They went to the show-ring – besieged by cars which encircled it like a cordon of beetles – and saw the farmers and their sons, labourers, girls and old men, leading the slow-padding cows and heifers and bullocks around the edge of the ropes. Each beast had a number glued on to its haunches; each was led by a rope, and as they passed the loudspeaker van the M.C. recited their prize-winning points and the litany never ceased. Most of the men leading the animals were shy, even among so many others and in an open ring, surveyed by very few spectators, many of them blushed or hung their heads as if expecting – and feeling that they deserved – to be teased for such excessive display.

While Wif concentrated on the cattle, Richard looked at the men leading them. All sorts; the older men who walked with the rope between their fingers, seemingly forgetting about what was at the other end of it, far too concerned with a brooding which began and, it appeared, ended three inches from their noses; farmers' sons, stalking the sodden grass with a constant tug at their animal's head, reiterating to all that this beast belonged to them; boys who shuffled around, continually trying to release one hand for time enough to allow them to comb their hair; and an occasional very old, or very large man, striking by reason of his singular confidence, who walked in the Grand Parade as in a victory march with all the honours of the world fit to be borne on his shoulders. From the top of Grike or Crag Fell, it must have looked like a pageant as formal, perhaps, as those of the Druids. The very density of the congregation in such a lonely area gave it a significance beyond its function. But it was the shyness of the faces which most impressed Richard. Such reticence he had forgotten about. And yet it was neither unmanly, nor stupid, nor backward; simply an expression which his way and place of life over the last few years had never recognised, it being lost under those complicated defences which fear everything that might characterise a lack of sophistication.

Again he saw it in the Industrial Tent which Wif took him to once the Parade and the speeches were over. There, in a massive marquee, were the spoils of a whole community. Flowers, vegetables, eggs, fruit, every sort of home-baked cake, knitting, sewing, paintings, woodwork, metalwork, everything neat, worked, well displayed, and again their makers shyly mingling with the

45

close-pressed crowd almost embarrassed to own what they had so patiently made. There were the most amazing things. An iced cake which had been decorated on top with a complete farm, all the buildings and machinery and animals made out of different colours of icing. An altar cloth, embroidered so intricately that you could only imagine a life's work in some airless room, with Chastity and Dedication the sentries. A number of shepherd's crooks, their heads carved so deftly you would have thought them turned on a wheel, and the choice of heads unaccountably macabre, with snakes running down the staff and minute antlers pricking out of the top; one was in ivory. On one stand, there was a special prize given to a young woman who had made a scale model of Ennerdale village out of infinitesimal pieces of slate – the whole model implying such disinterested diligence as was out of Richard's comprehension. There were scones, rock-buns, chocolate cakes, apple pies, teacakes, loaves of bread – now being distributed as the prizegiving was over.

The Industrial Tent was the only big tent. There was a smaller one for agricultural machinery which Wif examined scrupulously – as if he was about to seize on a loose bolt or a scratched surface which would confirm an unspoken theory as to the decline of workmanship, but no opportunity was given – otherwise, besides, the sacred beer tent and its two acolytes, the Ladies' and the Gentlemen's, there was little else but stalls, cars and of course lorries. There must have been well over a hundred lorries, all parked at the bottom of the field and it was there that Wif finally went.

This was the centre of it. Gangplanks shuddered as animals were heaved in and boxed up. Straw spread all over the ground, sticks whacked against haunches, the enormous vehicles shifted out and made off with their loads, rosettes plastered on the windscreen. Little boys scampered around delirious among the crowded business. The beer tent, wide open at the front, pushed its customers out from the bar into the sunny afternoon and women sprawled on mackintoshes surrounded by catalogues and newspapers. The competitors for the riding events were preparing themselves; old military-looking men, one with a face flayed purple by drink and fresh air, a shiny black bowler screwed on to his head to offset the damage, his twiggy legs shivering on the flanks of a bay chestnut; young girls, like Diana all of them, high in their saddles, one particularly beautiful, immaculately spruce

46

in a finely cut coat, her face white cream patched with red, the little nose repudiating the air itself as she tossed backwards and forwards on her arrogant way; men in heavy tweed, their faces as leathery as their bridles, scruffy jodhpurs wrinkled above half-polished riding boots, the whole aspect between rakish and bucolic, a cigarette burning in their lips. All knew each other. These riders moved around from show to show, almost as a travelling circus, daily jumping off the surplus money of land and farms for tin cups and crepe flowers, cantering into ring after ring with their numbers strung across their backs, the bumpy field uncertain under the hooves, the wooden jumps often as not cramped together too tightly. They were the standard-bearers of the day. They knew it, and everyone enjoyed watching their performance. No shyness there.

Richard looked out of the Show field in a direction away from the cars. Again he was bemused by the stillness not a minute's walk away. In a few hours, the Show would be over, tents down, litter cleared, and all as if it had never been. Why that intrigued him he did not know. Perhaps because such a temporary congregation was more touching, evidence of a real willingness to be herded together in voluntary communality and yet proof of the transience of all assemblies. Whatever, the mere sight of the land-scale beyond the field gave him a particular pleasure.

"See her," said Wif, pointing at a young woman of about thirty leading a grey mare up the slope to its box, "that's Anne Duvan." He waited for the reaction. "She jumps on television. I saw her there only a week ago. She'll be up for the Horse of the Year Show again this year. At the White City in London. My God, she can make that thing go. It's called Hebe. Hee-bee. It can fly."

Richard watched her for a few moments, saw the respect in which she was held by the way in which younger riders kept passing close to her, looking out for a nod, laughing outrageously when she passed a remark, glowing in the light.

"I just have time to get the presents before they start out jumping," said Wif. They went over to the stalls – two or three broken lines of hooded trestle-tables selling toys, sweets, trick things, pots and pans, all gaudily displayed, and other-worldly bargains. "That's what makes it an expensive day out for a working man," Wif grinned, "by t'time you've bowt presents for iverybody – it runs gay dear." For Agnes he bought two small ornaments,

47

which might have been Toby jugs except that the figures resembled demented dwarfs; for Janice a half-pound box of chocolates, and a fluffy rabbit for the baby.

Wif bought these things with a grand disregard. Although his money was scarce, he did not fumble or hesitate. He earned eleven pounds fourteen and fourpence a week at his job and after thirty shillings rent and rates, the coal and electricity, food and other essentials, there was little left. Agnes had once worked and still wanted to but was prevented in it by two things. The first, Wif's reluctance to have his wife working – this coming from such a long habit of fixing the woman in the home that it was truly painful to him to see it broken, and to Agnes to feel how much he was offended and diminished by it. The second was more singular. He started work at seven – cycling to it – and returned, in winter at about four, in summer at five; and he liked his dinner to be waiting for him. He did not make a fuss about this or claim it, as some men did, as the inalienable right of their inviolable masculinity, but he liked it to be there. And Agnes liked to have it ready for him. So any extra money was made through the odd jobs he did in the evenings, and through Agnes's sewing and knitting, incessant work which yielded about fifteen bob clear in a good week. That had more or less dried up since the birth of the baby. But none of the pared budgeting made Wif anxious; he remarked on it, he was conscious of it, he was not unaware of the disregard for justice in a society which sanctioned – thrived on – it, but that was his lot, he was too old to fight, and he would trim his material life to it. If he could not have the luxury of money, then at least the lack of it was not going to corrode his self-respect.

The presents were parcelled and hidden in his large pockets and they went across to enjoy the jumping, squeezing in front of a shooting-brake to get ringside seats. The competition was not strong and Anne Duvan won everything she entered. As the summer afternoon passed gently away, Richard became mesmerised by the repeated actions of the horses, the continuous cosy patter from the loudspeaker, the man at the microphone knowing everything about everyone and announcing engagements, past triumphs and personal idiosyncrasies of the riders as well as calling mothers to lost children, warning people to keep this and that clear, giving out police messages, reminding the spectators of future shows, popping on a military march between events, his sole concern being to encircle the Show field with sounds from his Tannoy; and with all this, Wif's observations about past and present shows, the reminiscences which certain names or people seen brought up. Quite a few of those there knew Wif, even though Ennerdale was out of his parish, and Richard was sometimes left alone while Wif scrambled up to go and have a talk with someone who hailed him. He shared his bait, Richard bought four bottles of beer, and they sucked happily at the brown spouts, the sun whipping a flush on to their faces, the noises of lorries and horses, loudspeaker, stall-criers and children all gradually mingling to one harmonious hum which seemed to spin off the hot afternoon as appropriately as the light clouds flitted across the hill-tops.

Intermittently he would start awake from this lapping vortex and then he would see only faces. It seemed to him that the faces had not changed for hundreds of years; that a group of men straining to tumble a beast up a slippery ramp could have tagged along to Canterbury with Chaucer's Miller; their expressions were clear and each feature appeared as a metaphor of a characteristic. The slim girls on the horses could have waited for a decade in castles or sat patiently in Capability Brown landscapes tiredly pleased to indulge the tentative requests of the portrait-painter hopping out from behind his large canvas like a rabbit; the younger men, with plastered hair and clothes that would not settle on their shaping bodies, with only one or two lines across their brows to indicate the long fall before them – they would have followed the drums to any war from Marston Moor to Ypres. Only the dwarfish, the deformed, the birth-cursed – those who have witched both industrial and rural landscapes and literature for so long, giving to England a physical oddness as strong in its flavour as the eternal peasant gave to Russia – only *they* were not conspicuous this afternoon – but here in a warty nose, there in slightly shortened legs, their spell had not quite left off.

In London he had rarely noticed faces – or never in a way which engaged him as these did. Yet in cities, too, the continuity was there; only his own haste had blurred the images. Perhaps he recognised it so clearly here because the faces resounded in his childhood which, though passed in a different area, had not been dissimilar from that in which he now found himself. And the faces gave him a feeling of span; he was not surrounded – as he had been in London – by that bright and uniform aspect which marked the hot-house product of one generation only and, by its uniformity, cancelled out any association with others, and so left that one segment in a vacuum, at once disturbed at its isolation

49

and proud of it. Here, he was a part of all generations; there was no rush, they would all pass, and in that last security he felt that he finally accepted the union between himself and his newly chosen ground. This cosy conclusion would once have prompted a quick laugh at himself; but now his guard was down. He felt no need for it.

A special announcement. The Show Jumping was over. The ring was now being cleared for the Grand Parade to be followed by the Games – the potato race, musical buckets and so on. "But before that, a special treat, give a big hand to something we don't see very much of nowadays. A pair of Clydesdales – large greys – completely dressed like they would have been thirty years ago – or even a hundred years ago ladies and gentlemen – led and shown by Mr. Hector Lowell, aged eighty-one, who has rescued these horses from the knacker's yard and kept them at his own expense so that others can have the same pleasure as he does himself in seeing these magnificent beasts. Aged eighty-one, ladies and gentlemen! A Big Hand for Hector and his Clydesdales and here they come in the bottom of the ring, just beside the ice-cream van. I'm going to put on 'Military Marches' played by the Welsh Guards. Here he is. Eighty-one! Hector Lowell!"

"Well I'm blessed," said Wif. "I was hired alongside Hector for seven year down on a spot called Curthwaite. Eighty-one, eh? Aye, he'll be that easy enough. Well, I'm buggered!"

In came the two huge mares, fit to plough for twelve hours at a stretch, to haul cannons through mud, households across a country, and they trotted together up the field. It seemed that no one guided them until Richard spotted a pair of brown leggings scampering along between the huge hoofs. It was difficult to know whether one was more impressed by the size of the horses, their manes garlanded and intertwined, their tails bobbed, plaited and regular as braiding, their skins shiny, hooves polished, nostrils shuddering out hot air even into the hot day, or Hector himself, diminutive, stern-faced, a new cap not quite able to contain his white hair, the brown overall, though of the smallest size, too long and flapping half-way down his calves, prancing along as sprightly as his horses, knees pummelling the bottom of his overall, alternate corners of his mouth twitching infinitesimally as he commanded his charges, his arms suspended high above him as he clung on to the bridles; it would have taken only a flick of the head from both the mares to lift him clean off the ground, and still, Richard felt, he would have pummelled his legs,

50

spat out his curse and kept unbroken the cemented composure of his face.

The crowd had laughed and clapped on his entry, but Hector soon made it clear that he was no laughing matter. He walked the horses, trotted them, hooked them together facing different ways and made them heave at each other so that all could observe their power, he petted and patted them, and then, in league with the loudspeaker, he pointed out their various parts while the words of praise sang out from the Tannoy. His sternness held it all this side of a circus act, while his seriousness compelled everyone to realise what a treat they were enjoying. Finally, he stood at the top of the ring, waited until a new record was put on – Hector's signature tune, it was announced – blew his nose with a mighty handkerchief, got himself into the holding position and then, to the strain of Colonel Bogey – which his audience clapped to immediately – galloped his mares right down the field, sprinting between them, his feet only toe-touching the grass.

"Let's away and see him," said Wif, who, perhaps alone on the field, had smiled throughout Hector's performance. "My God, I hope I'm as fit as that at eighty-one."

They walked round the field past the lorries to a corner which Hector had made all his own. A few people stood around, passing comments to each other – but none to Hector who was far too busy at his work to be bothered with them. Wif went up to him, introduced Richard, and Hector, having vocally acknowledged that Wif knew what a horse was and so could be considered for serious conversation, told them all about it.

"Mind you," he concluded, "it's an expense. I've nowt but me pension, you know."

"How do you manage?" Wif asked.

"I manage," said Hector. "I walked them here today. Seven miles. Walked them. Thowt I was going to miss the damned Show when Penelope played up at Wathbrow. She would not settle. I don't know what comes over her. Then I get a fee, you know. Oh yes. A pound an appearance. Two pounds sometimes. But I don't ask."

"It must be terribly hard work to keep them as well as you do," said Richard.

"Work?" Hector replied. "What work?" He paused. "I'll tell you what, though, it's all finished, Wif. They'll soon have forgotten how to dress a mane – won't know what a tail's for. Aye.

It's all over. And I'll tell you summat else. I'm glad. They were always more trouble than enough."

"When did you take this up, then, Hector?"

"A year ago. Anson laid me off farm-work, you know. Stupid sod. I could outwork him any day of the week. Then I felt I was getting stiff. I can't sit down, man, I can't stay inside, I can't do nowt. They want you to stiffen up. Then you're not as much trouble turning into a corpse, eh, Wif? They get you used to t'idea. Not me, laddo. I'm still runnin'.'"

"Are you staying for t'Trails?" Wif asked.

Hector hesitated. While talking to Wif, his eyes and body had gambolled with goblin energy – the words but a trivial indication of that energy. At Wif's question, however, he slumped on his flat feet as if struck. "Nivver again, Wif, nivver again," he said.

Wif nodded.

"And will you be walking the seven miles back to-night?" Richard asked.

"To-night? This minute. Unless you've a ten-ton truck up your sleeve that can carry these two."

To match his words, he turned and grabbed the bridles and moved down the field. Wif and Richard with him. He walked with the conscious modesty of a star; catching every stare that was thrown at him, noticing each smile and nod of congratulation strutting out with his two great ark-fit animals, and yet acknowledging none of it. Richard observed that Wif grew far more embarrassed and self-conscious. He himself felt like the server who, by virtue merely of an accident, is allowed to accompany the bishop as he beats the bounds.

At the gate they parted, and as Wif wanted to get back for his supper, the two men set off for Crossbridge, leaving the Potato Race in full sweat, the loudspeaker ringing out O Dear What Can the Matter Be?, the Hound Dogs come for the Trails yelping in the bottom field, the Industrial Tent sagging as they slackened the guy ropes to emphasise the end of its usefulness. Their backs to the field, they soon lost touch with individual sounds – except for the shout of a dog – and the Show diminished behind them.

"What happened to Hector when you asked him about – what was it? – the Trails, was it?"

"Hound Trails," said Wif. "It's a big sport round here. T'dogs run round a seven or eight mile course following an aniseed track. There's a hell of a lot of gambling on it – and Hector used to be one of the worst. Mind it wasn't only dogs. He would bet on owt.

52

Aa've worked wid him when he'd bet on how many plops would come out of a horse's behind when it started – you know. He would give anybody double or quits for anything. Double or quits every time you had a drink, double or quits about who pays t'bus fare, double or quits wid shopkeepers – aye, and collectors in a church if he could get away wid it. His wife left him, you know. He lived with a married daughter for a time, then she chucked him out. And then he was really in a bad way. When I met him he was entitled to live in, you know, like any hired man, but he wangled hissel a five-bob bed allowance and just slept where he dropped. Oh, I forgot, I saw him once bet a fella that he could spit on to a roof – and by God he did it. And he kept a pair of beetles in a match-box – he would race them. Anyway, at this time he was a disgrace. You wouldn't recognise him. He nivver washed, he had no money for clothes, he wouldn't shave until he could bet on it – he once bet Tommy Wallace, a barber, that he couldn't shave him clean without lather or anything – and by God Tommy did it – gave him a haircut as well. Well, says Hector, when it's through – thou's won. Yes, said Tommy, and I've wasted half a morning givin' thee a free do!

"Two things kept him going. First was, he was a grand worker. He's just a little fella – you noticed that – well, that little fella could shift more in a day than men twice his size could look at in a week. And his was smart work, always tidy, you know, his tools had to be just so, whatever he did had to be just A1. He was never short of work. And the other thing was – he didn't pinch, see. A lot of them, when they start bettin' heavy, well nobody knows where they are. They're forever cadging and pinchin'. Hector never did. He would rather finish a day's work and then work half the night for somebody else to get himself some money. Folk respected that.

"Anyway, these dogs. Hector got interested, you see. And he knows a bit about dogs. So he started to follow these Trails. They have them every night you know – in season. There's always one somewhere. Well he would bike all up and down. I tell you, there was meetings where they wouldn't start t'trails til Hector rattles in. Anyway, he thought he was on a winner. And by God, he knew his sport – he knew everything there was to know about those dogs – pedigree, performances, what their owners felt, how they ran in wet, how in dry, whether they knew the ground, how they were with sheep, whether there was any barbed wire around, what they felt about barbed wire – some dogs go right over it, you know – the lot. And he was daft, Hector, but he was nivver stupid, if you get my meaning. He would always have a bet, but he would always have a chance. Well, one year he started to coin it. He did. There were some bookies stopped taking his bets altogether! It came to that. He wasn't perfect, you know, but he was winnin', there was no doubt about that. He was givin' the bookies a hiding.

"Well, there's a lot of twistin' in Hound-Trailing of course – or there was, they've cleaned it up a bit now – so they say – anyway there was a lot of twistin'. I mean, they're run right over the countryside and they're out of sight of the start-and-finish field most of the time and so what some folk would do would be to nip out and catch one or two of the dogs, maybe the favourites say, and hold them back for a few minutes. There was all sorts of dodges. Well; they said that Hector had interfered with a race. They said that they'd seen him holding back a favourite, and he was barred. He denied it. And I believe him. But there was these two said they'd seen it happen – and he was barred.

"You've nivver seen a fella as cut up. Even though he denied it, you know, and even though he proved that those two men were mates of one of the big bookies he'd been stinging – didn't matter: Hector went round looking as if he'd gone through all t'crimes in t'calendar. He gave up his work and took to tramping. Aye. On t'tramp he was – oh, for a good few months. Then this wife that had left him dies and he comes back for t'funeral, and finds himself another. He was a big fella among the women, you know, before he started serious gamblin'. Always a bit of a dandy.

"Well, this new wife – Mary Alice Freeman, she was, from Seascale, I knew her brother – she fetched him up. In two ticks he was one of the smartest fellas you ever saw again. And now he's got these horses. Mind you, I didn't know about that til today."

"Is he really eighty-one?" Richard asked, after a pause in which he'd waited for more. "He doesn't look anything like that."

"No? Well, it's right. But those old men, you know, who got through that first war and everything after it, if they're alive at all, they're very lively, haven't you noticed? There's another, just out of Crossbridge, Alec Rudd – just the same. Mind you, he hasn't got Hector's stamina. I mean, Hector'll just keep going full blast till he drops dead. You see, spare time and rest and holidays and all that – they mean nothing to men like him. He was raised to go

54

like a steam-engine – and that's what he'll do till he cracks up. He can't help it. They were all like that."

The rest of the way back, Richard asked for more details of Hector – and Wif obliged, just as he had spent most of his free day obliging Richard. Without fuss or regret Richard had been taken into the older man's company, and as they neared the cottages, he realised how much he had enjoyed being with Wif, and realised also how much he had imposed on him. That stumbled out.

"Oh, don't worry yoursel about it," Wif said. "I was glad to see you. You get a bit down if you're just on your own, you know. Nobody to talk to. I can't see how you can like it in that cottage of yours just on your own. It wouldn't suit me."

"I like it. I've been surrounded by people for years. It's nice to be my own boss."

"Trouble is, you're your own labourer as well!"

"I don't mind that. And if it gets too bad, I think I'll advertise for somebody to come and clean once or twice a week."

"Cheapest advertising in Crossbridge is to tell Mrs. Jackson. She beats any newspaper. Instantaneous it is, with her. Instantaneous."

"I'll remember that. But I *like* being alone, you know." He hesitated.

"Oh yes. I suppose some have got to like it. It wouldn't strike me at first sight that you were a natural for it. But there we are."

"But I really like it," Richard insisted. "I was sick of being surrounded by people all the time, having to meet obligations that I don't want to meet when I think it over, seeing people for no other reason than that they're there, tramping around in a perpetual tribe with none of them nearer to me than chance acquaintance – one or two perhaps – but – you see?"

"No," Wif grinned. "To tell you t'truth, Richard, I didn't understand a word of that."

"Neither did I – at the time!"

"Well, we're both comfortable then."

Comfort. On that broad-bottomed word, he would never sink. The Show was comfortably way behind them and Hector comfortably set on his way, the day was coming into a comforting summer evening and there was a comfortable cottage waiting for him. The word made him hesitate at the moment it made him secure.

For after his depression, or "virtual nervous collapse" as the doctor had called it – "quite common" – comfort had been the most desirable thing on earth. And here he had it. He slept long and tenaciously, no more troubled by the hurtling spools of image, memory and nightmare which had slithered wildly through his helpless mind until he became afraid to close his eyes. He no longer shivered and thought that he would die at odd moments – no more! – to recall how he had been was dangerous. No. Comfort was what he wanted. And yet, as they turned into the lane which faced them up to Knockmirton and led them to the cottage, he was apprehensive of the calm, and gentleness. Perhaps to transplant himself so drastically was as bad a thing as he could have done. For, at that moment, walking beside Wif, he felt unrelated to everything around him – and why? After such a calm day, why? Why did he feel that his feet were sponges on cotton ground, that the hedges would wither away if he brushed them, that, among all this solid world, he alone was so insubstantial as to be non-existing?

"Cheer up," said Wif, "it can't be as bad as all that."

"Sorry."

"You were looking a bit down. It's a long day out if you're not used to it."

"Oh, yes. It wasn't that."

"Look. Come and have your supper with us tonight. You can't be forever on your own."

"Oh no. I couldn't – Mrs. Beattie has enough to do – I don't mind eating on my own – I. . . ."

"Well, you're very welcome, Any time."

Wif's gentleness. It was a mark of Richard's tentative state – which was there still, despite his increasing confidence – that he should plump so completely for any and every quality in the old man. A few weeks previously, this discovery of virtues in an "old countryman" would have been quickly dismissed as being "patronising" and absurd. He would have accused himself of being an anthropologist, treating the village as some quaint tribe where the glitter of the noble savage could still be seen by the "discerning". And the accusation rose up now; it was a "joke" rather than an accusation, the "let-out" – the nervous insurance against commitment of any sort. The obvious was to be avoided, his creed had said, at any cost; and the best way to avoid it was to admit it and show you were above it.

Yet, even if his attitude was patronising, could not patronage still be an action coming from sympathy not wholly untainted with appreciation? To hell with it! Wif was gentle. It reminded him of his own grandfather and the rich equation he too had appeared to discover between the world and himself. A walk to the pub after supper, back with an ash stick he had hacked off a dyke; whistling to himself whatever; along the road, free-wheeling down Crowther Hill on that old bike, the handlebars juddering as the old man's neck strained to catch all his eyes could see. Content, it appeared, and in some way innocent of contempt for life. Richard laughed.

"That's better," said Wif. "And here's Edwin."

Edwin came up to meet them, or rather to meet Wif. It was obvious that he wished to talk undisturbed and Richard made off, thanking Wif for the day, suddenly glad to be on his own, to have no real part of anything more demanding than acquaintance-ship.

CHAPTER SEVEN

Dressed in a tidy sports jacket and flannels, with a tie and polished shoes, Edwin, as usual, looked scrubbed, scraped, ready. He was consistently scrupulous about cleanliness, washing and bathing as if preparing for some hygienic confirmation. Yet it made him appear only more exposed, his face daring comment, raw.

Eventually, after the boniest of small-talk, the very existence of which in Edwin's mouth warned Wif conclusively that a serious matter was to be discussed. Edwin came out with it.

"Janice," he said. "Janice. Well, I've been up to see her once or twice you know, while she's been getting better, and I've talked to her but I want to talk to you as well."

"I see. Won't you come in and say it? She's upstairs all these afternoons still, you know."

"I know. Well, I won't if you don't mind, Wif. It's not that I've anything to hide – as I say, I've said it all to her – and thank you for asking, I'm grateful for that, but if you don't mind, I'll say what I have to say standing here. A cigarette?"

The packet was put out with that brusque manner which dis-tinguished all the young man's movements. It was as if – but no comparison is needed, because it is true that Edwin had con-scientiously learnt his manners, everything coming to him

57

slowly and fitting him ill, so that his determination – and success –
in "doing the right thing" was often painful to watch. No sooner
had Wif taken a cigarette than, without bothering to take one for
himself, Edwin stuffed the packet back into his pocket, unscrambled a box of matches, cursed a teasing tail of wind which
darted out of the soft evening to blow the match out, and only at
his third attempt succeeded in completing his gift by lighting the
cigarette.

The two men stood without talking for a moment in the quiet
lane, listening to a lorry hawking through its gears as it mounted
the small rise on the main road, spot-lighting the end of the long
summer day as the evening slowly spun in around them and isolated them.

"I had a word with her," Edwin began, after clearing his nose
with a flapping handkerchief, "and of course I didn't want to upset her when she's just coming out of a sickness, but I let it be
known to her that I was still, I told her, like I'm telling you, that I,
it made no difference, I mean it makes me feel stupid even to say
that but some people have to say stupid things just to get to the
next thing, you know, Wif. I have, anyway. Wif, what I'm saying
is I told her – I hoped she would know like, but I thought I'd tell
her again just to be sure, I said . . ."

"You told her you still wanted to marry her."

"I did."

Wif nodded. Edwin, blushing fully but staring into Wif's face
until the last atom of his last words disappeared, finally looked
away and took out his packet to give himself a cigarette.

Wif, in one way, could have wished no better. He liked and
admired Edwin, and respected profoundly the way in which he
had treated Janice. Yet there was no getting over the fact that
Janice wanted nothing to do with him. Or said she did not. And
this was where Wif grew confused and ashamed for Janice. There
were times when she was with Edwin when it was clear to anyone
that she more than liked him, and her behaviour would have led
to that immediate assumption in any other young man's mind.
And there were times when she spoke of him so affectionately
that, it seemed, Edwin need only pop the question and he would
be accepted. Yet, she wanted nothing to do with him.

Nor was it, she insisted – though Wif did not believe her – anything to do with Edwin's looks. She called his smile "tender",
his expression "manly and kind", anyone who spoke dispara-
gingly of him in her presence was rounded on. It was simply, she

said, that she did not want to marry him. But there were other times when Wif was equally certain that she did, or at least would not have minded. That these latter times almost always coincided with low spirits and such a boredom as exhausted her only made it more complicated.

"Well, something should be settled between you two one way or another soon," said Wif.

"Now I don't want to rush it," Edwin replied, "I'm in no rush. I want you to know that. I wouldn't want her to think that I was crowding in on her."

Wif almost replied as Mrs. Jackson had done – that it might have been better if Edwin *had* "crowded in" – but he repressed the reply. For he could not have it both ways. If he thought so much of Edwin's constancy and care, he could not suggest that it was misplaced; that, he considered, would cut everything from under the young man's feet.

"I know you wouldn't, Edwin. But for her sake as well. I mean, she's got to get it off *her* mind as well. I don't mean to sound as though I want it out of the way – but it should be settled."

"Well, I just wanted to tell you where I stood."

"I know you did, lad. Thank you." Edwin shifted slightly, at the compassion in the words. "You know I think a lot of you," Wif went on, unaware of the valedictory nature of his phrasing, "you know I would have liked nothing better. Yes. Well, I'll talk to her."

"Don't please, unless you think she – I mean, don't. I can't tell you what to do."

"I won't harm anything. I promise you."

Edwin looked truly tortured. He saw tactless remarks growing to malicious obstacles and preventing him from ever having any chance. And chance it would be, he knew that.

"Would you like to come for a drink?" he asked.

"No thanks, Edwin, I'd better be in."

"Sure?" The young man strained his neck around to locate the position of the pub, as if his discovery of it would somehow make valid the nature of his offer.

"Yes. I'm late as it is. Agnes'll be worried."

"Oh."

It was Wif who moved away first. He had to wrench himself from Edwin – and he left him as a submissive version of the state Munch painted in "The Cry". Only Edwin did not howl with his mouth, his entire body stood, listing with tension on that track as he sent out his will after the older man and drew on to himself, without a shudder, the despair he knew would certainly be his. It was Wif who shivered.

He went in, hauled out his presents and had his supper, thankful to use the day's experiences to fill in the chasm now widening dangerously between all three of them. The kitchen reeked of the baby. Nappies and plastic pants hung on a line by the fire, little piles of baby-clothes were stacked on the sideboard, safety-pins on the mantelpiece, bottles in a neat row, the baby herself rolled up in the crutch of the settee. She was called Paula; the only interest Janice had shown being in her insistence on that name.

Agnes was becoming more and more exhausted. In order to shield Janice from the accusations already flying around in the village, she persisted in doing all that she had done previously so that kindling might not be found for the crackling rumours in the observation of her own retreats. But she was finding it difficult even to keep up with the child. Janice did, virtually, nothing. She never fed her baby, only occasionally washed her dirty clothes, only with an effort leaned over to chuck her under the chin or play with her; and did that out of such determined sympathy for Agnes that it was painful.

It had been tolerable during Janice's convalescence because then, for both Wif and Agnes, there was an excuse which, however it diminished daily, had served to help them accept a situation which upset and frightened them. But now, and for the last few days, Janice had been coming down in the evenings. She was well. She sat in an armchair, a book sloping out of her hands, all her concentration, it appeared, directed to keeping everyone in the room outside her thoughts. Illness had made her tired-looking; her body was still stiff from the birth; only her hair gave her the impression of what she could be; she brushed it and cared for it as if she needed one thing at least to remind and encourage her. It was thick and long, dark yellow with lighter streaks of hay touching it to a nervous surface; her face was surrounded even guarded by it. Her expression reminded Wif of the look she had had so often when younger. Wif had never got over the change which had been forced on his attitude towards her after that early illness. She had been anaemic. From that time, he had based his manner towards her on some obscure idea of what was due to an invalid; and as she had become wrapt up in books, grown further and further away from the other girls in the village, that manner could only harden. Though he still longed to, he could never feel that she was *his* as he had done when she was a little girl.

Agnes was waiting for her moment. For every reason under the sun, as she saw it, Janice had to come to look after her own child. But she was prepared to wait, a little longer.

"That Richard, you know," said Wif, "your mam tells me his house is covered in books."

"That doesn't prove anything," Janice replied, sensing a wish to have her reconnected with the world; she wanted none of it at the moment; not even her father's concern; no concern.

"Your father didn't say it to prove anything," rejoined Agnes, plumping herself heavily on the settee and cradling Paula in the crook of her right arm, negotiating the bottle towards the quiet face. The baby had been "no real trouble". It was simply the total helplessness which demanded total responsibility – and that was wearing the older woman out.

"He writes for magazines, you know," said Wif, as a rejoinder, thus giving Richard a legitimate claim on his books, "I suppose he'll need to read a lot to do that. Won't he?"

"Oh father, *I* don't know! He could be the most stupid Philistine there is and still write for magazines. There's nothing marvellous about that."

"I like him," Wif continued, after a pause, "Philistine or Palestine." He smiled, "I think he's wastin' his time dawdlin' about up here, but he's a nice young fella. He sort of "catches" at everything you say. Have you noticed that, Mam? He seems to "catch" at it, as if he'd never heard anything like it before."

"Bessie (that was Mrs. Jackson) "was saying that he'll stop and talk to everybody. Just the same. Even Edna Parkinson can talk on for hours on end and he'll listen. Bessie says she thinks he's maybe writing a book about all of us."

"My God! Just let him dare do it!" Janice's expression was as tight as her fist. "If he thinks he can write one of those "visits to odd corners of England" books on us, well, let him try!"

"Now then," said Wif, cocking himself back on his chair, "I wouldn't mind being in a book. Would you, Mam?"

"No. As long as they didn't say what I looked like."

"Oh let him do as he wants! All I ever hear now is "Richard" this and that. I'm fed up with it."

"It gives us something to talk about," said Agnes, quietly. "We can be thankful for that at the moment."

"Why must we talk?" Janice murmured, wanting the last word, wanting to retreat on her own terms.

"Because there are certain things that need to be said," Agnes concluded.

The baby's feed being finished and the burping tentatively turned into a game by Wif with Janice firmly behind her book, Agnes took the child upstairs. It was eight-thirty and she was already thinking of the midnight feed. While Agnes was out, Wif turned on the television and began to roll himself a cigarette.

On her return, Agnes tidied up, made a cup of tea all round and then flopped into the settee and stared at the flickering screen. The set was always out of order and Wif was baffled in front of it. He could wire a house for electricity, mend a watch, strip a motorbike and tinker with a wireless, but he knew nothing about the television and whenever they took it up to George Wilkins to be mended, off it went again in two or three days, with two pounds down the drain. So they watched sliding frames, snowstorms and a washed-out sepia picture, with a love story struggling to get out. It was Wif's favourite series and the others were silent until it had finished; Agnes knitting and yawning, Janice reading and occasionally staring at the screen with fierce detestation.

When it was finished, he went out to his shed to work. Janice watched the news and then turned off the set. Agnes was asleep. The house, silent.

Janice took out a cigarette and stared down into the fire. Outside the heat was re-intensifying as a storm made to build up. Summer. But still the fire. Hearth the focus. Pocus. She kicked it. The coal broke open and a burst of yellow flames leapt at her leg.

"What was that?" said Agnes.

"Nothing.

The older woman squatted on the seat, her knees wide apart, making a sheet of the old cotton dress she wore, her knees shoved out at its edges, the underskirt dropping its fringe almost to her ankles. Janice could hardly bear to look at her. For about a minute Agnes dug her fists into her eyes, kneading out the sleep, using the action as an opportunity to gather herself for what she wanted to say. Just to begin to say. But it was time to begin.

"I know what you're thinking," said Janice. "Now that Father's out you've a chance to say it – but I haven't changed my mind! You know that! I haven't. I won't!"

"Don't be so upset," replied Agnes, tiredly. "Don't be so nervous about it. Nobody's going to force you into anything."

"Oh yes they are! *You* are! You don't say anything – but I know that you – look, Mother, I told you, I told you, I did tell you, I did!" She was already shuddering with passion – and Agnes had never been able either to follow her into this mood or to get her out of it.

"I know you did. I don't mind."

"But it's terrible for you! You're wearing yourself out – you're tired, you're ... you're just sleep-walking most of the time – I can't stand it." She paused. "But I – refuse – to – do – anything. I refuse. If I did – it would all be finished. I'd be stuck with it for good. It sounds horrible to you – it sounds horrible to me as well. It *is* horrible!"

"No it isn't. There's many a mother –"

"I m not a – I don't *feel* like a mother, I don't *want* to feel like a mother."

Agnes repressed the fury that grew in her against her daughter. She, too, had a temper, but she had found that mere anger broke over Janice's determination like a push of water.

"That little girl'll want her mother soon," she replied, quietly. "I like looking after her – believe me, Janice, I like it. It was a disappointment to me that I could only have the one baby myself. But every child needs its own mother."

"Why?"

"Because it does, Janice."

"But why? Why? As long as somebody looks after it well. I wouldn't be half as good as you. You're trying to say that I'll harm the baby if I don't take it. That's not true – you'll be better. I'd harm it a damn sight more if I did take it."

"But it's a pleasure. Children are a pleasure. They are. Oh, they might ..."

"Can't you understand? That baby is no pleasure to me. None. Not one bit. I wish the last year of my life could just be wiped away. I'm telling you the truth, Mother. I can't pretend. I'm telling you the truth."

"And what d'you think's so wonderful about that? If everybody went around just saying what they felt and saying it was the truth – what would happen?"

"It couldn't be worse than what happens now."

"Oh yes it could! The truth! We all feel bad, we all feel down – but we feel good sometimes as well. It just depends which side you want to take. Why is it always the most awful thing that you pick on in yourself and say that *they* are the truth? Why's that?

Have you stopped feeling good things? Have you? Don't look away like that. Janice, that's being a coward. You used to be full of people's troubles. I've seen you cry just when somebody was killed in a newspaper. Where's all that gone?"

"It hasn't gone."

"Hasn't it? Who do you care about if you don't care about that baby? Tell me that! That baby came out of you. No! You can't get away from that. It worries you, does it? Well let me tell you that you've been worrying me and your father these last few weeks! We didn't spit at you, we didn't pry – don't you think *I* would like to know who that father is, just to *know*! And . . ." Agnes stopped. She did not trust herself when she began to shout.

Janice went back to her seat and took up her book. The shouting had restored her control over herself. She was, she thought, perfectly calm.

"It isn't right," Agnes whispered, eventually. "That's all."

Let it end there. Let it pass. But again, that insistence which was within her, which would refuse to allow her to let herself be worked on or touched in any way when she did not want it.

"I have no idea what's right and what isn't right," Janice answered. It was too cruel just to leave it there. "I think that it could hardly be called "right" to be born in the first place. It's just an accident – or an instinct – and I can't see that it has anything to do with right and wrong in any sense in which I understand those words." Her own words bludgeoned her mother's phrases; coarse drum-beats blocking all melody.

"There's only one way to understand them," she replied.

"No, there isn't! What's right here and today is wrong tomorrow somewhere else. Killing, cheating, lying, helping people, looking after them – they can all be right or wrong depending on the situation you're in. And if such a thing as killing can be right or wrong – and if we were born accidentally anyway, and if there's nothing to believe in – don't look like that, you know that's what I think! – then what's wrong or right about me wanting to lead my own life without that child?"

"But it's yours."

"It was given to me," said Janice viciously, "it was kept because of you, I gave it to – the world if you like – and . . ."

"That's that? Is it?"

"No. No. If you weren't there . . ."

"I won't always be."

"But you are now."

64

Agnes looked past her daughter and saw the mirror. An oval of glass imprisoned on the hub of a score of bamboo spokes. The room was full of ornaments, knick-knacks, it took a good hour to clean them all.

"You see I want to understand why I'm doing it," said Janice, softly. "I know I talk too much when I start, but – oh, I wish I could explain all the things I feel and all that I think – then you would understand. I want you to."

"I never will, Janice. I never will."

She got up, feeling her ankles ache as she stood on her feet. She did not like to leave her daughter huddled like that on that big chair, looking half-savage, half-shocked out of her wits. But she could say no more this night.

"If you don't want a cup of tea, I'll be off up."

"No thanks. Can I make you one? I'll bring it upstairs for you. You could have it in bed."

"No, love. I don't like tea in bed. I always slop it."

She moved to the corner door that opened on to the staircase. Turning from it, she made one last attempt.

"You mean to tell me, you can look at that baby and feel nothing?"

"Don't ask that."

"I am asking it."

"What I say will only hurt you more."

The older woman nodded and went upstairs. Janice let her book fall on to the ground. Her parents still bound her. However she tried to be independent, they made her feel eternally part of them, and, in being part, she could see herself only as evil. Beside those two, she was bad – and she feared that she might come to believe that herself if she stayed on. She was only half opening, she felt, only beginning to comprehend that she could have a life on her own terms, only starting to breathe airs she had never known but which were somehow meant for her – and back she had come to this flesh-chained dungeon and been treated as if she had never changed since childhood. It was worse that she loved her parents and was proud of the way they lived their lives – really, childishly proud of it, feeling they had made something of themselves. But she, too, wanted the chance – on her own terms. And the love she felt only forced her to extremes to demand those terms. When she was most violently opposed to her mother – that was when she was most afraid, for she knew that she had to beware of the merest glance or inflection, for then she

65

was shrill and uncertain, and the slightest temptation might cause her to give in. Perhaps she was unclear about what she wanted to do or to be, but one of thing she *was* certain; she had not to give in to them. However tenderly you were bound, it *was* bondage.

When Wif came in, he found her ironing a pile of babyclothes and he waved down her offer to make him a cup of tea, putting on the kettle himself and, all the time, chanting some verse he had learnt about tea-brewing "from an old Yorkshireman". Janice resented the description. She did not believe in special Yorkshire virtues, or particular Italian characteristics, or any lumping generalisation about people except this one: that each was different. But as her father chanted the spell again and again, the resentment appeared to her to be far more pedantic than her father's careless chatter and she smiled at the solemn fool she could be.

"Anything you want ironed?" she asked.

"Just my tongue. Eh, I talked that much this day, I think my tongue's been in a race. He doesn't say much, that Richard, you know, not to me anyway."

"What did you talk to him about?"

"Oh, "the birds of the air and the animals upon the ..." Damn. I used to know that bible off by heart. "The birds of the air..." "the birds of the air"– do *you* know?"

"Father!"

"Well, I need never have known if I can't remember that. I thought I would never forget that."

He stooped over his tea, cuddling the cup between his hands as he looked into the dying fire, pleased at the slap of the iron on the board.

"Have you made any fresh plans yet?" he asked, eventually.

"Not yet."

"Ay well, there's time."

"Not enough." She waited to be pressed, but Wif never forced her. He had become separate from her at her instigation, but it was he, and not she, who was the more consistent in following that through. "What would you like me to do?"

"Whatever'll make you happy."

"You can't just say that. You must have some idea. "Whatever'll make you happy" is just next door to "I couldn't care less." What d'you think I ought to do?"

Wif laughed and, looking at Janice as he did so, he drew her into the laugh.

"You'll twist anything," he said. "You really will. If somebody offered you a five-pound note you would turn it against them."

"No I wouldn't." She paused. "I didn't." Then, "Have you seen Edwin?"

"Yes. Saw him tonight."

"What did he say?"

"Now you know that as well as I do, Janice. You must like him more than you think if you want to hear it repeated. He said to me what he said to you. He wants to marry you."

"Did he look upset about it?"

"What d'you want to know that for? No. He didn't look upset. Edwin has himself measured out too carefully for that. Mind, I know he'll be upset – if you – if you don't – you know? But he'll keep it to himself."

"Do *you* know something, Father? This time, I really liked him. I mean, I know he's supposed to be bad-looking and he isn't smart or anything – but when he came this time, I really did like him. I was surprised myself. He's strong, isn't he?"

"He's a man all right."

" 'He's a man all right,' " Janice grunted, and smiled. The ironing finished, she cleared everything away, came to sit by her father and continued as if there had been no interruption. "He is, though, isn't he? He's far better than any of those arrogant little ex-schoolboys I met at College. He's better than any of them. You know, Edwin isn't *so* strong. But he's so clear in what he is. He never does anything that he doesn't consider, he's clear about everything. He makes up his mind to something – and then carries it out. Like friends. He made up his mind that he hasn't the time to knock around with men his own age – and so doesn't. Ever. That takes some doing. And he's made up his mind that he should be neat and tidy – and he is, even though everybody laughs at him for it. That isn't all. He wants to "improve himself" as he calls it – and he tries to – without any of the bitterness people usually have about those things. I respect him."

"His ears'll be burning," said Wif, cautiously.

"No, they'll never burn. He isn't really interested at all in what people think of him, or say about him. Not even me. He wants to marry me – but he wants that only. I doubt if what I *said* about him would have much effect. You see, that's what's so nice about him. The only thing that would have an effect on him would be to do with what *he* wanted."

"He's strong-willed, that is true. How long's he been after you?

Five years, maybe more – ever since he came here and you were at school. And I bet he hasn't so much as looked at another lass."

"There's something horrible about that, as well," Janice shivered. "He ought to have. If I can be the only woman for him – entirely – then he must be peculiar in a way."

"Twist again, Miss Beattie."

"I suppose so." She stood up and stretched herself. "You know what I *really* like about Edwin? You know? If I married him, I think he would forget all about me – and that means that I could forget all about him. That would be worth something."

"Very little, to my way of thinking."

"It would mean I could be free to get on with my own life."

"You want it both ways."

"No I don't. I can't even think of one way – let alone 'both'. No, if I married Edwin, it would be so that I could forget about a lot of things."

"Well, my advice is don't marry him if you think that. What would be in it for him?"

"He would get what he wanted."

"Don't be so sure you know what he wants. Anyway, I don't like to hear you talking like that, Janice – "forgetting about things" – you can't live a life just "forgetting" about everything."

"Why not?"

"Because it's impossible to forget."

"I could forget Edwin the minute I married him."

"That's bad talk, Janice. That's treating him like dirt. He deserves better than that."

"How can you work out what people deserve?"

"I can. If you can't, that's your affair. But I can. And I say he deserves better."

"Perhaps I will marry him. That would startle everybody, wouldn't it?"

"It would. If that sort of thing pleases you."

"It does sometimes. Just to spend my life startling people. That would be one way."

Wif was silent. She had gone right away from him. He looked at her tired face and hoped to be able to feel sorry for her – and then forgive her, bring her back into his range. But there was an expression on it which was beyond him. Something unknown, spiteful or intoxicated, he did not know which. Whatever it was, he could not understand it.

"I'll be off to bed," he said.

"Good night then," she retorted, immediately. Wif was stung by the dismissive cut of her words, but he ignored the provocation and left her alone'

She went outside, unable to bear the small kitchen any longer. The night rubbed against her skin like felt and she stood quite still for some minutes, letting her eyes wander into the banks of darkness, calming herself by the hot sweet-smelling peace of it all. She was wearing black – a sweater and a skirt – and, lit by the open door, her hair gleamed alone in the dark. This was the first time she had set foot out of doors since Paula's birth. Her body seemed to creak in the still air, as if some breeze were tugging at it to launch it, and she put her fingers on her sore hip-bones, easing them into movement. Everything about her she felt to be lumpy and stiff, and the night was there to smooth her to what she once had been.

Closing the door behind her and without bothering to take a scarf or coat, she set out for a walk, making for Cogra Moss, a small tarn in the basin of Blake, Middle Fell and Knockmirton. It had been a reservoir as long as she could remember, but still on summer evenings such as this her father had taken her with him when he went to fish, she had picnicked and bathed there with other girls from the village. "Cogra Moss is peace itself," her mother said.

She paused as she came to Richard's cottage, curious to see inside without actually entering. Listening hard, she heard a quartet being played on the wireless or gramophone, tried to name it, failed and refused to pursue it, and that, combined with the flickering firelight against the curtains and the enviable liberty of Richard's whole enterprise – such as she knew of it – made her almost grimace with distaste and annoyance and she hurried away.

Through the fields which led to the tarn she moved, with only her own rustling feet in the grass to disturb her. She was fugitive and she relished the way the night swallowed her up so that she could move inside it, like Jonah in the whale, with that which was enclosing her unaware of her. The further she went, the more free she thought herself to be and she imagined herself as this or that heroine, always pursued or pursuing, as a nocturnal dryad, Madame Bovary and Anna Karenina, her two schoolgirl heroines – although of course, they were bound in what Janice considered to be such slavish shackles – marriage vows. She had not thought of them for years and the memory pleased her. And she called up

69

all that she had been forced to suppress over the last months, the endless adventures that she could have in life, what she had begun to dream of while studying on her own, what she had felt she was entering into during her few terms at Carcaster College. When she had seen that she could live a life entirely her own – in the ordering of the day, the books she read, the people she met – on and on she to knew not where; when she had sprung from her coiled and tight-bound background and let herself be shot into whatever wave cared to lift and carry her. And the first big wave had carried her right back to Crossbridge.

She had wept about that but now it was beginning to be over. Now she felt only exhilarated and as she climbed over the stile to cross the fell-dyke road her limbs emphasised the returned excitement; they were soft again, and pliable, she felt her legs rub against the skirt and was not irritated but pleased with that scraping pressure.

A bicycle headlight bobbed down the hill towards her and she drew into the hedge not to be seen. It was Edwin who, having changed back into working clothes, had gone across to Kirkland to do a job for someone. He saw her, but saw only her back, and, understanding at once that he had been recognised and was not welcome, scarcely interrupted his passage, but free-wheeled past. She ran across the road and went into the field that led up to Cogra Moss.

Further down the road Edwin pulled up. He was used to taking action according to an instantaneous reckoning of her mood, and practised in wringing out of any chance at least something for himself. Now he convinced himself that she was not well enough to be out alone at such a time and he determined to shadow her. Not to be seen, not to be there. He lifted his bike over a gate and hid it behind the hedge. Then made across the field to catch the path he knew she would be on.

He had never understood this liking of hers for solitary walking. He, brought up in one of the small industrial towns, considered a walk as a treat, an outing, a special event. Nevertheless, he had walked with her, aimlessly as it appeared to him as she walked, all over these fells and he knew them. Cogra Moss he had never liked; it was bleak, few trees, nothing to be seen but the bare sides of the hills as they curved down to the hollow; there were iron railings around the tarn – broken down in some places – it was easy, in the dark, to miss a step and fall in. Thinking of this, he ran, made a noise, Janice heard him.

70

CHAPTER EIGHT

"Edwin! Is it you?"

He stood quite still.

"I know it's you!" She paused. "If it's you – don't answer!"
This followed by a light laugh which slapped against his mouth
and stopped whatever he might have said. "Well, you've proved
your existence by silence," she said, eventually. "That's as good
a proof as there is."

With this nonsense she went on, halting once or twice to enjoy
the satisfaction of Edwin's clumsy reaction, touched that he
should wish to guard her and made even more happy in the
knowledge that he would leave her entirely alone.

The only trees between the road and Cogra Moss were a short
avenue of poplars which suddenly sprang up at the side of Knockmirton Fell, as if someone had wished to turn this ancient basin
into a landscaped Arcadia and then come up against the empty
hillsides and abandoned his project. The truncated avenue remained, however, and, the moon now beginning to lift its top
edge over the thick outline of Blake, Janice could see the tops of
the trees, unbending, like sheathed plumes. She felt that she had
only to stretch out her arms and she could run her finger-tips
along the soft bark, flitting from one to the other until the trunks
would speed past her with the same attractive rhythm as that of
telegraph poles outside a train window.

Beyond the avenue was a small pumping-house which drove
the water, and then the tarn itself. She walked along one side of
it for a hundred yards or so, trailing her hand along the tipsy,
rusting railing, and then she found a seat – only to jump up again
a few minutes after sitting down, and go to lean against the
railings, hearing Edwin scuffle up in the heather to find a watching
position.

"You can come down here with me if you want, you know.
Only I don't wish to talk."

Again there was no reply and she shrugged.

The moon by now had cleared the tops of the hills. It was
swollen, grainy, pendulously dominating the sky, overbearing,
as in a painting by a child or by Douanier Rousseau. So near did
it appear that anyone on top of the hills could reach out and
touch it. The stars were mere ticks of light, their hardness and

71

clarity dimmed by this gross moon. Its reflection was perfect on the scarcely lapping surface of the tarn and when some stray disturbance sent out a ripple over it Janice shivered. It had not to be broken – it was better in the tarn than in the sky – for there, on the water, its pouchy galactic expression was glassed, it appeared a magic orb. Across the tarn, moon-shadows lit up the scree and at the other end there was a dense black bush, concealing swampy land, above which the fells rose, their bowed ridges silvered by the moonlight.

Janice remembered that she had been at that spot before on such a night a few days before taking her first major exams at school, when all the world was in balance, and she had thought then that Ophelia or The Lady of Shalott could not have had a better setting for their deaths. She, too, had once played with the idea of ending her life, but it had never been more than a game – an easy way to give more importance to her existence, like deliberately crying herself to sleep by imagining her father was dead. Now, as she recalled it, even while she laughed at the memory and indulged it as juvenile, she panicked a little as the notion wormed into her.

She had walked too far on this first outing and now she felt sick. That baby! When her mother went out to do her work, then Janice, left in charge, sometimes spent the entire two or three hours looking down into the baby's face. She *could* be drawn to it, if she allowed herself she could be bound to it, she could love the baby and then, alone, her mother's confident claim "you really love her – you can't help it – I can see it" appeared true. But she would not. The pain of the birth came to her mind, almost to her rescue, to give her a proper resistance to it. And behind the pain, the words – "idiot", "fool", "useless, useless" to let it happen. The father, Paul, who had been a lecturer at the College, seemed not so much a destroyer as the fate her own stupidity deserved. Instead of having the strength to follow her own will when she went to College, she had fallen in with his, believing that such an act of yielding was the greater proof of her separateness. He had talked to her and carefully shown her around the few – to her, limitless – experiences and information that he possessed – all when she could have done it much better by herself, had she not, as she now thought, been amused by the degrading flattery of a man's attention. A man who had talked to her of what she wanted to hear: books, ideas, possibilities. Not that she had given in to him. Severely, rather uglily, preserving her virginity, she had

72

withheld – until the night when he, drunk, impatient, threatening, bitter with words which had stunned her that they could be directed at her, had pulled her on to his bed, pretended to himself and to her that her struggle was only the protest of one embarrassed, not unwillingly, and taken her. Raped her. She had refused to see him again, he had left the College before her state had made it necessary that she too should leave, and his letters, messages by other mouths, protestations by proxy – all had been met by a shake of the head. She wanted never, never, to look on him and see how much she despised herself in him; never again.

And Paula was a corruption of the Latin for Girl, wasn't it? A good name for the baby. The final proof that she was finished with her father, she thought. *His* name, corrupted, also, Puella, Puella, Puellam. "Puellae, Puellae, Puella," she recited aloud. "Puellae, Puellae, Puellas, Puellarum, Puellis – did you hear that Edwin?"

No reply, not even a sniffle. Perhaps he had gone away while she had been standing there.

Still the moon and she felt sick. Her stitches were sore after the walk and, though it was a hot night which retained the heat built up earlier for the threatened thunderstorm which never came, she felt cold, the damp of her perspiration cooling clammily on her skin. To float on that orb of gold, the worm wriggled through her head. To float, a drowsy abandon stirred inside her, her tiredness and the spectral strangeness of the place thickened to a tilting compulsion so that she began to sway on her feet. The black water, the bright black water, to fall on that and slip through, ten thousand fathoms down, to rest among the pitch of tress-waving weeds. The choice was the ultimate act of separateness; but the action was not an alternative, merely oblivion. Yet now she was caught in her own suffocating rhapsody; she gripped the railings and her hands trembled on the cold, scraping rust; her body felt as if it were being whipped, now gently, now savagely, by its own blood. Still holding the rail, she collapsed on to her knees and, closing her eyes, saw a swirling galaxy swoon and swing before her.

"Edwin," she muttered. There was no power in her voice. Pressing her forehead against the railings to waken herself. she called louder. "Edwin. Ed-win! Please come down. I don't feel well. Please."

No reply; and then the cough of a sheep. He *had* gone. "Ed-win. Please, Edwin."

Only her own voice, half echoing back to her. And now she seemed to go out of herself, so that she was on the fellside looking down at her body kneeling beside the tarn, and yet another self saw both these figures, and yet another – she half cried, half sobbed to crack these mad mirrors and her breath was like a hot wave in her mouth, the sound she made a crash of terror in her ears. She got up and ran along the path. At the poplars she stopped and looked around for Edwin – but there was neither sight nor sound of him. Only the leering moon which seemed to have grown even larger, sucking all attention into its dulled face. She ran on, stumbling over stones, aching all over her body at this violent movement, feeling that other self darting along the hill-tops behind her and mocking her.

She came to the fell-dyke road and could not open the gate which led on to it. She knew that it was latched with string, but it was an old gate, and after the string had been unhooked it had to be lifted out of a rut. She tugged at it – and it jammed. The more she hauled at it, the more it stuck. She tried to squeeze through the small gap between the post and the gate but could not. She considered climbing over, but her stitches were by now hurting so much that she dare not. Another attempt to lift it. Failed. Taking the rickety gate by its top bar she shook it, shook it as hard as she could until it rattled, damply, in the hot night.

"Let me do that for you."

Janice jumped away from the gate as Edwin appeared from behind the hedge on the other side of the road. The shock seized her, frightened her, and then shot through the fragments she had become and drew them suddenly into a whole once more.

"Why did you go?" she demanded.

"It just needs lifting up sharp," said Edwin, bending to the bottom of the gate, opening it, "there!"

Janice stood where she was.

"Where did you disappear to?"

"When?" Edwin's innocent query, an apology for a lie, infuriated her.

"*You* know when! At the tarn. You followed me – I know you did. And when I shouted for you – why did you go?"

"Did I follow you?"

"For Christ's sake, Edwin, don't be so stupid. What I want to know – oh, never mind."

She went through the opened gate and on to the road, impatient that some obeisance to manners compelled her to wait while he fussed the gate back into position.

"I thought that you wanted to be on your own," he said, his back to her. "You just stood there – and you'd shouted that I hadn't to join you – so I thought: 'I won't interfere if she wants to be on her own and she can't be on her own if she knows I'm here' – so I went away."

"And what are you doing waiting for me down here then?"

"I just wanted to make sure you'd get back all right," he replied, flatly. "You shouldn't be on such a long walk after your – after you being ill – so I thought I'd just keep an eye out."

"Which one? Oh, never mind." She paused and then, with such an effort that he flinched before the compliment, she said, "You're very kind to me, Edwin. Thank you."

She moved away to the path which led through three fields to the cottages.

"Do you want me to set you back?" Edwin asked, quietly now, not resentful.

"No thank you, Edwin. You've got your bike."

"I could leave it. I could collect it later."

"It's – I would rather – you see it isn't very often I get a chance to think on my own these days."

"I see. Yes. Well then. Good night, Janice."

"Good night. And thank you."

She went on to the path, knowing that he would wait until she had truly disappeared from all his senses until he left the spot. A husband? Why not, if husband there had to be. He would leave her separate.

Now, ordered, calmer, she thought only of reaching home so that she could rest. She did not look back on the moon, letting its presence recede.

Coming towards Richard's cottage, she heard a splash, then an intaken cry followed by a swishing and sluicing of water. She looked through the hedge. Richard was in the water-barrel, his head popping in and out as he gripped the rim of it and moved himself up and down. He was shivering, whistling and revelling in it all. Finally he ducked down, submerged himself completely, and then hauled himself out. She saw a white body, made steely by the moon, briny with water. He shook himself, using his right hand to sweep the top water off his skin. He jumped up and down for a few seconds and then he darted into the cottage, opening a beam of light on Janice as he opened the door, so that she froze, not to be spotted. And long after the door was closed she stayed as she was, to be sure.

Edwin was not in, nor waiting for her, and she was relieved. She was afraid of what she might have said to him – too much or too little – in her present mood. She tried to laugh at the picture of Richard dancing about naked, but could manage only a smile. Reaching her own house, she turned for one final look at the moon. It was nearer than it had been before, sagging over the fields, a slow-invading threat. She stared at it and then spat, before turning her back on it.

CHAPTER NINE

In the evenings it was as if some benign fate had anointed him. Richard stared at the flames and stretched out his toes until they tickled against the hard fender. Bacon and eggs, fried bread and tea were inside him, whisky was waiting, and around him a litter of books, magazines and records, with no rush, no hurry. He went over the whole day, remembering as many of Wif's stories as he could, seeing again the Show field and Hector slung between the two bucking mares, letting it loll and float in his mind so that it could ease up all resembling memories and become saturated with associations. He picked up a book.

'Some people say that life's the thing, but I prefer reading.' He could not remember who had said that – someone whom quick modern scorn would have skewered or languorous boredom found quaint – but at this moment it had, for him, an attraction. 'Up, up, my friend and quit your books,' Wordsworth could say; but he could add, immediately, 'we have a world of ready wealth, our minds and hearts to bless.' A strong alternative.

It was a collection of Auden's poetry. One stanza he had marked the previous evening and he reread it.

The sense of danger must not disappear:
The way is certainly both short and steep,
However gradual it looks from here:
Look if you like, but you will have to leap.

He applied it directly to himself. A belief lingered in the

psalmist's promise that we become what we behold. But it was not easy to leap from an armchair. Yet Auden could not have excluded himself from 'the sense of danger' – and the odds were that the words had been written in some comfort. The sense of danger, then, had moved away from its primary connection with action. It could be in the setting up of a home, reading, a look. Yet didn't danger imply the proximity of death? The bomb was near enought to everyone. Or the testing of an established pattern of life? That was done with every invention. It was complicated. Take a single man. Did Lawrence have the sense of danger more in blowing up trains for Feisal in Arabia or in becoming Aircraftsman Shaw in the concrete certainty of a peacetime air force?

"We shall never know."

The phrase popped up like a goblin. 'We shall never know.' One of the current catch-phrases – guaranteed to do just that – catch any phrase and prevent it running to a paragraph. And it was on such a note of mildly satirical aplomb that most of his ramblings ended. It was a primitive and Philistine reaction – caused by the nervousness that thinking and learning, however useful, are fundamentally suspect since they require uncommon privileges – and he ought to have got over it long ago. It was unlikely that he ever would.

Like his guilt about doing 'nothing', it had roots too set to dig out; they could be ignored for a while but no more. That 'doing nothing', for instance, was measured by the marker of his grandparents' way of life, where work was at once necessity, virtue and proof of capability, and it still clung to him as a measure, however preposterous his life at and since University made it appear.

Solitude had not clarified his thinking. He continued to hop around like a sparrow on a lawn.

He got up and put on a record. It was Monteverdi, and he thought of the sensuality of Venice, Byron riding across the sand with Shelley, Thomas Mann disappearing in its silted streets, the austere Teuton hot for historic sin, mad Baron Corvo acting as a gondolier to pay for his boys and shame his rich patrons, Ruskin's troubles, Browning's baubles . . . He changed the record. As if in inflamed reaction to his day with Wif, he could not stop this ticking of names, an embalmed multitude of writers forever tramping across the runnels of his mind without any thought for the stain of their print. He had brought some pop-records: he put on 'The House of The Rising Sun'. Then he pushed back the furniture and danced to it. Too much was evoked again by that beat. He went outside, leaving the needle clicking in the end groove.

At the back of his cottage was a water-butt. He paddled his fingers in it and was sluiced with the impulse to jump in. He looked around carefully, and then smiled; there was no one who would see. As he pulled off his clothes he savaged the lilt of self-ridicule which, on cue, pipped into his brain. Drown this watching, twittering self! He stood naked, and shuddered. The water looked bitter. Hooking his leg over the rim he hauled himself in and gasped at the chill, metallic bite of the water. He bounced up and down and then ducked himself right under, experiencing such a frigid slap against his ears that he thought he would go numb. Staying a second after he had determined to get out, he finally pulled himself free and darted into his kitchen. Rubbing himself with a rough towel, he heard a door bang. It might have been Janice. She was the only one he thought of, and the thought of her made him stiffen. He wanted her. He had done from the moment he had seen her ....

Along the lunar fields, Edwin cycled like a spectre from the old wives' tales which bandaged the folk-history of old Cross-bridge with careful cuddliness. None of it meant much to Edwin. He had his cottage and he had his job and the job was there because of Janice and the cottage was waiting for her. Now he free-wheeled and cursed his bitter luck at not having been there when she had wanted him. 'I shouted for you,' she had said – and all he could do was put on his innocent act, worn like the skin of an ichthyosaurus, and babyishly pretend that he had not even followed her. "I shouted for you." And he had already scudded away, a shadow even to his own shadow, somehow riveted to the belief that she must not be imposed on by him, she must not see him unless she asked, she must make the first, the second, the third, and all subsequent moves – for he would serve only by standing and waiting.

Though this belief had come out of a crippling idea of his inferiority to her, and though it still attended that notion, it contained in it a whispering seed of arrogance. Because he loved her so much, he thought, then she must love him so much in return; so much that she would need no tender inflexions of voice, behaviour or attitude – the rattled reminder of entrenched intention would have to be enough – she would need never to be

78

beckoned or encouraged or, in the end, courted, pursued, or in any way made to enjoy any of the games which desire arouses; she would have to bend to his will on his terms. That she was far and away the most attractive woman for miles around only made it more necessary that she should fall to him in a way he would have expected of no one else.

He could wait a while longer – but soon he would have to shift. His apprenticeship was up and, as a skilled welder, he could be coining money in any of the nearby towns. His trade was not so common now and yet with the endless increase in the number of cars it was more in demand than ever. He could see a way to making a good deal of money. But he had to get moving soon. The sooner the better.

Finally he arrived at his mother's. She had the house ablaze with lights again – never going to bed until sleep caught up with her somewhere or other in that cottage when she slept on the nearest chair or bed she stumbled to – and there he was, hammering on the double-bolted door, even though he always brought her weekly money on this night. When, eventually, she admitted him, he took a quick breath to get used to the stench inside, and then held himself very warily while he accustomed himself to the dirt, the untidiness, bordering on that confusion which suggest some kind of madness – and her face.

His mother was dressed in a tatty nightgown which was transparent and this was ignored completely by her. There was nothing he could say or do to make her dress otherwise when receiving him – and the shawl she had clutched around her shoulders as she opened the door was immediately thrown off. Therefore whenever he looked in her direction he saw the grey, pore-opened mass of old skin, old breasts, old hair – obscene. He walked over shoes, coats, petticoats, knickers, brassieres, hats. Newspapers, tins, jars, cups – the whole entrails of a house and its inhabitant, littering the floor as if some demon had plunged his arms through the windows and pulled the insides out of the place. And when she spoke, he saw the face she had given him. The less he saw of her, the more ugly he thought her. There were times when he could forget his own ugliness, forget the criss-crossed defences and countermoves which, since first consciousness, it had trained in him, forget the unforgivable injustice of it, the unalterable fact of it, the infamous burden of it. But he could never forget her. Head like a sucking-pig slashed for public show, head like a monster on a pike, hair wreathing the pike shaft like pythons, head like a skull which some Frankenstein of the universe had laughed to patch with flesh – all these and more images he had thought up of his mother, to distance her face from his, to make her so grotesque to himself that he would feel he had no part of her. One look at her exploded all that. He was her son and carried her marks.

He accepted the offer of a cup of tea because he always did and it would have started an argument had he refused – not but that she grumbled when he accepted. He sat on the arm of a chair as he always did, thus both distancing himself from the squalor and preparing himself for an early departure, and he closed his mind, his eyes, closed every nerve-end to his surroundings, as he always did. For the meeting had to take place and he had to look after her.

Mrs. Cass took her time about the tea. Edwin did not come to her often and, when he did, she wanted everything out of him that she could get. Not that she liked him very much, or if she ever had, that liking had been so deeply buried beneath her myth of maternal love that neither his childhood, nor his adolescence, nor his youth, nor any single act at any stage had ever been able to resurrect it. Her affection was of the sort taken so much for granted that in the end it is taken right away and never granted. However it was, he was hers and part of her life and essential to it first for the money which she took, checked, and then pushed behind a cushion, and then for his progress-report which rarely varied, was met – or rather beset – by scorn from her and which, nevertheless, had to be provided because it was there.

He told her about his work and she wheedled out of him about the customers; about his extra jobs and she got the price of them, about the one or two things which had happened to him which he thought interesting – those she dismissed – and finally, after his regulation half-hour, just as he was moving towards the door (there was no point in attempting to hint at leaving; the action alone was effective) she went for him, as usual, about Janice.

"Still playing Lady-Kiss-My-Arse, is she?"

"No."

"What is it then? She got herself caught – didn't she? Who does she think she is? She's a little bitch, that's all – just like everybody else. She's got you, all right. She's got you exactly where she wants you. And I bet you haven't laid a finger on her."

80

"No."

"Well that's nothing to be proud of, believe me. You're wasting your time – she's leading you on. She's a tart and she thinks she's high-class. She'll ruin you yet."

"No she won't, Mother."

"You don't give her money, do you?"

"You know I don't."

"D'you think I believe everything you say? I'm going to ask her next time I meet her."

"Do that, Mother." He had been threatened before. "Yes, Mother, do it. And you won't see me again. No money. Nothing."

"She's a tart! She's a whore!"

"Good night, Mother."

"And you're nothing of a man to put up with it. You're worse than nothing! You're just a little boy."

"Good night."

He left and, as usual, was so spellbound with fury and self-pity that he walked his bike for the first half-mile, unable to trust himself to get on it.

When Agnes came down with the baby for the midnight feed, she looked so haggard that Janice, aching, wide-awake exhausted from her walk, yielded. She would take the midnight feed. The midnight feed and the eight o'clock feed so that both of them could have a decent rest. The bottle. That would be all she would do. And though Agnes cried a little as she went back up to sleep, cried with relief, there was still the hard lump of fear there because she knew that it had not been done for the baby's sake. Not at all.

As she fed the child, Janice tried to remember the tune that Richard had been whistling. She smiled a little as she recalled his white body. He was a fool to jump around like that, she decided

CHAPTER TEN

When David and Antonia arrived, Richard was in bed. He was beginning to feel that he could now break the habit of these massive sleeps, but as yet he preferred not to. It was so luxurious

81

to wake up in mid-morning, with the edge taken off the day, the colours settled, people steady about their day's work, no rawness, no rush, no feeling of being ejaculated into the world with unrubbed eyes and that shivering warm stomach of dreams which chills before the breakfast table.

David Hill was one of the new Northern lads. The wave which had carried the North of England – its writers and bright young operators – into London, much, one imagines, as the Scots had flowed in under Gladstone and the Welsh following Lloyd George (and the North, too, finally furnished itself with a Prime Minister), that wave had deposited David on a welcoming metropolis which was impressed by his fauvism, amused at his urgency and slightly contemptuous of his directness. Now, in the mid-sixties, the tide was ebbing and to be born north of the Trent was no longer regarded as proof of access to some superior source of life, but David had been there near the start and his wave had landed him on a very agreeable stretch of lotus-land, established and secure. His boyhood accent, after being painstakingly lost at his grammar school and university, had been reclaimed, dusted, and refitted, until now it could be said to be an almost perfect imitation of his father's. His clothes, having been neat and conformist, through school uniform, army uniform, CND uniform and professional ambition's uniform, now burgeoned with contemporary idiosyncrasy, caring nothing for 'appearances' and yet riveted to progressive fashion. His ideas, which had come out of his own and his parents' background, ironed through steamed reading to an aggressive radicalism with one foot on Trotsky and the other tickling Lawrence, were now smooth as running cream, able to appreciate even the Tory party and once brought out – it was known – in defence of the monarchy. ("She's all right," he had said judiciously.) The one thing that had not changed was his ambition. Or his shrewdness.

Now his ambition thought it time to make a move. He was thirty, after all. He had made three moves before and he knew the feeling. First he had gone into the theatre – on the management side, ending up, very quickly, as House and Company Manager to a good and left-wing theatre. Then he had moved into television, first as a script editor for a successful series of new plays – mainly by Northern writers – then as executive producer of the series. Finally he had shifted to the assistant editorship of a new magazine which, taking its cue from *Playboy Magazine*, had put beautiful, naked girls between highbrow short stories, wrapped the thing up in glossy paper, shot it through with skilful fashion photography, toughened it, occasionally, with a feature article on slums or stuff like that and made, as expected, a good profit. It was there that he had met Richard, he who had employed him, in fact, and he who had been most angry when Richard had quit. For he was a proselytiser – of himself; he wanted Richard to be like himself, to be like himself particularly in regard to his career. He wanted plenty of confirmation that he was going the right way about things and what better reassurance than comes from creating a disciple? Richard had all the ingredients – and something other – a certain carelessness which David had found at once irritating and beguiling. Something difficult to grip. Yet there was talent which David could, by association, recognise; and that he was certain of. When Richard had upped and off, he had felt insulted.

Antonia, the latest of a long line of women all referred to as "me ladybirds", was introduced as "a deacon's daughter, for Christ's sake". She was bright, shining with that particularly smooth, well-exercised handsomeness which quite incredibly comes from bags of hockey and early-morning riding; intelligent, nervous, slim, and dressed always with stunning elegance – vividly of the moment – now bebooted mini-skirted, swathe-haired. She was David's secretary, or 'assistant' as they were now called.

Having bullocked Richard awake, David sent Antonia off to make them all some coffee and sat down to explain the reason for his arrival. As always, he began on top C and held it for as long as he could.

"It's time for another move," he said broadly, setting his suede-booted feet on the table and unfastening the buttons of his bottle-green mock-Regency jacket which might otherwise become too creased. "You've got to keep on the move or you get left behind in this game. And I've got to get out of London for a bit. A bit of what? Thereon lies a tale; I hope. You see – all these bloody carry-ons – institutions, television, magazines – they're all alike – they're always looking out for somebody new. You know that. So to get on, you've got to get out. They always look outside for a man to take over the latest cushy vacancy. It's this youth kick. It's turned into a new-at-any-price routine. And the end-of-Empire bit (will it ever end?), next man isn't necessarily the best man, let's shake it all up anyway and see if the salt'll come faster out of the cellar this way – you know what I mean? But the *new* thing mainly. I mean New has become entirely a qualitative word – hardly descriptive at all, don't you think? Look at all the junk they're painting now – you know, a bottle of jam stuck on to an isosceles triangle and called Studies 15. Well, it's never been done before (naturally – no jam) and the turd gets away with it because it's New. True. Am I right? I am. You just go to any of the galleries and there's this rubbish on the walls and then read your *Observer* or your *Times* or your *Telegraph* and you'll find out that it's all about relationships between material and environment, 'space and time', 'density and linear mobility', etcetera etcetera, and it is *really*, but *really*, taken seriously – solemnly, reverently – because it's New. What's new is good; No News is No Good." He paused, but not for breath, still less for a reply; to add point to his declaration, perhaps.

"Same with jobs. I'm known in London – therefore limited. I've got to clear out and send back exciting signals from some heartland of true England – voices off like those Greeks – they had the right idea, your big kill is in the wings – very true – and then, in a year or two, I can go back – say three years – and then find something *really* big. I've been playing with it so far. So there's this opening for a Controller of North-West Television – not bad, £4,650 plus perks, I can take the drop in cash, not a bad little company, can't make it any worse than it is – therefore a good time to join – Controller equals a big boss level, get used to the idea, practise in a pond, you know, let other people get used to it – means I've got to live in this God-forsaken part of the country, but I'll sacrifice art to life for once – so, here I am – 'sniffing it over'".

"Christ," said Richard. "One thing, David, you bring it all back."

"He's been waiting to tell somebody that for ages," said Antonia, as she manoeuvred the tray through the kitchen door, "for two days at least. What a lovely view you have from that kitchen window, Richard. It's *terribly* pretty."

"Bloody nature, is it?" David asked.

"Yes," said Antonia. "Bloody, but unbowed, wouldn't you say, Richard?"

"I need some coffee, he replied. "I feel as if I've been trampled on by your friend, Hill."

"I'm not her friend," said David. "That might imply a social parity qui n'existe pas – does it not, my dah-ling?"

"He's so sweet with his class business, isn't he?" said Antonia. "He reminds me of my father talking about 'those brave men in the trenches'. Exactly the same thing, isn't it?"

"No," said David, "it isn't. Your father was speaking out of ignorance while I speak out of prejudice. Very different."

"Coffee," said Antonia, "quick."

"The trouble with Antonia," said David, "is that she's been born at a time when the words socialist and socialite have become interchangeable, in *her* world, anyway. So the poor girl's never been able to define herself in any way that makes sense either to her background – which she thinks of as dull – or her ideas – which, mostly, she's too dull to think of. So she floats around people like me, thinking we're strong types, little knowing that the type went out of stock a generation ago and if it ever found its way on to the pages of my little life, I'd delete it with a bulldozer."

"He spends so much time telling me what I am that I sometimes think that he rather likes me," said Antonia.

"She spends so much time thinking whether people like her that I sometimes have to spend *my* time telling her," said David.

"You two ought to marry," said Richard.

"We get on too well to need that," said Antonia. "Besides, David would *hate* to be *related* to me."

"I like the relationship as it is," said David. "Master and servant. Anyway, Antonia would have about as much idea how to run a house as my mother would have about wearing a mini-skirt."

"If she *did* wear one," said Antonia, "like *my* mother does – then you'd *really* have problems."

"I like problems. They generalise my self-importance."

"Yes," said Richard. "You need a little help to keep you going."

"I need to keep going so as not to cry help."

"Oh God," Antonia replied, "will it never end?"

"What," said Richard firmly, "happened to Frank?"

"Oh my dear," David replied, "he made a real balls-up. You see – well, Antonia says this is what happened and I can't credit her with the invention to have imagined it – he got himself in with Kelly's lot...."

Richard found that he was enjoying hearing the gossip. He rose to David's bouncy way of talking, groaning at the constant stampede for effect but, despite that, entertained. Despise him-

85

self for it as he might, the chatter had in it the validity of something discovered for himself. At present, it was more integral to him than any solitary penances on the hills. He thought that he had cut himself off from London – but he had merely gone away from it. Frank was discussed, then Jane and Andrew, Julian's latest coups were unveiled – and so on until Richard felt himself finger-tip touching the entire world he had left. Once David had settled down, he forgot, a little, about his vendetta against Antonia and she, nestled in the corner of an armchair, with her skirt hooping up to the top of her thighs, lost some of the combative tension which she found it necessary to have in order to deal with him, and her manner softened, her air lightened, she became more girlish, herself.

"So what do you get out of this rustic hidey-hole?" David asked. "Cider with the local yokels? I must say, I was expecting some Countryman's Diary pieces from you at least. You know, 'Today I saw a sheep caught in barbed wire on the top of a beautiful mountain where yesterday three orphans lost their lives – the sun was shining, the birds were all a twitter and, lo and behold, here was the Grounded Roof-Robin with a broken wing.' No? What was it Dylan Thomas said? 'They're all bloody robins to me, except the seagulls.' I never imagined you on this mother-earth jag, Richard. What do you get out of it?"

"Peace and quiet," said Antonia. "I should imagine that to some of your friends that might be a cause worth fighting for."

"Come on, Richard," David continued. "Why? Got a book in the oven? No? Another lovely film script? No? Back on the old songs? No? Well. You won't be able to do many more articles, you know. They're all from memory as it is. They'll be turning into fiction next – and we've got another department for that. We don't want Art from you. Come on."

"For God's sake," said Richard. "I just wanted to clear out for a few months."

"But why? It was *exactly* the wrong time. You were just getting your foot in. You should have stayed and kicked a bit longer. Indispensability is essential for drifters. You've put yourself in a very bad position." He paused and glanced at Antonia. "Was it Sally?" he asked.

"David!"

"No," said Richard, "or yes. Maybe. I don't know. She was one of the reasons. I don't want to think about her."

"Well, she's stopped thinking about you as far as I can make out," David replied. "She went straight back to old greased lightning Philip Carlton-Smith. No messin'. You should have dug in there, my lad; she's a real swinger."

"Thanks."

"I give up," said David. "You've ruined yourself, my boy and all you can say is 'thanks'. Well then. I don't mind your clearing out – but why come and live in the middle of the steppe lands?"

"I like it. I was brought up in a place like this."

"Oh God! Enter the Womb. What a scene! At your age!"

"Your psychology was always subtle," said Richard. "Everything's a womb, a penis, an anus, a . . ."

"Did you hear that one about Tony?" asked David. "He came back from a year in Greece – and you know what he said – 'It was an anus mirabilis, my dear!' – Good, eh?"

"No."

"O.K. Well," he got up, "since we're stuck in this bloody agricultural paddy-land, we might as well go for a walk. Isn't that what you do? Prance about the hill-tops and get into communion with the Almighty Invisible, All-whitey, so-risible, God only wise, Wogs only please? Yes? Come on then. Have you any armour I could wear? But first – to P or not to P . . . ."

"Upstairs."

"You mean this house can support a first floor? God, those Saxons were clever."

He went upstairs. After making sure that he had definitely gone and would not suddenly reappear, Antonia, her legs curled under her so that she seemed rather like a lost kitten in the large chair, hurried to talk to Richard.

"Sally was terribly upset *really*. I saw her just after she got your letter – but she said that you'd been so honest about it all that she *admired* you for it and she thought it would be unfair to pursue it any further. Besides, Philip was going to Germany and it would have looked *odd* if she hadn't gone with him – especially after the *fuss* he'd made. But she was very moved by your letter, Richard, I know that. And I think she thought you were *right*. She said that all you could do would be to *ruin* each other's lives – and as you'd given her a chance to get out, she would take it. But don't believe David."

"I rarely do."

"Yes," she replied softly, "*he* isn't as confident as he looks at the moment you know. . . ."

87

"Thank God for that."

"Yes," she drawled. "No, I mean, he's made a *success* of that magazine, but people don't *like* him – and I think that was getting him down, you know. I mean, when you're at *his* stage, it's terribly tricky – you've *got* to be liked to get the sort of job he wants – and he could *do* them very well, no one questions that. But I think that most of the reason for his even *considering* this telly job is that he feels his luck's run out. People *resent* him for having gone so fast. They're jealous. And I think that *he* thinks that if he does something really *stunning* up here – in a sort of semi-administrative capacity – it'll be somehow *solid*, you know? Anyway, I think that when you felt he was upset – he never expected it – even though he half drove you to it by the way he worked you."

"It's pressure more than work. The articles themselves were hardly important at all."

"Yes. The articles weren't very good – aren't very *good*, are they? I mean, David always thought that yours were the *best*, but, even they – well they were *meant* to be sort of superficial, weren't they?"

"No. But they were. Thanks."

"Yes. And you see, David really *has* talent. I think he's getting fed up with that sort of thing."

"What sort of thing?" David, reappeared, demanded. "Aha! Silence. So, you were talking about me. Yes? Why does silence always mean consent? Why can't it mean – contempt, for example? No? Well, I've broken up that little lot. Richard, from your mean-sized floor windows I saw hills or things on all sides but one. So, no walk. I suggest we take the side without hills and go through the English countryside my style, in a blaze of petrol fumes, at sixty m.p.h. heading for the nearest pub you know of which serves good hot meals and good cold beer, as Mr. Hemingway would say. D'you remember that, in *A Movable Feast*? He says his wife 'made some *good* sandwiches'. I like to think of her setting out to make some *bad* ones. Mind you, the man was trying to resurrect the word Good, I'm sure of that. It must be mentioned ten times a page in that book. That's probably why he blew his head off. Good is dead and Ernest lacked the faith of our Early Fathers to do more than stub his toe against *that* little obstacle. Death. Well! Are we ready? Do you always wear those filthy jeans and things, Richard? What about your Brummellamania? It was *you* who got *me* started, you know. I was a teenage square until I met bright young, talented young, witty young, Young young R. Godwin who 'taught me how to dress, yer Honour, and that's where the trouble started'. Right! Away. Let's flee past all those fields and muscled men reaping or sowing or whatever they do at this time of year."

"Hay-timing, isn't it?" asked Antonia.

"Just finished," Richard said.

"When you two have stopped auditioning for the Archers, we might push off. And for Christ's sake get changed, Richard. It's bad enough your living here without seeing you dressed for the part. I think it's affected for you to look like a country bumpkin. You should have more respect."

"I think Richard's dressed *terribly* sensibly," said Antonia.

"Sense has got nothing to do with clothes in a civilised community. You wear them to look like a peacock – not to keep warm. They're plumage, not feathers."

"You'll end up on TV in front of the Archbishop of Canterbury and the latest Pop Group if you keep talking like that."

"Better men have had meaner ambitions. Come *on*!"

They did as he had demanded, ending up at The Trout in Cockermouth where they had a large, long and talkative lunch. Afterwards, declaring that it was just the sort of fine summer day which demanded that you look at it – and what better place to look at it than from a sunny room! – David insisted that they went into the lounge where they drank more, had tea, and then waited for the bar to open. Throughout this time both he and Richard went on non-stop about London, their friends, politics, anything that came up, the conversation having that rabid tone which in London itself appeared urgent and amusing, in Cockermouth appeared hysterical and garrulous. Antonia again, as she had done after her opening lines on entry (well-rehearsed, it would seem), now curled up tastefully and seemed to be getting her own back on both of them by the indifferent responses she made when asked for an opinion. They were talking about success.

"I can't see any other motive or reason or whatever you like to call it," said David. "I mean, what other reason *is* there for doing things? Honest Emulation – to make it sound better. What else *is* there?"

"All your success amounts to is Greed," Richard replied. "A greed to dominate or to own. Anything'll do as long as it makes you successful. The measurement of something in its own

89

terms is hardly important. You can be successful now merely by being known, although the reason for your being known in the first place might be nothing to do with talent or worth or anything other than sitting on a television panel-game."

"That isn't as easy as it looks."

"I didn't say it was. But it isn't *enough*, that's all. I got fed up with chasing around after the well-known – mind you, the job itself was nothing else – so maybe I'm having an over-severe reaction as *you* might put it."

"You just got fed up with being the one who did the chasing. *You* wanted to be well-known for a change. You wanted to be chased."

"Chaste?"

"For a change." David paused. "Small change," he added.

"But don't you see what I mean? I just think there's a better way to live, that's all. I may be wrong, I don't know precisely what I mean, etcetera, etcetera, but I simply think that chasing success – which, as you say, is all anybody – anybody *we* knew – does now (they won't admit it, of course, but being *known* is the thing) – I think that that isn't all that absorbing any more. I want to see if there's anything else." Richard was nervous; he had to be convincing but it was too soon, he himself did not know clearly his direction.

"That's opting out. It wouldn't be so bad if you had something to opt out *for* – but you haven't." David replied, curtly. "One or two articles, tinkering with those songs again – what's that? You can't just sit and think all the time, can you? Well, you can, I suppose. Like Bertrand Russell going away to think about the *Principia Mathematica* for seven years (a very biblical number, I'm sure *he* noticed that) – but that was a thesis. You're no intellectual. What's your thesis? That you don't like the way you were living. Well. Change it. You can't just run away from it – especially not to this desert."

"Why not? Is there anything so essential about living in a city? I know that we are supposed to be in the age of Urban Man, and if you live out of sight of seven million people you're somehow defaulting – but why? I know it *is* a city culture we have, de-dah, de-dah, that people will come more and more to see life through a car window on a street of skyscrapers – but how does that change anything that matters? The way someone feels, behaves and thinks – the way he acts?"

"All right. So you want to work out your relationship with

90

the Human Race. Very noble. To do it in isolation seems to me to contradict your intention totally. Never mind. But what happens when you finish? This success-thing – it's easy to sneer, but it *is* the only thing there is, you know. I mean, as a mood, as a general urge – and you can't discuss General Urge out of hand, or into the bush for that matter. Nobody, now, lives a life so that they can go to heaven – or very few; *that's* gone. Nobody – or few – live for others in the old public service, local charity way – *that's* gone. The race for posterity seems to have been abandoned – anyway nobody I know considers it worth while to enter. Sex? Well, that's all right, but it's a sport rather than an ambition. Poetry, Scholarship, all that – they don't draw in great numbers of people who want to be informed by it as they used to; they've become strictly private, exclusive. No, what people want now is to be known, to be successful. They want to be seen to be Living Well now, at this instant. It's to do with the sort of politics we've got, as well. If you have equality of opportunity (which we haven't, but we mouth the intention often enough) then that implies that there's going to be a fight after that – and also that it's going to be more power to those who win. Equality of opportunity is like saying On Your Marks; Get Set – that's Freedom of Choice; Go! – that's when we all scarper and show that, however equal our opportunity, our talents, my friend, are *very* different. And it's to do with the social carry-on. Who cares about Lords now – except Labour Party back-benchers? Who looks up to politicans? Not many. Who really believes that the Church gives a lead, or the great capitalists are worth listening to (especially as they're all Boards and Directors anyway or financial citizens of Panama)? So you have to have a greasy pole. You *do*. A hierarchy. For no other reason, if you like, than that we've always had one, and we'd invent one far quicker than we'd invent God if we found ourselves without. So who tops the hierarchy now? I.e., who do people talk about with that mixture of reverence, jealousy, contempt and wonder that used to be reserved for the baron or whoever? Who? *Personalities!* The successful. And that's what we all want to be – and it's second-rate to pretend to ignore it."

"David Hill. Collected Essays. Volume II. "How to Succeed in the World's Business by Really Trying.' "

"Exactly."

"Well, I must be second-rate then."

"That's too easy. And it's nauseatingly self-pitying."

"All right, then. I want to be successful on my own terms."

"What are they?"

"I don't know. But I don't want what you want! I want to see the weight of the life I live, to see what a day passing means, to allow some sense of other things, irrelevancies if you like, chat, accidents, to come into my life. I want to get totally away from your success-thing – because however much you gain by it, I think you lose more. You know the state I was in the last few months. That was wreckage. Or I think it was. I want to find out."

"When you do, bring me News, that I may come and be de-wrecked also. It's a load of nineteenth-century blarney, Richard. Obsolete!"

"No. It's your success-story which is jaded. However you dress it up and try to make it exclusively contemporary – it's been going on for centuries. Enter callow ambitious young man – younger son of an impoverished duke with six derelict estates, or son of a vicar or a doctor, or an orphan, or from an under-privileged class – and away he goes to make his way on his wits and become a success. You're at the fag-end of something, not at the beginning. Wolsey to Wilson, Pip to Joe Lampton – same thing. *You* are obsolete. Useless word. When so many people can live comfortably, with all the machines, those material gains which were like so many stripes along the self-promotion trail now seem less and less important. So you get a slightly bigger house, a bigger car, etcetera etcetera – you're doing nothing different, you're merely tampering with degrees; you're not leaving a hellhole, but shifting your behind on to a slightly thicker cushion. That's all. All the old fattening up for dead men's shoes. Prehistoric! Or you become well-known, a success – well OK but so bloody what? You know something of the forces that have manipulated you into that position, you don't respect them much, nor yourself much for being malleable, and you know that you can be manipulated out again any day. You're part of a system which needs you – but it needs you to stay *exactly* as you were when I found you. And however exhilarating it might be to live out part of your life in public, it soon changes to living out part of your life *for* the public – and that may be pleasant, desirable and so on. I don't think so, that's all."

"But you don't get away from it all in a country cottage any more, Richard."

"Why not? Isn't it just as boring to opt out in one of these

Swinging New Places – to go to Katmandu or San Francisco or wherever it is now, take the drugs or the drink or whatever – in a way, you could say that was just as lemming-like as what *you're* doing. Anyway – I couldn't give a bugger. I wanted to live here. *Wanted* to. I'd forgotten that I ever could want anything as limited and direct as that."

"It seems to me that you're bending over so far to avoid being fashionable that you must have a really *serious* dose of it yourself."

"That was bound to come up! There's no argument against it. No argument – only what I do."

"Hm. You'll have to wait on your own. And it *is* becoming fashionable to be unfashionable. Latest thing."

They had one or two drinks and then drove back to the cottage so that Antonia could change. David had somehow heard of a 'great' pub in Workington where they had a number of acts – a man in drag, two blue comedians imported from Bradford, a new raving pop group and, to top it all, a Palm Court trio who played light classical between 8.30 and 9.15 to a churchly appreciation. He insisted that they should go there, and there, among the crowded pints and smoke-stained brown-papered grease-shiny walls, with the amplifier winging away on its own at times to provide an unnerving electronic wail, the juddering of cheeks, restless legs, tight retorts of laughter, beer-swill, crisps, the limbo of the leisured hours – they got drunk. Antonia enjoyed herself marvellously and spent half the time tugging at her mini-skirt, the other half hot under the stares that followed its steady creep towards her navel. David spread into an even greater caricature of himself and was awash in it all, calling up the orange peel and glamour of the Victorian mob, and, at the same time, shrewdly watching Richard, wolf-eyed observing Antonia's antics, relishing his postion as the most initiated and yet the most detached.

"Tribalism!" David shouted. "You need never have left London."

Oh to be in London, now that summer was here, with the swinging chicks in the Old King's Road and the pretty boys all in their gear, with the rapid conversation, running free like ancient cheese, and the rat tat tat tat of the brave new world with only yourself to please. And who *is* yourself, Mr. Godwin? Well that's a tricky one, Fred. I don't know the answer while living, but someone might say when I'm dead. To tell you the truth, Mr. Godwin, Yourself doesn't exist, you're a circuit of characteristics and only defined when you're missed. When you're missed, ah then, Mr. Godwin, we know just where we are, you're as clear as a hole in a wall, skin, smell and clothes on a star. The star was just for the rhyme, I'm sure you'll appreciate that, your sort appreciate *so much* these days, your mind has become like a welcoming mat.

Matt Monroe singing, Matt Busby managing Manchester United, Manhatten, Matlock, all change, oh dear what can the Matter be, maybe the guard wants to go to – and the alcohol swirled inside him until his head was forcibly jammed in a sway-boat, his two eyes the tugging ropes pulling it through the kicking fuming air.

Once again his mind jabbered with this ceaseless babel of flinching words. Like a spool on a projector, suddenly slipping off and spinning round faster and faster. Once he had tried to accept this, to let the words run, to lash them on – so that his mind became a simultaneous flickering, like those cellars in which the films, pitctures, stills, slides and plays are all performed at the same time to an equally compacted range of music. This way of thinking or reacting had become a metaphor for his life. But he could not embrace it. What looked like passion was merely heat. What looked like complication, nothing but an endless whirl of surfaces. Not distension, simply tension.

He drank to the bottom of his pint glass. Tried to listen to the singing. Touched the wet-topped table. Wanted to stay, to stay here, where he was; but the jabbering would not be silenced.

Sally! Forgotten! Never did think! Always a! Coherence. Make firm your joints, or joyces. That shot in the light succeeded anyway. There's the. Sally. For those who want to rub. Sally. Gone to her because – oh, mother, father, mother-earth, father-figure, a lovely figure, youth in its final fight with middle-age nipples sprung and raising all resistance so that the temptation thickened around her like an old plot – gone to her. Love. Said so. In so many words. Said so. But always doubted motives – motives, why were we born with motives then, why were we born at all, they're no bloody good to anyone – but you can't just trample on your considerations, they're more valuable than your instincts, aren't they? *Say* something someone and stop that comic telling us about the man with no arms and legs. Motives – dubious. A flippant 'affair' – or the other word, it's

too fierce, though, for the beer – the other word. Coherence.
Order, please!

Sally. More than any of the others he had talked to her and
yet not told her of the others. And yielded to her as much as he
could, *she* thought it was all, but always that dry spot in his
mind even at the climax. A little curled finger of – what? And he
had decided to leave her, and all of it, while sitting on a bench in
Kew Gardens, looking over to Syon House, and down the thick
Thames bending to Richmond. The light in the river rising like
spots of Seurat and then hazy, more like Monet, he sat there
trying to get in all the Impressionists – his first affair with
painting through the Impressionists, fifteen mornings in the Jeu
de Paume – like Monet then, sitting alone, eight o'clock a bell
went to clear the Gardens, the bell of Cambrai or near there, he
could not remember, the Bells of St. Mary's were nearer with
Bing Crosby, or the bells of Shoreditch, never once heard in all
his time in London, anyway the closing bell – a tocsin tinkle –
and Sally the figure with him in the 'Angelus' of Millet – even
then, the disintegration, which had made it necessary for one
of the garden guards to dismount from his bicycle and prod
the recumbent loiterer and suggest that he go out on to the
towpath as it was quicker, sir, if you don't mind. Level stare.
Those were the words. Life is the leveller. It's death that makes
the hierarchies. Clever – clever but not clever enough, Mr. Godwin. At a certain stage, *un certain âge*, cleverness should turn
into something *more*, don't you think? Something *other*. Quite,
Quite *Other*. He had to leave more than the Gardens, as, when
he walked along the towpath, there was no principle, no intent,
nothing whatever that he could see to prevent him from walking
straight into the river itself – but he did not. Self-preservation?
Cowardice? (Of course.) Hope? Whatever it was, it needed
nutriment because it could call on no support as things were.
And so to Crossbridge.

Meanwhile, back in the pub, there was David, his hand
publicly placed on Antonia's upper thigh, bawling out 'It's
Been A Hard Day's Night' and squeezing the bare flesh whenever he felt a particularly intimate relationship with the rhythm.
So 'it's fashionable to be unfashionable now'. Where the hell
do you go from there? If *every*thing is to be interpreted in
severest relation to the modern scene, if every*thing* is to be
judged not as to whether it's good or bad, right or wrong,
effective or non-effective, but simply in terms of whether it is

in the 'scene' or not, that 'scene' spreading from clothes or behaviour to inform the whole of activity with its demands, then what do you do? But get out. In some way now, fashion was compounded of competition and contemporary vitality, it was everything you had to be because somehow the past has lost touch with the present. Or was it? Had it? As soon as your depiction of the scene was as clear and crude as Richard's, then any hesitation meant that you were on the way out – one way or another – and the only way to leave was with your own consent. Only contempt could contaminate what you wished to ignore.

No. David and Antonia bounced around in the next bedroom and the sweltering night of heat and beer tossed his head like a ship's lantern. No. Maybe the heart *did* have its reasons that reason knew not of. Or any other cliché to see him through. No. He was not raking the roots of his impulses to uncover a pot of golden nature-man. No. He was merely changing the circumstances of his life in order that he might alter the way in which he lived. There was nothing yoked or raw about Wif, whose way was as sophisticated as that of David. No. But maybe here there was an outside force he would have to reckon with – but a city, *too*, has a force, for those who wish to, can, hope to, need to see, feel such things. No. David could bounce around all night. What would Janice look like when asleep? Would her hair catch the light through the curtains?

A strained 'good morning', 'good luck for that job', good riddance – over-emphatic, but necessary like all lines of defence – to David, a short walk to clear the head, back to bed in mid-afternoon. Sleep.

CHAPTER ELEVEN

Two or three times a year, Agnes gave a tea-party for many of the children in the village. She had once met some children around Christmas and asked if they were going to any parties. They had replied that they were not, had never been to a party, and so she had given one for them.

The summer one was usually on the last Saturday before they went back to school. On a good day, as this was, Wif would put trestle tables in front of the cottages – the tables borrowed for the day from the Institute. They would be laid out making a long line which stretched almost from Edwin's door to Agnes's. Seats were a problem, but the combined resources of Mrs. Jackson, Edwin and Agnes usually made enough, and Mr. Law was willing to send as many more as were necessary. He always provided a quart of full cream and a basin of raspberries for the occasion. For such it had become. Without ever over-organising it, Agnes had made it into an Event, with all the formal excitement of that word yet without the embarrassment and boredom which could attend it, since her ambition was simple and limited – that is, to give the children a lot to eat.

Edwin would help to get the place ready in the morning, lay the tables, clear the path, obey any whim of Janice who now wanted a treasure trove dug out with sixpences under certain sticks, or a water-butt filled with bobbing apples, or whatever fancy she thought to remember from her own childhood; he would also undertake to provide the lemonade – cherryade, dandelion and burdock – the boy's favourite – limeade, orange-ade – the girls' favourite – and always, just before the first arrivals he would make up some excuse to disappear.

Mrs. Jackson, who complained of the noise, pretension and waste of it all with increasing bitterness as the day drew nearer, would suddenly catapult herself into it on the Friday night, coming in to help Agnes with the baking, almost knocking the other woman aside with her fussy bullying, but from that moment as devoted to the party as if she was taking her revenge against it. And when the children arrived, she provided the useful function of the enemy; much of their pleasure came from teasing her, doing what they knew would enrage her, ducking her blows.

Wif and Janice took to it in exactly the same way. They gave up their day for it and embroidered as carefully as possible on Agnes's plain design. Many of the little boys fell in love with Janice, many of the little girls liked to help Wif with the hutch he was building or the bicycle he was mending.

From his bedroom window Richard saw them arrive, hesitating down the path in twos and threes, hair plastered on to scraped faces, socks persistently falling down and as persistently tucked up, pleated dresses lifting out above skinny knees while the white bow sagged on the top of the head. Heads popping around the corner while shoes scratched nervously against a bare calf – giggles, retreat, a stone thrown over a hedge, and then finally

97

the ejection on to the battlefield followed by a complete full stop on sight of the heavy table. From there to be beckoned and coaxed to squiggle on to a chair and there slump, nudging the neighbour, feet waving above the ground, waiting.

It began when Agnes brought out the teapot which made them all gasp. It was the Institute's Urn, with many a "Jerusalem" sung to its warm brown spout. Everybody had tea *and* lemonade, so that it was at once ordinary and, so, comfortable; proper – because it *was* tea-time; and a treat – because the tea itself did not matter.

The scene, the children between the stone-fronted cottages and the late summer gardens, saturated with smells and wilting luxuriance, settled like a little convention on the only animated patch of countryside for miles around – their chatter and activity stilling any sounds, quelling any movement from anywhere else – this, as Richard watched it, seemed so innocently bucolic that, perversely, he felt himself react against it. David's visit had unnerved him and he saw himself as someone playing out a whim; again it seemed that it did not matter whether one did good or bad, whether one "contributed" or took away, an impenetrably complicated inevitability would determine what happened.

As he watched them, he thought his despair too easy – and yet it was present; he thought his collapse the months before self-indulgent – and yet it had happened; he thought the life he was now leading artificial – and yet it was the only way he could think of without distaste. And he thought himself a failure – yet that got him nowhere.

He watched the openness of Agnes. Paula had been brought out into the sun and the little cot stood apart from the long table, peeped into on request by the girls, walked around as if it were a landmine by most of the boys. Agnes kept her eye on the baby, saw that the scones and cakes were attacked, wiped splashed dresses, blew runny noses – *her* life needed no expiation, he thought. All had been consistent – open, true to herself, and beside her he felt dried up with sapped indecisions, lies, secrets. What had he to do to achieve that sort of equilibrium in himself?

Janice. It was she he was watching. He longed to have again the straight desire he had felt on thinking of her that other night. But at this moment, with David's words, his atmosphere more, his bombast still resounding through him, he could only pick at her with his eyes, observe the way she pandered to the boys, notice that she avoided the cot, smile at her undercutting of Mrs.

98

Jackson's fending glares, watch the tawny hair scattered with sunlight; and then go back to his desk and stare at the article he meant to get off by Monday morning. He remembered how boldly he had arrived and was sickened by his feebleness, went out by the back way and left the scene.

Agnes had been exhausted before the day began, and only the enjoyment of the children kept her going. When they left, she had still the momentum to do the washing-up, see that Wif cleared all away outside, resettle her own kitchen which had been the fall-out shelter, but finally, as she began to make up the baby's bottle, she turned dizzy, upset the pan. and fainted. Mr Jackson and Wif got her upstairs where she came to immediately and rejected their suggestion that a doctor should be sent for. She would be all right. All she needed was a sleep.

Wif came downstairs and sat there, unwilling to leave the house, even to take refuge in his shed. Janice fed the baby, put her to bed, and then made his supper.

"I've never seen her go like that," said Wif. "Never once."

"It's too much for her. Baking all night. It's just tiredness, that's all. She takes too much on herself."

"Aye. And there are other things that are forced on her," he replied.

Janice checked herself, but as the intermittent conversation continued to yawn between the gaps of accusation, she set herself to put her case. No matter that her mother was in bed, that her father was antagonistic – it was at these times particularly that she believed she had to make clear what her intentions were.

"I was thinking," she began, "that I might go back to Carcaster this autumn."

"To College?"

"Yes. They said I could come back whenever I wanted." She rushed on. "They'll renew my grant and everything. What I thought was that if I took some sort of secretarial work in the evenings, I could earn enough for Mother to employ a girl to look after the baby. It wouldn't be difficult. I'm sure that one of Mrs. Patten's lot would do it. Iris has just left school and she hasn't a job yet." She paused. "She likes children, as well. She's more or less brought up that family. It would take the strain off – Mother."

"I don't understand you, Janice. Not any more. Do you think your mother would have somebody else in this house to look after that baby? I mean – whether she *should* or not's a different thing – but do you think she would? Do you? I mean, you don't know the first thing about her if you can even consider that. That's what I mean. I don't comprehend the first thing about you – well, maybe that's only to be expected with your College and everything – but you don't know one thing about *us* any more. How can you not know that? Eh? I'm not angry or anything. But how can you even suggest that when you *know*, you must know, it couldn't happen and all it would do would be to upset her altogether. I mean – don't you realise that?"

"I don't see that it should."

Wif shrugged and took up a newspaper. He could find no way of making any move which would bring anything but a row, and pain.

"What do you expect me to do?" Janice demanded. "No. You can't hide behind that paper. What do you *want* me to do? Stay here, dependent on you. Gradually taking over that baby because Mother gets more and more tired? Is that it? Marry Edwin? Look for somebody else, go out to dances on spec? Is that it? I *can't*, Father. I'll just give up here. There's nothing I want to do in this place. How often do I have to say that– and hear you say that you agree and see my point – and then – back where we started – you *don't* see, you don't! Well? What do you want me to do?"

"Strange as it might appear, I'm more interested in what your mother's going to do. You have a chance to look after yourself. She hasn't. It's *her* I'm worried about in all this."

"That's a hellish thing to say."

"No it isn't, Janice. You won't let me worry about you." Wif spoke thoughtfully. "How can I worry when I don't know what the trouble is? Well I know, of course I know – you want to get out – that's all right – but the *way* you want to do it – the way you *are* doing it – it leaves me high and dry, Janice, and how can I worry about you, I mean help you – I'll always worry, there's nothing in that – how can I, when everything you say just makes me think you've never known us?"

"Of course I know you. But that doesn't mean you have the right to say. "*We* are unchanged and therefore unchangeable." Something's happened. There's a baby. Now *I* want to go away. *That's* unchanged as well. I'll have to provide for it – in spite of what I say to Mother – so *I* have to change. All I'm asking is that you *consider* a way. That's all."

"But can't you see, how can we consider anything when you

treat the baby like – well, I don't know, I've never come across anything like it. I mean, it's just – well, I don't understand."

"Well, try to – for a change. "I don't understand." That's no argument. Where do we get to from there? I've told you – I said and said and *said* that I did not want that child! I haven't changed – that could be understood, couldn't it?"

"But you *have* changed a little bit; maybe you'll change more."

"Oh no. You well know why I'm feeding her and that; I don't want Mother to be fainting every five minutes. That's all."

"Is it?"

"Yes. Yes! Stop trying to wrap everything up in this sort of muddled mysteriousness. You *can* understand what I'm doing – but you shy away from it by pretending that what I'm doing isn't very clear. It is. *Very* clear. I'm where I always was. I'm trying to get out."

"This minute?"

"Oh Dad. You're blackmailing me, you know. Yes – if you like – this minute."

"Blackmail? I blackmail you? What things you say – do you realise just *what* you say some of the time?" Janice did not reply. "If you care for my opinion then – I think you should wait a bit."

"Why?"

"Because of your mother, mainly – I suppose that's blackmail again. And – I'm going to say it, Janice, however much you don't like it – maybe a bit more time would give you the chance to change your attitude .I think if you just rushed off now, you might regret it for the rest of your life."

"If I don't go this autumn. I'd have to wait a year."

"Well, I would wait. That's my say."

She knew that she would accept his advice. Somehow, the exhilaration she had felt at the thought of being free of the child had overreached itself and, in curling back to her, had brought in an uncertainty. Agnes. Her own fear of facing everyone again without being totally confident that she could carry it off. And the grit had rubbed away the smooth passage she had hoped to make.

A year to wait, one *year*.

It would have to be organised or she would lose all will.

She went upstairs and looked across to Richard's cottage. She had seen David and Antonia with him and been jealous of the three of them. David had reminded her of Paul.

She rumaged among her files and brought out the reading lists

101

Paul had once drawn up for her. Very neat. History, Classical and Modern; Literature, Traditional and Contemporary; Political Thought; Science, Psychology; General. The usual ambitious ragbag stemming from the World's 100 Best Books with a few of Paul's idiosyncratic preferences thrown in. Perhaps he was to be one of the last of that long line which believed in broadening the mind through narrowing the eyes. Anyway, for Janice, with an empty year to be filled in, it was something solid; a calendar, a conscience.

It was appropriate that Paul's list should be her conscience, she thought.

CHAPTER TWELVE

Bowness Knot stands right against Ennerdale Water and marks the end of the public road. From there on is a forestry path which follows the water to the marshes at its head. The Knot falls steeply into the lake, but here and there are flat, jutting slabs on which you can lie, hidden from every view – for the lake itself is deserted. Richard had not yet seen a single boat on it. Here he would lie in the late afternoon and wait for the sun to strike across from Angler's Rock which stood opposite. Then the lake would spring a billion silver reflections, static under the water's surface, each reflection as clear as a silver strand. He was reminded of the old English game-cocks on Mr. Law's farm, the ancient fighting-cocks now kept merely for breeding, with their plumaged tails, scarlet comb and, most magnificent of all, golden crests, long slim cords of gold which fell deep down their backs, as beautiful as Janice's hair. The unexpected vividness of their appearance – such hard, equatorial colours in a landscape where all was modulated in endless delicate combinations by mellow-dour light – was like Agnes's description of the potters' rich crockery. And here too, beside this lake, bracken, heather and moss on the hills, rock, slate, gorse and thistle, suddenly this cold, immoderate silver.

It was Wif who had taken him to see the English game-cocks – Golden Duckwings the breed was – and it was through Wif that Richard put such names as he could to what was around him. For though brought up in a large village, Richard was not a country-man. He had known the shape and smell of the land, but the

102

details of his life had been found in the small streets, the cinema, the school, the footnotes of urbanity.

In the garden, Wif had shown him the Dorothy Perkins roses which he himself had introduced to Crossbridge after the First War. One evening he had taken Richard to see a badger's set and, getting on the right side of the wind, they had seen the whole family crawl out of the ground. The fells were riddled with interconnecting badger holes as they were raked above ground by the lean walls. He had seen the black-backed hares which ran up Knockmirton and no beagles could catch; the kestrel hawks which nested on top of Blake; old-fashioned lupins and wild kale more yellow than Van Gogh; the barley preening its whiskers like a kitten; the skylark rising like an arrow from the ground. A nibbling of knowledge, as often forgotten as remembered, more treasured for being given so kindly than for the information itself.

He could have stayed there for ever, he thought. No sound but the light tap of the lake against the rocks, the silver glittering: perhaps it was the tresses of hair of that virgin who had thrown herself into the lake after being chased over the hills by a pack of starved hounds – the only persistent legend associated with the lake.

Eventually he got up and began to walk, taking a track across the fields, now waving in the late afternoon, the yellow grass as long as hay. His legs had stiffened and he strode out to shake off the cold which tightened him. He came to a field which had been mown a second time and an enormous flock of crows were pecking at the stubble. Black on the shorn honey carpet. He licked his palms and clapped, hard, several times, and the crows lifted and wheeled, whirred around his head blocking the clouds, settled in the hedge, lifted again as he approached, calling each other into inexplicable formation. Farther up the hillside he looked back. They were settling once more in the mown field.

David really had thrown him – for it was clear now that there could be no isolation by simple distancing. Wif was as much part of things as David; he too could make day by flicking on a light, he too was dependent on a thousand specialised activities for his weekly wage, he too, in one hour's television, could see war in Vietnam, famine in India, a Prime Minister's arrival at Heathrow, the world champion egg-eater, an Irish pipe-band, ice-skating, and a short item on Picasso. He too was acted on by all those forces which extended and substituted his own powers of

103

movement, reaction and thought. It would only be disturbing, not useful, Richard thought, if here, as was happening, he regained a stronger personal sense of touch and smell and sight. What could he do with "one impulse from a vernal wood" when a supersonic bang would shatter it to smithereens? Yet there were degrees. In England now, the entire wash of its past, traditions oral, literary, feudal, industrial, rural, urban, primitive, sophisticated – all co-existed as equal ways to live, the Englishman's home was his cell and no cell had walls. Yet how to live with yourself when it seemed true that "the visible world is no longer a reality and the unseen world no longer a dream"–that could only be found alone. So the loneliness of these fells was still valid, even as a metaphor; presenting an apparent isolation which Richard was daily more sure he had been right to demand.

"So what'll you get if you gain your whole soul and lose the world?" David had asked. Richard smiled: he had been looking for the exact word to describe David and now he found it: *prat*.

He came to the top of a hill and went over, glancing back on Ennerdale Water, now so still as to seem cut out, a liquid carpet fitted smong the hills. Back towards the cottage where he would glimpse Janice but not see her, wait to hear her but not talk.

She had isolated herself – of that, no doubt. From the village he had gathered information about her – how she had read and read after her illness, tired before everything but her books. How she had swept up scholarships and prizes at the school and won entrance to Cambridge only to turn it down to go to the newer place at Carcaster, because, somebody had said, she had told them she could be more certain of doing exactly what she wanted there. Richard had come to see her as having built her entire life from her own premises, with no concessions and no deviations – and her child appeared to him as the crude punishment always exacted on those who are vain or strong enough to seal themselves off from the world in a self-governing style. Yet already she was countering that. But how to get near her? Like Echo she retreated to her cave, self-imprisoned, inviolate; and he, Narcissus, immobile. One of them must move.

Coming to join the road which would take him back to Cross-bridge, passing the rams – tips – with their curled horns, bounding from him like stags, he heard shouting. A child's voice. He turned towards it.

On top of that castle-like ruin which had marked the big iron ore mine, a small boy was kneeling, grasping the rubble, his knees and hands pressed into the loosening brickwork. He could move in no direction without falling.

Richard ran up to him. Seeing the man, the boy's small cries grew in relief and he howled, his body shivering with fright. Richard tried to climb up, but the bricks were not safe for him and his pull on them threatened the whole wall.

He looked around. No one within miles. The boy's demanding need seemed incongruous.

The boy's howling stopped. He looked down at Richard pitifully and enquiringly, interested, despite his fear, in what was going to happen to him.

"Jump," said Richard. "I'll catch you."

The boy tilted towards him and Richard braced himself. Then he shook his head.

"It isn't far. Jump."

The boy edged forward. A sliver of rubble ran down from the top of the wall. He froze.

"You won't hurt yourself. Come on."

The boy had just had a haircut and his shaved neck shivered its spiky bristles. He wore baggy little jeans, a striped tee-shirt and black wellingtons. His face was old, already muted by a know-ledge which wizened the innocence; only his situation was boyish – perhaps that was why he could not comprehend it.

"Come on," Richard repeated, softly. "I'll catch you."

Richard braced his legs and opened his arms. At the very least he would break the boy's fall. The boy looked at him, the small lid of hair flopping forward on to the thin white brow. The tears had left dirt-stains down his cheeks and his nose was running.

"Jump."

The boy shook his head and Richard let his arms drop. It was impossible to climb the wall; the only alternative was to build a platform from the loose bricks around and stand on it to pick the boy off.

"Don't move then," said Richard and turned.

The boy shouted. But when Richard held out his arms, the boy shook his head so violently that he slipped, slightly, and he began to whimper. Richard backed away and the whimper ac-companied him as he gathered bricks to make his platform.

He had to walk some distance away, to the pit shaft, ineffectiv-ely protected by a few stakes, carelessly covered by a mere board. There were both bricks and spare planks there, and Richard made several journeys to it, the boy never for a second taking his eyes off him, the whimper unceasing. Two cars passed below on the fell-dyke road, but neither of the drivers could have been over-curious about the dusky figure who walked between the sil-houetted rim and the cordoned shaft, for neither of them even slowed down.

It was steady work building the platform and, when it was high enough, Richard discovered that to heave himself on to it would threaten it. He went to look for a long plank to serve as a stair. When he returned, the boy had slung himself down from wall to platform to the ground and stood, hands in his pockets, head bent.

He would answer no questions. Richard had not seen him in the area but, assuming he came from one of the more remote hamlets, left him. He walked down a field to the stream which he could follow back into Crossbridge. Finding some stepping-stones, he walked across on them and turned to look at his path. The boy was gone.

It had been an easy action. No cause, no consequence; no struggle. Perhaps it was right that the only way anyone can be free is to struggle. Even with himself; dull combat.

He came through the gate and down the last field. Janice was walking back to the cottages. He stood and watched her. She had seen him, but did not turn back. Not yet. It was his move.

CHAPTER THIRTEEN

Each was aware of the other as two fishermen on the same stretch of idle river. Each had been burnt, in the friction of a chosen world, but this new flame which licked them served a double purpose by cauterising the old wounds at the same time. In Janice, the flame came through ice and was watched, scornfully, as a pitiful thing, to be regarded out of curiosity perhaps, maybe even approached to flaunt frozen hands over it – but not to be felt or acted on. Yet it was there. In Richard, it came out of the rubble, blazing away the tangled debris of his confused emotion, simply leaping to find more to burn. He expanded, she contracted.

Janice was interested in him. Dismissively so – but she was well enough prepared in her defences not to be so foolish as to refuse to recognise it. Something kindled. Interest was the correct word;

106

that safe investment which can be made recklessly. He was the only person she had met since leaving Carcaster – always making an exception of Edwin – who *could* be invested with interest. He was good-looking, intelligent enough, had some experience, she decided. That ought to anaesthetise him. Over the next few weeks, when they met, as they did, more and more frequently, she deliberately played herself down. She was brilliant at that tone of voice learnt at University which categorises all encounters, however long, as casual meetings. She never went out of her way.

She did not have to. Richard, now for the first time given a real pursuit, primed himself for action. He would glance at himself in the mirror when getting up; flex his arms, look at his body's profile. The two months or so in the country air had toughened him. He swam in Cogra Moss – enjoying the way his body had to clench itself against the cold water. He ran up Knockmirton. Until he glowed, almost glowered with physical well-being.

One thing which he had not reckoned on was a rush, an avalanched return of confidence. In Crossbridge, till now, he had been boyish, awkward, cautious. He had felt himself to be all these things – seen no shame in it, looked for no way out of it, for he was a stranger, largely ignorant of rural economy, uninformed when daily life ran in deepest ruts of generations' knowledge; he had been hesitant because he did not know where to go, uncertain because he was perpetually wondering what on earth he was doing there anyway, enclosed, distant, submerged. What he had shown of himself was the tip, the eighth or sixteenth or whatever; a part only, and even that part attended by little of what he had made himself in twenty-four years because it was determinedly clean and cleared, fresh antennae, willing and waiting to be guided on to a course which fitted the obscure instructions which supported it. The awareness of Janice – nothing more could truly be claimed as yet, but the awareness of Janice heaved him above ground and he changed.

Most important of all – and this Janice did not see, did not begin to recognise – Richard felt strongly in this situation. For he had been in love ever since he could remember. There had been afternoons, just a few months ago, when he had walked down Church Street or the King's Road in London and counted thirty or forty women with whom he would have been quite happy to have shared the consequences of passion for a week or two.

That all his affairs had ended; that never had he been more than

107

temporarily sated and euphoric; that their extension had seemingly inevitably given them a weight which oppressed him, and their regularity indicated an impulse never satisfied or understood to himself – all this he chose to ignore – but even this strengthened him because it gave him to believe that he was now able to judge, having so often been convicted.

He read less, wrote less, watched Janice, talked to her, walked the fields he knew she had walked, to wrap himself in the presence of her autumn way, looked for the light in her window and looked longer at the head silhouetted against the curtains, waited.

And in all this there was, he knew, something at least, at least something, there must be, of what he was looking for. So he held on to this saturating poise of attendance; for that, too, was different from any time before – and, to underline that difference, he would extend it. Let it spin slowly and mellow through him, through the early autumn.

Agnes forced herself into action again and was able, as usual, to summon a feast of decorations into the church for the Harvest Festival. It was strange that she, who had grown up in the dense snug and smog of a mining district, should be so fulfilling in her activities in Crossbridge, particularly in those which embraced much to do with the heart of the countryside – like a harvest festival. Perhaps it was due to that sort of pride which comes out of being constantly watched; back-to-back terraces are rarely breeders of privacy, and there a kitchen is a crossroads as well as a hearth. If you had a harvest festival it had to be right – and that meant sheaves of corn, massed fruit in large copper bowls and buckets, flowers in every niche, vegetables decorating the chancel steps, branches of evergreen thrust in limpid green sprays on the walls, horse-brasses on their leathers to symbolise the ploughing, sheaves of barley along the nave, the whole church a yellow-brown-green burgeoning of autumn. Although others helped her, the arrangements were firmly in Agnes's hands – simply because she was prepared to work harder than any of the others and was as excited at the display as if it had been for her own wedding. Moreover, she used this, as she did other matters, to give herself an unassailable excuse for being out of the house – and so forcing Paula on to Janice; she could see it doing no good, as yet, but it had to be tried.

Wif came home earlier as the nights drew in. There was little chance of overtime with the work he did and in winter casual jobs in the evenings were not as easy to come by, so he usually set himself something fairly big to do. The previous year he had made bedding-boxes. This winter he decided to collect the materials necessary for dry-stone walling his large garden into areas. The outside walls had to be done anyway, and within them he wanted to make three sections; one for the hen-run, another for the vegetables, and the third, with flowers, a bit of lawn, a seat and swing he would make – and maybe even a sand-pit – for Paula to play in, the seat for Agnes to sit out in through the summer.

For Edwin, the autumn brought a pile of work and, now that he was on full wages, overtime was really lucrative and he began to direct himself more specifically towards setting himself up. It was rumoured that some weeks his wage packet went over twenty-five pounds – not counting the extra he earned in his own time. He hoarded the money and used its accumulation as a shield behind which he hid himself from thought of the consequences of the alliance developing between Janice and Richard. He saw it but refused to fear it. His own approach was cemented in a consistency he could not, as yet, think of changing. So far, it had not let him down. Janice had never taken up with boys at Grammar School, as she might have done; the affair in Carcaster had taken her away from other men – not towards them. And she was more available to him these days. One evening they had a long talk about his mother where his usual restraint, indeed his refusal to talk about her, had broken down in a long confidence of bitterness. Janice had understood. Then again, he had expected her to go back to College in the autumn – he knew that she wanted to and believed that she would always do whatever she wanted – and yet she had stayed. If he allowed himself to dream – as he did – and to control that dream according to a careful assessment of the situation, then he saw a long wait coming to its close with success. For he might have said that her child made no difference to his regard for her – but it certainly brought her more within his reach; now that she was proved vulnerable, he began to see much more of a parity between them. Also, as his confidence in his work grew, and as the possibilities sharpened, his self-esteem took a sudden leap forwards. There was no swagger in him; but the shuffle was gone for ever.

CHAPTER FOURTEEN

Although Janice and Richard were together a good deal, their meetings, at this stage, still had the aspect of being accidental. Janice would not commit herself to accepting Richard's company as the natural consequence of their increasing interest in each other; she preferred the pretence that the time they passed together was merely an extension of the inevitable contact they were bound to make, living so near to each other.

Usually, he would meet her at about six and they would chat together in his cottage. She borrowed books from him, listened while he talked, nervously hearing himself explain his reasons for coming to the cottage, determined to be explicit – to be anything else appearing as a retreat. In return, she would tell him about her life, with that easy recollection of childhood typical of those who have just broken from it and are certain that they have swung quite off the course it set them on. Her ambition, though so private as to jib at articulation, was inclined to what he had left; to that sort of free-wheeling, in some degree parasitical, life which could, if you were resilient enough, enable you to bounce off the pins of your society without sticking on to any of its particular spikes. So, almost unknown to herself, she was being fed an attraction which, later, could grow into a demand.

This evening, however, she did not come, and eventually he went round to her cottage, only to discover that she was out. It was November the Fifth and she had gone, with Edwin, to the bonfire up by the church. Piqued that he had not been informed, or invited, Richard decided to walk through the fields, up on to the fell road, and possibly, later, join her at that bonfire.

Lately he had been so absorbed in himself that he had shut out the hills around him. Consciously almost, as if their infusion, though intoxicating, was useless for his present purposes; or perhaps the moods they inspired in him opened too many possibilities. He thought of them as being alternatively irrelevant and over-demanding. This night, however, with the pique acting curiously, as an impulse to cheerfulness, he walked towards them with his arms open. What effect such contours, shapes, smells, colours, mass, vegetation, rock, water, cloud and night had on other people he did not know; but against him they con-

110

spired as a solid force. He felt that the darkened landscape had to be reckoned with – and he felt, too, that, should he embrace it, it would close on him. Possibly this was mere fancy; maybe so. But as he went now into it there were plucked in his mind the murmur of a thousand apprehensions dormant until such times.

He reached the fell road and, for the first time, turned to see bonfire beacons lighting cones into the clear blackness for miles around. Some, just lit, were greedy yellow, callow flames gorging through careful constructions of cardboard, branch and tyre; others, half gone, were hugging the hub above their ashes, sucking a reddening arc back into themselves and bringing their makers to their knees to poke and push in potatoes for roasting; one or two were already dead, or driven under their own collapsed pile to smoulder in sulky secrecy till morning. And around and between them – for they were scattered across the whole area that was before him, right down through the fell village to the small industrial villages, alongside those isolated rows of blank-faced cottages, behind farmyards, in side streets, on roadsides, down to the coast towns where they flickered against the unblinking street lights and the fussy belching of the steel works, on the shore itself where dried driftwood danced its dying image on to the sea that had thrown it up – weaving in and out of this warning, spluttering spread of fires, their tips burning the raw night red, there banged and whizzed the fireworks. The fires were silent, and beside them the cheap reports of squibs, crackerjacks, flashers, bangers, atom bombs, thunderclaps, jumping jacks and all sorts of pencil-stubs of noise, cracked like the popping of guns when the centre of the battle seems still. And occasionally, rockets would go up, bursting into a star of sparkling, vanishing beauty. Roman candles popped up their baubles, Catherine-wheels fizzed around their pins.

He remembered a photograph of his mother, taken with a half-defective flash bulb, the light streaking all round the picture, just like the trails of the rockets, only her face untouched. She had been very young when he had been born, and he realised that the image he had carried round of her was now, to him, the image of a young woman, a woman younger than himself, with long black wavy hair, smooth cheeks and a smile that had never failed to prod his own lips to return it. He tried to imagine what it would have been like to have been brought up by his parents, but he could not. He had been left alone at too early an age, and then too well protected and raised by his grandparents to be much

111

more than wistful, and any length of curiosity soon snuffed out that wistfulness. For he would never know what his parents had been like. They had been pictured to him as without fault, any idiosyncrasy recounted only as it revealed them in a good light, their ambitions and possibilities being nipped off so soon, presented as inevitable of realisation. To have no sorrow for your parents, because you had never known them; only to be sorry because that was so.

He turned from the fires and walked down towards the church, and began to sing – hymns, as always, when so equipoisedly alone – those hymns he had heard and sung a thousand times at school, in church. He started "Onward Christian Soldiers , but that seemed too apposite to be anything but comic. He liked a long one with a good tune – that he could march to. He looked to his right, to the fells, cockily – wanting to shout something loudly at *them* also. Finally, he found it, simple and appropriately rural.

> "We plough the fields, and scatter
> The good seed on the land,
> But it is fed and watered
> By God's Almighty Hand . . .

The words came out clearly, but he had to stop. Yet again, his own observation of himself in action prostrated the act. A little too appropriate, don't you think? He walked silently for a while. There was nothing wrong with that; part of what he had come to Crossbridge for was to weigh and test these aspects of himself which, taken for granted, had proved rotten. To heighten a characteristic in order to see it as ridiculous or cloying, this was similar to those doctors who had once insisted on "feeding the disease" in order that it might run its course and expire. Or kill. Yet he wanted to make a noise. He whistled – "Colonel Bogey", then "The British Grenadiers", then "Rule Britannia"– that was better. A song his grandfather had sung from the Boer War –

> "Goodbye-Dolly I must leave you
> Though it breaks my heart to go.
> Something tells me I am needed
> O'er the hills to fight the foe."

Then there was the one that had started all the beat which led to Rock 'n Roll –"Cry"; "Hound Dog"; Bill Haley, Little Richard, Cliff Richard, the Beatles – "We can work it o-out."

They all came and he swung down the road now whistling,

now singing at the top of his voice, not so much free as in a vacuum, quietening down as he passed the first farm, which masked the cluster dominated by the church, stepping out to "pom, te di pom, te di pom pom pom", like the drummers keeping time while the band rests. Behind him, along that winding road, he felt he could hear the reverberations of his concert still trying to find a place to vanish to in the silenced countryside.

The bonfire was on a rectangle of stubbled ground which lay before the row of council houses. When Richard came to it, it was already levelled, spread about the ground, a few children throwing one or two branches or cardboard boxes into the centre to revive a flame, someone lighting a succession of sparklers, held at arm's length so that the face could not be seen behind the white unscrambled light, people drawn together by a man with some bottles of beer and a stack of cardboard cups.

He soon picked out Janice. She held the white cup by her side and looked down into the fire. Edwin was beside her. Her face was flushed from the heat, her hair covered by a headscarf. Richard stood well back, undiscernible. He recognised that solitude in company, he thought, and was imagining her self-directed aloofness when a small girl brought a sparkler over to her and Janice, taking it, suddenly whirled it as a lasso around her head and laughed as everyone ducked to avoid the flying sparks. Edwin said something to her and she shook her head; others came round them and they had more beer – someone offered sandwiches. Again Edwin spoke to Janice, and again she refused, but this time she hugged him.

Jealousy bit through Richard when he saw Janice's arms around Edwin. Janice was the woman he wanted; in her fused, he thought, all the women he had known. She seemed to stay in Edwin's arms for ever and Richard peered through the spluttering firelight to observe her expression. He stepped forward, and then hesitated. Perhaps she had been merely interested in him after all; Edwin was the one to whom she would go. His confidence scattered away at that moment, and then in a rush returned when Edwin moved away, went to his van, and drove off.

Leaving Janice. She looked so beautiful that he felt not so much that he had met her as that he had found her. All the others were half-discovered, rambling side-paths, diversions – Janice was the one he had found. He knew that their flesh would touch without any impulse to that impatience which is the first sign of a flaw; that she, to him, would be all he desired in a woman – in

113

her body, in her actions, in her thoughts. He stared at her, not wanting to move away for the moment. He looked on her with such a tenderness welling under his desire that it surged into gratitude – that he *should* have found her. This "found". It was the bewildering strangeness of someone not imagined until seen, someone stumbled on, not sought for, and yet someone whose exact image had taken time to press itself on his thoughts and feelings, and so, mingled with his realisation was an amazement that it had taken this long for him to see her as he did, and a shiver of apprehension that a thousand accidents might have prevented it. For what he had felt for other women – and what he had previously thought he had felt for Janice – was, he was certain, nothing compared with the force and tranquillity of what possessed him now. That tranquillity should mark him at all only rarified and verified his belief that he had *found* her.

And at the same instant, or so few seconds afterwards that it did not matter – or perhaps it was before, but got lost in the immediacy of the more powerful feeling – there appeared the convenience of this. Try as he might to thrust it behind him and hide it from himself as being unworthy, debased, shallow, any denigratory epithet he could think it – it was there. Convenient it would be. She need not be a divergence, could be the confluence; in her he would find that satisfaction, that completion which by remaining alone he could only consider himself lacking and which fundamentally appeared to him as the necessity for any existence worth the effort. Because of her he would find work, he would stay in the district, as he wished to do, he would find her unpocked by the plaguing fancies he had run from and so himself become cured; with her he could fashion a life which would have sense because it would have an effect on someone immediately outside himself. And why should convenience make his love seem a lesser thing? Was it not a natural accompaniment of any affection? Did not any impulse which presented expectations previously unknowable carry as a gift convenience with it? Nevertheless the presence of such a gift in this which should, he thought, have carried nothing in its flood but the clearest spring outburst, appalled him. It made him pause, wait for her to turn, watch her leave alone, let her get ahead of him before following her.

Something held him. Composed of that apprehension which he recognised as the indication that he was about to give himself over to someone else – and of that self-perspective which some-

114

times nips people at the beginning or at the end of things, when all things momentarily seem mild flickers, all lives arbitrary glimmerings soon snuffed – and exacerbated by the resentment felt at his mundane expectations – this weight kept him where he was until her footsteps died away.

He looked over to the fire. The children were still playing, their voices shrill over the silence that cosseted the burning sounds but shook off the high childish tones, people preparing to leave, the red arc pressing down close to the grounded stack.

Then he nodded, and ran after her.

CHAPTER FIFTEEN

She heard him running up to her but did not wait for him, deliberately exaggerating the firmness of her step as she had deliberately exaggerated her behaviour to Edwin, having soon noticed Richard's arrival on the other side of the fire. Especially in the hug she had given Edwin, whose evening it was to take down to his mother her weekly money; this he had put off and put off, with such a woeful look that Janice had laughed her amusement into sympathy and found a loyalty in the doggedness which had touched her to encourage it. Yet the hug had been more a flaunt before Richard.

People who ran to catch up with you always put themselves at a disadvantage, she thought. Their urgency sounded so pressing and when you knew the small matter which their arrival would stir, its manner of approach appeared ridiculous. And when the panting of the first few sentences, the leg-jostling to find an accommodating step, the expletives which pricked through the calm exchanges to justify the urgency of the build-up, and finally the silence until, perhaps, a sympathy formed. These and other thoughts fidgeted her mind, but as she herself began to hurry, she might have been aware that they came from eagerness as much as detachment. More. Her avoidance of men had arisen in part from a fierce ignorance which, however viciously, had now been impaired. There had been no excitement in her for men, she had thought, because all the excitement she had was preserved for herself. Now, this self – all other considerations apart, his look, his hand which had once rested on hers, the crouching

115

preparedness of his body when they sat together and she felt he might spring on her – this self was by her own choice abandoned for a year – with no linear compulsion, nothing to work towards which would show results of immediate betterment; she was pausing, observing, relaxing, for the first time as a woman, and in that time she found herself open to the breathing of parts of her mind and body she had hardly known. A thrill shot up her nerves as he came nearer; a quick relapse of that tension followed when he slowed down, stopped, only walked.

Still she maintained her fast pace, but now, she could judge from the weight of his step, he was not going to chase. Offended, she did not slacken; nor did he, but he was not gaining. Janice was annoyed at this, hard as she tried to rediscover the comic side; he had no right to treat her like that – to make his presence known, without giving her the opportunity of revealing that she *realised* it, and then to leave the decision to her. For it now became a decision, almost a declaration. To let him catch her up could only mean that she was prepared to make an effort to speak to him – which was not what she wanted to be acknowledged; but *not* to let him catch her up would be to declare that she did not want to acknowledge him – which was not what she meant.

She crossed the small bridge which gave the village its name, hearing the thin-banked stream foaming through the small tunnel under her feet. Half-way there. She felt foolish and re-sented his part in it – yet there was nothing to blame him for which did not include herself in the blame. Still, he *could* have run on those extra few yards and caught her up without all this fuss; but perhaps he wished to create such a fuss in her. That conclusion irritated her. If he thought he could incite her interest by such a trick . . . but her interest *had* been incited, and so he was right. So, obviously, she did not want him to have the satis-faction of finding his point proved. She kept to her pace, in-creased it even, as she considered that it might have been dragging.

This part was uphill. Well, people did walk more slowly when they went uphill and so there was no reason why she should not slacken a little, just a little more than that little, and soon he would be near enough to stop for. Because, from the start, she had made up her mind that a *certain* proximity would naturally necessitate her stopping – otherwise it would become absurd, on both parts – and that she wished to avoid, or a real battle, in which she considered herself not to be engaged. Yet, were she to slow down more than necessary, there was no guarantee that he would not do the same, and every reason to believe that he would notice the gesture and so feel that he had gained.

She did not slow down at all, but forged up the hill in the same gear. His steps now coincided with hers so that there were moments when she could not be absolutely certain that he was there at all; but she checked the impulse to look round as there was enough moonlight for the action to be noticed. Her feet stamped on the ground in temper; he had no right to treat her like this.

Perhaps – and this conjecture sprang at her so joltingly that she almost stopped completely – perhaps, having run to catch her up, he had changed his mind about the whole affair; thought better of it, given up whatever plan he had, resolved not to speak to her at all, was trying to get out of a meeting. Why should he want to do that? He had been keen enough before. Maybe she ought not to have hugged Edwin – no! for God's sake, *that* could have nothing to do with it, and if it did, then it simply proved how trivial he was. Or jealous. The word stroked across all the fibres of her mind like a furry bow. Jealous, Jealous, Jealous – she had never thought of that – *he*, Jealous!

Now she was near the turning which led down to the cottages, and still. . . . *If* he was jealous, then did that mean that he would sulk for so long? – for that was what he was doing, there could be no other explanation. Yet he was not the type for sulking. She could not imagine him sulking. He was simply not the sort of man who would sulk. He would have got over that by now – or never entertained the feeling in the first place.

Why did he not catch up with her? They were nearly there. She turned down into the lane, and, as she turned, slowed down. He did not turn. Dawdled. Still she could not hear his feet on the rough track. Stopped. There was no sound of him. Maybe he had gone on to the pub, maybe he had gone back; she began to retrace her steps; then she stopped again – maybe he was doing *that*! She laughed – louder than she need have done, and longer, and he came round the corner and right up to her.

"Are you all right? he asked.

"Why shouldn't I be?"

"I don't know."

She laughed again, this time even more loudly, and Richard, after watching her for a second, smiled, joined in the laughter.

"Why did you stop?" she asked.

117

"I thought you wanted to be on your own."

"So you just stopped?"

"Yes."

"Just ... stopped."

"Yes."

Again she laughed until she needed to check herself; Richard not joining in this time.

"Why did you run after me in the first place, then?"

"Because I wanted to speak to you."

"Well?"

"I thought you wanted to be alone."

"I did!"

"Then I was right."

"Yes. You were."

"Good."

Uncertain, not knowing why she had laughed, why she had gone back for him; what she wanted to do, what she thought of his explanation, what he thought of her, whether it mattered. . . .

"Would you like to come to my place for a drink?" he asked.

"What time is it?"

"Nine-thirty. Half past nine."

"I suppose it would be all right."

"I suppose it might."

"What d'you mean?"

"Nothing."

"Yes you did."

"Very well. I meant to imply that it was rather unusual for an invitation to be accepted so – so –"

"Guardedly?"

"Defensively."

"Perhaps your encounters aren't usually preceded by such an amount of tracking."

"They're not. No." He paused and smiled at her, knowing, as he did so, that this would make her furious – which it did. "Well. Shall we go?"

"If you want."

They walked in silence to his cottage and he allowed the silence to persist as he tried to rally the fire, got out the drinks, hung up their coats. She had been inside his place before, but never following such a direct and charged invitation. Utterly uneasy, Janice looked aloof, stiff and slightly bored. Richard smiled to himself, but, catching the web of panic and fright which lay over her exterior – only revealing itself for an instant – any adolescent pride in superior capability vanished and his wish to take her and love her made him more nervous than her.

All he wanted was to . . . but it would be as useless as charging after a fawn. And the opportunity might be lost for weeks he could not bear to think of without her. Straining, he began to speak – tittle-tattle which he was grateful to her for receiving so understandingly. Thus they each helped the other on to build props both longed, one knowingly, one unadmittingly, to kick away. Thus their intimacy began as the sort of exchange which had characterised earlier meetings – except that this time it was sustained not because its end – their parting – was assured, but because that end was feared.

"You ought to know about Paula," she said abruptly. "I haven't told anyone about her so far. Her father was a lecturer in Carcaster. It only went on for a few months but it seems now as if that time was most of my life."

She hesitated. Richard said nothing. Then she began.

Janice knew that Richard would certainly have heard of her past and part of her reason for detailing it to him was to eliminate the fabrication which gossip around the place had surely raised. Her principal reason for telling him was, however, less clearly known to herself. There had to be nothing withheld from Richard because that would have assumed a reason for wishing an intimacy which the revelation of a secret might destroy. More tangibly, she had felt, between them, the nights they talked, that pad of mutually recognised but unspoken fact which, fed by generalities, swells to a sponge of titillation and innuendo, finally stopping the words altogether and bringing about a situation which can demand unconsidered action for its relief. There had to be no unconsidered action. Yet she recognised that the 'confession', as well as clearing away between them that secrecy which attracted intimacy, also appeared, or could appear, as the stripping away before the commitment, the proving of trust in and affection for the other by divesting yourself of that which has not only been private but also protective. She could have been saying 'Now that you know all there is to know about me; do you still want me?'

The self-perception made her anxious, but she went on with her story and finished it. There was nothing Richard could say. He went into the kitchen to make coffee.

119

When he came back into the room he saw Janice kneeling before the fire, a newspaper spread out over it, the front of the grate removed to let in the draught. Both knew, he that she sensed his observation, she that he understood her awareness of it. Neither moved. Her hair, thick and loose, spread on to her shoulders and seemed to glow against the black sweater she wore. The sweater was pulled into a firmly belted pair of jeans and Richard's hands weakened as he imagined them touching the coarse material which sheathed her thighs. Finally, she turned and looked up at him, her face white as muslin, her cheeks dappled with rose, her chin timid, slender cheeks slightly hollowing down to it, a smallish nose, straight – nothing to suggest that which had ripped away her chastity, nothing to suggest any positive force which might direct that physical inheritance towards possession; merely a half-involuntary passivity, it seemed, waiting to be called. He put down the tray on the table, and went back to the kitchen.

Janice looked at the sheet of newspaper. The fire roared up behind it, the red glow picking out the black print, sucking the grey sheet into its long flames. She did not know where she was. There had been a softening and though, she was certain, this was merely on the surface, nevertheless there was nothing but the surface in Crossbridge now; that charge which she had driven into herself in order to project her out of the place had been exploded and consequently, though she did read and work, she was more recovering from defeat than preparing for victory and the silence of it, that self-hugged spell which is the main ballast for all strong solitaries, giving them the satisfaction and re-assurance that a singular course is being worked out despite and away from the world, the world's ignorance or indifference being their goad – that too was shot away. Richard had insinuated himself into the blurring, infusing it, moreover, with a tenderness she had not found to respond to before now, and calling on to this surface ungrown parts of herself which had never rooted in her because there was no room, but which now began to unfold; mysterious impulses, shyness, desires, confusion – the very opposite of that which her will had made of her life – these played around her mind, and she felt changed, attending circumstances.

The flames had begun to turn the centre of the paper brown and now the fire broke through the singed walls and leaped out at her. She made no move. The edges of the large square of news flopped into the centre and this made a bundle of flames which threatened to topple towards her. The heat glazed her face. Falling into the grate the fire flicked against her knees and then flaked into a messy rubble of fluffy grey wafers, scattering all over the green tiles.

"Build it up, then," said Richard, quietly.

"*You* build it up."

He came across and she moved away on to the sofa. After taking his time about putting more sticks and then coal on, Richard stood up and scuffled the newspaper's remains with his foot. When he turned, he saw Janice, her legs stretched straight out in front of her, hands clutching at her belt, her eyes glowering down her own body.

Richard sat down beside her, lit a cigarette, and stared at the fire. The next move was his; it had been prepared for, worked for even; there was nothing more to say.

Yet at this wanted moment, he checked himself. The physical straining of his body after her, which already many times had been hard to bear, lessened, almost disappeared. It would be the same old thing if he tried to make love to her now. The very words he had used in thinking of it, 'move', 'act', 'affair', these were mechanical; devices. It would not be enough, and that same force which had preened, stiffened and held him in his pursuit of her far more tenaciously than ever before, now reacted on him and pincered his instinct with the realisation that *more* was not enough; only *different* was enough now, if anything at all was to be made of his action in altering his life.

"Would you like something to eat?" he asked, eventually.

Janice started at his words, gruffly uttered, looked at him for a time which seemed minutes, and then giggled.

"Would *you* like something to eat?" she asked.

Richard laughed. Janice, suddenly relaxing and drawing her legs up on to the seat shook out her hair and Richard felt the cottage fill with her energy.

"Quite an opening." He stood up. "Oh *God*, how bloody stupid this all is. '*Would* you like something to eat?'"

"Yes. I would. Love it!" Janice, wanting to help, turned and reached over the sofa, leaning out for the tray, accidentally pulled it down – everything smashed on the floor.

"Leave it!" Richard commanded. "Leave it. If we got on our knees with dustpans we'd be sure to bump our heads against one another and then – Have a drink."

121

Janice nodded, nervously, looking almost afraid of the mess on the floor. Richard, on his way to get the drinks, saw the glance and went swiftly for a brush, swept the things up, said nothing. The crockery rattled hard on to the small shovel.

"Now," he said. "Whisky. It must be."

He poured two very large measures into green tumblers and brought them over to Janice, now in the last shiver of her laughing and seated on the arm of the sofa. They clinked glasses and drank.

"Why did you say it was stupid?" Janice asked, after a pause.

"Oh, let's forget it. Have some more of that." He poured in some more whisky. That would settle it; they would get a little drunk, go off to bed, get on with it – then take the consequences, if there were any. Anything else was too painful, and perhaps even more claculating than what he had been doing; yes, perhaps so; that cheered him up. "Cheers!"

"No. Why was it *stupid*?"

"Oh hell, Janice. Let it drop. Let it all drop. Obviously."

"You mean obviously we should have gone to bed," she said, so preoccupied with making her tone casual that Richard laughed again; the words seemed to drop out of her mouth like squashy plums. Too ripe.

"Yes, I think so," he replied, mimicking a military voice. "I think that the next move ought most certainly to have been a massive advance of my forces aimed at breaking through your flank, *ad hoc* tactics to pertain thereafter."

"Well?"

"Well – it would have been squalid. Particularly after what you've told me. What to toast this time?"

"Oh shut up!"

"Yes ... To silence!" He paused.

"What happened to you must have been horrible," he said eventually. "I've been behaving like a bastard. ... I'm sorry."

"When people say they've been 'bastards' – isn't it just so that the other person will say – 'No you aren't', so that they can feel a bit better and go and do it again later?" She spoke brightly, tensely.

"Yes. Yes, I suppose that's part of it. Everything's part of everything; that's the trouble." He smiled. "Thought for the week." Then: "No. I was a bastard to attempt to 'move in' on you in the way I did, knowing what had happened to you. And I *won't* do that again. Nor sooner, nor later." He bowed.

"Could I have some more to drink, please?"

"Of course." He held out the bottle and the whisky splashed into her tumbler.

"I think that your trouble is that you *do* nothing," Janice said, tentatively hovering over intimacy. "You talk and sweat away– I can see why. You don't have to defend it any more – but what are you going to do?"

"People have changed themselves."

"Saints!" she replied, witheringly.

"Not only saints. All sorts of people. You read about it every day – men who have suddenly decided that they won't put up with themselves as they are and *do* something about it."

"Sounds like *Reader's Digest*. 'I suddenly Realised I Was On The Wrong Path. . . .'"

"Pass."

"What d'you mean?"

"I mean Pass," said Richard. "If I can't explain what I mean without – rightly – being cut down, then I'd better shut up about it."

"That's rather feeble, isn't it?"

"No. If you can't protect something you believe in, then it's as well not to reveal it. My own inadequacies as a projector of these suggestions apart – why do we so 'naturally' laugh at a man who declares he believes in God, or Democracy, or Justice and so on? A simple sneer seems enough to tangle his ankles and bring him flat on his face. Why *is* there no energy to believe in that, when someone who says 'I believe in Money, Women, Power, Pleasure' – he's listened to, and respected. Maybe sex, cash, authority and hedonism are more credible than justice, freedom and faith; maybe they are more credible because they do, in fact, relate to the world as it is and has been. Maybe, like some people are now doing, one should dedicate oneself to following through these totems, bringing all to bear on them because only out of them can there be new births.

"But what if you DON'T WANT TO?" he went on fiercely. "What then? Do you give up and say 'I must be old-fashioned, behind my time, out of the "scene", not hip, without it, pre-historic' – and diffidently trundle to some cosy corner, leaving the stage to your moderners and betters? Well – I have; that's the first stage. And there, perhaps, you try to order that circus of acts which has been your thinking into some regular form; you read. And you come across phrases that seem right; like this one from Thoreau – I copied it down last night." – he went

123

and picked up the book – "'If a man does not keep pace with his companions, it is because he hears a different drummer. Let him step to the music which he hears, however measured or far away.' " He slammed the book shut. "That satisfies you – for a moment. Then you realise that it hinders rather than helps – for it means that anyone, whatever anyone does, is right in his own way. Goebbels heard a different drummer and so did Caligula.

"Besides, you further realise that Thoreau's statement can be made *only* when there is such a generally accepted standard – public and private – of behaviour that any digression from it could be encouraged both to let in air and to provide a relief – because it was given that the basic pattern would not change. But what basic pattern is there now? People generally conform – but what does that *mean*? Although most people practise a sort of monogamy, are there many who could defend it beyond convenience? So with other things. Very well – what's wrong with Convenience? Nothing 'wrong', except that it must ultimately lead to a society in which behaviour becomes a business relationship. Well, why not? Why not agree that your friends are buckets which can bring water from other wells, that your wife is a number of sexual discharges, a necessary ornament and useful to chatter to? That would make things easier. But it is repugnant. Convenience can only lead to that sort of brutality which people like to decorate with the word Anarchy. Anarchists in Love? A contradiction. For Convenience would be bound to rely more and more on the unalterable – and the unalterable is hand in fist with the intolerable.

"Then you come back to what I began with. I dismissed myself as a proposer of anything because of 'my own inadequacies as a projector'. Tidi pom-pom. That undercuts everything I've said since. Because you cannot talk apart from yourself. If you believe in any sort of action, you must try to take some steps towards it – given that you are not going to harm anyone by doing so. You have *got* to *make* yourself, at least, firm, or firmer, so that there is, inside yourself, that ballast of conviction, however vague, which convention in society used to provide – or which you find it essential to have. You see the water all around; the only way to feel it is to strip off and dive in. It's more in keeping with the times to swim fully clothed – on a drug, or wrapped in some cliquish extremity – and maybe that is the way. But one of the reasons I came here is because I believe that it isn't."

124

"What does that matter? If you solve everything, what's left? Why does it matter to you so much to be right?"

"I wish I knew."

"What would you do if you believed you were right?"

"I don't know." The words had ceased to be a substitute and became as substantial as he could make them. She had to understand. "Let's say that there is this noise, and the noise is loud, and you like it loud; but once, just once, you hear that loud noise chime in what you never thought of before – call it harmony. The noise goes on. You forget the chime. You don't know the word harmony. But the noise gets so loud that you begin to suffer from it – no delusion there, you do suffer, you become depressed. But that doesn't help. On with the noise. You remember that harmony. Listen for it. No sound. Begin to try to bring it about. Search for it; come to need it – nothing else matters; go on – the noise does – you must find that which you can then call harmony. End of part one."

"I see."

While talking, Richard had been unable to keep still, not pacing around the room but standing beside his chair, excused in that position by his intention to go to the mantelpiece for a cigarette, but at times trembling with the effort to convince Janice of exactly what he meant. As he talked, she thought, he became even younger; his face reddened, his hair flopped – but there was a current which informed him so strongly that she could feel it surge out at her. In his eyes – they were direct; groping, enquiring, but somehow bent on a passion, an ambition, which gave them, and him, a strength and attraction she had never before felt. Her replies at first had been brittle and had then become swamped under his monologue, and as they chatted on, he now calmer, purged, speaking much more detachedly, she softened to him. She found herself slipping towards that lassitude which needs little encouragement to be disturbed to sensuality. Unaware that this was possessing her, only of a dilation about her thighs, a sweet sting faintly rubbing her skin, her arms went, so slowly, behind her head and gently she pressed her neck, feeling her breasts lift up and forward in supple provocation.

Their voices grew softer. Now she was talking. He listened and cramped himself into the chair, subduing himself, recognising that he was on a brink which could be leapt, but even now, so wanting her that he forced himself to wait yet more, to be

125

sure, to be certain – and not to demand her body as forfeit for her displayed feelings. The way in which her arms twined behind her neck, her legs curled and then unfolded beneath her, her body became so enticing that it seemed like the slow shivering of thick silk – this unconscious abandonment stoppered any 'approach'.

And Janice entered into something that she, too, had not known. The wary eye she kept on herself closed as the small room stroked her to an intimacy she accepted with total and relaxed wonder. No man had let her be so close to him for so long without rattling her awake by the musketry of his urges. But here she swayed, hammock untouched, cradled in herself yet through him. Opened in her were those tendrils she had stamped on or ignored; like equatorial plants, they scaled her senses and clung to her with fresh delicacy coming out of each of them.

"You see, I believe you can think only if you have a particular idea you want to pursue," she said slowly. "Unless you want to work out an abstract theory – and even there you write it down and so on – you think about *doing* something. The rest is just scrambling about in the middle of things."

"But I *am* in the middle!" Richard laughed. She had, he thought, given him his chance. "Oh to be an emergent African with a new government to overthrow; or a Chinaman with Mao tucked in my pocket and the cultural revolution waiting for me to look after it; or an American even, with my problems of power and race and squalor and disintegration so violently declared and so important to the rest of the world that I would be thrown into the battle to wreck or erect. But here I am an Englishman – middling bright, middling capable, muddling through. Now if I don't go and ally myself to one of those world polarities – and I don't – why, then, what better than to paddle in the middle and see if it's possible to swim there? And I know I want to swim. That I do know."

"It's nothing very new," she said, "this business of people finding their society unreal has been going on for the last hundred years at least. It's just an excuse."

"I'm sinking. I know it's not new. Last time round. So much was redefined in the back end of the nineteenth century and the first part of this – in thought and behaviour, society and art – that somehow those who did it all now appear as the New Ancients, and cannot be questioned. But whatever has happened

126

in the last hundred years has not changed certain fundamental
facts about a life; that it's once-only, that it is largely, in our
society, made up of relationships between people, that each
man has the opportunity, if he's fortunate, as most of us are
here, to make what used to be called 'something' (a good ambition) of himself. What-thing? How-thing? That has not changed.
Knowledge has changed and so have cirumstances, and so have
possibilities, but the situation – to do or not to do, what to do
and how to do – that has not changed. Also, although all this
is supposed to have been solved – *I* haven't solved it. I accept it;
but maybe I should go through some of it myself – and so, the
great sacrifice, coming to a cosy little cottage with a thousand in
the bank. Amen." He was silent. Now it was right to move.

"I must go," Janice said, over-energetically. "I promised to
do the midnight feed. She sleeps through till morning after that
nowadays."

"I'll set you back."

"*Set*? Do you say 'set' as well?"

"Yes." He smiled.

They went up the lane, black under a moonless night, Edwin's
light still on, Mrs. Jackson sound asleep, though somehow one
ear would have registered those late footsteps, Mr. Jackson
free-wheeling in dreams of silence and coloured calendar cuties,
Agnes and Wif in bed – and most forceful sound that of their
own feet on the path. Near her door they stopped and, for some
moments, said nothing.

Janice spoke, quietly.

"My father sometimes says 'I'm sure I'm right, I'm sure I am.'
I suppose that's what you want to be able to say, isn't it?"

"I suppose so."

As her hand moved whitely across to the latch, he caught it,
gently, and turned her to him.

"I'm in love with you, Janice."

"Yes." Her voice was dry. "Yes, I know."

"Will you marry me?"

"I can't." This time the words were fully firm. "I can't."

He let go of her hand and nodded. Then he suddenly moved
to go. She touched his arm.

"You can't say that word," she said, softly.

" 'Love'?"

"Yes."

127

"You've got to, Janice." She felt his arm tighten and throw off her hand. He spoke so deliberately that she was afraid. "You've got to use it so much that it brands itself into you."

"I can't."

"Good night, Janice."

She watched him go away. Waited until he had gone down the track to the cottage that stood apart. Away from the three joined dwellings. Alone.

His door opened, the light flew out on to the damp hedges and then was gone.

CHAPTER SIXTEEN

Richard went round to her house the next morning and asked her to come out with him for the day. Agnes saw what it was, saw also that Janice wished to go, and encouraged her; she would take the baby. It was a Saturday; there was nothing she had to do in the village.

They caught a bus to Cockermouth and from there they went on to Keswick. It was a small country bus, single-decker, like a mobile village hall, picking up passengers as well known to the conductor as they were to each other. This took the top off any nervousness Janice and Richard might have felt at being together again in daylight, the previous night's intimacy far away. In Keswick they had coffee near the market square and then wandered through the slate-stoned streets to Derwentwater.

The sun was winter-bright, white behind the thin skidding clouds, stroking through the nerves of leafless trees, buffing the soggy grass to glitter, reflecting a diamond sparkle on the water.

They found a boathouse which stayed open throughout the winter, and Richard hired one of those long rowing-boats. Soon they were away from the shore, with Skiddaw Fell clearly topping the town. It was raw work, and Richard's face stung with the cold. There were one or two men fishing from boats, a motor-boat which churned around like a clock-work toy on a pond – otherwise the lake was deserted.

When they spoke, their voices had such a clarity that they lowered them. It was like speaking in a Gothic nave – the sound carried so far and so clearly that everything said smacked of assertion. They whispered, caught themselves at it, laughed, heard the laugh crack across the water, whispered again. Well out, past the first island, Richard let the boat drift while he lit a cigarette. Janice wanted to row and the flat-bottomed boat lurched perilously as both stood up and clambered past each other. She was even more unskilled at rowing than Richard had been, and soon they were soaked through. He came to sit beside her and, each taking an oar, they made for a small jetty behind which was an hotel.

It was one of those magnificent Victorian country houses, built out of the exploitation of man to celebrate a love of nature. Doubtful if more than one generation of the original family had ever lived there. Now an exclusive hotel, its resident life in this season circulated sluggishly through the shaking legs of old ladies and gentlemen with an eye for beauty. Janice and Richard had a couple of whiskies in the bar, the heat from a large coal-packed grate soon steaming them dry, and then they went in for lunch.

The dining-room was not very big – about fifteen tables – and almost empty. They sat in one of the two enormous bay windows which overlooked Derwentwater and were slowly attended to by a middle-aged waitress who looked at them, throughout, as if they ought to be ashamed of themselves for being able to afford to eat at such a select place at their age, and without even bothering to dress up.

The food was good and Richard had a big meal; vegetable soup, salmon, roast beef and Yorkshire pudding, Bakewell tart and custard. Janice would have only the salmon, but he persuaded her to take the 'Chef's Special' dessert which turned out to be a fantastic ice-cream structure, all colours, with wafers and sticks of chocolate for gables. They had three cups of coffee each, and by the time they were finished the dining-room was empty and their waitress was standing at the door, coughing angrily, flapping the notebook which was attached to her belt, as a prison wardress might jangle her keys.

Eventually, rather cruelly teasing out extra moments, they left, replete in the spicy afternoon. They went for a walk in the woods near the lake, passing an old man who stopped as he greeted them and coerced them into a discussion on the merits of the day and the prospects for the spring. He was very old, a sprig of white hair lifting beneath the back of his trilby, a black scarf from chest to chin, a black overcoat from neck to knees, little streaks of mud on the icy polish of his black shoes. As he left them he lifted his hat to Janice and walked on more spryly, glad of the rest and even more pleased to have gleaned enough from them to be able to describe, at length, a 'nice young couple' in evening conversation in the lounge. Rooks fastened their scaly legs to the tops of trees, heavy-bellied through the stripped branches, shadow-black. Richard and Janice turned off the main path and surprised a couple – schoolchildren, in their uniforms – who jumped up from the grass like pheasants and then, half-anxious, half-menacing, watched them go away. The sun had brought out a grey squirrel and they stopped to watch it bound across their path, scratch at the bottom of the tree trunk, huddle itself up against it, and then leap in clutching jumps back to its den.

Richard took Janice's hand, and she walked close to him, not quite confident enough to lean her head against him, but letting it brush him whenever a twist in the track or a stumble gave her the opportunity.

They walked in silence now, having talked throughout the lunch, and each felt that the other was looking for a place to stop and lie down, and each was too wilful to do more than glance at the bracken-bedded possibilities. Coming to the lake once more, quite near their boat, they stood and looked at the tranquil scene before them, as suffused with its loveliness as the lake itself was now infused by the reddening sun. All was gentleness. No waves to lash up fears, or unscalable rocks to rip at dreams, no endless water to awe or density of sameness to crush – the perfect proportion of hill and lake, with roads, trees, farms, villages, islands, clouds, boats – all exactly placed, it seemed, painted on the winter day with such docility as made it redolent of an imagined world. Janice nuzzled into him and he held her tightly, but that was all. Again, though he would have liked to believe that it was something in the rhythm and expression of the day which kept him so, though at one moment he would have given everything to have been able to have believed that of himself, he knew that his caution derived also from that exact judgement which did not wish to pluck at what it could not surely eat.

They went back to the boat.

In many of Turner's paintings the sky is such a scoured, braised red, so burnished with streaks of hard colour and lashed with whites and yellows, such a fury of broiling sunset and yet, at the same time, such a frame of calm, that it is difficult to believe there is anything in nature to approach them. This late afternoon sunset did. From the edge of the lake the hills rose up black, like a waistbelt, cutting off the water from the sky. On the sky itself the sliding sun, blood red, drew a great tumulus of clouds around it, clouds which leapt up and away from it like frozen oceanic waves, thick at their base, thinning to feathery-tipped edges – and all were blooded by the sun which seemed to be sucking in through them the fires of a day's blazing. Yet the clouds were few, clustered around the sun like the dust around a desert-marching army, leaving the rest of the sky clear – and that was of such a dense blue, of such a solid mineral sapphire shading to jet, that it was as amazing as the gaudy rubied clouds. And the water of the lake, split pearls the tips of the wavelets, turquoise plateaux the reaches in the distance, the water in the path of the sun a ruby-jewelled treasure chest. Through this, the black boat moved slowly, like the last homecomer in a dying paradise.

Richard's face was in the sun, and he was silenced by the beauty of it. Though he felt so close to Janice that the imprint of her cheek still touched on his, he let himself go into the ending day, sweeping out his mind so that the colours and the grandeur of it might infuse him. Janice sat back, her hair cascading with colours, her face pale by contrast, her hands bone-white sculptures on the dark of her dress. Again, as before, Richard believed in the power such a place could have on one like himself who wanted to be changed; that somehow such a strength and per-fection could be made an echo of a man's mind; intimating clearly that he *could* account for what he saw and come to believe himself in some way accountable to it.

A circle, cordoned by hills, canopied by the sky, supported by water – and outside that circle? The eye pulled back, and this scene was hung on a tilted frame in the corner of a crowded cellar. There was all the rest. The self-awareness clicked in his mind, even here the counter to all he thought or did. So you escaped into a picturesque location – shouldn't you be out among the junk, the tumbled traditions and bright plastics? Such peace here – it affronted the rest, except if it was ignored. And, if it were ignored, then what was it but an escape? He looked round the swirling landscape colours – this was part of what there was. That was enough. The nub need not be in the middle, the majority

131

need not be always right, if the centre did not hold, mere anarchy need not be unleashed on the world.

Janice sat and stroked her arm. Her skin felt so caressingly tense, she wondered that she had not noticed it before. Her body, which she had ignored until it had swollen before her, that, too, was lapped with uncertain longing and she saw herself naked, reclined, waiting. It seemed to her that her life, until now, had been a march; eyes front; left-right, left-right; atten-shun! But there was another rhythm in her body, one which had it ever tempted her, had been rejected till now: one which led her from her mind which now appeared dry and straitened. Yet her way was too set to allow much of this to be revealed in her face or actions; and when it was revealed, it came with that awkwardness which rightly made Richard flinch, for to snatch at it would be to shout at a starling. Nor was it recognised by herself other than as something new and powerful; with no name, with nothing in it which would invoke the surrender of her deliberate self. Action from Richard was needed to make her realise what it could be, and that action would, unless perfectly placed, be rebutted; she would retreat.

The boat bumped against the small jetty and they got out. As they went back into Keswick the sun slid down and they looked back only to see the last crimson tinges running down the clouds. The bus was in the station and soon they were back in Crossbridge, walking down towards the cottages, beside which they stood, irresolute, and then he watched her walk away.

She had not referred to his proposal. Nor would she, unless he mentioned it again.

CHAPTER SEVENTEEN

Edwin brushed his teeth painfully. The bristles scraped across them so harshly that they threatened to draw blood from the hard gums. He swilled water round inside his mouth, spat out, and then jutted his teeth at the mirror to check. They were clean, but, however hard he pursued his dental hygiene, they were never white.

He had shaved again since coming in from work, bathed again, again brushed the jacket which he had brushed in the morning, again pressed the trousers which had been under the mattress the whole of the previous night and day. His shoes looked waxed, a tightly ironed handkerchief was slid into his breast pocket, the loose change was carefully sorted so that there would not be too many pennies to spoil the line of the crease in his trousers. Clean underwear, clean white shirt, new tie – wine, a heavy silk-like material – black socks. The first haircut he had ever had which could be described as a "trim"; until now, he had let it grow and then sat patiently while Alf Hocking sheared him; this time, to "Denis"– one and six extra – but, instead of a shaven neck with the two large muscles from the top of the spine rearing up to the crown clipped and faintly blue, "styling", that is, less off.

Over his hands he took especial care, scrubbing at the nails and knuckles with a hard brush, removing every speck of oil and then bathing the raw appendages in thick suds. Still they could not be clean enough, there was something yellow in the tint of the skin which suggested constant fumigation by innumerable Woodbines. Even dressed, polished, ready, he could not resist returning once more to the basin and once more lathering his hands, trying to will some alchemy on to the soapy bubbles that their whiteness might impregnate his flesh.

The gold-plated cigarette case patted into the side pocket, money in the inside pocket. Car keys in the back pocket. Though it was cold out, he decided against a coat as it was of such poor quality compared with his suit.

There he stood, finally, in front of the bathroom mirror. Somehow, care and confidence had taken the tip of the sting from his usual self-disgust, and he nodded at himself. He looked smart, certainly, and as for the rest, well there was nothing he could do about that. He was just tilting into the attitude which would eventually make him think that it did not matter a damn how he looked – that in fact, he did not look too badly, that you took or left him, for he himself had ceased to feel shame and despair.

Before leaving, he put a bank of slack on the fire and once more rearranged the two cups and saucers, the plate of biscuits, the sugar, milk and Nescafé, even filling the kettle, ready to be able to invite her in when they came back.

Ah! His watch. He had forgotten that. He was a few minutes late. That shocked him – never before had he been late for Janice – and then he enjoyed the idea. It gave the last touch to his preparations.

133

He went outside and looked at the car. It was a Ford Anglia which he had borrowed from his boss for the evening. Already turned and pointing back up the lane to the main road.

Reluctantly, almost dallying, he made his way to Janice's house. Knocked. Went in.

"You should have got over knocking by now, lad," said Wif. "Sit yourself down – she's just fettlin' hersel up upstairs." Edwin pinching his creases between thumb and forefinger and hoisting the trouser leg to half-mast, sat.

"That's a very smart suit you've got there," said Agnes, coming in with the baby from the back kitchen. "Stand up and let's have a better look at it." He stood up. "*One* vent, eh, Edwin? I like that. And I like that tie going with it. Wif won't wear a tie. It took three of us to get him into one at his own wedding. True."

"Throttles me throat," said Wif, grimacing with relish. "I can't abide that stud bangin' into me Adam's apple."

"They don't *have* studs nowadays."

"Well, my shirts is made for studs. And I can't stick them."

"I've got him two shirts that don't need studs," said Agnes. "and they've both been in that bottom drawer for – oh – four or five years."

"I like to break things in slowly."

"You like to go round looking like a tramp, you mean. Look how smart Edwin looks."

"He's a young fella, Mother."

"Young or old – doesn't make any difference – a man should look smart."

"Oh dear! You've set her off. Now then, Mother, I'm clean."

"I should hope so!"

"And I could trot out wid t'best of them when I had to. But them times is past and that's that. Now then. No more. Here, pass her to me."

Agnes handed the baby over to Wif who immediately submerged himself in the child, his hair flopping on to his brow as he chuntered away to her. A wrinkled and cheerful gnome crouched over a fairy, it looked, and Paula smiled and crooned, happily biting on the stubby finger with her gums, her eyes gleaming with friendliness. She had never been much trouble and now, beginning to notice things, attempting to sit up by herself, she was turning into an equable child, always ready to return a smile,

134

constantly waiting, it seemed, to be smiled at so that she could return it.

"How's your mother?" Agnes asked.

"Very well, thank you," said Edwin.

"She must get a bit lonely down there. I often think I'll go down and see her but I never get round to it. Just laziness. It's that extra bit, after you leave the main road, that extra bit there – it's like walking into a no man's land. Father can remember when all that was one big estate."

"I can," said Wif, "and it was one of the best-turned-out estates around. I can tell you. A man called Spedding used to be steward – I think that's what they called it. didn't they, Mother? – steward, what you would call Estate Manager these days. He was just a little fella, you know, oh not much bigger than mother there, and he had one of those little 'tashes; you know, a little 'un – imperial, they called it, nobbut crept across his top lip as if he's missed it that morning. Terrible sporty fella he was – he would be out after anything that moved. They had a pack of hounds there and do you know, I bet he knew those hounds as well as that whipper-in – what was *his* name, Mother – Carrick?"

"I thought it was Harrison."

"No. No. John Harrison used to keep t'pit – he was nivver at a hunt in his life – he used to say "I keep thinking it's *me* they're after, and I can't bide it." No – summat like Carrick."

"Carter," said Agnes.

"No, not Carter."

"*Carter*," Agnes repeated. "I remember because I asked if he was any relation to Seth Carter of Wiston – and you said he was a second cousin they didn't talk about. Carter."

"No – that was another Carter a'together. That was Patchy Carter as used to keep a few hounds for trailing."

"It was *Carter*!"

"No, Mother. It wasn't! I've told you it wasn't and you're just clutterin' me up, Herrick! That's it. Harry Herrick."

"It wasn't, Dad. Harry Herrick was something to do with drink."

"Harry Herrick *did* drink."

"I'm sure he wasn't a whipper-in."

"He *was* a whipper-in and he *did* drink and I'll tell you how I can prove it – Billy Munn has a pewter tankard that Harry Herrick used to drink out of – always porter, mind, he wouldn't touch another drink – and that pewter tankard has H.H. on

135

it and underneath it has the family crest of them that used to run that estate and underneath that it says "Whipper-in the Fitzbridge Hounds"– and then it gives his dates – because Billy got hold of it from your Miss Wilkinson who laid him out. He had nobody, you know. Herrick isn't a local name. Anyway, it was Harry Herrick. And don't look like that, Mother, because I've seen that pewter pot. Billy Munn keeps it in his shed! Now then," turning to Edwin, "what this fella Spedding used to do . . . ah! Here she is. Well lass, here's Edwin been waiting on you for ten minutes."

"He doesn't mind, do you Edwin?" said Janice.

"No."

"That's what he says in front of *us*," said Wif. "Wait till he gets you outside."

"You wouldn't do anything violent would you, Edwin?" Janice asked, lightly.

"I don't know about that," replied Edwin, blushingly, staring at Wif, "what d'you say, Mr. Beattie?"

"I think Edwin can look after his own interests," said Agnes. "Now – away you go, I've got to change this baby and I'm sure Edwin doesn't want the sight of a baby's bottom to be in front of his eyes for the rest of the night."

"Are you sure I can't help?" Janice asked, obviously using the child as a pretext for dawdling. Edwin understood that.

"No," said Agnes briskly, "just you away and enjoy yourselves."

"Sure?"

"Certain."

Impatient, the older woman teasing the younger, the two men looking on apprehensively, masking that feeling by indulgent smiles – it seemed the quartet would never break up.

"Well?" Wif asked. "We've nowt in here for you."

Edwin stood up. Janice turned once more to the mirror and dabbed at her face. Agnes pushed her daughter, in a friendly way, but firmly.

"Go *on*," she said. "The lad's been waiting there for hours. There'll be no night left soon."

"What time should we be back, Edwin?"

"Whenever you want."

"We won't be late then, Mother."

"You won't have time to be if you don't get off."

Still Janice dawdled. It was now embarrassing Agnes greatly

136

to see Edwin so abused, and Edwin, on his feet, was loath to draw attention to himself by sitting down again; instead he leaned one hand against the television set and let his eyes search for some point of distraction. They rested on a calendar and he began to read off the dates to himself.

"I won't be a second," said Janice. "I've just forgotten my scarf." She went into the corner of the kitchen where the stairs led off up to her bedroom. "Won't be a minute."

"Eh my godfathers!" Wif exclaimed. "*I've* nivver seen a sek-like carry-on. Wher' you takun her til, Edwin, Buckingham Palace?" Agnes glared at him, sharply, and he said no more.

They waited.

"Whose funeral is it?" said Janice, as she eventually re-appeared. "I've seen a more cheerful congregation at the last rites."

"Don't be cheeky about that sort of thing," said Agnes.

"Ha! Best funeral I ivver saw in me life was up near Hexham. There was this old madam lived on her own, see, and mind there really can be some lonely spots up yonder. Anyways, she died. And this undertaker – Watson, he was called – he had to climb up through her top window to get into that house. She'd been frozen for a week when he got there – and that was just' start of it. This fella Watson –"

"Dad!" said Agnes. "They want to be away."

"No, go on, Father. What was funny about it?"

"Well, you see, this old madam had nivver had her corsets off for –"

"Dad!" repeated Agnes.

"I think we'd better be going if we're going to get anywhere to eat," said Edwin. His first and final intrusion. Janice nodded and went across to him.

"Don't do anything I –"

"Dad!" Agnes was flustered with embarrassment. "Have a nice time."

"Good night."

Both Agnes and Wif waited until they heard the car start up before saying a word. It did, drive away, sound of engine faded.

"I thought we'd have them here all night," said Wif. "I need a cup of tea after that lot. And look – even t'little 'un's fallen asleep on it."

"Pass her to me. I'll have to change her. I'll have to wake her up, that's all."

"Let's have some tea first."

"All right."

The baby was laid in the corner of an armchair and, like a catalyst, it consumed the discordance of their feelings.

Three men in Janice's life now, Agnes reflected; one the father of her child – of him she never spoke; another, long in love with her – him she treated with a whimsy which teetered not on uncertainty but on callousness; a third to whom, it seemed, she offered all the opportunities for intimacy without once speaking to her parents of him in terms higher than slighting. To Agnes, it seemed that play, which she could recognise – dallying, flirting, taking time, all that – had become the manipulation of others with full awareness of the process and its course. There was a consideredness about Janice which shivered her, and an irresponsibility which frightened her; no rashness, only misdirection; no impetuosity, only lapses; no warmth, only shine.

She wished Edwin luck; both Wif and Agnes felt it would be wrong if Janice accepted him, would not work; both would be relieved to know that she had finally turned him down; both had a hope that she would not.

Edwin had decided that his time of hoping was past. Now he had to do something about it all and see where he stood.

He had planned the evening most painstakingly and was worried only that they might not reach the hotel in time. There were many hotels around the Lakes, some of them seeming much more splendid than they were from the beauty of their site and the rates they charged which in terms of the earnings of those who actually lived near them appeared fantastical. Until the past week or two Edwin had not even noticed that they were there, driving if he had to drive somewhere, with his eyes on the white line, his head calculating the costing of jobs and the practicalities of deposits, loans and capital, Janice subdued, as she had come to be in his daytime activity, to some magic box in his mind, a box which could grow so small as to disappear, so large as to dominate.

But once he had decided to propose to her then he had started sizing them up. He would drive into the car park, go and stand outside a particular hotel, read through the menu displayed just inside the front door – but that was not so important as not only the money was no object, he *wanted* the dinner to cost him a lot; the more outrageous the amount, the more he would be pleased. What he really waited for was to size up the sort of people who went to these places. He did not wish to be involved in something which would make him so uncomfortable as to spoil everything – though he allowed for a bit of discomfort as the inevitable price of luxury – nor did he want to be worried over details. Therefore, when he finally found a place which suited him, he went to it, twice.

The first occasion had been nerve-racking; he had been plonked at a table in the middle of the room where, plastered in smartness, his face had been inflamed by the close, dry heat, and he had felt so many arrows of derision plummeting into him that he had become rigid, able to eat only by forcibly remembering how the process was carried out and obeying the fierce instructions he gave to himself. He had noticed nobody, been so shaken by the parade of cutlery that he had been quite impotent in front of the soup until a remembered voice – of someone from work who liked to pretend he made a habit of high living – had whispered "Start from the outside and work in", and finally, coffee having been brought, he downed it in one gulp and nearly destroyed the table as he jumped up to leave. Only to discover that you did not pay at the counter outside – that was for coats – and so he found himself hanging around until his waiter came with the bill and that blank look which to Edwin signified total contempt. More, outside, he had realised that he had not left a tip and so, determined that this must be the place, he had forced himself to go back in, hover until he saw his waiter, and hand him half a crown saying "I forgot to give you this."

In the van, which he had parked down the road, he had sat shaking for a full five minutes – with shame, rage, disgust at himself, detestation for the world of waiters; unable to start the car until he had reassured or strengthened himself by some resolution – that he would come again the next night, again alone, to get it really right.

The second time he had been alongside a wall. One flank protected. And the table was for two, not four as in the first visit, so he did not spend half his time fearful that he might be descended on by a highly polished group of strangers whose worldliness would strip off his pretensions. Moreover, the same waiter served him and was pleasant, chatted, was glad he liked the food. Edwin had not tasted the food, and even this second time he was largely numb to it. And this time, he sneaked glances at the people, particularly at the men, to see how they dressed. Suits. So that was all right. Most people murmured rather than spoke, many sat in silence, champing away at the food, some, he dimly realised, were anxious about their position in that place as he himself was. This time he sipped at his coffee, had a second cup, and waited for the bill to be brought.

They stopped taking diners at eight-fifteen and he drove very fast to be in good time. The thought of what he was to say to Janice, of her being next to him, of the car to be taken care of, the place to be reached – these kept him to concentration and fortunately prevented chat.

The hotel was beside Bassenthwaite Lake. Rather smaller than some of the lake-hotels, it had, to Edwin, that mellowed discretion of appearance which he recognised immediately and thought of as "really good". It stood in grounds of its own, and in the daytime you could see the lake only a few paces away outside the window. In decor and habit it was rather old-fashioned; the food was plain and plentiful, there was no Muzak, no piano, nothing to distract from the purpose of the place, which was eating. It had known better days, been the lodge for many a white-moustached party of fishermen and carried many prints and those artefacts of taxidermy which soothe the sporting soul; the furniture was oak, the carpets a little old. Persian and rich, the walls unobtrusively papered in warm patterns. Though it would never return to its former residential splendour, it was now enjoying a profitable Indian summer, which, the owner hoped, might be spring in disguise. He supervised the cooking himself, his wife looked after the bedrooms and arrangements, his brother served behind one of the two bars, In summer, it shuddered at the impact of coach-parties, but not only withstood them, welcomed them, and took no harm. In winter, as now, it was a middle-aged treat or a young experiment with occasional *aficionados* of Lakelandery who swore by the cold season now that the hot had to be shared.

Edwin was able to walk in confidently and was pleased to notice, as he did, immediately, that though Janice had made no extravagant efforts on his behalf, she was far and away the most attractive woman in the room. Eyes turned to her, and he was proud to be her escort. Escort her he did, almost marching her to the table – in the corner, he thanked God – manoeuvring her chair into position, picking up the menu as if about to study a battle order.

He wanted to tell her to order the most expensive thing they

140

had, but desisted. And was pleased by the modesty of her choice – it underlined her good taste.

Whether or not to order a bottle of wine had been a serious problem. To be able to have it and enjoy it would, undoubtedly, be perfect. But how to get it without exposing ignorance and how to enjoy it without encountering awkwardness? He had strained his ears on his second visit to catch the tone in which wine was ordered; he had the inflection, but the pronunciation would certainly defeat him. Then there was tasting it – that could only be a farce. He had decided against it.

"We could have some wine to drink if you wanted," he said.

"No thank you," Janice replied. "It makes me sleepy. But you have some if you want."

"Have some beer, sir'" said the waiter who knew he was at liberty to enter the conversation at any sentence he chose. "It'll go a lot better with what you ordered – and to tell you the truth, I think these wines are just a lot of show. Beer's what the normal English person drinks."

"Oh, I'd love beer," said Janice. "Half a pint, please."

"And you'll have a pint, sir? Good. I'll tell you, you won't get a clearer bitter anywhere round here. *Mad* on his beer, Mr. Rawlinson is. We've got some pewter tankards we use for Rotary Clubs and suchlike functions – I'll bring it in those – it looks very nice in pewter."

Edwin was pleased with all that.

After a fine mulligatawny soup, they had lamb cutlets with vegetables and potatoes and then the Chef's Mousse.

"Go on," said the waiter to Edwin, "spoil yourself. Have another. There's a few left downstairs and they'll go to waste. You know, I think this man's mousse is worth more than any dessert I've had outside the really big places. Would you like another?"

"Yes," Edwin replied so much was he now at his ease, "I would."

"And madam? Would you like one, love?"

"No thank you."

"I won't press. The ladies have their figures to think about – not like us men, eh sir? Right. Another mousse is on its way. Pronto."

They chatted so unforcedly that Edwin even allowed himself to tilt his chair back slightly – and more, recognise that it might be bad manners and have confidence enough to ignore the threat to etiquette.

Janice dallied over the coffee but eventually they left, Edwin leaving a five-bob tip and receiving a pantomime wink from the waiter.

He had chosen his spot for the proposal most carefully, but without the struggle involved in finding the hotel. It was a little road which ran down almost to the lake's edge – the lake flattening out beyond the road's end, hills lifting up from it in the distance, black as the water, a few lights like swollen glow-worms pricking out of the woods on the hillsides.

With the engine turned off, the silence sucked them into drama. Any word spoken would, he felt, be decisive. The purpose was stripped of all preparation and now waited only to be called. Nothing else would do but that it should be called. Diversions would diminish it, evasions muzzle its impact.

Edwin felt more conscious of his appearance than ever before in his entire life. In the hotel, he had seen Janice as he might see her for ever afterwards. Dressed well – for him; looking beautiful – for him; the whole evening's talk and movement – for him. Soon he had seen that she was the loveliest person there and pride in her, greed for her, humility before her – all had mingled with the love he had always had, inflaming his constancy until it flowed into that passion which had first provoked it. But now, in the car, seeing the whole moonlight pale her hair, her legs inches from his own with the soft skin so finely firm, he saw his hands knobbed and large on the wheel, felt that thin sweat come to his stretched white skin which made him aware of the bumpy contour of his face; even his teeth seemed ugly, too big for his mouth, the jawbone protruding as as a shovel.

"Janice," he began, "hear me through, anyway." He paused, not looking at her and, from her small reflection in the mirror, seeing that she was not looking at him. That made it easier. "Now you know my financial position so I needn't go over that . . ."

"That doesn't matter," said softly, more a punctuation than an interruption.

"But it matters to me. I have to have all that side taken care of. Now all I want to say about that is – I've got to move. There's a chance of getting in, on my own in a small way, at Whitehaven and I've made up my mind to take it. It's just an old garage as it stands now, but the overheads are light and I reckon I can count on a bit of trade carried over to see me started. There aren't many welders about, you know – not enough anyway; and it's a trade that isn't easy to pick up. So if I get going. I might get really set. Anyway, that's what I'm doing."

"I think that's marvellous, Edwin. I know you'll do it. 'Edwin Cass – Welder.' Will you live there?"

"Yes. I'll have to live over my work. I can't afford to hire anybody so even easy-looking jobs'll take a fair time. There's some rooms above this place – rubbish-dumps as now, but I'll get two or three of them in shape for living in. Now, there won't be much time for what you might call social life, there won't even be much time for reading books – but that takes care of itself because I always like a story going in my head and I'll keep it up one way and another."

"I'm sure you will."

"I'll be sorry to leave that end cottage. I've made it good and I'd like to have carried on there – it suits me. But there we are. And I thought that we – us two – might – I thought, if ever anything did come to anything, it would be handy for you next to your mam and dad. And I like them."

This time he waited for an interpolation but there was none. "So I'm shifting," he continued, strenuously. "And I want you to marry me. I won't be able to see you so much when I move – anyway – you know I've been feeling like this about you for a long time. I've been patient. But that doesn't mean much – except it shows – I've never, nobody else has – I want to marry you more than I want anything. If I told you how much I've thought about you, you wouldn't believe me. I've wanted it – well, it's thinking of you that's kept me going. There was nothing else."

"You mustn't say that. You would have . . ."

"Would have what? No. We needn't go into it. I wouldn't have. You've made me pull myself up into another world, Janice. If I'd stayed in the one I was born in, I'd be just as miserable as the rest of them. I'd be worth nothing."

Janice began to be afraid of him. If she said no, what would happen?

"This is the last time I'll ask you, Janice."

"Don't say that, Edwin."

"Why not? It is."

"You make it sound so threatening. I feel a bit frightened of you."

"Of *me*?"

"Yes."

143

"But you can't. You can never feel frightened of me, Janice."
Edwin felt that this was an evasion, but was so surprised at it
that he was halted.

"You should look around a bit more," said Janice, using the
pause. "You've seen hardly anyone but me. You can't be as
certain as..."

"I am."

Janice wished that it would begin to snow, that the black lake
might be flaked with broken lace, the hills capped in soft white,
the frost-glittered tip of the snow crunchy under the poke of an
index finger – a physical diversion present itself.

"Well," said Edwin. "I've asked you. You've known anyway
for years." He set his face so hard that the skin against his cheek-
bones was painful. "What do you say?"

Janice's breath was padded in her throat and dared not come
out. This fear of Edwin was quite sudden. His lumpy profile,
glistening a jaundiced yellow. Her skin crept into its pores.

"I can't marry you, Edwin. I can never marry you."

"Are you going to marry that other fella?" Rapped out.

"Richard?"

"Richard! I was listening the other night – I heard you. And
when you refused him, I was so glad I nearly choked. I thought –
he's just right for her, and if she won't have *him* – it must be
possible for me. But it is him, isn't it?"

"No."

"What then? You've hardly been away from his place this
last month. You never *once* thought of what I was feeling about
it all, did you? Did you?"

"No. I didn't."

"I knew it! Well this is my last offer, Janice. I can't stop thinking about you, maybe I can't ever stop that; but I can try to get
on without you."

"You'll be fine, Edwin. I wouldn't make you happy."

"How do you know?"

"I wouldn't. Anyway, I can't."

They sat. The heater was off, the car became cooler and then
cold. Edwin did not move. Janice feared that to move might
startle him to violence. His body, so large beside hers, untouching;
anything could come of it.

No cars could be heard from the small road they had driven
off. No movement on the lake.

144

Finally, Edwin's head fell down on to the steering-wheel. "I don't know what I'll do without you, Janice. I don't."

She saw that he was crying, without sound, and her hand went out to stroke his hair. He turned, grasped her by the shoulders, and kissed her. She couldn't move, so tightly did he hold her, but her nerves cringed with repulsion. Feeling it, Edwin drove his face deeper into hers and his hand snatched at her breast, grasping it so savagely she would have cried out had she been able.

He recoiled from her and she waited the opportunity to open the door and run.

"Don't you have anything to say?"

"No."

"After I did – what I did – touched you like that?"

"No."

He leaned towards her, she was unable to stop herself drawing back, unable to control the distaste, which appeared on her face. Edwin held back.

"Is that what you think of me?"

"What?"

"I saw your look."

"You're scaring me, Edwin. I can't help how I look."

"Neither can I! Don't you realise that? Neither can I!"

She nodded. No longer afraid of him. Tired. She had cheated him – but whatever she might have done, she would still have cheated him.

"It doesn't matter how long I wait or what I do, does it, Janice?"

"No," she spoke distantly, faintly; "no."

He started up the car. His hands were trembling and it stalled. He drove on to the road erratically and set off at a suicidal pace. Janice remained as she was, in the corner, not even smoothing out her dress. Edwin went round corners with howling of tyres, refused to dip his lights, and on one short straight stretch straddled the wheels across the white line and pushed the needle up to ninety. He said nothing. He said nothing when he turned down the lane, nothing when he passed the cottages and slammed to a stop outside Richard's cottage. Nothing until the engine's sound had disappeared.

"Now go in and tell him what you told me," he said slowly. "You've got to start telling people things straight, Janice. I'll leave here – and so will he. Only difference – I won't forget you, Janice, as long as I've memory." He spoke so deliberately that his words could have been nails, deliberately pounded into the boards which shut him out from her. "If you want anything – come; and if I can give it to you, you'll have it. Now. I'm leaving you."

She nodded and got out of the car. Richard had come to the cottage door and both of them watched Edwin back right down the lane and on to the main road.

Richard came across to her.

"He's leaving here," said Janice, simply. "He asked me to marry him and I refused. You should leave as well."

"You look – do you want a drink?" Coming close to her, Richard saw her white, set-faced, shivering in the cold night. "Come in – or I'll take you home if you want. You don't look well."

She nodded and turned towards his cottage. Inside, she crouched in a seat before the fire. Silently, Richard brought her some hot coffee and whisky.

Then he sat and waited. She sipped at the drinks.

"I wanted him to do as he wanted with me," she said, abruptly, softly. "Do you understand that? I know I would never love him – but I wanted him to do it." She paused. Richard said nothing, unable to meet her involuted tension. She began to sob, not loudly, not obtrusively. "I don't know what I want or what I hate. I don't know what I can find to love. It doesn't work for me . . . I wanted him to do it! Like Paul."

The silence between them was so rigid, Richard hardly dared to move his eyes from her.

"I will marry you," she said, in the same tone, still looking at the fire. "If you want me to marry you, I will."

Richard said nothing. Then Janice stood up, the movement appearing to come through waves of entangled, drowning thoughts all pressing to submerge her. She went across to the door. Wanting to say nothing, Richard knew that some sentence had to be risked to bring her into contact with the outside once more.

"Think about it. You're too upset as you are. I'll set you home."

"No."

"It won't be –"

"No!" For the first time, she looked at him. "If Edwin asked me again, this minute, I think I would accept him. But it's you. As long as you know that."

146

The winter afternoon levelled the countryside with a flat grey stillness. The sky was leaden and low, clouds so dense that they did not appear to shift but were as immovable as the fells. The grey roads trickled between barren hedges and fields with all the colour taken away from them. The coned peak of Knockmirton still stood clear but any slight sag in the cloud and it would be hidden. Everything was evened out under the grey light, all tones moved to grey, wagons seemed grey, houses and roofs even more slate-coloured, and from any viewpoint the whole scene spread out with that inanimate coldness which made each traveller burrow into himself and each seed and bulb grab deeper hold under the ground to prepare against the frost which would sink stone fibres into its roots.

At such times, this part of England looked changeless. Whether car, horse or hunter went across it, whether aeroplanes were heard above it or long-prowed boats climbed its rivers into the lakes – none would have changed the feeling which was given off. It was as if the scales of successive ages had laid themselves over the landscape so consistently that it could no longer be changed, could no longer yield and was sullen at it.

Janice, pushing the pram, had wandered far beyond the usual boundaries of the little afternoon walk wihch Paula received as often as possible. The shield was across the front of the pram so as to keep out the wind, and the whole thing suddenly looked to her like a strange black box, springing on high wheels between the withered hedges. Janice herself had taken a scarf and now it was wrapped around her neck, covering her chin, so that the steely wind would not cut at her throat. The wind was low but it had such an edge that it drove all blood from the surface of her face and she looked tensely pale.

She had gone down towards that tiny huddle of cottages which protected the sub-post-office and now was on the road which led to where Edwin's mother lived. But she was largely unconscious of her route. The previous night's events had riven her.

She did not know why she had been so afraid of Edwin and so troubled at the manner of his acceptance of her decision. She

147

did not know why she had agreed to marry Richard or why, later, in her bed, she had cried aloud to stop the pressures in her mind from sliding her into that uncertainty which she could not bear.

To marry or not to marry – either course, it seemed to her, would bring her loss: the one of liberty, the other of company. She wanted to make love, but desired to keep from the acts of love; she wanted to live with someone like Richard, but wished to live alone; she was elated at the thought of his departure and delighted at the notion of his remaining, depressed that she might be spurning love, depressed that she might be mistaking it; prepared to dream about a future with him, nostalgic for a future without him. She was pleased that he countenanced her moods, and pleased that he found some of them tedious; she liked the persistence of his thinking and liked the contempt with which he referred to it. Now when she saw him her body blushed, now it froze; she wanted to rush out and see him, she never wanted to see him again. To trust herself to him was her wish, to trust herself to no one her ambition; or had been.

Pushing a black pram along a grey road, her ankles chapped by cold. Snow in the air. Chipped pebbles under the thin tyres.

She looked around and found herself miles from her normal walk. Paula was moaning gently, not complaining; she rarely did, Janice thought, and peeked in at her, seeing again resemblance neither to herself nor to Paul; as if the child had escaped both of them.

Grey was thickening to dusk and she turned in her tracks to set off back. As she came to the cottage in which Edwin's mother lived, the old woman came down to the gate, a clagged and tatty fur coat held with nicotined fingers around her petticoat, hair bobbing out of fierce little curlers, silvery hinges flopping on wasted dry waves; she had seen Janice go past and waited for the return.

Janice knew Mrs. Cass but still found her eyes retreating from that face. She was not ashamed of this; it had always seemed to Janice that Mrs. Cass flaunted her ugliness, blackmailed one to sympathy through disgust.

"That yours?" The pram.

"Yes."

"Let's have a look." She came through the gate and peered in, gripping the sides of the pram so that her coat fell open and the petticoat, a blue one, flopped her body out. "Doesn't look like

148

you. But they never do when they're that age. I'm sure they could swap them all around in hospitals – that's what I used to say to Edwin – son, you're too good for me, I used to say, he was always very particular you know and then he started on that paper-round and gave me half – I didn't ask, a paper round in the morning and milk at the weekends – in the dairy, bottle-washing – too good for me, you must be a swap, I said."

The two of them were quite alone on the road. The young woman could have been visiting her mother; the older, seeing her son's child.

Mrs. Cass grew playful.

"He bought himself a suit," she said. "He didn't ask me about it and he wouldn't have told me either if I hadn't smelt something – got it out of him. I know what he bought it for as well. I knew. He didn't have to tell me that, either."

She had left the pram and now stood inside her front gate, hands gripping the coat once more, eyes rolling in loosened rims of red smarting in the wind.

"Come in for some tea."

"No thank you, Mrs. Cass. I'll have to be getting on. The baby's already late for her feed."

"Give it to her here. What? Is it off the breast?"

"Yes."

"I put Edwin off his first day. It spoils you for good. I don't think it did any harm. Mind you, a lot of people were shocked. But I wouldn't have him. Same with you, eh?"

"I suppose so . . . yes."

"Well. Come in! Come in! Don't expect a palace, because that bloody Edwin doesn't give me enough to buy a duster on. And he's coining it in now, the sod! Yes, that's what I call him – he's a sod. All men are. Keep away from them. Come in!"

"No, I'll have to be going back, really, Mrs. Cass."

"You don't want to, eh?"

"I can't."

"You're in a bloody hurry all of a sudden aren't you? Are you too stuck-up to come into my place? It might not be *good* enough for somebody like you, but for somebody like me, it's where I live, you know. And Edwin sees to it that I live somewhere out of reach – oh, I know his tricks, the bastard – gives his own mother a cottage in the middle of nowhere – I'm used to a bit of fun. I'm *used* to it!"

"No, really, Mrs. Cass, I have to get back."

"I keep telling our Edwin he's a fool to bother with you. We're just not good enough for *you*, are we? And I don't know how you can speak, brazen-faced with that kid belonging to nobody. I suppose you're just walking round doing nothing at the moment. But *I* know you're after it. Your sort can't get enough of it."

"I'm going."

"That's right, run away! Run away, little Miss Stuck-Up! I hope you bloody well don't get hold of my Edwin, that's all. And he's coming here tonight. And I'll tell him I saw you – just *looking* for it. Anybody can tell that. You're a tart. You're rubbish! Rubbish!"

Janice pushed the pram on further away and then, feeling that her guilt at refusing Mrs. Cass's invitation had made her ashamed where she need not be ashamed, she turned and shouted:

"Oh shut up! You should think yourself lucky that Edwin gives you anything at all! Every time anybody sees you, you're complaining. And the way you talk about him is disgraceful. He's a better son than you deserve!"

"What's that?" The gate opened, the coat flopped open, Mrs. Cass slipper-pounded up the road halting a few yards from the younger woman. "Say that again! Go on! I dare you! Say it! You rubbish!"

"I'm sorry, Mrs. Cass. I lost my temper."

"You! Sorry!" She spat out. "That's what I think of you being sorry!"

"I am going this time. Good-bye."

"Good-bye!" Janice began to go. "Good-bye ... Good-bye ... Good-bye!" The phrase so crudely mimicked that it contorted to a jab of venom. "Good-bye ... Good-bye ... Good-bye! You think you're the bloody Queen of Sheba! Well, you're a slut! You think you're too good for anybody around here! Well you're not! That's right – run! Run! Run away! I hope you break your bloody neck! Run! Run! Ha!"

The pram bounded on its thin high wheels and Janice's scarf winged out behind her. She did not stop or turn round at the crest of the rise, nor did she slow down until her legs were so weak, her breath so painful that she was forced to do so. She looked to see if Paula was all right, perceived her anxiety for her daughter and then unbuttoned the pram-cover, took her out, and hugged her. The child, who had not cried, now began to whimper.

Janice pushed the pram with one hand, in the other carrying

the baby. Though it grew so heavy that she feared her arm might become cramped, she would not put it back in the pram.

It was darker now and, as she turned on to the main road, a lorry suddenly swept round the corner and threw on its head-light, almost blinding her. She flinched aside and half slithered into a shallow ditch. Paula was like a lump which had grown in the crook of her arm, or lodged there like a boulder, but Janice would not let her go.

Even as she walked the last half-mile on that side of the village triangle which led from the sub-post-office to the pub, it became full night. Three or four more cars swept down on her, and each time she feared they might run over her. One went so close to the wheels of the pram that it caught the outside of the hub and the pram jolted out of Janice's grasp.

She took the short route through a cow-track which led to the path down to her own place. Half-way down her own path, Edwin's van passed her and as she turned into the cottages, he was waiting for her.

"Something's wrong with the baby?"

"No." The baby's weight was now so dense on Janice's arm that to have put her down would have been like having her torn away.

"You don't look well."

"I walked too far – towards the estate – and then I met – I'm tired. I must go in. Paula's starving.

"Did you see my mother?'

"Yes. Yes I did."

"She say anything?"

"It's all right . . . I must go, Edwin, please."

He let her pass. As she reached her door, he shouted out, "Don't worry! I'll settle her. And don't worry about me; I'm leaving!"

She had neither the energy nor the impulse to reply to that second announcement, which contained an appeal, a final offer, a threat even.

Inside the kitchen, she handed over Paula to her mother and then insisted on feeding the baby herself. Wif and Agnes were quietened by her paleness, anxious as she shivered and started at no sound, no report.

"Did Richard call?" she asked.

"No."

"He's still there, isn't he?"

151

"Of course he is. What a question. Of course he is."

The baby fell asleep half-way through the feed, and Janice rocked her until she, too, fell asleep.

CHAPTER NINETEEN

When Janice and Richard finally made love it was in his cottage just before Christmas. Edwin had removed his last belongings that afternoon, wishing everyone a stiff-backed farewell except Richard, whom he ignored. Nobody blamed him for that, especially not Mrs. Jackson who raised tears for the occasion and and so amazed herself at this that she followed them down her cheeks with squinting eyes and finally had to excuse herself, supposedly to recover her poise, but really to look in the mirror to see how far they had got. It was a Saturday afternoon on which he left and quite a few people happened to come along to see Wif or Mrs. Jackson or even admitted to coming to see Edwin himself, so that he was given a proper send-off after having had tea with Agnes and Wif and tea again with Mrs. Jackson whose main worry, now that the tears had run out, was who was going to occupy the end cottage, be her neighbour; she wanted somebody respectable but they must, she said, be friendly, because when you have three cottages so isolated and yet so snug together. friendliness was worth more than everything else put together, and Edwin had always been friendly.

Janice was quite willing to join in the departure scene but the fact that everybody clearly regarded her, so she thought – and she was not wrong – as the instrument of Edwin's flight, made it uncomfortable and so, without even inventing an excuse like a headache, which would have made matters worse, she just kept out of the way and played with Paula indoors. Paula had not been well since that run back from Mrs. Cass's house, her temperature had gone up to a hundred and five the same evening, or morning rather, because she had woken up at two o'clock crying, and though Agnes said don't worry yet, it's probably no more than a cold, the doctor had been called for and pronounced tonsillitis which meant staying indoors for a week or so. So there was an excuse for Janice if she wanted to use it.

She was sorry that her sensitivity to the feeling about Edwin's position took her indoors. For she would have liked to part in peace from him, not only no grudges, that wasn't the point, but a feeling of settlement, comprehension, that is what she would have liked. Selfishly, she realised, and was confirmed in this by Edwin's behaviour which, though correct, was unyielding and said to her quite plainly, you'll regret not taking me. She did not regret his leaving.

Wif did. He was more moved by it than ever he thought he would be, for over the years Edwin had done so many things with him, he had watched him fill out from the spindly, sheared figure, a boy of sixteen proudly renting a cottage for himself and unable to look at Janice without choking back embarrassment, then getting a trade, a lonely one, few others went in for welding, taking in books from the travelling library, almost creeping up to it behind the hedge so that nobody would see him and then all thumbs in the small van until Miss Steele had taken him in hand and told him how to get going – mainly the stalwart of Edwin's ambition and way of life he would miss. Though he had never thought he would make a son-in-law, he said to Agnes, he came as close as made no difference to thinking of him as a son.

Then, this enterprise raised him in Wif's eyes. Edwin had started from as near to nothing as you could get without the minuses of being crippled or deficient, and here he was, just out of his apprenticeship, off to a derelict garage in a back street away from the centre of the unbusy town of Whitehaven to set himself up against the lot of them. Wif would never have dared that, and, having seen how Edwin had come to doing it, he had more respect for him than for anyone else in the village.

Richard knew about the departure and was silent. It would have been nice to have been able to shake Edwin's hand and wish him luck, but it was impossible that he should do it without awkwardness. Edwin had to do it. Which was why Richard stayed in his own cottage even though he would have preferred to go up to Cogra Moss and see the beagling, he stayed in his own cottage so that he would be available if Edwin wanted him. Had he not been there when Edwin called, then it would have been bad – manners, feeling, action. So he went up to his bedroom and positioned himself so that he could see but not be seen and watched the cardboard boxes, the ornaments and bedding, the carpets and curtains (the heavy stuff had been taken the previous afternoon, Edwin having been given that afternoon off by his boss, who perhaps wanted a future rival to go away with a mark of obligation on him), people helping and watching, jars of jam being given by the ladies, a box of teacakes and fancies by Agnes, some Cumberland sausage from Mr. Law of the farm. Richard saw all this: at the edge of the dour little row of cottages it could almost have been a carnival, and he tried to avoid, unsuccessfully, the feeling of self-pity which, to be accurate, never developed into a consuming lump, but did linger around him. It reminded him of his own leave-taking for University, the neighbours there, and how the very fraternity of co-inhabitation had made even more felt the loneliness of being without father or mother. Beside all, he admired Edwin; it was a pity they could not know each other. So he waited, knowing Edwin would not come.

When all was ready and there was no more to be last-minute-remembered, the small group of people seemed all to put an avenue for Edwin to Janice's door. They looked away or turned to chat as he went to say good-bye to her, all knowing that she had refused to accompany him, all sorry for Edwin because of his patient courtship, yet also feeling that the spark which this departure represented would sooner turn into a blaze without her than with her. Richard watched the cottage and Edwin stayed inside a long time, coming out finally and walking straight over to his van, into it, a quick wave, and away. For an instant, Richard was certain that all the people turned and looked at his window and he ducked his head, but when he looked out again, most of them had gone, only Wif chatting with Mr. Jackson and Frank Semple, and he thought he might have been mistaken.

He went out of his back door, over the low wall, into Robson's bottom field and away up to Cogra Moss – but the beaglers had moved on and, hard as he strained to hear them, he could not. He wandered around until dark and then found that he had arrived in Kirkland where he had a couple of pints before setting off for Crossbridge.

The light was on in his cottage, the fire was crackling, the curtains drawn, a meal ready to be prepared. But instead they went to bed.

There, with one small light, on the white sheet, she lay under him, her hair glinting against the pillow, her skin so densely cream his lips could not stop rubbing it. Arms around each other they clasped so tight that her breasts buried into his body; hand stroking her brow, her thigh, her back. They made love, and then again, lay back and came again together.

154

And the fret smoothed away, the apparitions vanished, she opened herself to him, finger-tips stretching to the edges of the bed; he spread into her until all hardness between them dissolved and they swam in one chrysalis. Unconsciousness came as they folded round each other, slowly her legs circled round his body; unconsciousness within complete activity and that was what he wanted, what he had always been wanting. Through this dying, he could live again. The quest *was* over; entanglement became service, the one swathing the other in lapping play; became command, he driving her in fierce possession; became affection, she stroking him in love.

They were married soon after Christmas. Agnes feared that Janice might have given up, rebounded to Richard, being stuck with the child, Edwin gone, and tried, the best way she could, to tell her that there was time, there was no rush, no panic. But, after the surprise of the announcement, she came to like Richard increasingly and, on the day, was glad. Wif was pleased, even more so when Richard got himself a job as a teacher over in Cleator Moor and prepared to take it up after Easter. They would live in the end cottage that had been Edwin's; something had been settled and it was that, above all, which made Wif glad.

Agnes had wanted the church so much that she scarcely dared request it of them; they went there to please her but Janice wore a two-piece suit of blue.

There was snow everywhere. Slushy tracks outside the church gate. Brown clogs of dirtied snow on the good carpet which went by the font. Edwin sent them a glass-fronted bookcase.

For the honeymoon, they went for a few days to Edinburgh, coming back a day earlier than expected, both wishing to get into their own house, their own bed, for they made love constantly, wanting only to be naked and wound into each other's body.

PART II

EVERY TREE OF THE GARDEN

'Of every tree of the garden thou mayest freely eat. But of the tree of the knowledge of good and evil, thou shalt not eat of it; for in the day that thou eatest thereof thou shalt surely die.'

Genesis, II, 16-17.

CHAPTER TWENTY

The snow stayed until Easter. There would be days when it was gone, and then another morning all would be white, sweating under the clear winter sun. Only the hedges were marked out then, the boundaries, the confinements of property, they soon straggled out of the communal mantle and stood free, free to guard against any liberties which might be taken with the ground in their care. Unlike the walls; those walls which always seemed so much part of the fells that they might have been the old skin of the first thing which slithered across them, they were hidden under the snow. Though not quite invisible because, here and there, you saw a hump of snow where a fall or a drift had been checked, and deep under that would be a wall.

The district was silenced by it. The roads soon turned to brown slush which, with council grit among it, flew out from the lorries' wheels like fouled spray, but landed softly in the ditches. The dogs disappeared indoors. No tractors worked the fields. Engines which drove the electricity plant at the hall and could sound 'like thunder at rehearsals' (Agnes said) now bumped along, choked quiet by the weight of snow. People walked wadded and intent, their step as clumsy as in summer it was languorous, with gloves, scarves, double pullovers, Balaclavas, mittens, coats, Wellingtons and double socks – and if they hailed each other, the words cracked out crisply and then bolted into the absorbing snow, leaving no trace. The greatest activity of the day was sweeping the steps and the paths of sludge. This was done in the evening by the men, in the mornings by the women.

It was then that you realised how small a place Crossbridge was. For those smooth-buttocked hills, the fields leaning down into the stream perpetually running under the thin gripping ice – they were bare of sledges and snowmen and snow-fights. Down by the church a few of the cottage children had made a little track, and at the weekends you saw a small posse dragging their squat wooden sledge, the runners scraped with steel wool from the previous year and, if the father was friendly, rubbed with oil – but that was all. Otherwise, from the top of Knockmirton, where Richard once went, there was no movement, save the postman's brick-red van, tying the flung cottages together, occasionally stopping dead with ice under the wheels, unable to move, no noise coming up to the top of the fell, only the minute bright van stuck in the snow. Yet behind him, among the hills which went on as far as he could see, there appeared movement; for the snow had slid down, left patches, rushed, drifted, been shrugged away, it seemed, from the ancient hide, and the effect was of the hills heaving, dislodging the snow in their progress; while the flat land was still.

The cottage at that time was a brown and secret burrow. The fire was always piled high, the air so densely cosy as to make only semi-conscious many actions within it; they rose late and went to bed early, spending much of the day reading or planning what they should do. His money had almost gone; a job would soon be financially necessary and he was glad of it. Teaching, he thought, was an honest way to make a living and he sent for all his history notes and books which he had left, for storage, with a neighbour of his grandfather. Working through the notes again, he enjoyed the neat formulation of cause and effect, the sound of the names and battles, the rattle of certainties. The work he had done at University now seemed to find a much more relaxed place in his mind; perhaps it was because the area in which he now lived, so scarce in the monuments of post-Conquest history, seemed to contain so many reminders of the continuity of men, in stones and manners, in approach and feeling, that the scraps and scrapes of Plantagenets, Tudors, Stuarts, Whigs, Tories, City, Country, Reform and Riot appeared as a mere bag of tricks hot-headedly complicating only a tiny section of time. Yet, in the complication, there was pleasure; and, maybe because of the scheming and politicking in which he himself had been involved in London, he saw the patterns, not as stiff manoeuvres over dead issues, but as the peddling and wheedling of men ambitious, principled, greedy, idealistic, or all these; the history he was to teach took on the nature of gossip, and that relieved it of the portentous weight it had assumed at University.

Some of these notes had to be copied out again, and Janice helped him to do that. She, too, enjoyed the work. And when Richard started to write songs again, she helped to find the verses for them. He had found himself humming tunes again and written down a few of them. He knew that the chance of their getting anywhere without being put on to tape or, better, made up into a demonstration disc, were so slight as to be equivalent to winning the treble chance, but he sent them off to a music publisher he knew and was happy to have this long shot looping around the limited activity of his life.

For it was now gloriously limited. After the marriage. The soft-lined jar of the fact of marriage. The browsing in his own mind, the fratching over his thoughts, that had gone in his love for Janice. Each day his imagination painted new virtues and qualities and beauties on her whom his eyes saw as more perfect each day. As the fact of his love grew, so did the thought of it, and each mote of his mind was charged with passion for her just as each part of his body spread with desire for her. He was like one of those plants which keep tight-inlocked and inviolably contorted until one sudden day they flourish open and, with trumpets and strongest scents, drive off all memory of their green and twisted state. In achieving their full purpose, they abandon and abolish the straining after it. So Richard threw off his introversion, finding enough in Janice, in Paula, in Wif and Agnes, in the people in the village, enough in knowing about love and seeing it prise open his affection to humour and trust, stability and hope And he believed that he had found the style he had come to look for.

It was a style not of doing, but of accepting; it was not to build something for himself but to see himself as part of others, not only in the present but in the past, not trying to prove or to convince himself that that which made life rich and worth-while was the same now, yesterday and tomorrow, but living according *to* that. He had been afraid – and now he was no longer afraid, no longer thought about it, acted as lover, husband, father, son, friend, neighbour, teacher – as someone part of the place, though that place had no particular magical qualities; it was himself, not the place. Had he given himself the time to think over what was happening, then he might have suspected that he had not fathomed a life but crept into an inlet; that you could not, now, merely live, you had to test your footing at each step because there was neither reason nor instinct enough left over from slaughters and bombs, from technologies and organisations, to give you any trust in the ground you walked on. But he did not consider this. Here he had found, he thought, for the first time in his adult, suspicious life, the unifying qualities among people. And though that vision might explode, be lost, become streaked with flaws unmendable, it had been entered into and no better had been felt or seen any time in his life.

It was at this time that he really grew to love Agnes. What she gave off was not exactly cheerfulness, though it contained that, nor happiness nor well-being, though it was informed by these – what she gave when she moved was hope. Not that chirpy optimism which springs you up to bump you down, nor that everlasting clerical promise of better things which, by faultless repetition, turns all things to flat progression; a hope, she had, in the minute itself, in the movement she was making, in the way she was looking. Where she had been, there was hope, like the fragment of a song which stays in people's minds after the band has marched away. She had had no easy life herself; she was no lamb when her tongue felt moved to unleash her grievances; she was not pious nor was she spotless; she was, in all she did, neither ignorant of evil nor unaware of complication, yet hopeful for life, for the possibilities in being alive.

Agnes took to Richard and soon the two of them were much as mother and son, the law running into the blood. It was his proximity that gave their affection strength, as it had done with Edwin. When she saw Richard's openness to her and to everyone, his passion for Janice, his love for Paula, his decision to teach and, from the way he was preparing, to do it well; saw, finally, that he was not teasing out Wif's quaintness which she recognised in her husband and alternately laughed at and enjoyed, each way nourishing it because it was part of him, whom she loved – then she actively engaged herself in understanding. To Agnes, the notion of being an orphan was desolate. It was the work-houses she could remember outside the mining towns, gaunter than the town hall, black as the office on top of the pit shaft; the crocodile rows of little children, boys always so barbered that their necks seemed to reach the crown of their heads; it was that part of the loneliness which made every step a step away from nothing, with no one to look back to for encourage-ment or even a command. And however much Richard protested the kindliness of his grandparents, part of that image entered into her feeling for him and she saw how it was with as much relief as apprehension that he found himself marrying not just a woman but three generations of a family.

In this deep mid-winter the only fresh news brought by Wif was of the death of Hector. Insisting that his horses needed exercise no matter the weather, Hector had taken to walking them along a track behind his place. Up and down he would go, dangling between their heads like the diminutive groom of

162

some ancient charioteer, up and down until they had covered a fittening distance. This even when the ice covered the track. He went out beforehand and melted the ice – or broke the worst parts, as he had previously shovelled away the snow. A dog got among the horses' hooves; they reared, haunches swollen with muscle, lifting Hector with them, still holding the bridles; he tried to knock the dog away, snarling now around his feet, and both horses, thunder-horses, the Clydesdales, panic-eyed pulled him until he let go of one and was pulled over by the other and by a hoof was cracked on the forehead, to die immediately. "He was the last of them," said Wif, solemnly. "Now he's gone. He kept his promise though, eh? He said he would never bet again as long as he lived and he didn't. Not once." He paused. "I expect they'll have to shoot them horses."

And one other time the snow was not cover enough. A few weeks after they were married, the seed which was to tumble into the foundations of that marriage and root beside it was sown. Casually, Janice asked Richard if he intended to stay always in Crossbridge, reminding him that her wish had been to get away from it. That halted him, but he replied that he wanted to stay and would do so until she asked him now, now that they were married to take her away. With this offer feeling his hopes fling out and scatter, uncontrolled, once again, by himself. But she calmed him down, said she was happy in his happiness, told him to forget it.

It was an early Easter and the ice and snow left. The streams, gorged with water, crashed over the banks with their brown brothing force, put Crossbridge, the bridge itself, under two feet of flood, rolled the loose boulders down the fells, mashed the tracks to miry sloughs, sated the greening fields in marshy pools. Soon, only unsunned ravines had their streaks of snow to bear record. The rest of nature bathed in the water and lifted to that first lushness, the hint of loaded abundance which precourses spring. And Janice discovered she was pregnant and the ice which had left the earth entered into her.

CHAPTER TWENTY-ONE

She had to force herself to give the news to Richard and her parents. She put it off for days, sometimes found that she had forgotten it altogether and then she was happy; but finally forced herself to tell. The attention and delight she received as reward for the news grated her, the blood truly seemed to run even colder, the smile she returned was ordered into place.

Richard went off to school and she was on her own for long parts of the days, and she tried all she could to repress the fear and distaste she felt for the swelling child. She took Paula for walks, she helped her mother clean the church once, she attended a meeting at the Women's Institute. She began to practise on the piano – Miss Wilkinson had given her free lessons for a few years until Janice had decided she had no time for it – she revised her reading list and pretended that she might yet go to Carcaster. All of this left her with a dry-tongued panic ready, it seemed, to tipple her to disaster.

She began to stay indoors all the time, did, read, nothing, listened to the radio, could not bear to hear a voice, could not tolerate the concerts and recitals, filled the small cottage kitchen with the electronic rhythm of pop, rose late, was sloppy in her dress, left dishes unwashed, any excuse to get Agnes to look after Paula, which Agnes did, grateful to help, afraid that the pregnancy was reviving memories too hard to bear, believing that acquiescence and vigil were the best help she could give.

Janice tormented herself. She did not know why she could not be content, only that she was not. She loved Richard, this she told herself in reproof, in despair, in hope, for help, a thousand times each day. She loved his gentleness, his persistence even when it ran to doggedness, his resolution even if, at the moment, it led to dullness. For all was dull once more. It should not have been, she knew, it should not have been so. But the groaning in her mind was of boredom. Or that was what she called it, being too frightened to go further.

She had grown up so very much on her own that, although in a city people can be just as solitary, all those contours of the country which work for separateness infused her until she believed herself to carry her own destiny entirely and, while very young, roamed alone in the day-dreams which had become fibres of her mind. They were always the same. She would be a free woman, knowing things; she would be constrained by no person or place. This was simple, harmless enough as a dream, but into it she had driven all her ambition and her ambition had driven all her life. There was nothing around her which she wished to live for; not for the season or the animals, not for the countryside or the village people, not for emulation of her parents, for her way was totally different from theirs.

In her love for Richard she had flourished, but in ways foreign to her made life. Where she had been the will, now she was the willed, the follower not the leader, rather the wax than the seal itself. And in this she did flourish as her body softened to his; her features began to lose the tension which had pressed their refinement too often to anxiety; her mind eased out of its hermetic self-possession and the words between them made malleable and approachable what had been forbidden. For the price of her way of living had been a central void – or void presumed, felt almost, as a definite place in her head – the place where there were no questions, where all irrelevancies went to be scorched, where her spirit was kept in chains made by her intentions. And this, too, had been broached.

But when she knew that she was carrying another child, with a rush of consciousness all snapped back to where it had been before she had met Richard and, however hard she tried, she could not prevent it. She despised her retreat from Richard and employed every tactic she could so that he should not notice it, knowing that she was unsuccessful, but observing that he understood she had fears and would be ready to help while being unhurried in any pursuit of the cause of her private discontent. And the more to be loved for that. So much to be loved in her life – but the life chilled her, iced her reactions so fiercely that many evenings she could do no more than slump in frozen desolation, the only feeble flame to come from her being the excuse that she was exhausted, which was true as the struggle was exhausting her; for she was losing it, and yet she could not help believing, at moments immediately curbed, that it was winning not losing, winning her way back to herself.

The weather was no help – a spring as dully grey as late autumn, the torrential break of the winter having tired things, it seemed, and they plodded in grim growth, struggling, not leaping, pushing through the ground, not springing from it. She went with her mother on her few excursions out of the cottage by day, and once they called on Mrs. Cass whose treatment by Edwin – he had stopped paying her money on that same evening on which she had frightened Janice – had harassed Agnes. For though Agnes found it difficult to think badly of Edwin, who had at last done what everyone had seen provocation for over the last five years, he had, nevertheless left his mother in trouble. And she found it difficult to have any sympathy for Mrs. Cass – a woman who raked up distrust and disturbance at every possible opportunity – and yet, there she was, alone, with a fair proportion of her small income cut off. Agnes went with the intention of proposing that Mrs. Cass take a part-time job – there was one vacant at the hall for a cleaner, offered to Agnes herself who had enough to cope with, and she had recommended Mrs. Cass for it and now came to tell her about it.

Such a visit was a bonus to Edwin's mother and she spent it very carefully. First, she got them all in the house, once inside making a great fuss about her bronchial chest which made a melodramatic entry the instant she bent down to pick a slip from the floor. Then she insisted on their having tea and, more confident of her power seeing the unease of the mother and thinking she was forcing unease on to the daughter by the revenge contained in this triumph, brought Agnes into the kitchen and imposed on her the grease-thick, slop-pailed squalor which she instantly bemoaned as evidence of her abandoned state. Further, she would have the baby fed and Agnes assented to this, though it was she herself who boiled the milk, sterilised the bottle and teat and administered the feed.

So the three women sat in this lonely cottage, cold rain pelting against the windows, a poor, slumped fire drawing in the melancholy of the day rather than fighting it off, Mrs. Cass now on the arm of the sofa, now picking her way over her debris, one hand clutching the lapels of her quilted dressing-gown, her face leering with contentment. Agnes made the offer as tactfully as she could, but not even the Lieutenant of the County could have brought such news and got away with it. That was what a son did for you! Left you in the dirt as soon as he got a bit of money, as soon as he got fancy ideas. His own mother who had come to this bloody rotten hole to be hidden away because he was ashamed of her, unable to get any entertainment, she had just stayed because he wanted her to be near him and now he had dumped her just like his sodding father. You were lucky he

166

didn't marry you, she said to Janice, because he could be sweet as sixpence if he wanted to but that for show and nothing else – once married, he would have treated you just as he treated me. Like dirt.

No, she said finally to Agnes. No. She was going to White-haven and if Edwin threw her out when she got there, she would find a place to live and at least be in a town where there would be a bit of life. And if he thought he was going to get away with what he had done – he had another think coming! And one more thing; she would be glad to get away from this hole because the gossiping against her had made her sick. Everybody wanting to know everybody else's business and sticking their noses in where they weren't wanted. She had a bellyful of Crossbridge, it was nothing but an ignorant dead-end. She was used to this. And so would Janice be before she was much older. A good-looking girl like her didn't want to be stuck away for ever in this dump. She predicted that Janice would be out of it before the end of the year; Janice was like she herself was, game for a bit of fun.

No, she repeated, as, reluctantly, she showed them out – that is, blocked their progress to the door until Agnes was forced to slip round her – you could tell the people at the hall what to do with that job of theirs. She'd had enough of being a servant. That was what was wrong with the whole bloody lot of them in Crossbridge, she shouted, as they went up the hill, they were servants because they knew no better and never would. Again she stood outside her gate, screaming into the wind, threatening to run after the two women whose brisk step was thus made to appear like a scurry.

Agnes thought she was right to go to Whitehaven; even though it would be hard on Edwin, it would be much harder for her if she stayed alone. In speaking of her, she never once said 'poor woman'; in fact her single remark on Mrs. Cass's character was derogatory; there was no need, she said, to flaunt your troubles like a beggar. When she returned to her own cottage, she recited all to Wif and agreed that she would go down once more to offer her the use of Mr. Robson's cattle-truck for her move, Mr. Robson's permission having first been sought by Wif himself – Robson proffered this aid unfailingly – and Wif was to travel with her to see her settled in, Agnes to follow a week or so later on one of her infrequent trips to the town to make sure there was nothing she had forgotten.

Janice had felt no repugnance, no pity and no fear. She had come because her mother had asked her, stayed until it was time to go and left with neither distaste nor pleasure.

Her mind seemed to have been sucked of its resilience. The more so by contrast with Richard who was enjoying the teaching and replete, each day, with his day's work. Though it might not be the work itself so much as the fact of having worked which cheered him, that was irrelevant. To all appearances, he was exuberant and Janice longed herself to be ignited into his enthusiasm yet could not be.

Janice attended to being a wife, now moving so slowly through the empty days that the cries of her daughter scarcely reached her and the concern of her mother escaped her blank eye, unseeing as she stared ahead, at nothing.

CHAPTER TWENTY-TWO

One evening, a Saturday, was really spring-like and after supper they went to the pub, had a few drinks, played dominoes. Janice knew everyone and was known well by them, but until now her position in relation to others in the village – that is, the position she had made for herself since adolescence – had been uncertain. She had little to say to most people and granted few of them even that little. Her attitude had, not unnaturally, earned her the reputation of being snobbish, strange in the head and with something to hide. The mysterious baby – coming out of the unusual action of going to Carcaster College – and the sudden marriage – coming out of the expected climax to Edwin's courtship – followed by this unremarkable domesticity, had confirmed all the more extreme opinions and promoted many new theories. Her arrival, just noticeably pregnant, in the pub itself on a Saturday night salted the theories very strongly. The manner of her evening threw most of them out of joint. For, encouraged, perhaps, at being on firmer ground than Richard, she played the guide to him and, in doing so, opened to a friendliness with the customers which made one or two of the most inventive theorists throw their previous elaborations overboard immediately and conclude that she was a secret drinker, the alcohol clearly bringing her out to best advantage and this fact having been kept quiet as Agnes would not approve and the College, if it had been discovered, would not take her on.

That she should go so far as to enter the domino school was extraordinary. That part of the darts room was the kernel of the pub, confident, intimate and vociferous. All women were challenged to 'join in'; few and only the most self-assured accepted and then for no more than one or two hands. Janice stayed at the board for an hour, sharing a hand with Richard, clearly excited and able, through this excitement, to encourage that sort of enjoyment which produces, in the minds of the participants, gossip already spinning into 'That night she came down here, I was . . .' And when Time was called, she took them all through with her into the other room where the accordionist played on for half an hour, songs that everybody knew, everybody singing together, a curious semi-drunken serenity on most of their faces, more like Christmas Day than a Saturday in spring.

She ran back to the cottage ahead of Richard, who let her go. He was disturbed rather than elated. For there had been a desperate flirtatiousness in her which he had seen in other women but never before in her. In them, it had presaged a war – to victory, defeat; whatever it was, a decisive action. In any other company but one consolidated to caution through co-habitation, he guessed that she would have provoked more than one attempt to get off with her and he would somehow have been dragged into a fight to prevent it. She was saturated with a recklessness which the pub had been totally unable to assuage.

Inside their own cottage the fire poked into life, drinks not coffee, out, she turned on the wireless, fiddling with the dial until she found Radio Luxemburg going full belt through the pop tunes; and, having pushed back furniture, she began to dance, impelling Richard to join her, yet not allowing him to hold and hardly to touch her. As soon as a tune came on which was not hard or thudding with rhythm, she raced across to the radio and switched to another, louder station.

Disturbed as he was, Richard himself grew intoxicated at this, his own pleasure in jumping about to music being called in to overlay the chill which entered him, doubting the sanity of her mood. Since his reaction against her showed not the slightest signs of influencing her to stop what she was doing, he joined her, out of pleasure but also out of a determination to be with her. Soon he, too, was gyrating in the way which, on observing *her*, he had found a little ridiculous, too strained, too sophisticatedly, awkwardly, clumsily primitive and somehow an affront to the small space of the kitchen, to the evening they had spent, as incongruous as tom-toms would have been beating out a voodoo evensong in the small stone church. Moreover, though she danced well, she was straining so hard to beat herself that savagery replaced suppleness, no delight but violence. She jumped on a chair and landed in a crouch at his feet, throwing back her hair as she stretched herself back, back, shaking her belly, her arms quivering; she went from the chair on to the table and leapt from that, using his shoulders only as a break-fall, lifting her hands off them instantly to swing her head low across the floor, her hair swishing the carpet. Again she jumped and Richard realised what she might be trying to do, but before he could believe it she had jumped once more, landed awkwardly, writhed clutching her stomach in agony. The doctor was called; she had a miscarriage.

CHAPTER TWENTY-THREE

It took Agnes longer than she thought to find Edwin's new place and she had already decided that it must be the five o'clock bus she had to catch back to Crossbridge, not the three o'clock she usually took on her Hospital Help days. The difficulty was that Agnes would never dream of taking a bus within a town and Edwin's garage was on the outskirts which she knew scantily, almost all her activity being in the centre.

When she did find it, she was tired out. It was a hot early summer day and the last part of the journey had been uphill, past shanty shops and amputated terraces screening allotments and slag heaps which went down to the sea. The sea itself was more grey than blue but still it shone under the sun, tempting for bathers as the coal dust wafted along the streets, but barred to them here by a coastline which was slimy beaches and dirty rocks; to swim you had to go down to St. Bees whose cliffs soared out a few miles south of Whitehaven's port, or even further, to Seascale where there was sand. There were no ships and the port was still, only a railway engine shunting along dock-rails. Agnes had been born around here when there were pits every few hundred yards, but now they had been closed down and their works stood like abandoned siege engines, the attack having been given up. She had no nostalgia for the area.

Edwin's garage stood on its own. On one side a few small shops ended with a Second-Hand Outfitters then there was a gap which served as a cars' graveyard; on the other, a cinema, boarded up, began a row of large terrace houses which had long ago been turned into bed-sitting rooms hired by a few bachelor labourers, fewer prostitutes and seven West Indian families – the only coloured settlement in the town. Edwin's was a low-built garage with no gaudy petrol pumps to advertise its function nor any exterior activity at all. The roof jutted out at the front and threw down a long shadow which ran along the ground, back into the garage itself whose doors were wide open and black. Like a little turret glued on to a child's toy, there rose, above the garage at the back, the living quarters.

This was Agnes's first visit – much later than she had intended, but Janice's accident had kept her more at home than she could have expected. The rumour was that Edwin was doing very well; Billy Munn had gone to see him and found him 'knee-deep in it', 'up to his eyes in it', 'a bellyful of work he had there', and she had been pleased, though not surprised. Mrs. Cass had set off for her son and the report on that was that she was living in a room near the docks, though whether supported by Edwin or not, no one knew. The gossip was that she wandered around like a twenty-year-old, painted and powdered, in and out of every pub along the quayside.

Looking at the black hole, Agnes shivered, but that, far from intimidating her, gave her the impetus she needed to go in. Edwin was at the back of it, crouched over an axle, the welding-torch splintering flames over it, his gauntleted hands and helmeted face-guard giving him the appearance of a mythical mechanic, set alone to do a task which would amaze the world. She waited until he had finished what he was doing and then moved to him. He came across to her immediately, pulling off his gloves, pushing back his face-guard.

"Mrs. Beattie!" He smiled. "Well, well, well. I thought you were never going to get to see us."

"Hello, Edwin. I've been meaning to come but – you heard, did you?"

"Yes. She all right now?"

"Yes. She's very down about it, you know. It's a terrible

171

thing to happen to anybody. But – well I think she's going through the worst of it now. It can only get better."

"That's good."

He stood, awkwardly, and Agnes had time to see how the few months of independent work had altered him. He was even paler, the bones of his face, which had always been prominent, now razoring against the skin; his hair was dry and appeared thin, flopping down listlessly about his ears; eyes which had been sunken were now deeply socketed, almost clenched and closed in the grip of the bones below and above them. His nails were bitten so far back that the pad of the fingers grew back over them, and his hands were filthy. More than anything, however, he looked driven to exhaustion.

"Would you like some tea, Mrs. Beattie? I generally get my lad to brew up at this time of day but he's away taking something back."

"I'd just love some, Edwin. But don't let me interrupt. I can make it for you. Where are the things?"

"Well ... I usually have it down here, Mrs. Beattie, but we can go upstairs – it's a bit rough here."

"No, no, no. Let's do as you usually do. I never have drunk tea in a garage before. Ah! This the ring? Where's the tap?"

Taking the kettle, she bent down over a tap which grew two feet out of the ground and spurted water so violently that her shoes were swamped. There were two brown tin mugs beside the gas-ring, a jam-jar of sugar and half a pint of milk; the tea had a caddy which she herself had given to Edwin on his setting up house in Crossbridge.

"How are you then, Edwin?"

"Oh, not so bad. A bit pushed at times, you know. But all right."

"They tell me you're doing very well."

"They know nothing at all about it! But I'll tell *you*, Mrs. Beattie, I *am* doing well. In fact, I'm thinking of maybe taking another fella on."

"That's marvellous. Edwin. I think that's really grand. So you are doing well."

"I've got to build fast or else I'll just fold up on this site. There's one big garage in the middle – and all the little ones *say* they can do welding, you know – and they're all in the centre. I'm the only little garage specialising. It was lucky I could bring my customers, some of them anyway, with me. Thanks." He took the tea offered and continued, talking more about his business to Agnes than he had done to anyone, grabbing the opportunity. "You see, it would be safer if I just built up slowly – but if I do go slowly, I'll just get into the way of doing that for the rest of the time and never be able to shift. I work myself, well – about sixteen hours a day, sometimes only fourteen – no days off – and I try to deliver at least two days before the customer expects it. I give him a shorter estimate than he would get anywhere else anyway (*and* I quote a lower price) and then I send him a card – I've had some printed with my address on and everything – telling him that it's 'now ready'. You see. He's surprised at that and I reckon he'll tell people about it. It's like a bonus. Same with the price. I estimate *below* what I know other garages charge – and then I knock a bit off that as well if I can. I only do it if I can knock off a bit that he can notice. Then he talks about it again. Well, you can only keep this up for so long, particularly as the price business can work against you, because people don't always like things cheaper – except repairs, you see – but even so, this means I have to keep labour costs right down. The lad I've got – he's on minimum apprentice wage, learning the trade, and I've been lucky because he's quick at it. What I need now is a fella who's just finished and willing to take a chance. You see, I would give him certain parts of the work and pay him a commission. That would get *him* going. There's plenty of work going in this business, it's just a matter of getting as much as you can at the start, getting established while your overheads are small – then the thing should snowball on its own. These next six months are very important to me."

"Well, if we had a car, we would send it straight to you."

"I've already heard what you've been saying," Edwin smiled. "Arthur Carter was in last week and he says 'Agnes's telling everybody to go to Edwin – even if they get a flat tyre she thinks Edwin should be paid to blow it up'. Thank you for that. But you would support me whatever happened, wouldn't you, Mrs. Beattie?"

Agnes was uncomfortable at such a direct appeal. "Now that doesn't mean you can just go off and do as you like, Edwin. You can't run around the streets terrifying the life out of everybody with that welding-gun of yours. I wouldn't support that."

"But I know you would support just about anything else. I

173

am glad you came, Mrs. Beattie. I was expecting you and then I knew that you would be restricted after what happened to Janice. *Is* she really all right now?" He had to be sure.

"Yes, Edwin. She's depressed about it, of course, but that's normal enough. She blames herself for it though – and it couldn't have been more of an accident, Richard says. They were just playing about and she jumped off a chair and fell badly. It knocked her back a bit, though."

"And how's Paula . . . and Wif . . . and Mrs. Jackson . . . and did Billy Munn . . . ?"

She was pleased to give him the gossip, taking, from the interest in it, confidence that he had not changed, she thought, not *really* changed, which, to Agnes, was the most important thing of all. 'He's changed' or 'She's changed a lot' were almost invariably statements of distrust only rarely followed by praise or enthusiasm, mostly concluded with a full stop which did not conclude at all but pointed firmly towards further conclusions, all of them disturbing. But Edwin had not *really* changed.

Agnes wanted to offer to do out his rooms – in her bag there was a duster and furniture polish and scrubbing soap – but whenever she hinted at that, he deflected her, and when she stated it outright, he dissuaded her, saying that he preferred to talk to her the short time she was there and anyway, he wanted no one to see those rooms; his things had simply been dumped there on the first evening, the bed was rarely made, greasy frying-pan and half-opened boxes – that was all part of his past life which he had maintained so scrupulously at Crossbridge and which now demanded no energy from him. It was appearance only.

He did not want Agnes to leave. As she stood there his mind, repeatedly invaded by the knowledge of the work yet to do that day, kept reorganising the efforts he would make after she was gone and yet he did not want her to be gone. It was as if he wanted to draw out of her every last bit of friendly sustenance, not only sufficient to salve the loneliness of the past few months but enough to store away for the solitude which faced him.

When she had to go, he insisted on driving her down to the bus station. His lad had returned by then and could look after the garage for a few minutes – for hours or days were he to employ all the instructions given him by Edwin – and Edwin relished the protests Agnes made against his generosity. He told himself that he would do anything for her.

174

They reached the bus station.

"And your mother," said Agnes, tentatively, "is she all right?"

"Yes."

"I'm glad. Well, Edwin, I'll have to make for that bus. Wif'll be miserable without his tea. He just goes into his shed, you know. He won't eat if I'm not there to make it for him."

"I know." He leaned across her and opened the door. "Will you – you will tell Janice I was asking for her."

"I will."

"Thank you."

He watched her walk slowly across to the station, arms hanging with heavy baskets, her step slow, but dainty, just as her coat, though very old, seemed, to Edwin, special, as her face, though worn and, he thought, more tired than usual, was still as delicate as if it had led a shuttered life. If only she had been his mother.

He set off back, and the moment he turned away from her, he found anger against his own mother. Oh yes, she had turned up – at eight o'clock one night with a lorry-load of stuff – and he had been forced to take her in and then forced to pay her to get out. He knew about her place down at the docks because he went there, as he had once gone to the cottage, to pay her to keep out of his way. He resented this so much that it almost choked him to think of it. This time there was no feeling of duty to salve the cut of having to give her money. He paid her to stay away because, had he not done so, she would have caused trouble. That she had so ruthlessly taken advantage of his present vulnerability and made him go back on his word never to give her another penny – that she had won – this almost suffocated him with fury, but he bided his time, unable to do anything else. And the once she had trailed up to see him had been the one and unexpected afternoon when his former boss's daughter had visited him. And the mother had come tearing and larding in, drunk, beating her breast about the 'deadness' of the town she found herself confined in by the trickery of her son who wanted a slave to keep his house but *she* was not going to do it. Bewildered, the woman had run away.

Janice would not have run, he thought. Janice would have laughed or at least given as good as she got. He thought of Janice so often that he had come to accept it as nothing special, nothing particularly to be noticed, it was like his business, always on his mind, but Agnes's visit recharged the ferocity of his thoughts and he groaned aloud at his loss as he skidded the car to a stop on the dusty crest of the unprepossessing hill of which his shanty garage was the crown.

Agnes had recognised that Edwin's love for Janice had not retreated and she sighed over it on the bus going back. But there was no use in being depressed about it, she thought. Richard was a good man, and he was Janice's choice. If only that choice had not come out of the hopelessness she had seen on her daughter's face when she had announced it to them. But the choice was made.

When she got back she found, as anticipated, that Janice had offered to make her father's tea but that offer had been refused. She was happy in that, finding in it the reassurance which predictability produces. Richard returned from school and came in to say hello, bringing Paula with him, reluctant, it seemed, to return too quickly to his own house but, as soon as he himself became aware of this reluctance, standing up to go there.

Paula was put to bed, after sploshing and shrieking through her bath, slithering off her mother's knee like a fish as the attempt was made to dress her for sleep, flailing in Janice's arms as, finally, she was carried up the stairs, as reluctant to leave the day as the light itself that summer evening.

Silently, Richard and his wife ate their supper and then both prepared for the long interval before their day ended. Prepared to ride the silence which had settled after the 'accident', now punctuated by regrets, occasionally soothed by mutually conciliatory chat or resolution. Now that there was no reason for her child not occupying the centre of her life, Janice found herself relying entirely on its appetites for her daily rhythm and that was shaking her worse than anything had done.

Richard picked up a book and looked at the wall. Outside was still light and warm, quiet and undisturbing; they could have gone for a walk, gone fishing, even reached one of the lakes in time to take out a boat, worked in the garden as Wif and Mrs. Jackson were doing – but they sat, each pretending to read and observing that the other was not doing so, avoiding the questions which would prick the silence for fear they might burst it into argument.

His main concern was to watch that Janice did not slide into such a sullenness as would make it impossible for him to follow her. Both were aware of the purpose behind the accident but, whereas Richard had deferred his shock to look after her, Janice embraced hers, so tenaciously that she seemed to want to nourish it.

There he was, married, with a child not his own but one he loved, a wife he loved, whose parents he loved, in a place he loved. Yet the word 'love' slapped his ears damply. There was only apprehension in him. He had freed himself of his self-consciousness but this struggle with Janice was forcing it on to him again. He feared it.

"If you would like to go out for a drink, we can," he said.

"No. No thank you. I'm not going there again."

"We could go to the other place."

"No."

"Is anything wrong?" he asked, after the pause.

"No. Why should there be?"

"I thought you looked a bit down."

"No."

"Look, Janice. If there *is* anything you want to say, say it. It's better."

"Is it?"

"Yes. It is."

"Why?"

"Oh hell! Well, maybe it isn't. But at least if you told me what was wrong, I wouldn't be jumpy all the time. Not that I could put it right. But at least I would *know* about it instead of being in this humiliating position of having to guess all the time."

"Guess what?"

"What's wrong with you, for Chrissake?"

"Nothing's wrong with me."

"Good. Full circle. But our circles are empty, not full. And anyway, I don't think that circles are the best shapes for talk. Lines would be better."

"Don't run away into your nervous clever-cleverness again," said Janice calmly. "I hate to see you like that."

"Ditto."

Janice put down her book and looked directly at him. Paused. He deserved explanation. "I feel so greedy for everything, it's terrible," she said. "I can't be satisfied with anything. I'm so selfish that I daren't do one act because I'm afraid that that will lead to a great rush of selfishness. And I know I'm dragging you down. I hate to do that. But I – honestly – I can't stop this feeling that I'll be burnt up if I don't consume myself in my own

177

wants. All I am is wants, Richard. And I don't know what I want."

"Yes, you do." Richard calmed, even though his hand trembled taking a cigarette, it was the shiver of relief. "You know very well what you want. You always have done. And I think I know something of how badly you want it. It's Greed." He smiled. "I must have passed it on to you."

"What are *you* going to do now?" Janice asked.

"This minute?"

"Now. Now that you have a job, you're married and settled. What're you going to do?"

"Try to make it work, I suppose. Do you expect more?"

"Don't *you*?"

"No. Not at the moment. I'm content with what is here."

"Are you?"

"Oh, don't ask that in such a *profound* way! Yes. I am."

"I know that you'll get fed up, Richard," she said. "You've already had to cut off so much to stay here. I watch you – you force yourself to read for those long stretches, you force yourself to walk – nobody walks like that over those hills; they stop and look around; to you, it's a forced march. You're cutting yourself down, Richard."

"No I'm not. I'm doing less, that's all."

"You're not doing anything. You're still trying to find out how you might do things. And you won't even talk about *that* any more. When was the last time you told me about 'a better way to live'?"

"Oh God! Whenever it was, it wasn't long enough ago."

"Are you backing out?"

"No! I'm trying to forget the talk and do something. You seem to think it isn't enough. I do."

"That's because you've confused action with achievement. Why don't you just *do* things – and bugger the consequences?"

"If it doesn't lead to anything, it's movement, not action. And bugger that. You can move in a room just as much as on a new continent."

"But you ."

"Look! Somebody called Thompson came to me at the school yesterday. He's a Labour councillor – youngish, thirties; and he wanted me to join the party and work for it. At first I thought – what the hell, what difference would it make to anyone, I hate the de-socialised Labour Party probably more than the Tories by now. Anyway, I couldn't give a sod for any of them. And then I saw that that didn't matter. He did it because he thought it could better be done by people like him than by others."

"So you agree to work a useless system."

"It isn't useless, exactly. It's difficult to feel, let's say, enthusiasm for it." He smiled. "But yes, I'm going to do some things for him."

"That's exactly what I mean about cutting yourself down to fit in with an idea. You'll end up as dutiful as a church warden. There *is* a pious streak in you. Why didn't you take David's offer? I saw the letter – it *was* addressed to both of us. Why didn't you tell me about it?"

"I don't want to do that again."

"Why not? It's only Carcaster. Not much further than you go now. And *I* think you would look nice on the telly as well."

"I don't want to."

"You mean – you would like to but you don't think it's proper and so, measured by this stupid divine scale, you've convinced yourself that you don't want to – even though you know that you would enjoy it."

"I don't mean that at all. You are very confident of my feelings. I wish *I* was half as confident."

"I wish you did things that you would do with confidence, that's all."

"Don't you realise that there is nothing better than anything else until you yourself have found the relish of your own life? There was a man on the magazine who once spent an entire evening telling me about the development in printing methods since the introduction of the glossies. Most people would have bored me and themselves insane. But he didn't. He was delighted at his work – I knew that I was not. There are people like that everywhere. They have somehow got that central – oh God! Off again!"

"Go on."

"No."

"Go on!"

"You have to know where you stand. You have to be able to say 'Here I stand.' The best of all is to *have* it said, to *be* it, without declaring it. But if you don't have that – then it is the only thing to work for."

"I know." Janice hesitated. "But I'm not a stoic, I don't ever

179

want to be one – and I think you do. I don't want to endure, just to endure; I want to do what I want and enjoy it."

"Want. Want. Want. Three wells make a river. I wonder what three wants make."

"Richard, I want to go back to Carcaster in the autumn. Please let me."

"So that's what you want. Still."

"Yes. I'm sorry."

"Don't be sorry."

"I am. What else can I be?"

She began to make the arrangements in the following week. Agnes was shocked and raged at her daughter – to no effect – and so she locked up her anger and agreed that she would look after Paula through the week, though Richard insisted that he would take her in the evenings.

Janice became more cheerful immediately. Wif had never seen her so pliant and gay as she was that summer. She grew more healthy under the sun and was more of a daughter to him than ever before. Sometimes she would grow anxious and say "I won't go", "I didn't mean it", "I can't leave you" –and Richard would reply "You must". By the end of the summer, his money was almost done and he found no alternative but to teach again. None of his songs had 'done anything': he had not the inclination nor perhaps the confidence to write articles again. He would teach in the same town, not changing his school to follow her. That was an implied condition.

Janice went to Carcaster in Mr. Robson's van. Richard saw her settled in and then returned to the cottage. Unable to bear Agnes's company at first, for he knew that she found neither kindness nor reason in the action of either Janice or himself, he went out and helped Wif build the wall in the garden. They worked together until it grew dark.

CHAPTER TWENTY-FOUR

Janice had never felt better. She found that she had a little over from her grant and from what Richard sent her to buy some clothes – which had never interested her before, nor did they now except as ribbons proclaiming her independence. She wore them because she felt so cheerful that everything about her, her walk, her chat, her work, even the clothes, was forced to match this feeling.

She was in a position of peculiar freedom at Carcaster. There had been no trouble about coming back; indeed The Authorities had fallen over their own rules in the rush to display liberality and generosity: she had asked to read English Literature and, although the list was full, she was welcomed in; she had discussed living accommodation, not wanting to stay in the College buildings, and had immediately been encouraged to take a tiny flat near the College – and a special grant-in-aid had been raked up from some fund to help her out. This latter demand was not a spoilt insistence but necessary, she felt, because of all those who knew of her reason for leaving – those now in their third or fourth years but still with the memory to pity and nudge. Not that she felt uncomfortable often, but still, she wanted to avoid the possibility of pity and particular attentions. Then again, as a wife and mother single among the randy flowers of England's youth – it was felt she needed a certain protection and the flat gave it her.

This flat became much dearer to her than either her own home or her mother's. She decorated it very simply and spent as much time there as she could, rushing back from the lectures to make herself some coffee, take a few apples, put a record on the second-hand gramophone Richard had bought for her, and then, curtains drawn, reading light only on, she would sit deep in the large armchair, drawing up her legs, reading, intoxicated by the freedom of it all.

That the freedom was, in part, founded on the service of others bothered her occasionally but did not disturb her. She knew that Paula would be well taken care of by Agnes, and the more she considered it, the more she came around to her initial opinion – that it was Agnes's duty – Agnes who had persuaded her not to have an abortion. Agnes who had said, repeatedly, that she would look after the child and be glad to do so. And now that the baby had passed her first year, there was not so much work in it, especially as she was beginning to walk and the cottages were ideally safe for her to potter around. While Richard – staying in Crossbridge, that was his business – again she felt a qualm at the harshness of her dismissal, but again that was mitigated by the consideration that Richard had freely made his own choice.

This freedom seemed to curl around her every minute of the day. Not to have to listen to voices she did not want to listen to; not to have to follow a routine of needs and sleep and shopping imposed by others; not to be confined in the radius of other's needs. And freedom To. To rove as she wished through Carcaster, to go to the pictures, to read, to laze, to dream – Crossbridge became a dour knot in her past which the plane of her life had mercifully slid over. Above all, she was free to keep to herself; she made no friends and treated acquaintances with caution. In fact, the person she saw most consistently, and even him not very regularly, was Richard's friend, David, now in charge of North-West TV.

Her flat was near the Castle. Carcaster Castle, built by Henry II, put in its present shape by Henry VII and renovated at each Border War since, stood at the north of the town on a picture-book site. To the south, east and west, the ground sloped down easily and yet not so gradually that the domination of the walls could be dismissed; to the north was a sheer rocky drop down to a flat plain and river. The town was not large – about 70,000 – and the Castle, the Cathedral – with its beautiful thirteenth-century windows – the Tudor Town Hall, the Courts, the City Gates, and, from the Victorian Age, the Railway Station, the two red-brick Hotels, the Museum and the College – these civic structures tempered its whole mood. Moreover, spreading through a large part of the southern end was a large market bringing farmers, lorries, beasts, auctioneers, dealers, all the business of the countryside, into the place. Such new estates as there were had been displaced outside the old city limits, encamped on what once were quartering grounds for resting armies, and encamped there with about as much care for comfort and grace as the most sullen army tents; awaiting, it seemed, the invention of a new bulldozer which would shovel away the lot of them and build houses in place of the barracks they resembled.

In the town there was, of course, the juke-box circuit; the cellared electronic fruggers sucking suspect cigarettes, the flip side of everything from the swinging age – and it was this world which David had taken over, become bored with, and elaborated for his own sake, all in a couple of months since arrival. But Janice was not interested to follow him there; for there, too, was the herd, just as herd-like as the Institutes, Rotarians, Churches, and Social Activators. Maybe . . . sometime . . . but not now, now she wanted to be on her own, and the Parks, the older parts of

182

the town – these, perhaps because they were dead, were visited only by people 'putting in a couple of hours', never concerned to live there or conceiving that they could get life from there, these places, with their forlorn utility, their withdrawal from the functionary world, cosseted a desire for solitude but not as the hills around Crossbridge, nothing imposed or stamped on – they permitted it, kindly.

The life she now led was one she had believed she would lead; it was, to her, the life she was fitted for and it was the *other* which appeared unnatural. She saw no merit in obligations, none at all, and although her closeness to her parents had led her to accept many, she had done so for peace; not from any feeling of duty inevitable. To Janice each person was entirely on their own from the moment they saw the world in themselves. That burgeoning of feeling which had led her to marriage now appeared as a digression, not a weakness, for that would have implied that it was strong to be alone whereas she thought it essential to be alone.

There were days in Carcaster, mornings, afternoons, in the mild autumn, when she went up to the Castle, because few people went there except on a Saturday, and walked round the ramparts or across the large courtyards or dawdled in the small Military Museum, and it was as if every single thing she saw and touched had such direct effect on her senses that she became heavy with the weight of the external world. The brown stone brought into her mind the brown of winter heather, the brown of the hills, the labourer's corduroy, the muddy tracks, the lichen-bitten walls of the church, the glow of her own brown-papered room. The clouds rolling above, across the Eden Valley over the Solway Plain to the hills, brought the reflection of the seas they had crossed and risen from and in their grey weight was the substance of her dreams. All colours, the paint-red of the uniforms, the bowed green of the grass in the parks, the plastic tones of the cars and shop-fronts down in Castle Street – all imposed on her, striking the colours of her childhood with such reverberation that the rainbow turned in her mind like the Big Wheel. And the sounds, and the smells, and what she touched and what she tasted – and then, these times, she could scarcely drag herself to her favourite place, a bench in the Cathedral Close.

There her mind would slowly swarm with images and she would indulge them all, leaving her thoughts to madness but pitching that madness on a firm site. Not craziness. The madness

183

of seeing the extremes of things: the absurdity of a woman walking across the close; the comedy of two men with simultaneous briefcases swinging, harried eyes bent to business chattering about the ambitions of life they had metamorphosed into accounts; the lunacy of those old people clinging to the benches with the sun never to come through again that day, their heads nevertheless pecking at the sky for a last reflection; the absorption of a child squatted before a dead flower-bed poking a small fingered hole in the gluey soil to bury a paper-wrapped sweet. She would see all this and more people, more people, and think the world a place where nothing at all mattered, where all were caught with their backs to death, spun around as in those spinning tubs at fun-fairs which pin you to the wall, where each day the act of being was no more than a re-invention, a remorseless will to act, to encompass passion and fear by any business – a hole in the ground or a regular bench – which would serve to take the burden off the mystery and console the dreams by blocking them out.

For to dream alone, to feel, in the world, all that you could feel, to let the fragments cascade into the mind and be unsorted – that was everything, she thought. There were no rules, either of convention or from desire; she did not wish to order, as Richard did, she did not wish to lash reality to a way of life, she did not wish to have a society at all, quite content that it should decay or regrow, or do anything it liked as long as her participation was not called for. That she was fed, clothed and materially supported by the work of others obliged her not one scrap. If the things of life were to hand, she would use them, that was the circumstance in which she found herself, other circumstances might evoke other responses. All that she saw was even, all the ground under snow which might have individual contours but they were hidden – the snow was a condition of life. Whereas Richard wanted to make a choice, could not bear the retreat, the surrender, the abnegation which he saw in such a complete acceptance that all things are mere alternatives among a crowd rushing towards the same leveller which would mock all choice and did, daily; Janice would have there be no choice, none at all. Not that she saw the world as a particularly primitive place, she did not look for nature red in tooth and claw, nor did she sympathise with those who see motives as realities and view life as ceaseless psychological warfare; she merely saw no reason to erect anything, preferring, instead, that the world be images, and she a reflector and hoarder of images, and her life the satisfaction of such images as pleased her, and her ambition ignorant of all rules. If she wanted something, she thought that the deed should run with the wish: regret came when she fell from that purpose.

Richard, she realised, could *feel*, he *knew*, that certain things, certain actions were wrong. The sense of their wrongness impregnated his mind. It was the tepidity of his intelligence, its poisonous involution which prevented him from being able to prove that something was wrong; and perhaps a certain modesty, a distrust of his own experience in relation to his conclusions, this too, made it possible for him to say "wrong". Yet he knew it. Janice did not. As instinctively, she did not. At some stage in her life, she had cast out other people and abandoned herself to her own certainties where right and wrong knew no place, their position being occupied by ambition and will. What she did was her own affair. What anyone else did was their own affair. Totally. If she happened to get mixed up in something, then there were no judgements which applied; only desires, as ephemeral as a day, but as intense as a day. And who would judge a day, right or wrong?

As soon as she reached Carcaster, not gradually, but on the instant she took her flat, the desire she felt for Richard diminished. She no longer wanted him to make love to her and the return at the weekends was the price she paid for having been born as she had been born; in a few years, as few as possible, that too would be paid – she would then be alone for ever. Again, she did not recoil from the memory of their passion; she had been as submerged in it as Richard, and the black bedroom had bound her as wildly tamed as she had never dreamed to be. But now she no longer desired it, preferring, instead, to walk with Paula even and watch the wind go into the winter, tossing the spent leaves across the shrunken grass.

CHAPTER TWENTY-FIVE

One Sunday he persuaded her to come for a walk with him in the morning. He did not enjoy having to persuade her but this time he was determined not to let the short time slide over without some effort to halt, to make a mark on it.

They went up through the fields to the fell-dyke road and then kept to the road, the fields too waterlogged for comfortable walking. This road was quite deserted; not a single bicycle or car passed them; the countryside too seemed deserted, no cows in the fields, no men working, the mountain sheep huddled in some ghyll, out of sight; and the sky, lowering so thickly with grey clouds that they must have been miles deep.

Janice walked about two yards away from him, over-consciously looking straight ahead of her, that atmosphere around her which suggested that if she were spoken to or touched, she would spring away violently or chill the hand which touched her. Richard did not tempt that reaction, but as he walked he could scarcely keep his eyes off her face, scarcely keep his hands from her body. And he thought she realised how much he desired her and titillated that desire by such enticing detachment,

Richard loved her now more than he had ever done. He spent much of the time when Janice was away longing for her to be back, dreaming of what they could do together, merely wanting her with him, to see her, to talk to her. He loved her so much that he had become afraid to declare it.

The first time she had returned from Carcaster, he had proposed to go back with her – not to the job David had offered him but to take a teaching post there.

"If you like," she had said.

And such disenchantment was in those three simple words, such badly concealed resentment, that he knew he could not go. She wanted to be on her own, to make her own way, and if he respected that in himself, he had to respect it in her.

This he had explained at length to Agnes whose bewilderment at the manner of their parting, the "shuttle service", she called it, of their marriage, he had not been able to clear up with all his talk of independence, wishing happiness to the one loved and so on. "Your marriage comes first," Agnes had said – and to that, though he could find a reply. he could give no answer. He had married her to be with her, and he did not follow her away; this contradiction resolved itself only in the struggle to go on as he was doing – it led to no conclusion. "Why don't you just make her stay with you?"

She wore a bright red coat which was wanton on the grainy grey road. The coat was held with innumerable buttons from neck to navel where it flared out to skirted pleats, short, above the knee, and then the mirror-black wellingtons, her hair tousled and honey, the three colours blending so perfectly on her that she moved apart from the landscape, like a painted apparition in a drudging dream. The buttons crept over the line of her breasts, so closely following that line that Richard wanted to open them, to see the nakedness and hold tenderly the white skin heavy in the palm of his hand. Her face, into the wind, was again, as on that day on the lake, milk-white and deepest rose-red, the brow so fine, pale, the cheeks so deeply tinted that nothing it seemed ever had or ever would touch her. It was this inviolability which gave his passion its constant swell.

They went down the hill and under the bridge, past the quarry and on to the brow which overlooked Ennerdale Water. The lake now hissing with clouds and vapours, the wet trees on the steep fells gluttonous with foreboding, the peaks seeming to intone to the clouds, all the colours shifting between blurring browns, molten greys, and a blue which was fathoms dense.

It began to rain, a few large drops plopping on to their heads, long and fat drops which had been suckled in those clouds for miles and came first, the favourites; you could see them hit the road, each making an individual splash and sound and, as they broke, breaking the ground-hugged smell of the earth so that the soil's pungency was released. Faster they came and smaller, the clouds shifting open as they relieved their weight, and cream-backed light streamed down in intersecting rays. Then the way open, the rain sluiced down.

Richard and Janice ran over to the abandoned iron-ore works which was still sufficiently roofed to give shelter. They laughed at their soaked state and took off their coats. Richard looked around for something with which to build a fire, but there was nothing.

The works were on a knoll from which Ennerdale Water was hidden. The shaft had been boarded up but someone had burst the boards, and it was deep, had not been filled in. Where they sheltered was under a few boards which had once made up the shed next to the shaft; there were two whole walls left, the other two half-stripped. Looking out, there was nothing but an ordinary wet field, such hill tops as could have been seen in the distance now obscured.

Richard put his arm round Janice and then kissed her. His hand went to her breast and from there, eagerly, to her thigh. She pushed him away so firmly that he rolled quite apart from her.

"Why?" he said. It was the first time he had asked her directly.

187

"I don't feel like it, that's all."

"That's obvious."

Why go further, he thought? If she did not want sex, well that was her right. Yet it was impossible not to believe that such a refusal was a refusal of more than her body, and impossible to be married, to love someone without making love to them. Then, not to talk about it at least, to do something about it, that was cowardice, he thought; it was accepting less than there ought to be. To do that was to let circumstances, once more, take control.

"Look, Janice. I know you don't feel like it – and you haven't felt like it much since you – after you lost – did you want that miscarriage? – you did, didn't you?"

"I don't know."

"Yes, you do. I saw you. I saw your eyes just before you made it happen."

"I suppose I did," she said softly. "But I didn't think about it like that – at all. I didn't want another baby – but I didn't expect that pain. I just did it."

Richard nodded. The shudder which he had withheld now disappeared; he no longer dreaded so much what had happened.

"All I want to know is why we don't make love any more. I want to. You don't."

"It's just these last few weeks."

"No 'just'. After you lost the baby – got better – I've been thinking about that – we went back to what we had been before – was that because you knew you were leaving? Why did you marry me, Janice? Why did you want to marry me?"

He was shouting. As always, that made her, who had been anxious under his attack, calm.

"I did. That's all. If you start to dissect these things – all the reasons are everybody's reasons."

"What's wrong with "everybody's reasons"? You loved me – right? That's 'everybody's reason'. You wanted to live with with me – yes? Another reason for everybody. And I loved you, wanted you – all so ordinary, so very ordinary – but what better reason has anybody found? But we skimmed across the word "love", we scampered through the "living together": we acted as if we had no reasons but convenience."

"Maybe it was convenience. But I love you, Richard; or I don't love anyone. And if I wanted to live with anyone, it would be you I would choose. What more do you want? The rest *is* convenience."

"No. I shouldn't have mentioned love. We can't talk about it. Love gives: what we have, takes."

"That isn't true! If I hadn't known you loved me, I would have killed myself. I would have killed myself or killed what I wanted to be. Only that kept me alive then."

"But once resurrected, it was no longer needed, was it?"

"Not in the same way."

"What other way is there?"

"As many as you want. We both have things to do – you here, with the life you are trying to make for yourself – me in Carcaster. Friendship – affection is more important than passion now."

"Affection is a loss, Janice. It is no way to live. It helps pass the time pleasantly, that's all."

"What more is there? If the time passes pleasantly then we can ignore the time and do the things we want to do. If it doesn't – all our energy is taken up fighting with it. Can't love be useful just helping to pass the time pleasantly?" She paused. "You want me to be honest, don't you, Richard? Well, I think that you felt as you say you did, I know it. I did not know that anyone could submit himself to me and I to him in such a way as both were forgotten. I would never have believed it. But it's changed."

"Well?"

"I had to go back to what I'd always wanted to do. I could feel that I wanted to, even when – even when what we did was marvellous. It was there in me to go away. But it was only through your love that I could leave – because I would have shrivelled without it."

"Yes. You are right to go if you want to. There *is* nothing more to say." He hesitated. "Except that I miss you, Janice. And the whole business of living up here in the wilds, and teaching and trotting around for the Labour Party, it all seems so ludicrous now."

"But it isn't ludicrous! You mustn't think so! Don't!"

"No." Or yes, he thought wanly. It little mattered. "I don't. That was just blackmail."

They were silent again for a while and she saw his face harden from the hopeless openness its expression had worn to that baffled deliberation she admired in him so much more than the fixed determination of even the best of the other men she knew. She was afraid a little of his physical power – not that he was violent with her or brutal – but the power he had to make her

189

sodden with warm ecstasy – and afraid, too, of his persistence, for though he would not stop her, he would not stop himself from trying to understand what was good and what was wrong in what they did.

The rain had stopped and the sun came clearly through the clouds, spotlighting the fields it touched, leaving the rest obfuscated by the dreamy vapours of the rain. Janice got up and impatiently beat her red coat, trying to slap out its damp creases. She went to the shaft and pushed her foot against one of the remaining boards. It creaked, loudly, sharply, and a fizzing ooze came from its drenched joints, Holding on to a post which marked its edge, Janice stamped on the board as hard as she could. It split; she stumbled forward as it gave but soon righted herself. Now it swung down the shaft like a half-opened trapdoor. She went round to the other side and kicked away at the spot where it hinged on to the shaft's sides. This held. She picked up a stone and knelt down, striking the wood with the sharp end of the stone, Richard still watching her, smiling at the concentration now bewitching her, the long hair down to her knees as she crouched, striking the obstinate plank.

"It won't give," she said. Stood up. "You try."

"I like it as it is," he said.

"Oh, come on. Here." She threw the stone at him; he jumped aside and it landed near his feet.

"That could have broken my toe."

"See if you can do it."

He ignored the stone and went to her position. The plank was toughly held. The best way to break it would be to jump on it – and that would take you down the shaft with it.

That halted him.

"Can't be done," he said.

She looked at it, made as if to go across to it once more, changed her mind, lost interest in the project entirely and turned to smooth her coat.

"Your feet will get soaked through the grass," she said, looking out, away from him.

He came to her and put his hands on her shoulders. She did not yield but neither did she resist. When he had tried to make love to her the previous evening, she had lain so still that any move would have been an assault; it was as if she had willed herself to drive all feeling from her body, knowing that his hands would grow cold and stumble, his desire would be forced to clambering lust and so would be checked. But now, there was some life there, some pressure under his hand, not the retreat which left the flesh an object.

He pulled her gently towards him and slipped his hands down to her skirt which he unzipped. She turned to him, making a shrug of the movement but not sufficiently cutting to disturb him, and her arms went round his neck, her head leaned on his shoulder as he undressed her.

Yet even though she was soft against his body, though she cried out and bit his foraging lips, he knew that what she really wanted was for it to be over. And there was nothing he could do to call her up to him. Except to want equally.

As he moved away, for a second he knew that her sigh was his – and that sounded in his mind, relieving all the fear he had – for even if it were only for a second, in that one second they had belonged to each other and so there was hope – and he knew that he had found his love, could never leave her, would not wish to.

CHAPTER TWENTY-SIX

"Holy Night, Silent Night
All is calm, all is bright,
Round yon mother, virgin and child,
Holy infant so tender and mild,
Sleep in heavenly peace.
Sleep in heavenly peace."

The two boys waited until the last treble tone quavered around the corner and then the taller of the two took hold of the brass elephant on Agnes's door.

"Knock knock the napper,
Ring ring the bell,
Please give us something
For singing so well;
If you haven't got a penny
A ha'penny will do,
If you haven't got a ha'penny
God bless you."

The door opened and light shone on the cold faces struggling out of the motherly wrapping which padded the throats. They

191

took the few pennies and ran to the top of the lane, to the light, where they counted and divided them and decided it was too early yet to go to the pub. It was better later when the men were "all drunk."

In the black church, moon-rays caught the silken wax of white candles and milked a gleam from the brass. The holly bushed from the windows and a large kissing-ring swung over the porch beside the east door, catching the draught which came down the tower.

Mrs Wilkinson folded and refolded the parcels of gloves and stockings and scarves she had knitted, unable, as ever, to decide whether they looked better rolled in a tubular parcel, which was more practical and used less paper, or in a square, flat parcel, which looked better but then might just be that little bit too showy. One was larger than the rest and that was for John Talbot, a pullover, his wife had died in the summer and he had refused to move in with either of his married daughters, sticking to the house he had been born in, gradually retreating to the kitchen and there mouldering among his untidied mementoes.

There was no snow on the fields and the children knew that there would be no snow, as there had been so much the previous year and you could not be that lucky twice running, but the fields were something white under the old moon as the cars sped between the spiky hedges, their drivers best-suited, hair flattened, off to dance, hoping the other front seat would be warm before midnight.

In the Women's Institute the streamers, well hung, in geometrical cross-patterning, pastels all, blue, pink, pink holding the day, were still taut, after the Old Folks' Tea, the Children's Party, the Institute Social, the Dramatic Society's first and only night, and the Crossbridge Christmas Ball. From that latter, there were still chalk skids on the floor and some one had cracked the portrait of the Queen, but Agnes had not been in to tidy up yet and all that was needed for the New Year's Eve Social was a few more balloons. Those there now, this night, were either popped or shrivelled, dangling from their string unmoving, except one, a green sausage in the centre of the hall, as tight-skinned and shiny as after its first blowing up, ripe for pricking.

Richard had been working overtime for the Labour Party on a scheme suggested by himself – and so left to himself more or less alone to implement – which aimed at renovating a decaying part of the over-optimistically large Labour Club, painting it,

192

fitting in chairs, tables, finding magazines, getting up the subscription for a daily coal fire – and then giving it over to the pensioners. It had not been easy, because there was a lot of pride which Richard did not want to hurt, and would rather leave alone than impair; more important, it was difficult to put across the idea – which he held to throughout, despite opposition which would have had the place a card-carrying cemetery rather than accept any notion tasting so strongly of luxury – the idea that there was this large comfortable room in the middle of the town, with a fire, magazines, daily papers and tea at three-halfpence a cup, biscuits at a halfpenny each – and that was all. A few sets of draughts, dominoes, a fives and threes board, those were the available sports. For the rest, people could do just as they pleased. Through Agnes, as the town was near Crossbridge, Richard had organised a rota of women who came in, seven of them, one each day of the week (another fight to keep it open on Sundays) from ten to eleven in the morning to tidy up. This simple plan had taken most of his free time and energy for two months and even now it needed looking after carefully. What he wanted was to avoid the least, the smallest hint of any sort of coercion and to keep himself anonymous had been hard work, unsuccessful in the end and that made the effort to do so appear foolishly misplaced.

On Christmas Eve Agnes kept open house and the cottage was never empty of people coming in for their glass – Janice seeing that they were all comfortable. Wif mercilessly badgered into a sports jacket and flannels for this occasion and then taken by Agnes to the midnight Mass for which he changed yet again into his suit. Richard and Janice cleared up and drank and talked until the old couple returned, when the presents were opened and Wif, having been to Mr. Law's for the goose and plucked it in his shed, departed to bring it into the kitchen where he set about cleaning it as he always did, at this, the last possible minute "so that the goodness stayed in it."

Richard's mood was volatile. Now happy, now almost tearful, some strange alchemy of joy and sentimentality breaking on a scarcely relaxed tension of foreboding. And Janice he found so poised that he all but complained to her of it: this communal activity, which she now re-entered from the outside, brought up in her all those colours in her character which he most liked – and which, he knew, she could display because the situation was temporary only.

193

But a Christmas Day passed, as good as he could remember, he ate the goose, plucked by Wif and cooked by Agnes, that Janice had embellished on a serving plate, that heaved with roast potatoes, apple sauce, stuffing, turnips, boiled potatoes, bread sauce, while Paula banged her spoon on the tray of her baby chair and the room steamed up for the Queen's Christmas message, somnolently observed.

On Boxing Day morning, with Wif back in normal dress, Richard followed a fox-hunt and came home later in the afternoon, blowing healthy and tired, lifting Janice off her feet and twisting her around the room and then on to Kirkland for the dance where both danced more than they had done on any previous single occasion in their lives. Janice adored Richard in this happy mood, energetic, laughing, always moving to do something. She would never love anyone else, she thought: she would never need to.

And that week through to New Year was marvellous. They made love again. Paula, walking now, toddling along after them on their walks; mountaineering over Richard and the sofa, crying to bed because she had enjoyed the day so much.

On New Year's Eve, David arrived with yet another girl – a "skinny", he called her this time, a model – and the four of them went to the Crossbridge Social where the skinny was a sensation, reaching for the balloons in her mini. "Auld Lang Syne" was sung, the dance went on and they left at about two o'clock, Richard slightly drunk, tightly hugging Janice who responded to him more warmly when he was drunk than when he was sober – control over uncontrol – the muttering again the slow-tread heart-milching words of Burns –"The Korean National Anthem that tune is," David announced, happily, his skinny having become almost boneless, dangling around his shoulder – all of them back into the cottage to welcome in a New Year the "best way", said David, "Scotch *without* tears".

CHAPTER TWENTY-SEVEN

"I resolve to be randy and "invest in all things that give pleasure'," said David. "Especially momentary pleasure. I resolve never to miss the opportunity to doing myself a good turn and I dedicate

myself to discovering new meanings in the word "indulgence".
I resolve to have no regrets, except the sort that titillate the
sense to greater efforts. I believe that man is free and that his
freedom can find no better course than self-satisfaction. Therefore, I bid myself to go out into the highways and byways and
bring in all parts of me considered lame, beggared or ashamed
and set them down to the wedding-feast where myself will marry
my ambition, the toast being Health, Prosperity and Success."
He glanced at Richard, hoping he would rise, then lifted his glass
and imitated a celluloid gangster slugging back his drink.

The four of them were bunched round a high fire, settled for
the rest of the night with bottles of whisky, mince-pies – delightedly produced by Janice to the skinny's horror (her name
was Fiona; on arrival in the room she had sought the largest
armchair, folded up in it like an elfish marionette, and peek-a-
booed at the company from then on) – and David was making it
quite clear that he intended to greet the New Year with words.
Any loss of spirits which might have been noticeable during the
trying period when he had been jostling for the new job had now
vanished, for the job had been embraced –"I'll give myself two
years"– and already the changes he had made had brought more
publicity to NWTV than ever before, while his great news, con-
spiratorially whispered earlier in the evening, was that there was
a good chance of getting one of his programmes nationally net-
worked – for the first time in that region's history. So he was
fairly pleased with himself.

"Oh! One more thing. On the serious side. I resolve to have
stuck such a mighty broom up the tight little backsides of our
Board of Governors that by the end of the year they'll have
offered me an unprecedented – mark that word, Godwin, it'll be
useful for your politics – an unprecedented – it's another of those
"class" words, isn't it? I say un*press*edented, the turds who consider that an education has something to do with sleeping in all-
male dormitories and being banged on the head with the Shorter
Latin Grammar say un*pree*cedented – something to do with
irregular verbs, I bet, though which verb is not irregular given
half a chance, that's what I'd like to know – where was I? yes –
up the governor's backsides – perish the thought, God, *I* would
perish right enough up there, there's one of them, a bishop, I
think he imagines that heaven will be full of hard benches, anyway, he's padding himself up a right treat (as we say in the north),
he's got enough there for two – maybe that's what he wants? the

195

sly old bugger – yes! I resolve to be offered – and to graciously, modestly, unwillingly and all that well-bred jazz, accept – an unprecedented – going, going – rise – gone! There we are, end of New Year resolution. Come on, Fiona, your turn."

Fiona thought. Her long legs unwound and rewound in earnest of that activity. The shapely chin was cupped in the long, rose-nailed hand and her large baby-brown eyes misted to a glamorous texture beneath the expensively scattered brevity of her one-tick-ahead-of-the-minute hair-do.

"I'd like to get on a front page," she said.

"Resolution, Fiona! That's just a wicked little ambition you're proposing. Resolve, like me. Something to do with your character."

"I resolve"– she paused for dramatic effect; it was like playing "I Spy", which she had always hated –"I resolve to be nicer to people."

"Oh Fiona! You'll have Richard round after you if you're not careful. Is that all?"

"Yes."

"Ah! The naïveté of youth. How sweet the name of Bejesus sounds. More Scotch?"

Richard shoved out his glass and watched the sparkling brown trickle splashing up against the sides of the tumbler. Then he looked at Janice and winked; she smiled back.

"You two want to go to bed?" David demanded. "God! I should have thought you would have put lust behind you being married. You ought to have a bit more respect for us unattached people, you know. Anyway, it's disgusting. *My* marriage will mark my retirement from the world of Desire. 'Till death us do part', I'll be saying, meaning, It's death do us join, my chicken. Here, top up." To Fiona who blinked as the whisky came across once more into the glass.

"You know," David began, never, really, having stopped, "Richard", speaking to Janice, "should have taken that job I offered. Not as the regular link-man – we need an honest-looking man for that, and believe me, we've got one – but I would have liked him as the main hard reporter and the introducer of this posh series I'm starting. When he puts his gear on, he's just right, you know. Trustworthy, "frank-looking"– nicely spoken, classless, very flip is our Richard, that is TV flip, that is common denominator flip. Mind you, we would have to keep him in a dark room for a few days to get all that health out of his face. You can

196

have a tan – preferably in January and then everybody knows you're the type who goes skiing but prefers not to boast about it – but you can't be sort of stinking of health from the fields. No, really, I still need somebody for it. Come on."

"No. Don't be such a drag, David."

"Now what d'you make of that?" He turned to Janice, arms-open appeal. "Here I am, giving the lad the chance of a lifetime, to become the hero of the silver screen in regions as far-flung as Dumfries and Barrow in Furness, to be stopped in streets by shopping mothers and toffee-fingered children who will ask for an autograph on a sweet-bag and accept a free invitation to their favourite television programme, to be patted by pretty girls in blue overalls all in the name of make-up and dine with the cream of Cumberland society all in the name of communication – all this, and yet, without so much as a cock-crow to go by, he denies me thrice."

"No can do." Richard shook his head drunkenly. "I'd rather teach."

"He hates it," said Janice, briskly.

"Aha! I thought your silence a little suspicious. Is it one of your duty-free stints you're on again?"

"I quite like some of it, in fact – Janice is wrong."

"You're not for teaching," said David. "I've nothing against it – except the children and the pay, and the sort of work involved – but there are hundreds of people who want to teach."

"I'm one of them. I'll have some more of that whisky if you can let it go for a second."

Soon, Fiona fell asleep, and rather than wake her to send her to bed, David swung her armchair round so that it caught more heat from the fire while, at the same time, shielding the three of them from a full view of her sleeping beauty, posed even there. David wanted to make a night of it. Indeed, there was something merciless about the way he made it plain that a night would be made of it.

"I'll make some more coffee," said Janice.

Her exhilaration had gone quite away. While enjoying David's company when they were alone together in Carcaster, she resented his carping persistence against Richard whose tolerant dissensions she thought too soft. She heard him, still going strongly.

"No it's right. At all the American Colleges now they have what they call "role-playing sessions", I read about one where they had to "role-play" what would happen on the first night of marriage. Straight! And one of them said "Some of the girls really opened up!" It's all mad. But you've got to join them."

She wanted to be back in her room in Carcaster. Thinking of it, she panicked for a second. Someone might break into it while she was away – she had been unwilling to let it, preferring the expense of keeping it on to the thought that someone else might inhabit the place – and she wanted to return, the next morning, to make certain that everything was all right. She wanted to return that instant.

"Everybody painted Christ and now nobody does, that's all," said David. "Remember when we did that story on Sotheby's and they had that day at the end of the season when they sell off all those nineteenth-century acres of canvas – "all done by hand", as the man said – platoons of dead Saviours, descending, ascending, all over the place. You just don't get it any more, Onward Christian Corpses – no more!"

The words, they came through in those excited sentences, prised away from anything which made sense to her. People could talk. What did she mean? People could talk, but the talk denied more than it admitted. There was a flutter in her mind; she understood what they were saying, but somehow, stated, the words bit away the experience proposed. People were more real than their words, but they would not be content, as she herself was, with silence. She took her time making the coffee, afraid to have that silence which she had built up attacked so fiercely when she was so tired.

"No, it's the working classes who have the phoney morality today," David again. "The middle classes are so permissive – except their lunatic fringe, female or syringe, which is resolved to vaccinate everyone with the hormones of god-sent genes from the ghost of England's past – that it's difficult to find a piece of ground that hasn't been mined. I mean, your working-class lad is still a bit worried if he gets his girl in pod, whereas –"

"Oh, for Christ's sake!" Richard interrupted. "You just can't talk in those sort of terms with sense any more. Don't pretend that we can say anything that means anything about class, not at this time of night."

"You can't push it off like that," said David.

"He doesn't push anything off," said Janice, resolved that she had to come in, otherwise the duration of her absence would be remarked on, which was the last thing she wanted. "Hasn't he told you about his Old Folks' Rest Room?"

"No. But I heard about it. "An example to the County," said the *Maryport Evening Star*."

And Janice, having made her entry, but wishing to exit as soon as possible, put down the tray and, just casually enough, said that she wanted to go upstairs to read. She left. In the bedroom, she smoked, knees hugged in white sheets, and stared at the yellow curtains, counting the days until she should return to College.

"I know it's there," said Richard, drowsily, talking to curb his impatience to follow her, "but somehow it's all beyond me. Same old thing. How can you work for people if you haven't a clue what you're working towards? I went on a march once – on *one*, half the way, I stopped at Slough, of course – thus was my crusade nurtured – but what in anybody's name did it do? It was so depressing that the alternative was to get out or to lose your sanity. Maybe to find it, I don't know. But you wanted to say to everybody: "LOOK YOU ARE IN DANGER STOP FROM ACCIDENT OR DESIGN IT DOESN'T MATTER STOP TOTAL EXTINCTION STOP." A World Telegram! And we were led by the great conscience of the Labour Party – who voted for nuclear weapons to be retained as soon as they got to power. Oh, they said, we do that only to stay in power. But what the hell has that do do with it? They took a vow, let's say of chastity, and then went and poked every whore in the district in the name of hygiene. So. If people cannot rouse themselves about their own destruction – what is there? What? You help to get an Old Folks' Club going – and maybe to want or attempt to do more is vainglory – but to what end? I'm not panicking about the Bomb – but shouldn't I be? Shouldn't everyone be worried by it? And in so far as they aren't, how *can* they find the resources or whatever to worry about anything else?"

"You've been on your own too long," David replied, enjoying Richard's confusion.

The coffee, undrunk, grew cold and the fire, having glued itself in a canopied heap, shuddered down into the grate, waking Fiona who blinked entrancingly and would have snuggled back to sleep then and there had not David prodded her up to bed, returning to state that he "preferred it in the mornings in winter, anyway". The remark smelled of over-use and Richard regarded a little sourly his privacy being comandeered in the name of some sort of therapy for his friend; for David very self-consciously loosened the tie and kicked the Cuban heels over the traces of

199

young executive responsibility and overblew his attitudes in a way which was meant to indicate a contempt for what he was reacting against, but unfortunately that contempt ran into his present attitudes and was offensive. He was on a real "chatting" jag.

Richard's thoughts swirled around behind the words that he and David pushed across to each other, the thoughts so potent that the words seemed pawns, the thought so distended with nostalgia and uncertainty that the words seemed the only thing solid about him.

At one stage they decided to go out for a stroll, opened the door, found the night cold, and returned to the ashy grate and dwindling whisky. The greed for company which had been at the centre of Richard's impulse to see out the night in this way sickened, and he was unhappy at the feebleness which made him grab what he was leading his life to do without.

"No," said David with considerable emphasis, "you can't just go on ignoring things. You're trying to put the clock back. And it's an alarm. Nobody can do that. Nobody should want to. And it isn't as if you're doing anything wild up here; I mean, you're doing nothing that hasn't been done before. You're trying to be middle-aged, that's all. You've got some idea of "maturity" in your head, I bet. Well, maturity's finished. Believe me. All that is over. You go as far out as you can or you perish. It's no good planting your behind on the collected volumes of the Renaissance and talking about beauty and a balanced life or whatever they talked about; once you've cracked the living barrier – as most of us in *our* position have, i.e., I before 'ee except at sea, we aren't afraid that we can't make a living, we aren't afraid that there are wonders of the world we shall never see, we feel that we can knock along quite easily – once that has happened, then you find that the spirit or drive of *this* hangover age is towards what's new. And what I'm suggesting is that if you don't recognise that, if you don't play that and keep on looking for New this and that, then however hunky-dory the world might seem, you're missing the point of your own lot and, what's more my friend, let me predict that all will lose its savour because it's in the Newness of things that the excitement now lies – and to miss the excitement of your own times is such a shame."

"All you're saying is that it's better to scamper after every new fashion that pricks up its ears," said Richard. "That's always been happening. Nothing new. And what are these New

200

boys doing? They strut about with their distortions – which become empty of all effect sooner than a slogan because, as Wind says, 'You can blow The Last Trumpet once. You can't blow it every day.' So they distort – forgetting that a norm is needed for distortion to be even viable never mind effective. And they clamour for violence; but what do they produce? – hysteria, mostly; violence had something to do with hitting and cursing, madness and blood – forgetting that violence is in us and can be disturbed into life by the slightest reawakening. A true description of a street could bring more violence to our response to that street than any amount of horror. O K, so maybe you're right. Maybe we should accept or believe that the best thing to do is to take a fragment of our experience and lay out all the capital we have on it. Maybe that's right. Maybe we should all or each, each one of us live by abnegation of the past and in contradiction of all that seems offered in the present. So maybe that's what I'm doing as well."

"Except that what you've got is dull."

"How the hell d'you know?"

"No need to growl. It looks it, that's all."

"You mean, it isn't very good 'programme material'. What d'you get out of your lot, David? Speak up for the New Boys. Come on!" Richard's drunkenness leapt to belligerence.

"Oh for God's sake – I have a good time. And if I don't then I worry. That's all. To drivel on about anything else is phoney and a waste of breath. Everybody who has any sense or opportunity wants a good time and if they have any energy they try to get it. I know it doesn't fit in with all those snobbish hangovers of yours about 'the purpose of life' – but it's a good enough purpose for most of us. You've forgotten how much you once enjoyed yourself, that's all. This place has made you into a prig. There we are, an old-fashioned word that fits you exactly; there isn't a contemporary term that applies."

"I *do* remember – and it wasn't all that enjoyable. I like drinking Scotch, but if I drank nothing else, all the time, I would be stoned out of my mind in a month. Everything we see that is strong is, you say, extreme; people are empowered by exaggeration; all that glitters is gold; the further out, the further 'in'. Chase despair, man, hop on disgust, hog lust, spray the world with froth of slap-happiness – but one at a time or you can't be serious – but never, never, sit and idle and let yourself live. Never take time to discover if the things you think you reject

201

do in fact exist. I know your pleasure. It's too bloody close to panic for my liking."

"Maybe," said David solemnly, "it *is* because of the Bomb, after all."

"Bugger off!"

"Extreme language again."

"Oh 'I want to be extreme in my normality.' That's your sort of remark. And to live without being swept along as rubbish by every latent brush of opinion – that is so dull, so very dull."

"That's right! Bloody dull. Isn't it? I mean, don't you *really* think it's dull to be a teacher?"

"No! Shall I shout it? NO!! Apart from everything else, the fact that you consider certain types of activity as automatically 'dull' is to be ignorant of everything but show. And how in sod's name do you know what is or is not dull? And why *dull*? The opposite – bright? So everybody should lead 'bright' lives – by your standards – always un-stated. Blamelessly, unblinkingly, blissfully Bright."

"Why not? Isn't bright better than dull?"

"In the morality of Everyman's Pocket Dictionary, each has about the same space allowed. Why don't you measure the longest entries in a dictionary – find all the words that have most said about them and live your life around *those* words? Then *you* could be sure you were getting the most out of life – *and* being extreme. Now why don't you do that, David? There's a great deal to be made of 'into', you could have a ball with that!"

"Have some more to drink?"

"No. I'm going to bed. I've had it. I can feel the rubbish assembling for immediate discharge and I don't want to be here to listen to myself. No thanks."

Janice was curled asleep and Richard looked at her but could not calm himself enough to touch her, nor did he want to wake her. But he could not sleep for regretting his talk with David. Whenever he tried to explain what he was doing some alchemy turned it to pontifications which sounded so hollow that the words began to clang in his mind like rusty bells announcing empty evensong. Yet, if he couldn't argue, then he couldn't maintain his life; expiation through explanation, was that not it? You had to be explicit because the surface was broken; there were no implications left. And though his words might bruise his feelings, like so many daubs on a blank canvas where should

202

be painted the dappled colours of a dream, rather let his feelings be bruised than bury themselves under that refusal of challenge which, in the end, leads to such a distortion, to superiority or inferiority, anyway to a binding of untouchability. He had to live in the world and talk in it and if his sentences rattled as cans on a dog's tail, then at least their sound might wake him.

He looked at Janice. Words were useless there, too. He had lost the way of making his love known to her. Maybe he had lost his love of her? He touched her shoulder. No! He loved her and could wait in that love. Lying there beside her, trying to feel that love, hoping that its call would reverberate in every part of his mind and body, he grew afraid. For there was nothing but quick blackness quickening to an impenetrable centre and in that centre no man could find a way.

David trod noisily up the stairs and his shoulder banged against the door. Janice stirred. The door handle turned. Then the knob clicked back into place and a cough took him across the small landing to his own room Richard had grown tense and he wondered why, could find no reason for it as he relaxed and let the stiffness go out of him; could discover none that would satisfy him.

New Year's Day. In the morning, Edwin would come at Agnes's invitation. His had 'always' been the job of 'first-footing', that is, being the first man to cross the threshold in the New Year. The man had to be dark-haired and carry a lump of coal and some bread. He brought the Luck. An excuse, Richard knew, drowsily, to get Edwin out of that garage for a day and cheer him up. The work and his mother were driving him to a transparent desperation.

Who lived their lives according to what? If only he could get that question out of his head he could sleep. He had interrupted David's grand night and that pleased him. David got too much his own way. Janice was beautiful. The whisky hung at the back of his tongue, thickened by the coffee to a sweet coat of stinging sugar, to sour in the morning. What did he want to do? To sleep. Erect ambition high.

And his head pounded as his self once more turned on him.

CHAPTER TWENTY-EIGHT

"Richard's a mess and that's all there is to it. More wine? Isn't a bad place, is it? Carcaster's Alvaro's this is. Still, the bread is good. No. What I mean is that I see the lad sinking. He's made up his mind to something and he won't let go – but I'm not sure that he's made up enough of his mind. I mean, he isn't *really* an intellectual, taking a few years off to solve the old problems of the universe, is he? He doesn't *think* much better than I do. And he isn't somebody with a natural knack for seclusion and all that wilderness bit. I bet he hates trooping around on his own with you miles away in the metropolis. So why's he doing it? He had a nasty crack-up in London but that's centuries ago now. Well I know why he's doing it – he wants to find out ... and so on. But it isn't doing him any good. I mean even his stamina's fading – couldn't make it to stay up all night New Year – remember? Bad, that. No, I think he's got some sort of perverted Destiny bug that's eating him up without his knowing it. The Man Without Destiny. He was a very bright lad, you know, your Richard. He's going to find it very tricky to jump back on to the band-wagon if he keeps beating his breast out in Siberia over there. Somebody ought to warn him." David wiped his lips with the linen napkin and with a very free movement of his arm he tipped back the wine. Janice was good, eye-catching company for lunch. They went well together, he thought, he in his neatly cut suit with a Paisley-patterned shirt and a gay, floral tie, she in a white bolero blouse and a short mauve skirt. He was finding that he enjoyed her company more each time he took her out.

"I don't think it would do much good to warn him," Janice replied. "And he's doing what he wants to do, after all."

"No, no. He's trying to *find out* what he wants to do. And everybody wants to do everything. So it's a waste of time. You commit yourself to your straight line and stick to it. Otherwise – a mess."

"He's chosen quite a few things," said Janice. "I think that his trouble might be that he's chosen them too obstinately too early."

"Yes – but all this business about 'What is it for?' I mean – it's dead. It's for nothing. Who cares nowadays? If he was somebody who was really going to do something about it all – he wouldn't be worried to argue it. He would just do it. It isn't the real thing."

"Are you so certain you know what a *real* thing is?" Janice laughed as she said this, guessing, correctly, that it would puncture David to a comically deflating rasp of derision. "But are you?"

"No," he answered promptly. "And I don't much care. That sort of thing can drive a healthy young man out of his mind. It's just 'How many angels can dance on the point of a needle' brought up to date. There's debate in it, I grant you; there might even be interest in it – for a few eunuchs and executive brain-men; but there's nothing in it for yours truly. Eat up! Thus, you refute unreality!"

"I admire him."

"Oh, *I admire* him. That's easy to do. I still think he's wasting his time. And his opportunities. God – with a wife like you! I wouldn't let you out of my sight for a second. *Really*. Look, there's an outfit who call themselves the Green Room Club, they're doing an adaptation of *Edwin Drood* is it? Some genius has written an ending to it. I have to go because one of the chaps in it is supposed to be good material. All of which leads me to ask, why don't you come?"

"I'd have liked to – but I go back to Crossbridge tonight."

"Stay until tomorrow morning. I'm sure Richard would appreciate the call of culture."

"You *do* go on about him. Why does he upset you so much?"

"Perhaps," David leaned over and whispered a cod aside "perhaps I'm a repressed You-Know-What."

"Perhaps you are. And that would explain Fiona. What happened to *her*?"

"Oh – she went the way of all flesh. Flushed. I can't find any of them bearable after a week or two. Thank God we live in an over-populated country. There are about twenty-four-and-a-half million to go, by my latest calculation. Come tonight."

"Sorry, David."

"Please. Look. I don't go around asking women, begging them like this. But you're the only one who doesn't bore me to death. One evening – spare an evening, lady, to cheer up a pore ole man." He clutched her hand, theatrically, but when Janice laughed and tried to release herself from his grip he held on.

"Don't be silly, David."

"You're being 'silly' as you call it, not I. You can't see me as much as you do and then beetle off every time I ask you to go somewhere where we might be alone for an hour or two."

"Why not?"

"Because it makes you into a 'tease', my dear – and you're better than that."

"Oh no, David. That won't work. If you don't want to take me to lunch – don't. But just because I accept an invitation doesn't put me in your debt. Isn't that a little 'old-fashioned'? There, I knew you'd wince; the biggest crime I could have accused you of."

"Calm down for a second, will you? I want to be with you. What's wrong with that? Maybe this hands across the table business is all right for you –"

"It's *your* hand across the table. Mine, as you might observe, are trying to get back to their knife and fork. Thank you."

"Oh God, I'm going to have to be serious. Why can't I say 'Look, Love – let's have a bang tonight'? Now why can't I say that by my troth in all good conscience? Eh? I mean, *I* would like it; I flatter myself that you would find it not disagreeable, it's natural, the way of the world – friendly, a cheerful act – now why all this scene with the stalking-horses and the medieval strategy. It exhausts me." He flopped forward on to the table.

"You are a clown."

"Ah, but there are tears beneath the grease-paint and when the mask is taken off in the wee small hours then the portrait of Dorian Gray looks out at me and says ' *You* killed Cock Robin.' "

"I must get back."

"To what?"

"Shall I tell you? Yes? 'The moral intentions of the characters in the novels of George Eliot'."

"And for this she leaves me! – could I have the bill, please? George Eliot's greatest intention, as far as I can make out, was to be God. Do they teach you that? – bill! Thank you! He'll be across in a minute. Coat?"

They went across the heavy carpeted floor, dodging the plain-topped oak tables, almost lancing themselves on the Gothic spikes which reached from the baronial chairs to pierce the fat timbered ceiling, David nodding to quick glances and smiling through the explanatory whispers which followed and then out they were on the grey afternoon street in the endless surge of shoppers.

He watched Janice walk away and his eyes tightened, sealing off the facetiousness which he had allowed throughout the meal. For no one else would he leave the television studios, which were on the edge of town, and come into the centre in the middle of the day, and yet she darted away at the end of the meal as if she had been having a snack with an acquaintance.

He drove back carefully, always careful. The old equation worked out in him as in millions before him. The more Janice showed her indifference, the more he desired her submission. Besides which, he told himself, he wanted it anyway with her. *It*, his pride and glory, never suffered abstinence gladly and yet the more he thought of Janice, the less appeal other women had for him. He had gone to Crossbridge to see her, not that bloody husband of hers; for Richard's way of life mocked his own, he thought, and he could not tolerate that. But Janice was so cool; usually, when they were that cool, he swerved away, believing it not worth the effort. Yet there was a flame in her somewhere which contradicted the coolness and which, if he could catch and feed it, would leap higher than any he had known. How to do it – that could be his baby for a while.

Fully aware of David's intentions, Janice was amused by them. She could play David, eat his lunches and disappear; she had no compunctions whatsoever, nor would have, for she regarded his attitude to women as adolescent and cynical; occasionally it tippled towards a bewildered honesty and then she truly like him and sympathised with him – but that was rare, and her sympathy was *with*, not *for*, him.

As the bus bumped her along the road to the village, she composed herself for the weekend. In the beginning, she had attempted to continue her reading as if the change of location did not matter; that now was a strain which she preferred not to undergo. If she could fit in some of the work she wanted to do, then she did so; if it proved impossible, she put aside her worry. At the moment she was anxious about something else – the contraceptive she had had fitted inside her had caused bleeding and stomach-pains and the joggling of the bus, its stale air, made her feel sick. So as not to arrive in a state of exhausted nervousness, she got out at the stop before her own and slowly walked the half-mile or so.

It was a brisk March day, cloud-covered but with little threat of rain, the wind coming sharply out of the north-east. She had little luggage – a small suitcase – but that soon grew heavy and banged against her leg as she moved. She walked slowly and even though the wind cut through her coat to hurry her along, she let it smart her, sting her eyes, rather than walk quickly and escape it. These days, though she had settled herself in the determination to behave as faithfully as she could towards Richard, the reluctance she felt about returning to him often threatened that resolution.

When the doctor had fitted the contraceptive inside her she had wanted to tremble, but held herself steady, even smiling at him afterwards and walking out through the surgery door as if nothing much had happened, walking straight to the Cathedral Close where she had sat, blank-eyed, looking at the grimy lead lattice-work of the big windows. So there could be no more children. The burden of that relief came to balance the shock of the act.

Approaching the cottages, she felt sick. The cold had got into her; she was dizzy. At the corner, she stopped and leaned against the cold stones.

Wif and Richard were in the garden, arranging the stones which were to make the divisions Wif had planned for it. The project was now well under way, but Wif seemed to enjoy taking longer over it than it warranted. He wanted to make a dry-stone wall which would last as long as those on the fells. This had been stated tentatively to Mr. Jackson, transferred immediately to Mrs. Jackson and cried around the village as the first, but nevertheless, inescapable proof of Wif Beattie's immodesty which, it would not be surprising, might be no less than the first step to his getting his name in the *West Cumberland Times* or something like that. Paula, over eighteen months now and well able to trot around, played at the side of the sandpit which had been made for her. Despite the chill of the day, the three of them made up a calm, warm scene. In which Janice had no part. Nor wanted one.

Choosing a moment when all three were involved, she went into the cottage. As usual, the table had been laid for her supper, there were fresh flowers in a vase on the sideboard, the fire was solidly made up, the grate clean. Without taking off her coat she sat in an armchair and allowed the disturbance within her to rise so that it could be aired and thrown off before she met Richard. There was some generosity in her return home now, incongruous as that might appear even to herself when she recognised it; but she knew that she was coming back to the

208

cottage chiefly as a favour to them all and to keep the peace. She could do without it.

"Hello." Richard.

"Hello."

"You were very quiet. I thought that you had missed the bus, as we say."

He hesitated, awkwardly considering whether a kiss would be welcomed or not, falling between the two impulses, one which urged him to kiss and get on with it, the other which alerted him to her fragile connection with him at this moment and warned him not to damage it.

"Well?" She held up her face and smiled. He kissed her; but as his arms went out to hold her, he felt the retreat and himself desisted. "No letter this week," she said.

"Nothing happened, I'm afraid. Oh yes; Miss Wilkinson broke a hip-bone while sidestepping to avoid Arnold Somebody – or – Other's motor-bike."

"Arnold Millar?"

"Yes. End of six-o'clock bulletin."

"How did the canvassing go? Will your man get in?"

"He needn't be a man. He could be a bullock. Yes; West Cumberland is safe for the cause of Socialism."

"Oh dear! Disillusioned again."

"Not really. But, unfortunately, disinterested. No, that's not true."

"You still protest against yourself?"

"Too much. Don't you want any supper? Or 'do you want *some* supper?' "

"No thanks. I'll wait until later."

"Your daughter is outside."

Janice looked at him calmly.

"I saw her. Did Mother buy her that little duffel coat?"

"No. I did."

"It's sweet."

Gravely, Paula entered and then, seeing Janice, squealed with excitement and did a war-dance on the spot. Janice smiled, made no move to get up and go towards her, waiting for the child to finish her excitement, stand still, rather puzzled, and then tack over to her mother's chair.

The evening passed as many did now when Janice was at home; they hovered around each other in the small area and all but apologised when they bumped into each other. Agnes popped in and they popped back with her, and Mrs. Jackson stood single sentry, intermediate with winning disapproval. Paula was put to bed and they sat down to read.

Richard had long abandoned any fixed plans for reading; just as he had given up the regular attendance on his record-player. Those snug and self-consciously cultivated evenings, which nevertheless he had enjoyed, though whether in appearance or reality he was not certain, those were gone. All regularities were gone. He read, but with indiscriminate intentions; he had, at one stage, prided himself on the fact of his fitness, his control over the number of cigarettes he smoked, the hours he kept – all that was gone; and that gladly, somehow.

With Janice in Carcaster and his days taken up at the school, there was little to do if you did not act on your own. And the convenience which he constantly remembered having called up (only to reject, but it had stayed) when he had first wanted to marry Janice now recoiled in his face. For she was not there. Where before he had been alone because of personal choice, deposited, now he was alone as part of Janice's decision, suspended.

Perhaps he ought to have made a greater fuss about her leaving – but then on what grounds, as he believed in independence? Or follow her, even now – but for what? Amongst other things, to sit in the shadow of David?

There was no tinder in him. He did what he did – but knew nothing. Whereas Wif moved around his garden with ease from knowledge, Richard was still ignorant of plants, flowers, trees, and animals with an ignorance which became depressing as daily it cut him off from that which was the texture of his senses, the everyday landscape for the mind.

So again he had begun to learn the names of the flowers in the garden. Each evening, Wif told him all the names and when he went for a walk he would try to pick them out in the hedge-banks and fields.

So he would know all the names of all the flowers! He laughed.

"What's wrong?"

"Nothing."

"What was funny? Read it."

"Just something I was thinking of." He kindled at her interest. "Let's go to bed, shall we?" And by the slightest whisper, her face changed its expression.

Again, there would be a night side by side, slabbed bodies on

210

uncrumpled sheets. But it wasn't all that important, not sex, was it? He stared at her until she had to speak.

"I had lunch with David."

"How was he?"

"Oh, the same. He's got the first part of his rise."

"Good old David."

"He was cheerful."

"Better old David."

"Don't be so flippant, Richard."

"What else?"

Janice let that pass. But a scattering of shame shook on to her; she had helped to bring him down. And he was down.

"Did, did – how did the mock school-certificate exams go?"

"Lordy Lord! The efforts the girl doth make!"

And her shame was shot through with comtempt.

"There's just time for one," he said. "Coming? Thought not. Don't wait up!" He went to the door. "I can recognise a foxglove at ten yards," he said.

She read on, her concentration little disturbed, her conscience unstirred by his act. He was pushing himself into self-destruction just as blindly as he had pushed himself into everything else, she thought. But to help him would be to involve herself where, she was certain, she could do no good, anyway. Let him go his way.

CHAPTER TWENTY-NINE

Flight. She had told him of the contraceptive and perhaps that had been the tangible – 'stopper', would he call it? The thought of that prohibitive nesting smugly in the centre of copulation, bland in its plastic negative, made him wince. But it was an unequivocal declaration; of that, no doubt. Laugh? He could have died.

Flight. Go, go, go – indeed – 'Go, go, go, said the bird'; and his bird turned him to flight – wax of his temper, clumsy feathers of his strapped-on wings – conscience's things – guiding him to the sun, or any too-much reality, to a certain fall from the sky unobserved by the ploughman, Icarus in the painting by Breughel: 'how everything turns away quite leisurely from the disaster'. I love the man who creates higher than himself and perishes in this

211

way', with Nietzsche, himself perishing to insanity – Icarus once
more, and all because the wings were untrue. Or perhaps because
the sun would have been too strong, anyway – whatever the
materials, even if a Merlin had slipped in through the trapdoor
of an alien mythology and turned the boy into a real bird – a
sparrow-hawk, say. But even then the sparrowhawk might have
gone too close to the sun – because, simple thought, it wanted
to dare. Dangerous. Scorched instead of melted. Not as dramatic
a fall. A charred lump plopping on the ploughed field to become
humus. Whereas Icarus, the boy-bird, would one day be dis-
coverd – and something would be said about it – even if 'Isn't it
a shame?' was all; but more would be said than that; someone
would be curious and, perhaps, try it for himself and this time not
fly near, so near the sun. But then, why fly?

Flight to fanciful involutions. Richard was beginning to show
the effect of being too much alone. He indulged in that part of
himself most slight – his thought – which, bereft, it seemed, of the
power to charge his action to his proposed intent, stumbled
headlessly around the clutter of magpie lootings; facts and
fantasies sticking on to the skin of his mind like summer flies
on to those long rolls of brown gum-paper. Or maybe he had not
been sufficiently alone – where the drenched solitude of parched
coenobites or Simon Stylites or any man finding a wilderness?
No wilderness. England was all garden, with rockeries and rough
– but the lush vegetable patch was always at the end of the scrub.
Yes, he ought to have tried to be truly alone – but then, the
eccentric hermit would have been discovered by the *News of the
World* in twenty years and given a jolly write-up. If you went
into the wilderness in England, such wilderness, you became a
Robinson Crusoe and planted cabbages – and waited to come
back.

Maybe, Maybe, quite contrary, how does your garden grow?
With slivered bulls and cuckold fools . . .

He had barged off to the pub and drunk as much as possible
in half an hour. The company in the pub, who had now settled
to accept him in the only way they ever would – as a regular
stranger, like one of those goldfish in a plastic bag at a fair ('It'll
be dead in two days'), hermetically sealed in the incomprehensi-
bility of his uncertain position ('A teacher, is he? I wonder how
long *that'll* last?') – but accepted – oh, to hell with being accepted!
He could chat, play darts, listen and find the odd laugh. Drink
was the day's keystone now; not that he was a real drinker – just

a few, increasingly regularly, coating the mossy lining of stomach, ready.

He did not make love to Janice that night, but the next afternoon, surprised in the Sunday-newspaper-strewn sofa, he did. Remembering that time by the mine shaft when he had known she was his; knowing again that if she loved anyone, she loved him – but once more feeling coldness – a spirit's icy stab – even at the crest when with lotus-spreading quickness he entered her; barred. He would discover himself slipping once more into those eternal dreams where every woman was a nymphet, virgin expectant to each knight's errant lance.

Light-headedness in all things now. He saw Paula, his daughter-by-marriage as he had discovered himself calling her, and the concern which had once informed his care for her was now transformed to shallow heartiness; affection was in throwing her into the air and swinging her squealing round; love was in being kissed at bed-time by that bud-tipped mouth; concern was the automatic daily question to Agnes, merely, "Has she been all right?"

In the garden in the evenings with Wif the stones grew heavier and the cigarettes between each load so increased that it was almost two stones a packet now. Having been set the task of teaching Richard the names of things, Wif stuck to it, but when he lifted an eyebrow and said 'What's that?' Richard had often to restrain himself from saying 'Who cares?' It was so easy to say 'What does it matter?' Easy to swerve from everything in the name of nothing. The zero is the key to all construction. Zero was the cardinal invention. And nothing wields a power unappreciated; in its name all things bright burnish, all so quickly turns to dust and ashes that the world moves in a vortex of rubbish.

Knowledge, the keg of powder so carefully stoked by militant ancestors to dynamite the world into justness, had exploded and blown to the winds. That knowledge gave strength to such a man as Wif could be observed; yet the strength could have found the knowledge to grace it rather than being formed by the knowledge. No, blundering into Wif's preserves was no more than a respite – as with his marriage, as with the teaching; you could not stand for yourself by imitating the externals of others.

So he worked at the wall, unable to bear his incipient rudeness towards that old man beside whom he felt a wandy sapling yet, sure that he had to be separate from him.

Flight from Arthur Thompson and the local Labour Party with which, he decided, his relationship was either whimsical or desultory – certainly the commitment was more homage to the idea of what he ought to be doing than interest in something he believed in. He was not proud of himself for the low opinion he held of politics and politicans – but it would have been blind to have ignored the strength of it. The argument with Arthur came up over the local elections; Arthur had found a fairly safe seat for him and wanted him to stand – 'to get a few progressives in the council.' Richard objected to this Rotten Borough arrangement in name of the idea 'that a man should serve the interest from which he was elected'. Arthur laughed and hooted this out of the argument – but its point had penetrated. To Arthur's scorn, Richard replied in kind, and the two, companionable but never intimate, had ceased to be concerned with each other.

Richard had fallen into a new routine. Instead of catching the school bus back to Crossbridge at four o'clock, he would now stay on and correct all the homework in the staff-room. There, with the emptied school around him and only the occasional clatter of the caretaker's bucket to disturb him, he could mark the books at full speed and be finished soon after five. There would be time to make a cup of coffee, shake a little more coal on the fire and read a few chapters of the book he was on before going out to the pub. For, out of consideration for Agnes, he did not do all his drinking in Crossbridge. So between half-five and six he walked down to The Stag.

It was a small pub, in the middle of a row of terraced houses and indeed converted into a pub from two of them. The sign showed a nobly antlered stag perched on a hillock, nostrils pantingly flared, shocked still in mid-pursuit. The pub was tenanted by Mr. Johnson who had worked on a coal wagon through the day while his wife attended to the few lunch-time customers. They had a daughter, Margaret, a woman of about thirty-two who had come back to help them following her father's accident – when the coal wagon had backed on to his leg and crushed it – and it was Margaret who governed Richard's choice of that particular pub.

Once inside, he would take a seat by the window where he could look over the road, across the rubble of what had been a small jute works in the days of Victorian coarse capitalist euphoria down to a sunken row of council houses, new enough to look incongruously trim at the end of the debris, and beyond to the hills which soared free in magentas, purples, darkened weed-green and browning gold as the sun pulled away from them before sliding past the skyline. He had almost given up the rambling he had once been so fond of and now, with a pint in his hand, he would tell himself that the best way to appreciate nature – or anything – was through a glass.

He remembered the last long walk he had taken – guilty at leaving Paula yet again with Agnes, irritated against himself for the restless paralysis which was dominating his days and in the usual corkscrewed frame of mind about Janice – who should have been with him, had the right not to be, nevertheless, why was he not with her? He loved her, did that not mean living with her? Yes and no. Yes *and* no? Yes!

He had set off at top speed, bypassing Knockmirton to reach the inland fell area as soon as possible. There he had been determined to quell his turmoil or, somehow or other, force it to guide him. When finally he had stopped he was alone inside a well of hills. A few score yards in front of him was one of those black, flat tarns, with a tree or two sticking out of the ground as if stuck on to it by someone who wanted to leave evidence that he had tried, anyway. He looked around and everywhere were the same round-topped hills, now fissured by crag outcrops, now scattered with scree, but bare, all, and cold. After dusk grew to denser evening he had left, pulling himself reluctantly from the place, physically tugging himself away from it. The silence had sunk claws into him. His thoughts had been of Janice – all led away from her, back to her, they were with and against her; in the cold hollow he had seethed with a throttling passion which he had lost the means to direct in any way. On reaching the cottage, he had written in his notebook, 'To exist is all there is, for death is oblivion and no alternative.' That had satisfied him greatly and he had gone out to the pub to drink on it. On his return, he had read it again and, quite suddenly, found it so intolerable that he had ripped out the sheet of paper on which it was written and thrown it into the fire. The pleasure of seeing the page turn cringing sepia and then charcoal had encouraged him to dismember all his notes and serve all the same way. He had done the same with his songs. Then he had gone upstairs and brought down copies of the articles he had written; these went the same way and so, finally, did the few letters he had received from Janice. He remembered calmly laying the table for breakfast and having the best night's sleep for months. . . .

The Stag was crowded from about quarter to six until quarter past, as it stood quite near the bus station – then it would empty until seven-thirty when the regulars would begin to drift in. It was during that dead hour that Richard had come to touch wood, cross his fingers, count the beer-mats – anything he could draw chance from – to provide for his luck and leave him alone with Margaret. This evening he was unlucky. There remained a man not much older than himself, with a tense white face – the thin wall holding apart external pressures and some internal malady, a face already older than Richard's face would ever be, scoured by lines whipped across the brow and down the cheeks with pasty sweat ever oiling the marks; his hair was black, brushed straight back from his brow and flattened into submission by Brylcreem; his build was not unlike that of Edwin, ill-jointedly broad and knotted, as if lumps of bone and muscle had been added on to a thin frame grudgingly and uncaringly. He wore a rough sports jacket, grey open-necked shirt, a pair of jeans with a brass-ornamented belt, and Wellingtons with the tops turned over so that the jeans were stuffed into what was thought to resemble cowboy boots. Around his wrist was a broad leather thong, the loop of the lead on which he held a large, slinky, Alsatian dog which alternately padded morbidly in its narrow circle and crouched on the floor, ears pricked forward, a statue of mute expectation.

He asked for the dominoes and invited Richard to join Margaret and himself in a 'shuffle'. A stained old board was brought out, and then the dominoes – greasy shiny black on one side, discoloured ivory on the other, the spots like so many jet eyes – were emptied from the old Oxo tin, clattering on to the wood, and shuffled. They played threepence a knock, a penny a spot.

Richard found himself winning against his wishes for it would have been far more pleasant to have given money to Margaret than take it away from her – whatever the amount – while the man with the Alsatian was so hell-bent on winning that the ease of Richard's good fortune seemed an insult to his effort. There was nothing, however, he could do about it. There was even a game where Richard's last two dominoes were double-five and double-six (one and ten to pay if he lost) – but he still won.

216

"Let's play bob a knock, tanner a spot," said the man.

"No," said Richard. "This is high enough for me."

"Yes, I'm all right here," Margaret said, sensing Richard's motives and backing them up.

The man looked at the piles of cash; Richard's was the largest; Margaret, who had won one or two useful games, was holding her own; he himself had had to break into a pound note.

"Let's go up," he insisted. "I'm after me money back."

"Now come on, Edgar," said Margaret, "we can't all afford to throw our money about like that."

"You two'll nivver starve," he said. "Come on." He smiled. "Scared o' losing your life savings, are you?"

It would have been plainly unpleasant to continue in disagreement and yet Richard did not want to run away or surrender to the bullying so early.

"Let's stick where we are," he answered. "I'm happy."

"I'm not. I've to be away soon. This way I can get off quick."

The attraction of *that* was very strong. And it was said with such a merest whisper of understanding that Richard noticed the slightest trace of blush on Margaret's face.

"I'll meet you half-way," said Richard. "Sixpence a knock, penny a spot."

"Three games," said the man, brushing aside the trailers of embarrassment. "Two at your rules – one at mine. What could be straighter than that?"

"But I don't want to play for those stakes."

"It isn't going to bankrupt you either way."

"But – I was perfectly willing to play for the original stakes – it seems silly to go up so high."

"Toss you for it." He put a penny on the couch of thumb and forefinger. "Heads it's my rules, tails it's yours."

"No."

The coin was still on the two broken nails. Richard noticed that not only were the nails bitten, they had welts along them, black lines from the pale half-moon to the tip, as if they had been stamped on by nailed boots. The sight sickened him.

"Well, I'm looking at this penny," the man said, "and I'm thinking it's looking a bit lost just sitting there. So I'm going to give it a bit of exercise."

He flicked it and it spun into the air, falling on to the palm of his right hand which slapped it on to the back of his left hand. Then he uncovered it.

"Heads," he said. "My rules." He put the penny beside his pile of cash. "Let the lady shuffle."

Margaret looked at Richard and did nothing. He was not, he told himself, afraid of the man – and insofar as he was not unduly nervous at the possibility of a physical clash, that was true. But it was not fear which was besetting him – something else, obscure when it should have been clear; he ought to be able to stand for himself without being anxious over the grounds of that stance; the friction would have come, just the same; but it would have been in the name of something, whereas now even Margaret, he could see, was puzzled over the arbitrary nature of his wanting not to, yet finding no active means of carrying out that want. No will: thou shalt not wilt.

"O K."

Margaret turned the dominoes on their faces and steered them around the board. The man lit a cigarette and then placed it carefully on the ash-tray, like ammunition ready for the crisis. Outside, the swished purring of the occasional car, a boy shouting "Pass! Oh, pass!" and the soggy plop of a soft football against the wall. In the bar, the inevitable clock; how often had that tick been solo accompaniment? The melodramatic tock. The spring evening's flurry of quick shades to dusk was flattened by two electric-light bulbs, yellow-bright under white shades.

They picked their dominoes and played the first game. The man slouched against the bar, where before he had stood upright, tense over the liquorice rectangles, one against the world and fortune's wheel. The Alsatian coiled itself around his feet and, unprovoked, he prodded its ribs with the hard neb of his Wellingtons. The cigarette was allowed to burn and the long ashy stalk crept towards the brown tip.

Margaret won the first game with little money on the board; three shillings. In the second game, Edgar was left with six-three and double-five, after having knocked twice; that cost him eleven and sixpence; Richard took it.

"Let's draw for who leads this last game and double the stakes," Edgar said.

"No," said Margaret. "You two can, but I'm playing for far too much as it is."

"What d'you say?" he asked of Richard.

"I agree with her."

"You would. With that pile in front of me, I would agree with anybody."

"Now, Edgar," said Margaret. "You wanted to raise them. You lost, that's all."

"Isn't it enough?" He smiled at her. "Come on, you and your boy-friend here aren't going to go bankrupt on two bob a knock, bob a spot."

"No. I'm not playing."

"Well," said Edgar, placing the butt of his cigarette in his mouth, the long ash mould dropping on to the floor, "we shall have to play ourselves, won't we?"

He shuffled, noisily, not taking his eyes off the board. Then he passed one domino to Richard who passed one to him. The highest would start. Richard won.

"Thy mother must've been a fortune-teller. Set off."

While they played, Margaret wiped the glasses which she had rinsed after the rush. There was still about her mouth that tense pull which had come when Richard had been referred to as her 'boy-friend'; otherwise she was calm and self-possessed as usual. She was not beautiful as Janice was beautiful, but her eyes were grey, her face slim, a fine pull from cheek-bone to mouth without the strain which would crease into spinsterish lines. The notion that she was a spinster seemed so incongruous as to be mysterious – with the added piquancy that Margaret's manner was not such as promised easy, or any, insight into that mystery.

At the new odds the game went very slowly. Each man 'knocked' once – which put four shillings on the board. Edgar won the game, but Richard had a mere double-one left, which meant that he paid over another two shillings only.

Edgar picked up the money and began to shuffle once more.

"Five bob a knock, half a dollar a spot," he said, without looking at Richard.

"No thanks," Richard replied, "I've had enough."

"But I haven't," Edgar answered. "I want a chance to win that money back."

"If it's your money you want, you can have it," Richard said. "But I've finished playing."

Edgar stopped shuffling and looked up. All very deliberate, and so conscious himself of the menace in such deliberation that the movements drew themselves out a little in over-emphasis and plodded towards caricature.

"You mean you're offering to give me what I've lost?"

"Rather than go on playing, yes."

"D'you think I look *that* broke?"

"No," Richard paused. "Not at all."

"Well I *am*," Edgar said, leisurely.

Richard picked up his glass and sipped from it, the rim hard and cold on his lips, the beer sliding heavily down his throat. Edgar looked to Margaret for recognition of that stroke of repartee, but she was still with her back to them. He too pulled at his beer.

"So it's no go."

"I'm afraid not."

"Afraid? What's to be afraid of?"

"I don't want another game."

"You won't play."

"That's right."

Edgar smiled, the sneer running into vacuousness. The chance to provoke a nasty argument had somehow gone. Richard saw how easy it could be to win and how winning made no difference.

"Have a drink," he offered.

"I will! A short!"

"Fine. Whisky?"

"Aye."

"A double, please Margaret."

She jerked the small lever under the whisky bottle, let the measure fill and jolted it up once more. Edgar downed it in one, nodded, flicked the lead at his dog, and left.

Richard collected the money together. He had won about thirty shillings. The pile of coins filled two hands.

"Could you give me a couple of notes for this."

"I'll give you the pound note he gave me to change."

"I'll keep it in a special pocket so that he can win it back." He smiled.

"Why should you?"

"Well, he . . ."

"He's probably earning as much as you are. He spends it differently – that's all."

"Will he be earning that much?"

"He'll be on twenty-five a week – labouring. He's a piece-worker on the roads."

"What about winter?"

"He can take care of himself." She smiled. "A lot of people can, you know."

"Will *you* have a drink?"

He had never bought her a drink. The weight which lay on the answer to the question was too much for it to bear. He started to laugh.

"What's the matter?"

"I was thinking..." Richard paused, "it seemed very important that you let me buy you a drink."

"I'll have a Scotch, then."

"Could you get one for me as well?"

"I think I can manage it." She laughed. "You look so cheerful and sound so solemn," she said. "You know, I think you go around looking for trouble. Just like Edgar."

"Does he?"

"He's always fighting. He would have been after you if he wasn't afraid of being barred from this pub. There aren't many he can go into in this town now."

"I see. So self-preservation is everyone's salvation yet once more. It's a popular system."

"I don't think *that's* very original either."

"How long are you staying up here?" Richard asked suddenly.

"A few weeks more. Maybe a few months. There's something very pleasant about standing still after racing all the time."

"You too?"

"No," she shook her head, "my problems solved themselves. I like the fresh air here, walking in the afternoons – and being with the people I was brought up with. But still, here it's nearer stopping than going."

"Maybe it's better to stop."

"No."

"You're sure?"

"Oh yes."

"Better than being stopped – bang! like that."

"I suppose so. But few people *are* stopped – bang! like anything." She smiled, raised her glass, and drank in one mouthful.

"You seem to have everything worked out."

"I seem to?" She paused. "It's easy to seem." But this was said lightly, with no invitation to Richard to go further.

"I must go and make some supper," she said, "thanks for the drink."

He went back to his seat by the window, wondering why he had persisted so half-heartedly with her. Neither one thing nor the other. He had begun to 'flirt' – although that old word contained such relish as had been lacking in his action – to 'engage' with her and yet had done so in such a cautious way as

221

to take one step back for every one step forward. A rather pointless manoeuvre. He sagged. His shoulders were firm enough, but he felt the rest of his body slouch to wasted tiredness. He saw himself there, slouched. He was his own audience. Narcissus faced by a multi-reflecting mirror. That story of Narcissus – ending up inanimate, for ever condemned to nod over his unreality – that was the most chilling myth of all. A free man self-immolated.

As he sat there, he felt wan. He thought that everything around him was the same. Was there not a bloodlessness about everything? About the towns, so scabby from bricks and concrete that they lay down before the bus and the bulldozer like an ancient whore whose offering infects all that it deceives to comfort. And the hills were bare of song – too late come for that. And people – so plastered by sound and sound again that out of a din they were listless? And the men losing any feeling of essentiality, and the women of indispensability? And the whole world shagged out, turning listlessly round a sun which did not change. Nothing again. So easy to roll into that nothingness.

Margaret's mother came into the bar. An old woman, leather-skinned, her eyes bright, her grey hair straight and folded carefully round her head. Dusky clothes, one ring diamond-sharp on the freckled fingers, slack-skinned. She chatted amiably and Richard drank some more.

He missed the last bus – the 7.30 – and, knowing he would have to walk back, ate a pie and some crisps. Stayed until closing time. With Margaret he had no more direct talk. Listened to others.

A bitter spring night. He took the old road so that no one would stop to give him a lift. The whisky joggled inside him and he went as briskly as he could, feeling as topped up as a tub and twice as barrelly. There was no world outside his whiskied head – no cold, no night, no landscape. The alcohol subdued all to its own atmosphere. What was the name of the man who had left Captain Scott's tent so that the others would get on faster?

He must leave that school. This wanness was incubating his uncertainty into cynicism. What was the name of that man?

He was in the middle of a small, black road, the moon hidden by clouds, alone, he noted that, and yet he could not sing. All the singing was in himself, buried, and the next morning the whisky's litter would trip up his mind. Oh no! Margaret was – it was ridiculous.

Who was the man who left the tent? Oates? Oakes? Oakes — something like that. Just left and went. *He* went away.

No flight.

CHAPTER THIRTY

"It's the way our Janice goes on that's driving him off," said Wif.

"He doesn't *have* to stay here," Agnes replied. "Any other man would see that he was with her no matter what. That's a fact."

"What the hell?" Wif replied. "She doesn't want him about her. She's made that plain enough. If a woman made it as plain as that to me, *I* would let her fetch for herself. She's driving him away — it isn't right. I wouldn't be surprised if he upped and off."

"Just went?" Agnes put down the sewing she had been doing. Wif had become increasing critical of Janice over the last few months, irritably critical, as if some grain of her discontent had finally pierced his love and since then rubbed against it, gathering to itself growing bitterness. Agnes was upset at this, and surprised at its force, for even now, just returning from work and sitting down to his dinner, ready, usually, to put on his wire-held spectacles and gossip over the paper before going out to the shed or garden, he was prepared to talk about it. "You mean, you think he might leave altogether?" Agnes said; and Wif ignored the fright in her manner.

"He would have cause. To my mind, he would have cause. She isn't anything of a wife to him. I don't know, why she married him except that it suited her for that minute. She could just as soon have married Edwin. She told me once that she *would* marry Edwin because then it wouldn't matter what she did. Now I've never stopped thinking about that. What kind of woman is it says that?"

"She was in a terrible state after that baby," Agnes replied, unhappily. "She didn't know what she was doing. That sort of thing's an awful experience for a young girl."

"Granted. But he still took her on. And you couldn't have a more helpful young fella. She should have got over things by now — but they just get worse with her."

"She's never had much luck," said Agnes. "Goodness knows
223

what was going on inside her head when she was laid up all that time as a little girl."

"She should be over that now. Look at him. He never had anybody. He's all right. And Edwin had no easy time. *He's* all right as well. It's how you take it yourself. And she's let it turn her into something I can't recognise, Mother."

"You don't think he *will* go away do you?" Agnes whispered.

"I can't tell. That's the bugger of it. You just can't tell. He's drinking a fair bit these days, that I know. And he doesn't seem to have any "crowd" he goes around with, that I know. He was in with them Labour fellas for a bit, but it fell through – and I can't blame him. I mean, he can't just scallywag off with a lot of young fellas looking for lasses; and t'other young fellas that's married have their wives about them; and all of them that's left either sits at home or marries a pint pot. There isn't a great deal for a young fella like him to do up here."

"He should never have come in the first place, then," said Agnes. "He can't expect things specially laid on for him. Others manage; he should. He's been educated, he should be able to think of things to do for himself."

"How can he think when he's in a flat spin about his wife? He thinks the world of her yet, I'll swear on that. And her gallivantin' about in Carcaster there! He just wants to forget things – not to think about them. Besides, he might be educated, but that doesn't add up to much. He still doesn't know whether he's on his arse or his tip half the time. Excuse language – but it's true. And he's trying to find out for himself without taking what anybody else says as gospel. I can see him doing that and all power to him, I say. Most fellas just take whatever happens to be about when they're born. I did. I admire a fella that gets up and says "Hold on a minute, let me work it out for mysen." '

"He's been bringing you over to his side."

"It's no question of sides, woman. It's a question of sense. *He* isn't perfect – but there's few that are. And our Janice is giving him a dirty deal. I can't recognise her, Agnes. I mean, granted she might have none of me in her, I look for summat of you. But I see nothing."

"She has your eyes. And when she decides she'll do something, nothing'll shift her – just like you. Except, the things you want to do are quiet things."

"No. She's got nowt of me. And for you! You'd go a mile in a snowstorm to help a body, even if you didn't know them – if they needed help. But she wouldn't pick up a telephone. You're badly for a month if you think you've been and upset somebody by mistake – she seems to thrive on upsetting folk on purpose. You're a tender little thing, Agnes, always have been tender. She's hard, my daughter. I shouldn't say it but I do. She's hard."

"You *can't* say that about her." Agnes was near tears. "You can't say that about her, Wif. You can't."

"I can and do, love," he replied softly. "One thing I can't. I can't hold it in any longer. If I didn't talk to you about it, I'd bust."

"But what's going to happen to them?"

"I don't know. I don't want to think about it. The sins of the children are visited on the parents. That's all I see."

Paula trotted in from the garden, and Agnes diverted herself by covering the child with attention. The bath, the supper and the changing for bed had to be done early tonight as Agnes had to be away on an evening at the Institute where, once a month, the backward children from the surrounding area came for a games night. She made the tea and laid out the refreshments; others helped with the entertainment. Richard had promised to come and help her this night; he was going to meet her outside the Institute which was just next to the bus stop. So Paula was dealt with smartly, but with no obvious hurry to fuss her. To Agnes, the little girl grew sweeter every day; she spent hours chatting to her and listening to the responses gradually focusing on particular words. There were times when she would look at her playing in the garden, and have a double vision; of herself a younger woman, still hoping for more children, and Janice wisping about the flowers, herself a dancing petal. Then tears and pleasure would be so mixed in her that she would have to turn to something active to stop the crest of memories breaking into her mind and taking her quite out of the day. More than she could admit to herself, she was thinking increasingly of the past, and on her walks to the church or whatever, would sometimes pass her destination and find that she had dreamt her way on.

She found that she wanted to circumscribe her life, but, for fear of withdrawing from it, she resisted the feeling. More and more often she did not *want* to walk to the church to clean it, to the Institute to tidy it (she was back on that: Mrs. Carruthers had only managed for four months and then got water on the knee, she said), to go to Whitehaven and serve light refreshments

225

to the out-patients, to – then she would shake herself and march off over-briskly and tire herself out.

She remembered first arriving in Crossbridge, afraid of the countryside and the suspicion her neighbours had of anyone born away from the land. How she had never showed that fear but used all her energy to show Wif that she could be just as good a wife to him as any country girl. She had done things like digging over the whole garden one day – to surprise him – and then discovering that he had laid it to seed the previous week. She had roamed over the fields to collect flowers and branches so that the cottage had become a bower to greet him on his return home. He was such a gentle man; she found this gentleness so profound in him that, far from making him "soft", as her family had concluded, it gave her the strength of foundations so deeply dug that nothing but a natural catastrophe could impair them. She had kept his clothes so clean that he used to be teased at work for being a "dandy"– however old the shirt, it would not be frayed and never dirty. And he had been in awe of her, daily. His first and sole conquest, one who, he had been certain, would never take the slightest notice of a "tatty old labourer", and he had brought her to the cottage with a pride and gratitude which had scarcely diminished since that day.

All the more then was Agnes disturbed at Wif's hastiness and sourness over Janice. Janice who, when very young, had been such a beauty. In those days before Agnes had known definitely that she could have no more children the world had been completed by that small golden daughter who had rushed up the lane to meet Wif from work so that she could be piggy-backed home; pottered around the small patch he had given her for her "own" garden and leapt with delight when flowers appeared overnight; gone fishing with him and been lost, found paddling down the beck trying to talk to the fish. It seemed to Agnes that her mind opened to the winds and each mote of dust carried a memory, each one sparkling in endless sunshine or snug in cosy wintered contentment. Idyllic, idyllic – she would catch herself regretting that it appeared so idyllic and be unable to understand that regret.

There were other matters she could not push from her mind. If the actions which occupied such a part of Agnes's life – the organising and helping – could be described by Janice simply as "more trouble than they're worth", then what *was* she doing? She respected her daughter's intelligence – indeed, had been a little afraid of its solemnity ever since the little girl had retreated

from her bed to the back room which she had called her "study";
so white and drawn she was over her books, so determined to get
full marks for everything, so tense over those long essays. And
her daughter implied, clearly "What you are doing is, if not a
waste of time, certainly of little account in the world." Agnes was
sensitive enough to feel this attitude – it pierced her like a needle –
but she had not the sort of resistance which can fight against that
which it does not fully comprehend.

So she went her way, on this night, out to the Institute; but the
savour had gone. There was a dryness in her which she would
conceal, could not but conceal, but could not conceal from
herself.

Richard was not there and she went inside. Through the
windows she saw the bus come, stop, draw off, but Richard was
not yet on it. There was a later bus, the 7.15 from Whitehaven,
and she waited for that, joking to the other women – who had
been looking forward to having him to help them – about the
unpunctuality of people "who thought all the time". But he did
not arrive on that bus, either, and she made no more excuses.

Richard had deliberately missed the bus. Watched its shiny
old back disappear, bearing the sign "Watch your step! Accidents
can happen easily". He did not want to be with Agnes and the
children. He had helped her before, but in his present mood it
would be too complicated and phoney. He could no longer face
Agnes. As he had sunk from his purpose so she now appeared
heightened, inaccessible. She unnerved him – and he wanted no
more of that.

He went into The Stag to see Margaret. Again he waited for
the pub to clear, sipping his bitter with tasteless regularity.
The men were crowded at the bar and a damp sweat came across
the small room. The beer was heavy. Behind the bar, Margaret
served briskly and chatted to whoever wanted to.

Richard had twice taken her out for a meal and each time the
same thing had happened. Soup – and they were friendly, each
enjoying the other's company. The courses came and went. The
coffee-cups were refilled. She talked of her life, a wandering with
shorthand and typing, as boundaryless as the Dark Age monk
with his Latin, to America and Mexico, Rome, Stockholm and
London. Mainly London. And in time she had somehow become
so honed by the rub of her experiences that she had lost, she
said, all recognition of her own tone of voice. Sometimes she

227

would hear someone talking and be unable to believe it was herself. That was why she had so eagerly taken the chance to come and help her parents. And in the pauses of her talk, Richard recognised the two rooms sep, kitchen and w.c., the married man leaving his briefcase in the small hall, the cutting from roof-garden cocktail to surreptitious launderette, the smart clothes and the anxiety about the incontestably thickening waistline. There was an experienced plus and minus about her, a "gameness" in a way, something pawed, something proud, which reminded him of other women he had known in London, far from the sculpted inviolability of Janice. So what about you? she asked. And he saw what he wanted to expect of himself and was silent. It was no use. Instead of making him forget Janice, revenge on her, and, curiously, enable him to allow her continued independence, Margaret only defined Janice more clearly. So he took her home and left her at the door.

His interest – the word gave it away – in Margaret was forced. Yet he went on with it. Although the rarity of intercourse with Janice was hard to bear, he was not clamouring for sex. Exhaustion sometimes underlines abstinence with the strength of continence. But to pretend to himself that he *was* deprived, that he *was* missing it, that made counter-action easier. Yet the pretence led to insuperable tepidity.

The bar cleared.

Simultaneously Richard came over for a drink, the last man closed the door and Margaret laughed.

"Can you get away to-night?" he asked.

"I could. Why?"

"I would like to take you out."

"For a meal?"

"Yes. Or we could go . . ."

"To the pictures? Elvis Presley at the ABC and *The Curse of Frankenstein* at the Regal."

"To my place."

"I see."

She took the empty glass and held it under the pump's snout, looking down into it as the hard froth jetted down.

"It seems a bit – exposing yourself – to do that, doesn't it?" she asked.

"I suppose so."

"You *had* thought of that?"

"No. Funnily enough. But it's better like that."

"Wouldn't it make things complicated?"

"Yes it would.."

"Do you want that?"

"I passed the catechism first go, Margaret." He lifted his glass. "Cheers."

"This isn't like London, you know. Everybody sees. So far, you've been *just* safe. This would mark you. And others."

"Yes."

He said no more. To take her back to his cottage, to spend the night there and wake up with Agnes knocking on the door and Paula crying for her breakfast – that would pull it all down. Destruction can sometimes clear rubbish, sometimes it can break irreplaceable things. Margaret would come with him – but it would be no more than a bit of the usual for both of them; both would be mechanically keeping in touch with their past and memories would roll them away from each other, not satiety or even a thought of tenderness.

Yet he wanted her in some way. He wanted the gesture of it – let things break down, let Agnes be hurt and Mrs. Jackson smirk, let Janice find Crossbridge a sniggering secret and then tell *her* so that between them, too, there would be a stain and not this forever watchful tension, let there be honesty rather than secrecy.

"Thank you," he said to Margaret.

She smiled and leaned across to him. He put a finger on her lips and then went to the door.

"You've forgotten your change," she said and picked up the two coins. He cupped his hands. She threw them and he caught them, neatly.

He went into Whitehaven, down to the docks. The sea washed against the wall, the waves swelling leadenly on the surface; it was all too massive and tranquil. Leaving after a few moments, he made for the nearest pub, The Docker's Arms, where the committee for the Old People's Rest Room used to meet.

Richard had struggled. That the fight had been against himself made it no less a struggle. And only in the continuation of that struggle would he be free; that he had once paid homage to, now he knew it. He was cleared of fear of himself. But it was without fear, must it also be without hope? In Janice was, he knew, such hope as he had.

There, with her, was what he wanted. Until that was known, nothing could be got, or understood or lived for.

For love, being indefinable, defined all the actions around it, as a still centre would show the turning world. Love, being the body's action when all was done for passion, made sense of the frailness and flabby mobility of everyday movements. It was mindless because the mind was spun into blank ecstasy, and so all things from there could reach for a reflection of such happiness. Selfish through the open need for total satisfaction; selfless through that need being bound to the other's delight. In tenderness and fierceness, storm and tranquility it went beyond any other pleasures, leaving below it the plains of enjoyment and the chasms of pain clear to see and so understand. And around it were the humours whose essence could feed it, whose importunities destroy it; lust, greed, vanity, lies. They, too, could be stripped of their claims to inevitability and shown as they were. Such a love as he felt in him he had never felt before. He could not move from the seat, so suffocated was he even with such a small glimpse of its strength.

He would go and write to Janice, resign from the school, join her the moment he could – no! None of that was enough. He would go and see her *now*. He had to see her – if he did not make her understand now – he was convinced that there, in Carcaster, she must feel the power of his love and would be waiting for him, wanting him to come, waiting, as he was, to come into that passion which left the earth and yet fed off its roots.

CHAPTER THIRTY-ONE

He got up and went out. The docks were dark. He hurried along the quayside and was almost knocked over as a woman lurched out on to him from an alleyway. The bundle of her multi-layered body cushioned against him and then stumbled away, near to the dockside, guarded solely by a low looped chain.

"Why don't you watch where you're going, you sod?" Richard recognised the voice immediately – Mrs. Cass. She staggered in her own circle, dangerously near the feeble chain, on the edge of a yellow pool dripping reluctantly from a street light. Richard moved towards her, into the light.

"Mrs. Cass?"

"I didn't mean it," the voice whined back, "I was just going home – but I couldn't get in the house because I've lost the key. You see, I've nowhere to go," she tacked towards him while she was so plaintively apologising, "you see, I had it when I was in The Bull and I've been back there but they say they can't find it – I know I had it there – you *aren't* that young copper in plain clothes!" She stopped. Already, Richard was impatient of the meshy hooks the old woman had thrown into him. Yet he could not simply turn on his heels. She was in a bad way, drunk as a newt, and precariously tottering in that dangerous place. But he *knew* that Janice was waiting for him; and even catching a train right away would take him an hour and a half to get there. He had to go. "You're that bloody Richard that took my Edwin's girl from him, aren't you?" Now close to him, she reached out and took his lapel and it was all he could do not to turn away; her face was no longer simply ugly, it seemed to decay as he looked at it. He could not even let his mind register details; it was as if the ugliness and distortions had softened and were running. And the breath which came from her was the stench of foul clothes, of drink, tobacco-teeth and illness.

"You're a fine one," she said, now losing the fear which had kept her upright and hanging on to him, fiercely, "pretending to be that bloody copper. That bloody sod of a pimp hangs around here at nights just to molest and worry women. He wouldn't touch a man." She swung across the front of Richard and he caught her under the arms; she sagged and then straightened and, as she did so, broke wind. That rubbery breakage – the longer word more suitable to its sighing dolour – peeled off her wadded legs to lift from under her skirts and colour the air with the warm smell of port and lemon, mild and bitter, and the overpowering ripeness of intestinal disintegration. It turned Richard's stomach. No metaphor. He felt his stomach rise, lift from whatever held it, and then slump back into place, leaving a thin curdle of sick in the back of his mouth. Janice was waiting for him. Mrs. Cass in straightening up once more, belched – right into his face like the cracking of an old egg – and the mouth stayed wide-gleamingly open as a limp hand whitely straggled up and across to it, more, it seemed, to help close it than to indicate a certain politeness. The sight of that hand delicately looming towards the gaping hole, while the speckled eyes rolled in their watery sockets with crazy concern, was too much. He laughed – and then his own laughter encouraged itself, breathing in the stench of all, clearing through one shell of scents to encoun-

231

ter the dank oily fishiness coming up from the docks, the laugh a cold, isolated crackle across the water.

"You can bloody laugh. Let me alone. Let me alone!" He released her and, unsprung, she recoiled backwards to the edge of the dock. He followed her and caught hold of her coat, enough to steady her, and then he let her go.

"You should be careful," he said. "You'll fall in one of these days."

"And who would bloody care? Who would cry over it? My Edwin would've done until you pinched that flamin' tart of his. He would do anything for me up to then. He knew his mother and knew how to treat her right. I told him that she was a little bitch but you can't stop love." She sobbed – and again that action was gruesome, as if the tears seeped out from all her shuddering body and brought the grime with them; so much a mixture of affection and debility that they ceased to be the crying of one woman – yet "gruesome" was not the word; it was too cruel. For however dislocated tears seemed, she mourned, she wept, and, as it continued, Richard found himself wrenched by her solitary debris of misery. He had to stay to help her – and after that he could go to see Janice.

"He was in love like nobody's business," Mrs. Cass sobbed. "She was the only woman in the world for him besides his mother. He would even have given *me* up for her. Oh, that woman ruined him – and *you* did, *you* helped, *you* ruined him."

"Where d'you think you left your key?"

"I've told you I don't know. You silly git. Bloody standing there."

"Perhaps I could climb through a window or something. Where is it you live?"

"You're not smashing any of my windows. I lock everything up in this place, I can tell you. That bloody rotten son of mine brought me from the nicest little country cottage you ever saw in your life, where I was respected and never even locked the door – but this place is a bedlam. You can't get in without a key. He just dumped me here to keep me out of the road. *I* know – the bastard!" She paused, and Richard knew that she was craftily working out a move which would involve his being used. "*He* has a duplicate key," she said. "He won't have me go and see him where *he* lives, but I could go if *you* took me, *and* for a duplicate key. You've got to take me to him!"

"All right. I will."

232

She perked up and came to take his arm. Richard began to walk towards the town, and as he approached the dock-gates, a train came out of the station which was near-by and made along the coastline for Carcaster.

"You could be my boy-friend," said Mrs. Cass, sentimentally. "Have you got a cigarette?"

CHAPTER THIRTY-TWO

That walk was something he would never forget. Soon, Mrs. Cass was tired, and the tiredness allowed the drunkenness to come back through. She staggered around on the narrow pavements, rather seemed to throw herself over them, as if she were running apart so violently that she was forced to follow whatever prick of her body contained her centre of gravity at that moment. A scarf came off and lay wretchedly in the gutter, and as Richard bent down to pick it up, he had the feeling that she might tumble all over him as she hovered there.

Few people on the streets, but none of those few ignored by the bundling old woman. She caroused them all with her greetings and received the jeers which this drew on her as a tipsical queen might have acknowledged the baying of rudely sycophantic courtiers. The streets were her Court and Richard her Regent. She waved at her image in the navy-blue-blinded windows; stopped in front of a grilled jeweller's to observe and appraise the rings and bracelets lying there, pushed herself up against a young policeman whose Christian name she unnervingly knew, and danced for a bow-legged old miner who called her "Maggie May" and asked her to do a "trot" for him. Richard lost all self-consciousness, all will even to get her to Edwin's, became merely the arm of the law. And when she demanded a drink at the bottom of the hill which led up to the garage, when she sat down to cry should the drink be refused her, just a little eeny-weeny one – she had him on a string and went far beyond exploitation into absolute tyranny – then he was not conscious of any irritation, only a vacant, unbelieving bemusement that so much energy and wilfulness should come from this over-wrapped and flannelled woman.

In a pub she waltzed, one-two-three, one-two-three, to the bar, lifting the skirts of her top coat with a delicate gesture and

233

tripping over her own slippered feet to land thump against the counter, bowing to the cheers and grumbling of the men and women in there. A gin and it she wanted, gin and it with not too much it and this was her new boyfriend – cheers to the landlord, cheers to the landlady, cheers to the company and the drink was raised and slid out of the small glass like an oyster into that winey mouth. One more. Just *one* more – before she saw her son. Yes, her *son*. They would all know her son. He had the garage on the hill. A stuck-up little ponce he was but she loved him in spite of everything – going to show him her new boy-friend, that would – and the second drink caught the windpipe, seizing her body in such space-demanding convulsions that the bar cleared as she stomped a dervish dance with the landlord blazing out from behind the counter to thump her on the back and use the thumps to get her to the door and out – out! "The last time you set foot in here, you filthy old baggage – *you* too, you take her back where you found her"– and like the thin shadow that had escaped from an earlier incarnation of Mrs. Cass to come back and torment her in her dotage, Richard slipped on to the street to find her theatrically heaving around a lamp-post.

Up the hill, past the glow-wormed light from the cottages and the odd flash from the smashed rubble heaps, once living-places of some sort, with the docks just a seedy flicker below and the sea a quiet wash. They walked on the road for more room, Richard almost carrying her now as she hugged his neck with both arms and sang "The Rose of Tralee" into his ear, panting the words with great feeling and begging him, and all, to join in and sing. And then they were on the top of the hill where a cool flush of air was waiting for them and a bus swerved past them with hooting horn and window-goggled faces shocked and the bus conductor swinging on the open platform's rail, shouting his abuse – the bus marking the end of interference, for bright yellow lights could be seen coming through the garage doors and, sweating, trembling under her weight, Richard put an end to it by knocking on the doors with a desperate fist so that they shook and juddered and flung open, revealing Edwin.

Edwin stared at them, quickly flicking his eyes from his mother to Richard, whom he seemed to examine with a look sadly abstract, for the moment merely curious to know how it had all come about. Then he stood aside, motioned them to go in and, after looking outside to see that there were no others to follow, slammed the door.

Richard, duty, or whatever it was, done, wanted to be away, but Mrs. Cass, now fizzled out to a bedraggled whisper, clung to his hand and would not let him go, In the bare-bulbed light of the garage, with its oily floor, the cars jacked up, the benches cluttered with tools, the welding equipment just laid down with the visor like a lost helmet on the floor; in there, Richard flushed with a quick but sickening exhaustion which came to him and left him quite suddenly, as if reminder of another life he might have had, or the strain which Edwin's life would have imposed on *him*, or the freedom it might have given him.

With his back to them, as if he could not bear to look on them, Edwin wiped his hands on a large tatty rag, once a shirt.

"Did you come all the way through the town?" he asked, and he faced them now, the pasty haggardness of his face clearest proof of relentless overwork.

"We had to," said Richard. "Your mother's lost the key to her house. She said that you had a duplicate and I offered to bring her up here."

"Did she need bringing?"

Richard did not see why he should be responsible one way or the other for Mrs, Cass's obvious state; and yet it was difficult to think of a reply which totally evaded the acceptance of responsibility of some kind.

"Did she *need* bringing, I asked?"

"I heard you."

"I said I would get a policeman, Edwin," Mrs. Cass whined, unhinging herself from Richard and stumbling a few feet until she found a steady piece of floor, "I said it would be no trouble – just a key – but *he* said he would bring me here. I said you didn't want to be interrupted, I said you worked hardest this time of night, I said we had an agreement, I said –"

"Shut up! Shut up you stupid old – oh! what a bloody mother! What did you have to bring her through the town for – shaming me? I bet everybody saw you – everybody knows she's my mother now – I bet she shouted that filthy mouth of hers off." Edwin stepped towards Richard, and only his leg catching against the lever of a vice stopped him. "Just like you to want to shame me."

"Has he shamed you?" asked Mrs. Cass, lugubriously. "The bloody sod. He's always shaming you, Edwin. He shamed you by taking that rotten woman away when you were all set – a beautiful girl, she was – he's just trying to show you up again. With his white shirt! Sod!"

"SHUT . . . UP! I've told you not to come here. Remember what I said."

"No, Edwin, please."

"Remember what I said . . ."

"No!"

"Well you can bloody well remember it by me telling you. Come here once, I said . . ."

"No."

"Come here once I said . . ."

"No. No."

"Come – here – once – I – said – and – that's the last you see of me. Now see if I meant it. And *you*," to Richard, "you just did this to laugh at me and find out that I was working like a navvy. I know that. Well go and tell Janice. Go on! Tell her. But maybe you can tell her this as well. I've doubled trade every two months since I got here. Every *two months*! Work that out if you can. I put more than your wages into t'bank every week, I bet. Just chew on that! I could have hung around working for other sods, like every other stupid twat; I could have done that – but I got out and I'm making myself into something." He was shaking now, as if the onrush of words was more destructive to his physique even than any number of sixteen-, seventeen-hour days. "And I'll tell you something else. I know I've gone back to being coarser than what I was. Don't you think I stand here not knowing what I look like. And I stopped being able to read more than half a page of a book without falling asleep, months ago – but that doesn't matter. I can catch up on that kind of thing whenever I want. It isn't that that's important. I'm my own man, see. *You* can't say that."

"He's just a teacher, Edwin. He just runs and jumps when anybody tells him to. Teachers!"

Edwin turned to her and raised his hand. The first frenzy, at being surprised in his lair, had gone, however, and he shuddered at his own intended action, dropped the arm listlessly.

No one spoke.

Richard looked at his watch. "You haven't got a railway timetable, have you?"

"Yes."

Edwin walked heavily across the garage, to the back, to where the loneliness of a single light gave it the appearance of a cave. He searched around on the bench where he kept his tea things

236

and eventually came back with the pamphlet containing the timetable.

Richard looked through it and found that the trains were still running on winter-time; the fast one had left.

"Is there anywhere I could hire a car and a driver to get me to Carcaster?" he asked.

"Wilson Rowan might do it for you."

Richard nodded. The hope had gone already. He had not enough cash with him. That simple frustration was too stupid. "Damn." He stood, uncertain of what to do. He could have asked Edwin to run him to Carcaster, but that would be asking for trouble.

"Look," he said, "I've come out without enough cash. You couldn't either lend me a couple of quid or . . . or perhaps run me to Carcaster. I want to see Janice."

"And you want me to help you to get to see her."

"No. I want to get to her. I'll pay you for your help."

"What makes you think I would take your money?"

"Oh, for Christ's sake, don't be so edgy. If you can't do it, say so, and I'll go and look up this other fellow."

"You'll be lucky. He doesn't like to come out after eight."

"I'll find somebody else then."

"You're not in London now, you know."

"Fine. Thanks. Nice to have met you. Good night."

"Here." Edwin brought a key from his pocket and threw it at his mother. "You can go with him."

Mrs. Cass clutched at the key which landed somewhere inside the bundle of clothes and, after mutely thanking Edwin for this great kindness, trudged over towards the door. Those few moments when she had not said anything seemed to have weakened her. The whine had been some sort of energy; now she was silent, wilted, ill-looking.

"I think that she needs taking home," said Richard.

"You take her home, then."

"Don't be so bloody rude. You're her son."

"I've wasted enough time." Edwin shook himself back into his former state, the result of his explosion, like a bloodhaze before his eyes, clearing away. His gestures grew again to that agitated rhythm which clawed at the demand to work and build. He could not bear to be stopped in that.

"She knows the way," he said. "She'll be all right." He paused

237

and then, with hawking venom, added: "Nobody would touch her anyway!"

Richard felt sick at the violence of that remark, and turned to go. Mrs. Cass was now propping herself up against a wall, almost disappeared in the clothes, her mottled hair the serpentine halo around her livid face. When she spoke, her voice came eerily from the shawls, a babyish tone like the limp babble of an old and mad spiritualist.

"He says his mammy can't see him again. Her own little boy says that. Oh, he was a rascal, a proper rascal. They take the best years of your life. When you could be out enjoying yourself you're at home looking after them, clearing up after their little messes, looking after their little wants. *I* never wanted anything from him except love for his mammy. But he doesn't love her. He needn't pretend. He doesn't love her any more. She's been a bad mammy. A bad mammy."

The lonely wail, which curled around Richard's nerves like wet thread, pulling tighter with every ululated word, ended as whisperingly as it had begun, and the old woman stayed, unmoved, waiting to be pushed, or led, or attacked or abandoned; at the disposal of circumstances.

"I'll take her back," said Richard, and he reached out his hand to find the elbow's crook in that camouflage of clothes, and, finding it, he pulled, indicated, her towards him. Together they walked haltingly, convalescently, towards the door.

Moving swiftly, Edwin got in front of them and opened the door.

"I *did* tell you," he said, plaintively. "Nobody can run a business with that sort of carry-on going on. It's easy for you to pretend you're sorry now. Shamin' me again in front of him! That's all you're doing. If I say it's all right, you'll be drunk again tomorrow and making just as big a disgrace of yourself. You're the laughing-stock of this town. And what does that make me?" He spoke to Richard. "She gets herself drunk and then she talks to men and – she does disgraceful things. She's been no mother to me. Aye! Look like that! Maybe you've been lucky without one. She's been no mother to me."

"Just like his soddin' father," said Mrs. Cass, the last stinging vindictiveness flickering above the dead embers of her mind. "A rotten useless sod. He thinks he'll make himself a great man, you know. But he *won't*. Take my word. He *won't*. He'll bugger it up some day – you'll see."

"Don't say that. Don't say that!"

"I'll take her back."

"Take her. Lose her! Do what you want with her."

Out on the street where it seemed much colder than a few minutes before and Mrs. Cass hugged herself into him. Richard's thoughts about the encounter with Edwin were scattered all over the place. He found it impossible and irrelevant to judge what had passed – there was so much right on both sides, so much wrong in the expression each gave to the position adopted, and it was none of his business anyway – he felt only an abhorrence of what had passed, and that abhorrence was like a useless lump in his stomach; a nerveless pity akin to cancer.

She clung to his arm. This hold on life. A woman whom nobody wanted, who provoked one true emotion in one person only – and that contempt; whose days were a labyrinth of cadging, dirt, drink, unlovely mewling, with the solitary idea of the next few shillings keeping her going, the sound of it in her mind like a woodpecker's rattle on the silent bark; her feet moving on memories, her eyes open only, scarcely seeing, and lit by whimsical memory thrown up into the spotlight of her mind briefly, like an acrobat darting up from a trampoline, yet this woman, with all the passion and cunning she had, kept hard the props against death. If there was not an instinct, or a reason, or a system, religion, style to which life could be aimed, then perhaps taking the forces which work against death, from those, something could come.

To whom, for what, and how?

A car suddenly approached them from behind and slowed to a stop. The fresh paintwork glittered coldly in the street lights. Edwin leaned out of the window.

"I'll lend you the car to get to Carcaster," he said. "I can't do better than that."

"I don't drive," Richard answered, so promptly that he laughed. "I don't drive."

"You don't drive." Flatly, Edwin responded.

"No."

"Well, that's that then. I can't drive you there myself. I can't do that."

"I know. Thanks for the offer, anyway." Richard created advantage where there was none. "You might as well take your mother home as you've come this far. Rowan's is just up that street. I'll see if he'll do it on tick. Good night, Mrs. Cass."

239

He walked away quickly, not turning to see what might happen.

Rowan was out on a job, his wife said, irritatedly answering the door with a cardigan bad-temperedly thrown over her slip – the kitchen door down the short hall closed too sharply for anything but suspicion – out on a job and she *knew* he wouldn't be back until after eleven and he would certainly do no more jobs that night. There might be a taxi at the station. There wasn't.

Although the resolution to see Janice now lay heavy on his stomach, although he foresaw no easy entry late at night or in the early hours of the morning and knew that Agnes would worry about him – so there would be that for cold comfort along the way – he had to go, and he set off out of the town to hitch a lift.

CHAPTER THIRTY-THREE

Walking, knowing he would be late anyway, he made no attempt to get a lift until well clear of the town. The streets, to the hard soles of his feet, echoed a sorry mood. He turned from it.

Rather than think of Agnes or Margaret. Edwin or Mrs. Cass, and to prevent a build-up of obstructive fantasies about Janice, he turned to the melancholy which had washed beneath all his thoughts and actions over the past year, coming upon it with the jarring impression that he was fondling it. It *was* something to be fondled – and by giving it the name of "melancholy" it appeared much less wiltingly narcissistic than if it had been called Self-Pity. Odes to Self-Pity? None.

The most moving poem he had read on melancholy was Tennyson's *In Memoriam* – and there, the fondling, the sensuousness, was stated clearly; the loss of love was sustained through the love of remembering and glorifying that loss. The poem, as he recalled fragments from it, moved him in the manner of all recognitions, all kinships. Especially in that constant strain in it which acknowledges the triviality of the poet's melancholy. The belittling indulgence of it as compared to the affairs of The Great World, even as compared with the potentialities of the poet's personal world. Seen in such comparative light, the emotion was as a feeble flicker, and yet one which was fierce enough to burn, to inflame, to drive all else out of thought but its own pressure. To avoid due recognition of its power would be to distort feelings which might be feeble but were undoubtedly there.

Once it used to bother him, this finding of loose references to his own state in literature; as if there were something dead in him choosing liaisons with the dead, as if it were somehow reprehensible to take the forms of other's thoughts and apply them to yourself – a lack of Initiative, Inventiveness, Self-Reliance. And the blustering drum-beat of those imperial virtues rolled ever on in the receded traditions of his mind. But now he was no longer bothered. For everyone had their references – to family, church, group, to modern heroes, modern events – and literature, in that sense, was merely one more of the magnets of imitation. While in practical terms – the terms most often used now, as if practicability in itself held virtue – literature had the advantage of being more open about its feelings, more accessible, the contour of history's emotion. And always the same. So he thought of Tennyson, the years of melancholy wandering after the death of his friend, Hallam; between grief and nothingness, and from that rub, a form, a style. From loss.

And there was a loss in his own life – the loss of the pursuit of a love he had not had the wit or confidence to recognise. So, he saw melancholy in himself and from there it was easy to see it inhabiting the whole world – as it did Tennyson's, whose days were black, light was grey, streets bald, people phantoms, feelings shadows; and in the silt of retreated love, a furtive reality appropriated with inevitable ease to each circumstance; and underlying that fiction was the seeping ooze of draining life, each day the last.

Yet that was long ago! Now there were cures – or names. Sink the depth-charge of science and the blocking silt would be blown to freedom. Yet such freedom could alleviate only, it could not change such facts as loss.

"Thou shalt not be a fool of loss." And fool he felt no longer on this oddly calm, silent walk up the runnelled streets of the town, phosphorescent globes beaming myopically, road like a snail's glistening track, a door slamming, a motor-bike kicking up, the stage effects of night, and he, coming deeper into his clothes, flesh running into fibre.

Janice, long fair hair glittering flax-drenched in silking sun, standing waiting under apple-blossom, her breasts scarcely moving, shouldered with petals.

CHAPTER THIRTY-FOUR

Carcaster still had its four gates from the time of being a walled town, and Westgate was approached by a cobbled street which shuddered Richard out of his doze. When eventually he had set about trying to get a lift, he had had to wait for almost an hour – until a lorry-driver had opened his high cabin to him. The journey had been slow, and it had to include a stop at a transport café outside Wigton, where the driver had settled to read a chapter of his book, the chief function of which, judging from its cover, was to so flagellate and exhaust all erotic senses that keeping clear-eyed for night-driving would be child's play.

The lorry-driver pulled up outside Westgate, for he did not go through the centre of the town but branched north to join the border road through the Lowlands to Glasgow.

It was well after closing time and so the pubs had spilled out their customers and beds had shovelled them off the streets. A few quick night-birds, holding close to the walls as they walked, an occasional policeman, cars, freed from the clogging of the day's traffic, leaping from one traffic light to another with rips of noise, and the line of lorries, pulling through the streets, constantly shifting a country's supplies, in endless passage.

The city's façades demanded reverence and respect. It was not Learning which invoked that demand, nor Religion nor even Property – though all these partook of it – rather it was Order, a style, a declaration – contained in the buildings – that a settlement had here been made by those before you or stronger than you, and your place was to find the appropriate attitude within that settlement. The demands were very clear: this town is your fortress, know your post. Modern towns were built so that they could be shifted anywhere; put on wheels and rolled to Cairo or Detroit, fit in just the same. No reverence or respect demanded there; but maybe something worse, an indifferent power to quell.

In the College area there arose the feeling of piety and austerity which clung to learning despite all activities to contradict it. From the moment a special place is devoted to such a high ambition there is little help for it. Edifices to edify.

He hesitated at her bell and thought "Of course. I'd hesitate"

242

and pushed it hard, sharply, three times. His legs dithered at the knees and then he felt flooded with energy to each nerve-end. He stood back in the street and looked up, seeing first the light come on and the curtain nudge to one side. Suppose she were not alone? The nerves dried, bunched, and then flew back to hope as he saw her looking at him; she waved and came down.

She opened the door and beckoned him, finger to lips. Enquiringly. He went in and followed her up the steep stairs which creaked under his toe-cringing steps. Inside the room, with one purple-shaded corner lamp on, he sat down and felt his sound crunch against the sleeping silence of the place.

"Anything wrong?" Janice asked.

"No." No point in building padded tension. "I just wanted to see you."

"Oh." Janice yawned. "That's nice." She wore a white-transparent robe which flowed out from her shoulders to the floor as her arms spread out, shivering with the pleasure of their own movement. Richard's own body, which had seemed lardy and glotted for months, opened to hers, opened as it had done those first few weeks he had known her, but this time to dwell not in its own satisfaction but in the pleasure of both of them. "Would you like some coffee?" She smiled, perhaps remembering.

"Yes. That would be fine."

She nodded and, still blinking her eyes open, went over to fill the kettle and plug it in. As she knelt down to fix it into the socket, the robe split open from her hips, and Richard was momentarily dizzy at the sight of the white, smoothly tensed leg, the little, nubile folds of belly, the rub between the thighs. Feeling a clotting in his throat, he went over and knelt beside her. She continued to try to fit in the plug, soft fingers obstructing. Richard pressed his face into her thick warm hair, and held her around the shoulders, one hand stroking the leg, fingers gently trailing up towards the hip. Still she fumbled with the socket.

"I'll do that for you."

"Thanks."

As he released her to do it, she, without offensive movement, but quickly, stood up and went over to get out the cups.

"We could have coffee later," he said, still kneeling on the floor.

"Oh, we might as well have it now. Two sugars, isn't it? Besides, you haven't told me why you came."

243

She completed the preparations and then went across to an armchair, folding the robe in front of her, for convenience but also, undoubtedly, as a statement.

"I wanted to see you." He got up, hovered, and then went and sat on the bed. "I suppose that is a bit strange."

"No. It's nice . . . How's everybody?"

"Fine. Oh Christ, Janice! Why don't we go to bed instead of playing around like strangers? I came because I love you."

The bolt, too soon shot, plummeted inches only and landed bluntly in the un-intimate enclosure.

"Kettle's boiling."

She poured the coffee and brought him his cup, kissing him on the forehead as she bent forward to give it to him.

"I suppose it is a bit stupid, telling your wife that you love her. Is it? I don't know." He hesitated, but felt he had to talk on, however artificially. " 'What we don't know is exactly what we need, and what we know fulfils no need at all.' "

"That's good. Who said it?"

"It doesn't matter."

They drank their coffee. The incongruity of it touched on each of them but Janice did not give in to it for fear of further offending Richard, while he was impatient with the bubble of hesitation which so consistently bobbed up in any phial of intimacy.

"Is it so remarkable to say that I love you? You didn't answer."

"I didn't need to. I know you do."

"What?"

"What you said."

"Say it back to me."

"Don't be silly."

"Say it!"

She smiled, or rather imitated a smile, and bent her head slowly to sip the coffee.

"This is useless. Look, Janice – Janice, your name alone makes me . . . happy – I love you – that is the only thing which makes sense and allows any sort of beauty."

"Love makes the world go round," She bit her lip. "Sorry."

"Don't be. Truth can seem to be trite. As well."

"You came to make a speech to me, I see that," she said. "I've been missing those. And I agree, with everything you say." She put down her cup and pushed her arms against the resistless air. "Let's go to bed," she said, calmly. And repeated: "Let's go to bed." She waited. "It's very late, Richard, and I am sleepy."

He paused. "I want to give up teaching and come and live in Carcaster with you. I'll get a job here. Perhaps David has something. We'll have Paula with us – do you think of her much?"

"Yes, I do, sometimes. I don't want to look after her while I'm here, though. That would make things impossible."

"Would it?"

"No. Come if you want. You must do as you want."

"What do *you* want?"

"Richard, I'm tired. I *don't* want another of those futile arguments we have where the meaning of the universe becomes vaguer with every cup of coffee. That's pointless. I'm happy working here as I do. I have the life I've always wanted – nobody worries me, I go through things at my own pace and I like it. You know that. When I finish here and have to do something else – then we can talk about what *we* want. I've started to write – you weren't going to be told that until I'd done something I could show you. Perhaps I'll go on with that."

"Everything is so straightforward and clear. You make me wonder why anyone fusses about anything – ever. Is it always like that with you?"

"I try to make it so."

"Why?"

"Because I don't want to squirm in a fog all my life, that's why! I've seen enough of the sentimentality, all that sloppy accepting and patching with loving kisses, pretending that warmth is everything in the world. I was brought up on it. It's not for me. I want to know more, to experience more – don't *you* flinch this time! I don't wrap it up in all the moaning mystery about Life, that's all – I want to be absorbed and surprised and know exactly what I'm doing."

"And why?"

"I know why. It interests me. End of argument."

"Yes. End of argument ... So with you, there'll be *no* argument. Never a cross-road, let alone a lane, always the highway to the next fly-over. Pull the trigger and, given a vacuum, the bullet will travel in a straight line for ever, ladies and gentlemen! Given the vacuum – pennies in the box towards the vacuum. And no friction – no change of pace or aim or –"

"Don't be absurd! If you're trying to make out that I'm a machine so that you can sun yourself in the feeling that you're all animal intuition – O K. But please don't believe in it, for your own sake. Except if you need the comfort."

"I wasn't talking about comfort, or warmth, or sloppy fog or sentimentality! Do I have to bound over the threshold and hurl you to the floor to prove I love you? How *can* you prove it? How can you walk around it without in some way trying to share, to show it? It's only half a thing without that which it aims for. It'll wither or simply flake away."

"Then let it."

"Or be killed."

"I hope I can kill it!" said Janice savagely. "It's a pretty name for lust, that's all. I know. Let it be killed!"

"I want to love you, Janice, and live with you."

"You *do* love me. And I like the way you love me. You're gentle. You leave me alone. I love you. When there are no great silences, we get on very well together. I don't want to change it."

"I don't know where I am."

"If you could answer that, you wouldn't be here."

Name a thing and you limit and lose it. Why should that always be? Could he not name what he felt for Janice without destroying it? It seemed not, and yet they were not able any longer to move by unspoken mysteries – far too soon they grew into upspoken uncertainties. This was the mirror infinite.

Flaking away. The big chance, the big decision, the do or die – peeling flakes.

Janice went to bed and Richard slept on the couch. It was a single bed she had, but even so; he slept on the couch as if that were the most natural place in the world for a husband to sleep. Or to lie. For he was awake, feeling beaten even though there had not been a battle. The thought of the fight had worn him out, then? God help us.

She was well asleep. A bare shoulder rising outside the coverlet, her cheek smoothing out from the pillow. In unguarded sleep. But inside her, that safety net. The attitude which that permanent preventative signified – *noli me tangere* – keep out – thus far – not a chance. Her business, her business. So much there was that was her business, so much hers alone, two limited companies – what did you do? Merge? Impossible. Take-over? Impossible – although for a frantic second the thought of rushing to her and ripping out that thing and spearing her with the barest of all declarations. Sell-out? Fold? Declare bankruptcy? Wind up the company? The analogy threaded itself leadenly through the blankness of his thoughts.

There he lay. In him, he knew, was power, was love, was a

246

need to grow into something which would fulfil all the impulses, at present no more than fidgety nerve-ends: with no illness, no deformity, no unwillingness to look into himself – hotly he had started out and it had not been difficult to keep the flames going along the way – and the mere puff of her presence had extinguished it.

Then he should leave.
But it would be too melodramatic to steal away in the night.
Then he could stay.
But she had made it quite clear, she preferred to be alone.
So he too could be alone.
But there had been no bliss for him in solitude; he wanted love.
Find someone else to love.
He could not do that.
He loved Janice.
She had said that she loved him.
Why, then, was that not enough? Perhaps the greed he had found in himself in London was still there. Perhaps he needed to be plastered with proofs of love, tokens, sighs, declarations, looks, kisses, demands repeated on him until he was drained: then he would not be doing more than asking for fullest self-satisfaction, the optimum return on his emotional investment.

There they lay, a few feet apart. What dream was it that he wanted to enter? To lie, content not to touch, not to co-heave, was that not something as well? If what his 'passion' meant was sweat on the turning thighs – then why did he not pursue that alone? All that 'mystic union bit' – the old jeers came round like Sunday – all the 'two in one and fused spirit', and the 'sanctity of total giving' – was he on that? So he scratched and tore down what he had only lately erected.

No sleep that night. His mind like a sieve on to which his memory scattered a handful of ashes, and he caught at the lumpier remains, to juggle with them. The sounds began outside with the morning, the scattering of feet along the cold pavements, the isolated drone of a car, the bottle-shaking steps of the milkman.

And then there came peace. However much he turned on himself and others, the impulse that had brought him to Janice was as true as any he had. That and the feeling of the worth of goodness which Agnes inspired in him. He could not ignore these discoveries, however impossible he found it to live by them.

247

Breakfast was silent and sparse and they went out without having referred to the night before.

"Are you catching a fast train back for the school?"

"No. I'll miss it anyway."

"I have to go to a lecture. Sorry ... We could meet for lunch."

"I don't know what I'll be doing. Where do you eat?"

"I'll be back at the gates at one. If you're not there, I'll go on my own."

"Fine."

"Well, then." She stood, in her cotton dress, books in front of her, like a 'picture' of the clear-eyed student, others drifting to the College behind her, a mildly purposeful crowd walking towards that odd process by which the implanting of wedges of information was somehow to educate, to 'lead the mind out of' – what? And towards – what? Richard shivered his head abruptly, to shake off this jarring and insistent questioning which was beginning to resemble a cry *for darkness* rather than a cry *in the dark*. "I'll see you on Saturday," she continued. "I should be able to catch the early bus."

"Don't come if you don't want to."

"Don't be silly, Richard." She faced him, wanting to go with a light word, unable to find a place for one in his heavy presence. "Of course I'll be there. I really *must* go now."

"O K." He did not budge. "I think I'll go up and see David."

"Good." She hesitated. "I've been seeing David rather a lot lately."

"Have you?"

"Yes. There's nothing ... nothing – don't look so stern, Richard. You ought to know, that's all."

"I'm sure there's nothing in it," he replied, gloomily.

Janice laughed. Such a fresh, pleasant laugh as cut right through the implication and unspoken question which hung between them. When she laughed like this her face, her whole body seemed to glint with an extraordinary freedom. Richard laughed with her.

"No," she said, gruffly, "nothing in it at all. 'Bye." Pursing her

248

lips as a kiss, smudging the air with soundless, touchless lip.
"'Bye."

He turned, so as not to watch her go, for he could have stood there, rooted, for days; grown into a town tree, ready to be made limbless.

It was a hot spring morning, and the first beat of sun on his head made him leaden. His shoulders ached, his knees were feeble at pulling along his stiff calves, his mind strolled with aimless tiredness. What a stupidity his body was! It swooned with exhaustion for as much reason as it trembled with exhilaration; yet to have control over it meant, usually, to keep it in that equilibrium which fended off all feelings, which was flatness, sliding into walking somnolence.

The town enjoyed the morning. The gaudiness of the people's clothes, the lush squares of garden, mauve doors, yellow gates, the crackling white line on the middle of the road, hard yellow laburnum against the blue sky, a tricycle, abandoned, brick-red seat, blue handlebars, white glossed plate wheels; and, in the centre, the carnival colours in the shop-windows.

David was in his office. The morning's planning meeting over, he was, or said he was, delighted to have a 'chat'. Richard might be mistaken, but he thought that David behaved towards him differently; it could be suspicion only, but he thought that David was hiding something; it could be imagination, but he thought . . .

"Janice tells me she's been seeing you quite a bit," he said, after a few minutes of the chat.

"Did she?" David smiled. "That means I've even less chance than I thought I had. Joking. Yes. She's about the only female with a brain between her eyes north of High Wycombe as far as I can make out. We have lunch. Then she scurries away to learn all there is to know about George (was it George?) Eliot or somebody. Bright girl. Your wife."

"Yes."

"I'm trying to persuade her to come into telly when she's finished the ritual self-stuffing stint. Look at her on the screen! Cool as a mountain stream and sharp as your Ever-Ready razor. She could be the first big woman telly personality."

"What does she say to that?"

"She tells me to stuff it – in her own inimitable way, of course. But what else can she do? Grow plaits and do research? What a waste. There are enough people doing research now for them to set up as a nation-state – somewhere in Africa with a bit of luck. Or be something official like your Female Senior Civil Servant – horn-rims and a tight bum. Our Janice? No! From the people she came, and to the people she should return, bearing gifts. Have *you* come for a job?"

"Not yet."

"Just say the word." He picked up a piece of paper. "Look at the trash I've got to deal with here. It's all very well being the senior executive with your standard black-leather swivel-chair, wall-to-wall carpet and three tasteful prints around the walls – but in this outfit what goes with it is half a load of idiots. So I send our Ace Reporter all the way to London to do a story on the Royal Academy opening. Two others as well to cover cost – they're all right – but what does he bring me? The usual stuff about it not being 'modern' or 'progressive' or crap like that! Everybody knows that! Why can't he say that the Academy's got a fair chance of becoming the new Outsider. That all your real Establishment's with the with-it boys. That it's not only easier, it's *safer* to paint a pair of circles than a pair of twins these days. He *will* say that by the time it goes out, but – predictable? I can set my colour supplements by him. These new lads have no Philistinism, that's their trouble. And there was me trying to do a good turn by Culture."

"It'll teach you ... No, I came to see if you still had anybody you know I could write to about doing a few articles. I'm skint."

"They won't pay for much – anyway, what do you spend among the sheep?"

"I want some cash, that's all."

David hesitated, then,

"I could lend you some if you're stuck," he said.

"It's not that. I just want to be doing something again. D'you know anybody?"

"Peter's with *Nova*. Maybe has more pull than he used to have. And Andrew's on the *Telegraph* – jacking in teaching?"

"Maybe."

"You won't make a living from ink alone, you know. Not unless you've been baking a best-seller up there. 'Murder in the Mountains'. That any good to you? We haven't had a farmer as an ace detective. Detectives are out – he must be an agent. Bring a load of gypsy girls in and a mad scientist who's hollowed out that fell of yours to launch rockets on London and you're away. Chapter One: 'It was a normal day in Crossbridge, but Huckleberry Armathwaite smelt disaster. At first he thought it was pig-

250

shit, but as his fine country nose twitched further . . .' And he
could have learnt Karate at night classes in Maryport. What
about that?"

"I'll write it."

"I take ten per cent."

David chuntered on and Richard was soon with him, feeling
a return of energies, forgotten. There was no reason at all why
he should not leap over that desk and join the 'senior executive'.
David was cheerful, he was busy, he was engaged, he was full
of himself – he grabbed at what was going and if it did him harm,
let it do him harm, at least he was kicking.

In a paper bag.

Mere activity was no more valuable than mere inactivity, that
much he was certain of now.

The edge came into David's conversation – that it had been
great, just great, but the wide world wouldn't wait – see you
later? Come back for lunch – come again, think it over – telephone – in a minute, Anne – you should see her legs, and she'll
show you most of them, these provincial girls have no coquetry
(mark that word; it breaks down well), pull it out, lay it down
and – thank you, Anne, one minute – love to Janice – you don't
want to see the studios, do you? – Extending them, buying a
second camera – cheers!

Jolted out. The bank. A very complicated telephone call all
the way to Whitehaven to make sure that the company could
stand that five pounds demand. Did he know he had only five
pounds eight and three in his account? He did.

A pub. Outside, students walking in straggling procession
carrying placards about Rhodesia. A good case for bombing.
The automatic liberal reflex given spice by the prospect of a bit
of justifiable homicide. What they said would have no effect and
yet they said it. There was no being 'mature' about that. They
said it and he ordered big-deal Scotch on the rocks.

Late afternoon, bumping along upstairs on a red bus, so that
he could smoke, the sun striking his drunken face through the
window pane. Janice roasting in the back of his head. Turning,
on a spit. The ride through the dead coalfields slumped with slag.
And the heat burning the wispy hairs on his cheek-bones. Not
Margaret. No more. He would sleep with anybody – no complications.

The bus corkscrewed into the cool hangar which was the
depot and, so far away in his broiling blankness that he could

251

not be bothered to look even and walked with his eyes watching the wobbly procession of his feet, he turned to where the 'nice girls' – bloodless euphemism – lived, up by Edwin's. Maybe Edwin had bought up all their property by now; and turned them out. Better, bested.

CHAPTER THIRTY-SIX

He found the houses but no one was around. The sun had gone behind a row of flake-façaded buildings on the other side of the street, and a sheet of black stretched across, under his feet, and up the chipped steps which led to the houses he was facing. He walked up and down in front of them. From some came the shouts of a mother at bay, from another a procession of little West Indian children descended in single file as if off on safari. A van drew up and a salesman galloped up the steps, holding a clutch of suits at one arm's length; he had disappeared through the door by the time Richard got there.

He did not know which house or houses contained the women he wanted. And the deep shadow seemed to swish around his feet like a low tide. A woman came up past Edwin's garage and towards him. He stood and looked at her, stared. There was no reason why a prostitute should not go shopping. But could you stop a woman with a straw shopping-basked and say "Excuse me . . . ?" No, you would *know* as she came nearer – and nearer she came – and then it would be a mere look, hardly a look, a simple moving off together, as in London where you brushed the glance and swept down the plastic corridor and up the linoed stairs. So he assumed a drunken nonchalance and the woman, as she approached, stared at him with fear, tacked to the inner part of the pavement, slid past, and walked on faster, the shopping-basket clutched tightly to be used as a weapon.

The West Indian children were curious about him and played cricket just a few yards away, willing the ball to run free towards him and then delegating the most daring of their number to scuttle past him, snatch the ball, and breathlessly return, unscathed, to the game.

With two pounds thirteen and seven in his pocket and his health intact.

He looked at all the doors. Looking for one which had a suspicious number of bells. All did.

Then at the curtain. Perhaps a fancy display of lace would be the give-away. In which case, the street was a Casbah.

He was beginning to enjoy the non-experience as much as he might have enjoyed the experience itself when a tidy little woman in a bottle-green coat came on to the steps, carefully locked her door, patted her hair, shuffled her coat, examined the evening, lit a cigarette, and then swung down those steps on to the street, turning towards Edwin's garage. She had caught Richard's eye and no mistake – hooked it would be more accurate – but he had not caught the bait, being too distracted by his own thoughts to react quickly. He set off, after her, fascinated to watch the bottle-green swing of the hips, and overwhelmed by the knowledge that a suitable payment could result in the abandonment of that garment. Small she might be, but also shapely; she curved in and out with the certainty of painted line. She looked clean, too, and that was a consideration, though for it to *be* a consideration always bewildered him.

At the end of the row of houses, she stopped, and turned to him, a newly nipped butt between her fingers—

"Have you a light?" Without cigarettes there could be no more meetings.

"A light. A light. Yes. Here."

And the gob of phosphorescence spurted into flame which she drew through the spattered black end.

"Looking for a nice time?" she asked.

"Yes." Richard laughed. "Yes. A nice time . . . How much?"

"Depends what you want. Two ten minimum."

Ask for a description of the minimum.

"O K."

"Want to take me for a drink first?"

He wondered if she would accept a cheque.

"Provided we don't have to walk all over the town."

"There's a nice pub at the bottom of the hill."

"Let's go there, then."

She linked his arm and began to walk. "I saw you waiting," she said. "Just got in?"

"Yes."

"Are you on your own?"

"Yes."

253

"Let me guess." She hesitated. "You're a traveller, aren't you?"

"How did you know?"

"You get a knack. Where's your car?"

"Being repaired."

"Richard."

He turned. There, in front of Edwin's garage, with Edwin, was Agnes. The black shadow from the buildings stretched just to her feet.

"Richard." Her voice was so strange, not an exclamation yet not timid. "Richard, could I speak to you for a moment?"

"Excuse me," he said to the woman.

"I'll come with you."

"No – I – O K."

They went across to the other pair.

"Hello, Edwin," the woman said. "Changed your mind yet?"

"Shut your filthy mouth!" Edwin looked feverish and almost uncontrollable. He was wearing the clothes he had worn the night before, but now they were caked with mud as well as grease. His face, too, was splattered with dirt.

"Been playing with mud pies?" she asked.

"You're a disgrace – being with her!" Edwin screamed this at Richard who was watching Agnes. Her face had set, as unassumingly as she could manage, but somehow the set of it seemed to withdraw the skull deep within the skin, so that her soft cheeks and flesh hung about her, cold and dead.

"I'm sorry, Richard," Agnes said, "but I'm afraid I'll have to ask you to take me home."

"Of course. What's wrong?"

"What d'you care?" Edwin demanded and, then, quite suddenly, he began to cry. The action distorted him and he clutched his arms into his face, his shoulders, but exhaustion and fear came off as much as sorrow. Agnes moved to put her arm round him. Richard and the women looked, stared, at him.

"His mother's dead," said Agnes, quietly.

"Oh. Poor Edwin," the woman was truly overcome. "Oh Edwin, I am sorry I teased you. I'm sorry, Edwin." She went up to him, the better to transmit the message.

"How did it happen?" she asked of Agnes, withdrawing from Edwin's recoil.

Agnes shook her head.

"She slipped," said Edwin, as suddenly emerging from his

collapse as he had gone into it. "Last night" – he looked at Richard closely – "last night when we left you. I put her in the car and we went down to where she lives. I had to stop the car on the docks. I had to. You can't get it up her street. And when she got out she started – talking and that. And I got out to take her – you know what state she was in – you brought her. But she wouldn't let me come near her; and she slipped. I couldn't find a ladder down. There was no water along the edge so you could walk. She landed in the mud. Doctor said she must have smothered in it."

"Oh Christ," the woman murmured. "Poor old devil."

"I came to see if I could help," said Agnes, for the first time admitting herself to be on the defensive through seeing Richard with the woman. "And now I've got to get back home. Edwin has a lot to do here."

"I've said I'd take you, Mrs. Beattie."

"No, Edwin. Richard'll see me right."

"Can *I* help?" the woman asked Edwin. He did not reply.

Richard felt a lump of horror climbing up into his throat. The way Edwin had looked at him as he had described the death! The way he had butted through suspicions which need never have been suspected! Agnes's face, calm-seeming, but so dulled with the double shock, it looked bloodless. The lump pressed against his throat. The old woman, her face in the mud. He managed to get a few yards away before being sick.

He turned. The three of them standing silently, behind them the ripped end of the terrace, stairs and fireplace still visible, yellow wallpaper peeling. In shadow now enclosing all of them.

"I'll get a drink of water," he muttered. "Just take a minute."

The cool of the garage. He shivered as he doused his neck under the cold water tap.

"I'll not tell Janice." This, from the door. Edwin was standing, black in outline. "And you can be sure Agnes won't tell her."

It didn't matter whether Edwin told Janice or not. Why should he cover so quickly for him? – and now, now – Richard went across for the towel.

"She's laid out upstairs," said Edwin. "Agnes laid her out. I thought it would look better her being brought here."

Richard nodded. And, as he passed Edwin to leave, he smiled at him; and that smile was returned. That macabre, wordless exchange stayed in his mind.

Outside, the woman stood smoking a cigarette, a few paces

away from Agnes who waited, unmoving. Richard cried inside himself that Agnes should be hurt by him – but he had to go over to the woman first. She would accept no money, coldly looked at him, was affronted, it seemed, by his lack of tact. Or perhaps simply stunned.

He touched Agnes's elbow and together they set off. Not a single word was exchanged, and in the bus queue they waited thus for fully ten minutes.

The slow bus along the narrow road. And the sun setting threw up the most luscious lights of the day. The glinting, slag-despoiled landscape shot back a thousand tones to the copper spell of the sun, and wherever you looked, purples and thickest browns, lizard-backed greens and the mauves of richest lilac, soft-seamed whites, daffodil-yellow ochre. The flash and stab of raw veins of mineral brought out of the hacked ground and spindling through the heaps like tracks of snails or gossamer-patterned webs of spiders, these all sparkled and rolled back to that great portentous shield of sun which threw off all the tones of the day through thin clouds which submerged themselves in further colours from their own day's collecting. In the country-side itself the fells took in the show with the huge sighing of repeated glory, and the streams were like make-believe strings of diamonds, the bracken a magic felt, rich in browns and burnt, reds, the flowers and grass, the trees, with blackbirds, wrens, sparrows, thrushes, robins, crows, peewits, and the gulls come inland to follow the tractor, the quiet flutter of water-hens on the tarns – there, waiting to be walked into, was the happiness of a long day, happiness he had missed, had been ignorant of. And he wanted to go back and start again before it, again come from that fell-side point and walk unknown into the village, and if there was nothing new, nothing admirable even – then let that be; for he would enjoy the peace alone, the knowledge of himself as a thing among other things, not inanimate, not deadened by this partaking, but relieved by it, at peace, peace which he avoided yes *like* a plague, and which he now wanted, for in the heart of it he might be healed. Of what, to do what, oh no matter. The grass and the leaves, a willow-glade and the dart of a yellow-hammer, hawthorn and grace-punctured iris could heal him – of himself, self. And Edwin's mother? Too late. The wetness of her face in the mud.

Agnes beside him, her head half averted, holding the tears.

Protest! Against a world that savaged all hopes by savaging

all that hope depended on. Protest! Against the foulness of men who would not yet learn that injustice and cruelty and corruption and indifference necessarily reflect back the image given; that until some cord of goodness strums throughout mankind all else will be scrambling up the tilted ship, to slide back to the rats around the cesspool of that ever-sunken vessel. Protest! Again such violence unimaginable as burning chemicals on children's arms and averted gaze on old men's loneliness, and penny-in-the-pound charity on sickness's malignity. Yes, *let* the extremes come to the centre! Drum through the world now, however pitted and pocked you yourself might be – for it is inevitably so. Nobody can ever be cured. Drum through and raise a noise at least and stop this whispering in the dark, to yourself, self. And Janice's mother? Too late. The deadness of her face beside the window-pane.

The bus drawing towards Crossbridge now, with themselves the only two on it, and still not a word. And Edwin's crooked smile.

Oh, celebrate! If nothing more to celebrate, then let it be that wormy thing that seemed himself. Transform it by singing. Celebrate the self and so raise it from the pit which condemned it so pitifully. Celebrate Narcissus and Icarus, self-love and self-confidence, take out that weary little spirit for ever corrected and chided and tugged-of-war with and set it up and say – there, that is I, if I bury myself it is to little purpose and all I can see of my past is the digging of a grave; so I throw myself on a pedestal, a rock, and say – there, go and do, do what you find you can do, stop these dissections and deliberations for they shred you and do you no good and make you capable of doing no good. Take any road – and walk! Himself. And Janice herself? Too late.

Down the track to the cottages. Agnes leaning on his arm, to comfort him, to support herself, to be led because her eyes could not be relied on now she was out of other's gaze. The silence now frightening, for at least the bus had throbbed a little life beneath them.

He took her to her door and she moved her arm so that his hand dropped away. Paula ran up to him and he lifted her up, jogged her and then turned to find Agnes still there, holding out her arms for the child who stretched out for them like a kitten clutching at a tree.

And Richard went into his own house, sickened, his head swarming with unnamable dread – blasted from every course, even from those small tracks he had tried to call his own; too late.

257

Agnes was so silent, withdrawn, like a frightened hare trembling in the corner of a yard with the unheard sounds of the hounds making her flinch. The slightest touch set her off crying, no comforting words comforted, not sullenness but a vanquished understanding gave her that submissive inertia, yoked, yet immune to all pressings. Wif could do nothing with her. The only mood he could refer it to was that which had come following on learning that she could have no more children. But then he had understood the cause of her distress and been able to help draw it from her; now he could not comprehend and so could not help.

She repulsed any attempt to help. Either by a silent turning away, or by a plea which came out as irritation – the least potent of its faces – or by tears. And she acted like an old woman. Paula was too much for her, the housework was done with infinite weariness, she made slight excuses so that she need not go and participate in any of her undertakings in the village, she shuffled around the small kitchen in slippers. To the funeral of Edwin's mother she went and Edwin she saw one afternoon when they must have talked, but Wif could learn nothing of it. Richard, he noticed, was avoided, but then he himself was avoided and so it seemed no strange matter. Janice came, was greeted with scarcely any of the excitement with which Agnes had been used to welcome these weekend visits – as if each were a holiday, each a chance to start afresh, each a new promise. And Wif thought that it was Janice who had caused this, who had, in something she had said or done, left unsaid or undone, finally unsettled Agnes and caused her decline. Yet he dared not accuse and blame, too fearful of the consequences that his disruption of that undecipherable surface might provoke. But Janice! He could not think of her without anger.

He who had grown in innocence – ignorance – ease – or so it could be said, for though he had been as early proffered to disillusion as anyone else, though he had seen enough to break ignorance's bones and undergone that which made ease a pleasure still, not a habit – yet all the description applied, for the alchemy of himself and his life had glowed with an untouchable innocence; he, then, was finally warped by a destructive regard – and this grew within him towards his daughter. In its beginnings he had spoken of it to Agnes and she thought it a passing temper; now he nursed it and got so that to think of his daughter was to stab his own mind with jerking ferocity. The ice he now considered Janice to be burned him.

Agnes tried to drive all thoughts from her mind. She wanted emptiness, sweet nothings in her imagination, silences in her ears. She wanted a blank place, nothing, nothing to think or do or say or hear – just the emptiness so that all would go away. She saw Janice lift up Paula with clumsy disregard. Edwin, his face pleading for comfort. And the swinging of the bottle-green coat as Richard walked arm-in-arm down the street with that woman. She wished none of them any harm, could not really blame anyone, did not want explanations or apologies, wanted emptiness and longed, longed to be alone.

When she was alone, she would sing to herself, very softly as she scarcely moved around the house. Songs from all her days, lines, melodies, a few words, fragments, and hymns she sang. One in particular she sang repeatedly. This hymn came to be the chiefest of her veils for blankness, and she sang it softly as she moved in the empty cottage.

"God is working His purpose out
   As year succeeds to year.
God is working His purpose out
   And the time is drawing near.
Nearer and nearer draws the time
   The time that shall surely be,
When earth shall be filled with the glory of God
   As the waters cover the sea."

Low-voiced, a sweet voice from that hawthorn-blossomed face, dull now, but still with the fine, thin skin and the colours which could dapple, the grey hair silvery, caught up at the neck. And the plaintive words filled the cottage so that she met them wherever she moved. This bed, given by her brothers as a wedding present; carried by them the four miles from the sale. The Toby-jugs she had received from Janice from a school trip to Morecambe. The curtains she had made up herself. She would stand in the bedroom, her back to the window, looking at the calendar on the wall, and an hour would pass in a whisk. There were Janice's school reports she found in a drawer, under a tidy and

259

pressed collection of Wif's shirts – scarcely worn – and these kept her occupied for the whole of one morning. They had been very hopeful about her at the school. Agnes had never missed a speech-day and knew the titles of all the books her daughter had received for prizes.

If she had ever entertained a picture of her daughter and herself walking arm-in-arm through the village, gossiping intimately, people saying how alike they were, then she had lost it without pain, and the memories she did have were enough. She remembered the growing understanding that Janice was different and doing what she could to make that difference complete; the girl had never been dissatisfied with her home, never ashamed of it as some with a lot less brains were. She had argued with her parents, but only, Agnes realised, to try to pull them also through the barrier she was attempting, or in bewilderment, when she did not know what to think or do and wanted her father to be the honing-stone. And Agnes had accepted all that – allowing for intermittent anger and unhappiness – she had accepted it, as much in love with the wild flower as she would have been with the garden rose. Indeed, there was a strangeness in it, seeing someone change, make themselves into something else, which had opened parts of herself to herself that otherwise she would never have known. She felt that it was daring, and the whisper of admiration this evoked compensated for any sense of loss.

She found an envelope of photographs, old smoked studies in oval of her family, clustered in a band around the mother in the chair, standing as in a redoubt, not a smile, not a question, it seemed, all gleaming with sureness. Those she looked at, brushed with a handkerchief, and returned to their forgotten place.

So the days after the meeting with Richard passed, slowly as the time-masking afternoons of early childhood. And as the memories of her own childhood pushed gently into that slow time, the days were stretched in a still motion, where everything was reviewed and nothing in the present went forward to make new memories.

Richard was relieved to be avoided. Had Agnes not made it very clear that she wished to be alone, then he would have felt cowardly about keeping out of her way. As it was, he had time to himself, and, being cut off even from Agnes, he felt truly alone and he could sort himself out finally, and for good.

He had to be the author of himself and inscribe something.

What he would do came to him quite easily and so, still in his crabbed suspicion, he at first distrusted it. He would ask Janice to come with him but, expecting a refusal, prepare to go on his own. To India. He was aware of the weakness in such exotic extremism, but that he could accept. He would save from his wages until the summer, go to London, try to get employment in India through a United Nations organisation or through War on Want and, if that was impossible, then he would work for his own passage there and, once there, see what there was to do.

That he could do as good work in England as in India was unanswerable. That India, with its ring of Millions Starving, had the sort of glamour such a decision ought to be unaware of, that was also true. That to work for so many would be as pitiful in its effect as to work only for yourself – the one just about as self-indulgent as the other, one salving conscience, the other trying to create a conscience – all this, fair accusation. That perhaps to work for poor people was no more than to employ charity, charity which, he had thought was the first defence of the status quo and should be made unnecessary by a system which made it so – all fair accusation. That therefore he should stay in his own place, work with people and institutions he knew something of and so could have more chance of influencing – in short, make the Labour Party or the Independent Labour Party, or the Communist Party, into a real force for change, for root-change which would spread not the surfeit of affluence's benefits, but the structure of Socialism's aims for society – true once more. But you could move only where you had hope. That he had learnt. For himself it was so, if for no one else. Whatever seemed to be the logical and admirable course could seem so until doomsday but could gain no allegiance from him unless he personally saw hope in it. And this, too, was another face of selfishness; that the greater should contain his own lesser aspirations. But there it was.

These were the merest beginnings of arguments which could go on for ever, but he did not allow them to. He found that his decision came clearly, and though he waited each day for it to change, to be qualified, to lose impetus, it did not. He would tell Janice, tell Agnes, and do it.

Janice came over at the weekend, and he made love to her, if not as at the beginning then at least without that expectation of resistance which had frozen him. His visit to her, it appeared, had even softened her a little, for she was more tender about all things. It seemed as if she, too intuitively recognised that a new phase was to come, and on the Sunday evening, when they were lazily curled up with the litter of the newspapers and the comfortable ululation from the radio, he almost told her about the woman. He had no fear that Agnes would reveal what she had seen but no real impulse, as yet – until he had first talked to Agnes – to inform Janice of it.

Wif had 'words' with Janice, but they fell over her as harmlessly as water and the old man soon gave up, indeed avoided his daughter and devoted himself to the wall in the garden. There was but one half of one side to go, and then it would be finished.

Now back from school early, Richard began to help again, and half-way through the week only a few more stones were needed. Both men went out to it at about seven o'clock. It was a blustering evening, the new leaves thrown about the trees, the clouds streaming across the sky. Rain had made the garden a little treacherous and Paula slipped on one of the stones, Agnes coming out to comfort her and then get her ready for bed.

They finished in a couple of hours. It would not have taken as long as that had Wif not spent half the time going round the whole thing, knocking and testing it with concentrated care. Richard was as pleased as if he had done the whole thing himself. It was strange that such a job – which led to no greatly useful end, had no aesthetic ambition, cost no profound price of skill, no excessive amount of labour – should yet be so pacifically satisfying. He wanted to stay and smoke a cigarette within the walls, to tap them with the pad of his hand as Wif himself was doing, to extend the enjoyment that was, undoubtedly, in him. And he had done little enough for it! Wif's enjoyment – but Wif, it seemed to Richard, must get the same contentment out of whatever he did. There was in him something which relished the making.

It grew darker, and yet the two men felt disinclined to go in. A fine, blowy dusk, fresh spring, when all could be cleared out and made new.

He would tell Agnes about his plan, and try to explain to her about that other night. There was an obligation to explain to her, a simple one; he did not want her hurt, and as he had hurt her, he must do what he could to remedy it. There could be no better time for it. The fell behind them was darkening quickly, but it seemed a friendly darkening; the grass shook under the wind, one or two rooks wheeled and cawed, a few lights peeped from a distance. Richard felt that he was full of everything necessary for any life he chose, and he rested on his decision.

Agnes came out with a tray bearing two mugs of tea and some biscuits. She handed them to the two men, after picking her way carefully over the scattering of wet stones, the pile which would not now be necessary for the walls. As Richard took the tea from her, he looked at her for the first time enquiringly since that awful encounter. She returned his look, steadily, but with pain, a pain he could not bear.

As she turned and set off for the house, he could hold back no longer.

"Mother," he said, quietly, beginning to follow her. "Just a minute."

His tone was clear; he was going to tell her. She hurried on. Scenting her flight from him, and unable to bear it, Richard strode after her, faster.

"No," he said, "don't rush. I want to talk to you. Please!"

Now she walked with a trot; the last few yards of the garden she ran, fearing that Richard would grab her and tell her what she did not want to know.

"Mother!"

She turned, to say no, to say leave me, to say, go away – and saw Richard so close to her that she flinched back. Her feet went from under her on the wet stone and she fell, her back ramming into the upturned point of another stone. The crack was so sharp it split through Richard's mind.

CHAPTER THIRTY-EIGHT

It stayed in his mind, that sound – like a trapped echo, called up at the least whisper. He felt that it would stay there for as long as he liked. Everywhere, it jumped him. So he could be sitting reading, or walking along a road, eating or half asleep, and the crack would jerk back his head.

Agnes was taken to hospital. The spine was fractured, and the nerves at the base of the spine had been severely damaged, so that she was paralysed. She could lie with her eyes open and seem calm, as if resting; but her movements were mere twitchings, her speech an indecipherable gobbling which soon tired her. The hospital promised survival, perhaps for years, but were no more than sympathetically hopeful about recovery.

Her bed was surrounded by flowers and cards from people in the village, and in the corner of the small white ward the flowers made her bed seem like a jubilant bier. People came to ask Wif about the visiting times, and rotas were made out at the Institute and the church to prevent too many from crowding in and to allow the family some solitary vigils. The cottage became a gift centre as farmers brought eggs and fruit, children brought chocolate and committees brought cardigans the members had knitted; for a good three weeks after the accident, the cottage became a point of pilgrimage for everyone, it seemed, from all the area.

Janice was at home to deal with it all and look after Paula and her father. The term was scarcely under way, but the work she had to do consisted, chiefly, of writing a long essay on her 'special subject' – and, with the books around her, she could as well write it in the cottage, which she proceeded to do, giving Paula to the care of Mrs. Jackson for three or four hours of every morning.

The worst change was in Wif. He sank into himself, withdrew so far that Richard felt that he was meeting a new person. He said little, and that little either a short clutch of remembered pleasure with Agnes, or a fractious outburst against some harmless mannerism or act of Janice. He was given compassionate leave from his job, but tolerated that for one morning only, glad, it seemed, to be away from the cottage. Occasionally he would appear as he had never done before – as a very old man. He would be standing outside the cottage, barely able to answer some sympathiser, hands in his baggy pockets, his big-nebbed boots muddy, the laces loosened and trailing on to the ground, his waistcoat open, buttonless, but still stiff brown-fronted from shoulder to stomach, standing, only slightly swaying, as if something in him was reminded of once rocking on his heels, and then tears would come into his bright eyes, blurring and ageing them, and his face would tense greyly with the effort not to cry. The friend would see what was happening, pat his shoulder or touch his arm, and leave, and Wif would turn a little to his left so that he would have his back to the cottage, his gaze over the garden to Knockmirton, fuming in mid-spring clouds as if drawing volcanic wrath into itself, and Richard and Janice would see the silk back of the waistcoat shaking slightly as he wept. His head, cropped bare at the neck, still thrusting with hair where he permitted it to grow, would shake forward, his hands billow in his pockets, a boot stir nervously as if half-intent on kicking a stone, and then, as he prepared to come in, or more likely to go to his shed, he would start to whistle, like a schoolboy hiding guilt, and that strutting sound came out so brokenly that it was unendurable.

When he talked of Agnes, he spoke of times so far past that it seemed he was remembering not youth or manhood, not love or marriage, but life itself, calling it back into him. And when he turned on Janice, it was with short-winded irritation. He blamed her – there was no reason for it and he pressed none, neither did he state his blame straight-forwardly – but he did blame her, and it was written all over him. But, as yet, he was not much concerned to turn on her. He was still too robbed of all responses, queueing up for the visiting time in the hospital, changing the water in the flowers.

Janice smarted at what she considered to be the injustice of her father's unspoken accusation, but kept it to herself. Indeed, she was perturbed that such a small feeling could be so prominent as her mother lay paralysed. And even more disturbed that she should be able to devote so much concentrated effort on her College work. And think about it, about her own future, about David's offer – all that; think about it naggingly and consistently and never be able to get it out of her mind. Herself not only pre-eminent but clamant, as her mother lay unable to speak. The contrast between her own selfishness and her mother's helplessness was too terrible to consider for long, and so Janice shut it up in herself, was immaculately efficient in household matters, and, rather than examine the circumstances of her condition further – not helped to do so by Richard's sunken shock, not helped, either, by the retreat she thought she saw in all of the village when she walked through, and further exacerbated by the fact that she felt she needed no help – impregnable then, she remained, because she did not want to do the stoop necessary for that vulnerability which can eventually lead to understanding. She stayed cold as she seemed. And sometimes her coldness seemed a protection, and other times it seemed a posture, and then it seemed the essential part of her. She would *not* be swallowed by her feelings. By any feelings. In making the least attempt to yield to them she squirmed with fear or disgust, and a determined rationalism wriggled again to the top of her mind – even

265

as she caressed her daughter, saw her father's tears, heard Richard's groping misery in the night, stood by her mothers' bed – even then she set her aims in order, tightened her lips and remained enclosed in her determination to be alone, to make herself independent of as many people as possible, to be untouched.

One afternoon, when he was free, Richard went along to the hospital. It was not an official visiting time, but the staff were very easy, especially in a case such as Agnes's when all of them knew that she would be there for a long time. He went in at the time of the 'afternoon nap', as the Sister explained; but Agnes had her eyes open and so Richard was shushed to a bedside seat and left there with a finger-to-mouth warning.

Before leaving, the Sister tucked Agnes in, though the bed was unruffled since the morning, and all that could be seen of her was the upturned face, practically immobile, the white hair spread out on the pillow. She looked very beautiful. It was as if she had come to the hospital for a rest; her skin, always clear and fresh, now seemed like finest mother-of-pearl, with faint rosy tints on the cheeks by a painstaking miniaturist. The contrast between her appearance and her condition was tranquil and violent; her face brought to Richard's mind comparison with delicate works; the knowledge that under the padded bedclothes was a lump of plaster set round the small body like a stiffened winding-sheet, that when she would attempt to talk her precise mouth would slacken and dribble and the face run to a pain which looked as if it might set the expression for ever, so that you would wipe her chin and tell her that she need not talk and see her eyes trying to crowd all meanings into their still clear colours, so many things unsaid, and to unscramble them would exhaust her.

It was the first time that Richard had been alone with her and it had taken many false starts for him to face it. He pulled up his chair, wincing as it scraped across the bare floor, and positioned himself so that she would be able to see him without straining.

He wanted to tell her that he was sorry; he wanted to explain how much he loved her and why he loved her; he wanted to try to make it clear to her why he had been with the prostitute.

All of that seemed unnecessary and the very bottom of the pit of self-indulgence. She was paralysed, her life, as she had lived it, over; and that was a fact.

So instead, he told her about his own childhood, making it as

266

rambling and detailed as possible. For that, he knew, she liked. The area in which he had been brought up was so like Crossbridge in many ways that he could constantly bring in comparisons. He told her about his grandfather who was like Wif in many ways, and his grandmother who was like herself. About Temple Whitehead who was the last man left working on what had been an important railway terminus there in a country village – as Lord Yealand would let the line run no further since his wife did not want to see 'dirty steam engines' from her bedroom window, no requisitioning in those days, so they built a turntable. Temple Whitehead used to operate it, spinning the engines round like sausages on a plate – and he had seen his work go away, for eventually a tunnel had been made under Lord Yealand's flat land – but Temple would *not* go away. So first he had changed his job from being a fitter to being a cleaner, and from cleaner to odd-job man, and from that to watchman, until everything was cleared out, but he still watched. He would sit on the plate that had turned the engines round and keep it in shape, and although the rest of the yards rotted and rusted and wood from fences disappeared in the night when he was *not* watching (the hue and cry he raised over those fences!) this one piece shone and sparkled and would work, he said, 'any day anybody had a mind to use it'. Finally, when a watchman was no longer needed, he became known as the caretaker. It was never established whether the position was official, whether it carried any pay – and he was seen to collect his pension regularly so it could not have been very well paid, otherwise the pension would have been docked. But caretaker he became and he worked or dabbled or did what he thought had to be done in the yards from eight to twelve and one to five each weekday, contenting himself with a stroll through his property on Saturday mornings and the merest glancing over it on Sunday afternoons.

This might have developed into a lonely life, but Temple loved company, and he was someone whose gregarious nature did not have to reach out to others, for others reached out to him. There would always be at least one old pal 'up in the yards to see Temple', and the boys of the village went there for all reasons: to be shouted at and chased away if they threatened to destroy or filch anything; to be shown how things worked; to be given exact information about the make and construction of trains; most of all, perhaps, to be entertained, for Temple did imitations. Always had done. Of people in the village.

There was the postmistress – Miss Osborne – and he used to take her off to a 't'. She was. . . .

And he had come to tell her that he was sorry. Perhaps this clumsy story-telling was just as indulgent. He could only hope not. What did anyone ever do that did not indulge themselves in some way? It wasn't an academic mannerism of a question. He wanted to know, to live, knowing. But there was no time for that now. He kissed her brow as he left, not hesitating or wondering over the action until afterwards when, thankfully, it was too late. The skin was slightly damp, but firm as he kissed her and left.

With the tension in the cottage between Wif and Janice, he found it an uncomfortable place to be – but for that reason stayed there. Not only uncomfortable for that reason – horrible and awful because he was convinced that he was the sole and total cause of Agnes's condition and yet he could not begin to explain it. Many times he thought he would – but what would be the effect? Wif would be confused and take little notice anyway, and he would blame Janice for driving him to another woman in the first place. Janice would sweep it away as absurd or, taking it seriously, do something which could only further upset Wif and Paula and Agnes perhaps.

He wanted to say 'I did it.' 'It's all my fault.'

But at the centre of that confession would have been nothing but pain and further misery for others. And the last consumptive gasp of Indulgence and Self-pity. He was manacled in unbreakable, secret silence.

CHAPTER THIRTY-NINE

He slept less and less and, though summer came, was often shivering. Wif was moved to see him take it so to heart, but could only hold the younger man's shoulder and mutter that he must not take it so hard. Janice tried to find out what was wrong, but she had not the patience to hear through the tacking and testing which led to the first hint even of the trouble, nor did she want to entangle herself with him, having so much to think about herself. But she pitied him. All his zest had gone – and even though, before, that energy had concerned itself, as often as not, with a broiling self-regard, nevertheless it had smacked off him like the trembling spray off the sea. Now he was steady, and steadily shrivelling. He merely played with his food, he went on no walks, he did not go to the pub, he sat with the same page of a book before him for a whole evening or clicked on the television so that he could be distracted – and failed to be. He lost weight, cared not at all about his appearance, becoming sloppy and even dirty. She could see that it tired him to get up, it tired him to catch the bus to school, it tired him to mark the exercise books, it tired him to walk the slightest distance – even across a room; all things tired him and he went where she did not want to follow, into that depression which sucks in all who touch it.

Finally, Richard could stand it no longer. The truth, it now seemed, Truth – like a simply-formed force – was in him and had to be spoken to be known.

He went down to Margaret's pub one day after school, after meaning to mark the homework in the staff-room beforehand as he had once done, but falling asleep over it, waking up cold, though outside the sun shone clearly enough. He did not reach the pub until about seven and it was empty. Margaret's mother was behind the bar and so he waited. He had a whisky because he could not face the quantity of a pint. Not even of one.

When he went for his second drink, he asked, stammeringly – the stammer coming on him so suddenly that it felt affected, but he could not throw it off – whether Margaret was in.

She was not, her mother said. She had gone back to London. Her father was now much better and her help was not needed. She had the address, would get it for him, and Richard waited while the address was searched out, painstakingly copied down, folded and delivered.

He put it in his pocket intending to throw it away later. The nothing that that had been! It all seemed part of such a nerveless time.

Swallowing the second whisky so quickly that it slid into his throat like a stinging swab, he choked and coughed violently, his eyes streaming, his head jerking on the shoulders puppet-like.

When he got outside, he knew whom he must talk to, and caught the bus to Whitehaven, to see Edwin. The garage was closed, and it was only after hammering on the doors for a good few minutes that he succeeded in rousing Edwin from his seclusion in his own room, at the top at the back. Edwin did not want him to come in, and Richard did not fancy inviting him to a pub, so they set off for a walk.

They went along the top road, out of the town, to those terraced villages which clung so perilously to the scarred cliffs above the sea. The day had been fine, and the sunset was glorious, children were playing cricket on the waste land and men were digging their allotments, yet none of this calm – for it seemed that all things were tranquil and all was easy, pleasant and possible – none of it loosened by one part degree the tension in both these men.

"I haven't told Janice about you and that other woman," said Edwin, with such a mixture of virtue and slyness as made Richard want to challenge him to do so and then discover how brittle the supposed hold was. Yet he restrained himself. Edwin had to be told about Agnes. There were ways, ways – one way . . .

"I think that that was what *really* finished Agnes off," said Richard – and the words seemed too crude, talking about the woman he loved, now alone in the white ward.

"How do you mean?"

"She changed because of that," Richard said. "She seemed to give up. And it was when I was trying to tell her that I was sorry and to explain it to her – we were in the garden, I followed her – then she fell. She fell, running away from what I was going to tell her."

"No. That true?"

Richard did not reply. So he had told – futility. It was himself he had to tell. Himself had to decide for himself what himself would do. To ask for help was to ask for mercy. And he deserved none.

Edwin looked at Richard with something of triumph and something of relief. He stopped, shoved his hands in his pockets and took a breath deeply and said, with strained carelessness,

"Don't let it get you depressed, I feel a bit the same way about my mother. And it's daft, you see. I lost my temper a bit with her, and, to be quite honest, I could have got that car up to her house but I told her to get out. Well, you know how she used to shout. She shouted at me then and I got out to quieten her down. And I went across to her . . . to stop her screaming her head off so that everybody could hear. But she thought I was going to hit her or something. Anyway, she backed away, and that's how she fell." He paused and licked his lips. He knew that Richard had guessed some of this, or more, and was risking all by daring as much as he could – and so clearing it, once and for all. "So you see, I could blame *myself* as well – and I do – but that's just one way of looking at it. In a way it was *her* fault. And, really, it was an accident ... You didn't *want* it to happen to Agnes, did you?"

Richard made no answer.

"Of course, you didn't. Neither did I. So you can't spend the rest of your life blaming yourself, can you?"

Below, rocks going into the sea. Dull, vicious rocks, even in the glow of sunset, and black, as if they too had been saturated in the coal dust that smothered the cottages and the land around them. To throw himself on to them. Only more trouble for others. One life. No alternative.

They walked back towards the garage, and when they reached there, by way of saying good-bye, Edwin put his hand on Richard's shoulder, as Wif did, and gripped it encouragingly.

"It'll be all right," he said. "And by the way, I'll be seeing more of you soon. I'm coming back near Crossbridge. This place is too small now, and my trade'll follow me. I've got some premises – down where the forge used to be – you know that? That and the old school. The both of them. I should really be able to get going there." He nodded. "Welding's a specialised trade, you see. People don't mind travelling out of their way to get a good job done. And there's all the trade from the farmers." Richard nodded and left.

As Edwin walked away, his affection – based, entirely, on his own feelings of relief in finding, as he thought, that Richard was no better than himself and had no more hold on him than he had on Richard – shrugged off and, at the garage, he thought of Agnes for whom he would have done anything, anything in the world, the one woman who had always respected him and been kind to him, he had loved her, he told himself, yes, he had loved her. And that sod had killed her!

Reaching the hospital, Richard was told that it was too late for visiting, even for relatives, even as a favour. And Agnes was asleep now, would sleep until morning. He wanted to go in, to pull her back because she was dying, he knew, and dying she did not want to come back and face it all. He pleaded with the Sister, but she was increasingly firm the more he insisted, and he went away.

The last bus had gone and so he had to walk. He did not thumb for lifts and by the time he reached the cottage he was almost

271

shaking with exhaustion and he fell asleep in the chair, his mouth slightly open, a bead of saliva running from one corner of it; beaten.

CHAPTER FORTY

Agnes's funeral was at the end of August. She was buried in Crossbridge churchyard and most of the village was there. The small church was full, and the wreaths were so many that they spread over on to the two graves on either side of her own. A cross was put at the head of the grave, Wif saying that he would get a headstone as soon as he could, refusing all offers from others to buy one. Blinds were drawn at each house the hearse passed by, and the farmers kept their tractors away from the fields bordering the route.

Wif would no longer stay in the cottage and was going across the fells to a similar village to live with his brother. Janice was to return to Carcaster, having found a capable woman in the village who would look after Paula through the week. She would also see after Richard who refused to move, gave up his teaching job, and revealed nothing of his plans.

When the coffin was carried out of the church, and the people followed, the whole graveyard was covered in black. Richard could hardly look at the slim, short box. Lowered into the grave. Wif took a handful of dirt and let it fall on to the wood. Then he bent as if to go down one last time to his wife, and Janice held him, gently, taking his head on her shoulder. Richard felt the soft, wet earth in his hand and scattered it into the grave.

PART III

DANCE TILL YOU DROP

'The desires of the heart are as crooked as corkscrews,
Not to be born is the best for man;
The second best is a formal order,
The dance's pattern; dance while you can
Dance, dance, for the figure is easy,
The tune is catching and will not stop;
Dance till the stars come down from the rafters;
Dance, dance, dance till you drop.'

from *Death's Echo* by W. H. Auden.

CHAPTER FORTY-ONE

Janice looked down at the blank sheet of paper and picked up her pen yet again. The action was enough, however, and the moment her fingers touched the black plastic surface of the pen she abandoned the impulse to write. Since her mother's death, she had written nothing of her own and now the habit which had kept the essays going was fading too. She had been sitting at the table in her room for three hours now and not one word had been written.

In one way, there was dignity in such a paralysis. To have carried on for ever 'as usual' – as she had done in the first months after the funeral – would have stretched conscientiousness to unfeeling display akin to indifference. So at the back of her mind was a contentment with her inability to do any work. Yet as she dreamed and was vacant about herself that contentment slid forward and presented itself as something else; a relief, a reassurance about her own feelings, that she could be as was expected, which was the way to normality. But, as soon as she realised that she was nourishing the pain for reasons which came not from the cause of it but from its value to herself, its helpfulness was dissipated. It was yet another face of selfishness. Nor did she *want* 'normality'!

She had not cried at the grave. That was not exceptional. She had not felt the least prick of tears. As the earth covered the coffin she had seen the sleek wood despoiled and noticed that for Wif, and perhaps for Richard, the box was a shield too fragile, for them the earth landed on Agnes's face, her body, her quietly unclenched hands. For her, it was an event of which she was part, but she could find no whole on which all the parts depended. Everything had seemed isolated and untouchable. Her father's grief was private, there were others who were sad, the church walls were glossy with lichens, the grave-digger's spade lay casually across a settled mound, the drivers of the funeral cars stood together under the plane trees and smoked. Perhaps if Paula had been there; she had wanted Paula to come; she had wanted Paula to attend to while the service was going on, but Paula was put out with a neighbour.

She did not wish to explain or explore further, for fear of

what she might find. She had decided on what her life was to be and would stick to it, could not but stick to it now – for all else seemed so far away from her. If she could claim Richard, and her father, and Paula, and anyone from her past into this life she was leading, then she would be glad. That she knew. She was lonely. But – she had decided on her life and knew, from that broken time after the birth, that the loneliness within it was worth it, for outside of it she could do nothing at all.

David had said that he would be in for lunch – he had started to join her at the flat occasionally now, bringing a bottle of wine, some pâté, she supplying the bread and cheese to add to the farce of a French picnic in tolling Carcaster. This day, she looked forward to seeing him, as she had come to do, but much more now, because his jokes, though they were strained, and his pushiness, though it was sometimes boring, and all the unflagging operating that there was about him were all bearable now. He was as far away from her as everyone else, but at least he made the effort to flicker more brightly. Behind his bombast, there was a desire to be cheerful, to pass the time a little more energetically, to force the other to action, which she could reject but which, if accepted, had the definite aim of increasing pleasure. In a situation where everyone who wanted to enter her world demanded that she expand or change it to fit them, it was good to meet someone who, if he gave little, demanded equally little. And occasionally she was moved to think that David almost deliberately did himself an injustice. For he gave a lot; though brash, he was not violent, rejecting that mind-acted animality which besotted many like him; though garrulous, he was looking for answers as much as audiences; though ambitious, it was as much the understandable wish to emulate as the need to hoard success to himself. When he insisted it was always with a joke, in tone or word, which inevitably provided an excuse for the other, Above all, she felt, suffocated as she was at Carcaster by young men preoccupied with their place and baying at the pressures of the outside world, and at Crossbridge by Richard, gnarled over some private misery or mystery which she thought, alternately, silly, unnecessary, or too complicated and strenuous for her to wish to be involved in at this moment, David was air. She worked hard to convince herself of this reappraisal.

So she waited for him, wilfully, happily. She got up from her fruitless paper – it was not essential work, a prize of twenty-five pounds had been offered for an essay of 10,000 words on the subject 'Literature and Morality' and she wanted to win it – packed up the sprawl of books and notes on her table, threw a clean cloth over it and then, discovering she had only a little bread and that stale, went out to shop, leaving the door on the latch.

In the lazy street she walked, the slow wind pushing the skirt limp against her thighs. Just as sun did not burn her skin, powdering it rather with a softer bloom, so the gritty weather of late autumn did not pummel it stiff or blue-red streaked. Her hair was loosely bobbed now, for convenience, but still around her brow it lifted softly, against the wind, and its wheaty thickness sank against the neck with a richness which made men want to plunge in their fingers. Her figure had become even better, slim not as a colt but as a woman who had had the last grease rub of puppy fat and seen it roll away. Yet she walked not in that stride of flaunting narcisism which beauty explains but no one can ever excuse, nor in hustling modesty which claims even more than it presents, but she walked thinking about what was on her mind and as near unconscious of the effect she had as her awareness of it would allow.

David was there when she got back. He had laid the table and somehow made the room more comfortable, by throwing his coat over a chair, swinging the settee around to face the window, sprawling in it with his paper. She was more honestly glad to see him than she had anticipated and they picnicked and laughed through the meal until they reached the stage where everything said was to be laughed at and the laughter was a shot across the bows followed by silence while the sea lapped uncertain.

He was always uncertain of her mood. Now, he thought her exuberance came from returning to what concerned her. Besides, since her mother's death, he had been wary of her. On her return she had, to his eye, been ready for anyone's 'taking' and he had resisted only from some presentiment of the complications which could result from such an action at such a time. He had felt, for the first time with her, chilled; she was not urgently desirable to him, and the tip of that feeling reached out and tapped his urge each time it raised itself. That had made it easier to visit her, easier to be free with her, for he still enjoyed being in her company, though more to be fascinated by her behaviour and attitudes than, as before, to practise bemusement on a pregnable young woman. This day, her spirits were more unbridled than he had ever seen them, and he was doubly wary, suspecting some spring coiled hidden from him which would release a vicious jab should he more than acknowledge her state and accept it as he had done less open moods before.

"So how's Richard?" he asked, when the litter of lunch was settled around them and she gulping at her third glass of wine. Wild but rather grand, he thought.

" 'So how's Richard?' " she mocked. "It's like the pips on the wireless. 'So how's Richard?' " She said it gruffly, irritated her throat, and coughed spasmodically so that the wine slopped on to her dress. "No!" She waved him away. "No." Steadied herself. "I've got to reply just like you've got to ask. Richard" – she paused – "is still working his purpose out in the stone quarries – isn't there a song about that, *you* should know? – wearing himself out, exhausted and incapable of speech or movement most of the time outside his working hours, drinking a lot, I think, brooding even more than ever and to even less point and living in a pigsty." She paused, knowing that she had over-tilted, but, exhilarated at the moment by her unaccustomed lack of restraint, she abandoned all the devices employed to lock her secrets. "He scarcely says one word to me," she went on. "Sometimes he sits – in his working clothes, you've no idea how dirty he gets and I wouldn't care if it was attractive grime but it isn't and he refuses to clean up – though not out of a snobby pride, I think, more because he *is* too tired to do it – and he sits there all evening without reading or listening and I think he's working up to make a monumental decision – it becomes unbearable – and I say 'What's wrong?' – and he turns on me: 'Why should anything be wrong?' 'Why did you say that?' and 'What do you know about wrong, or right, or any bloody thing at all except your own sick ambitions?' "

"He sounds in a bad way still," David interrupted, unwilling to listen to more said against Richard, and rather disgusted with the malice in Janice's tone. Yet he knew that if she loved anyone, she loved Richard, and he was sorry for her, too, that her several frustrations were curdling to sourness. "I tried to talk to him just a few weeks after the funeral – you know. But nothing I said made the slightest difference. I mean I tried" – he smiled – "I used the old business of it being sheer exhibitionism to work in a stone quarry, but he didn't bat an eye. All he said was that he could not go on teaching and he didn't know enough to be a farm labourer and so, in Crossbridge, there was little choice left. But why Crossbridge?"

"Why?" Janice spoke over-loudly, drunkenly, David now thought, the dislocation between the rhythm of her voice and that of her body becoming noticeable and feeding itself by over strenuous attempts at correction. "Why Crossbridge? That's what I ask him. But he won't leave. And there's nobody there for him now, nobody – except Edwin, maybe. I know that he spends some time with Edwin at his new place."

"Did you try to get him to come here?"

"Yes," she said, shortly.

"I suppose," David replied, vaguely, "that he might want to keep an eye on that daughter of yours. She's still there isn't she?"

"Well looked after. Better than I could." Janice picked up the bottle and poured the small amount that was left to the dregs into her glass. "You're just like Richard. You haven't the guts to say I should be at home 'nursing the flesh of my flesh and watching its every change as a True Mother should' – but you expect nothing less, nothing else. The mother isn't necessarily the only woman who can mother a child, and sometimes she's far from being even adequate. I should be useless. That's that."

"Oh, I agree."

"You couldn't do anything else," she retorted, sharply.

"I wouldn't want to."

"Hm!"

"I mean, it's all right for him to go on as he had been – but for *some* time, not a long time, or it could turn out to be all the time. He's cracked up altogether though, as far as I can see."

"Since his marriage?" said Janice.

"Now then. Ask and ye shall receive." David smiled, put his arms behind his head so that his cuff slipped free of his watch and he could cheer on a deadline. He wondered, as often he did with others, how he had been drawn into his pursuit of this woman, now edged forward, hot on her seat, her eyes blazing at him, her dress sliding up her thighs, frenzied, he thought, and unbalanced, driving away desire with the whip of overbearing challenge. "Anyway, I'd like to help the old sod, but he won't have it, so that's that. It's funny, though; you think of the people you were with in London, and they'll be more or less successful, you know, the net's too big for them to fall out of. Something'll always turn up. Richard got away."

"I thought that you envied that about him."

"Maybe I did," David answered. "Maybe. But not now. His trouble is that he thinks the world's against him and to get it on his side he's got to find a magic key. Well, there aren't any. And the world's too busy to be bothered being against him. He's inventing enemies and opponents and grudges. . . ."

"He doesn't have grudges. And he doesn't need opponents."

"Maybe not." He yawned. "That wine made me tired. And I must be off. There's a Love-In at Bitts Park. We're covering it. I know the fella who's organising it – used to know him – I thought I'd participate in the latest sleeping-draught to intelligence – or conscience." He stood up. "That's what's bothering Richard, you know. His scabby old conscience. But it's no good, all that's finished. We all 'tune in and drop out' now."

He smiled, and held the smile as he leaned over for his coat and calculated his quick flight. There was a commitment or intimacy clearly expected of him and he was going to escape it. The moment would be uncomfortable, he knew that, yet anything but fast action would land him in trouble.

"Can I come with you?"

"Well, you *could*, but it wouldn't be much fun for you. I mean, it's just like Castle Street on a Sunday evening – a lot of people standing around – and our people are down there filming, I'll have to hop around a bit, I don't think you would like it."

"Such consideration."

"No. Come, if you like."

"No thanks."

"Well. I must be gone. I told you I'm probably going back to London soon on a new ITV deal that's being set up, didn't I? Yes. I'll be flitting there and back quite a lot in future. So I won't be able to see you as often."

"David. Don't be feeble as well as being stupid. Just push off to your Be-In like a good little boy and impress your engaging personality on all you meet."

"For Christ's sake, Janice!"

"Oh, push off. Sorry. But – well, you're O K. You're marvellously O K, David – but what does that add up to? O K O K. O K! O K!" She put her hands over her ears and stamped out the letters.

He opened the door and she stopped. Looking at her, he felt a fool to leave, an idiot to, he wanted, she was . . .

"Janice."

"Fine David. Cheerio. Please." She paused. "Have a . . . Please! Go away!"

Then she was alone again and wanted to write to Richard.

Opening that blank-sheeted morning file, she began and tore up the first attempt, the second, the third, the fourth. She got up and walked round her flat, still littered. Crowded in on her, would go to Richard this minute and say – but what would saying mean? What would she do? Do about it?

It would be convenient for her to rush to Richard now and declare her love, to have her fear appeased. But he would smell out the convenience of it in a moment and that fact would harden everything between them. Once he had said that it was convenience which had stoned their marriage. Both of them, he had said, had thought they were on to a good thing. Temporary relief. Temporary surface. The holes still unfilled below.

Dear Richard, Dearest Richard, my darling,
I. . . .
And there was no more that had not been abandoned by her, shot with unhappy suspicion by him, or traduced on the slab of their late meeting-places. Meat to meat in the chill bed.
Richard,
I. . . .

No more.

If David had slid his practised little palm between her knees, they might have opened this day. And for no better reason than that she had allowed herself to hover over past decisions, to heat up the stacked memories which could be culled to hurt but could also be forgotten. If she had taken him, it would have been self-willed payment for the price of her thoughts which she alone had succeeded in making unbearable to herself. That way led to the loss of everything. And she could afford to lose not a particle of what she had, for it would unseat all she had self-straddled.

So she tore up the final sheets and washed her face. Sat down and wrote out a page and a half of good sense about Literature and Morality. Calculated that she would need to rearrange her lectures and commitments the next day in order to finish it in the time she had set herself. Gathered together the books she was to return to the library. Burned the litter of the lunch. Made notes of the reading list she had to order for her special subject. Wrote a note to one of the lecturers, accepting an invitation he was giving to half a dozen students to attend an informal meeting to consider setting up an Essay Society. Changed her dress. Arranged her table in the way she insisted to herself it must be arranged with the ink *there*, the pens *there*, the lamp *there*. This was it. Literature and Morality, a further degree at a different university, and work, work, work she could control, enjoy, be independent by, be exclusive to, if she wished. And if men came, well she need not remain an unattainable careerist forever, but *she* would choose the man, the pace, she would control the intentions, the time. This was it. This had to be it, for anything else would destroy her as she wanted to be; ruin that which she aimed at. And that would not be allowed to happen.

But Richard, Richard, maybe he ... she saw Richard. She would see him, as usual, at the weekend. There was no reason why it should not go on 'satisfactorily' enough. He would get over it. Or not.

In the stuffy room, with the cigarette fumes still circling to embrace and dance with the swirls of her head, she saw Richard as a man in dirty boots, like her father except that 'like' had no place – no place for simile when there were no connections – sitting there unspeaking – maybe he did not speak because to have a conversation meant that you had to have connection and he realised her wish to avoid it – oh, it was no stylish wish, she had to cut them all away, father, husband, daughter, lovers, people all, as the chairs in her room were wooden, props outside the steaming swirl of her head which yet knew that it would smack freshly with proposals, resolutions and achieved activity. She saw Richard, but her feelings towards him went no further than to the surface of her own pores. Touch and be pitched into contact, and from there lose control and so, for herself, possibility.

And no more the country. There, where you were hidden as an ant in the garden, like Wif, murmuring about in service to its continuation, or exposed, as Richard now was, a blighted tree on a bare hill, eccentric to be a landmark, without nourishment or purpose. Neither of those. Nor the third way, to go back, the return of the prodigy, tacking herself on to what she had left, as a cleric returning to confess his father and mother, darting around in vacuum-tight certainty, able to patronise even men – as Edwin – because nothing could sting where nothing could affect. Janice, too, did not want to be affected, but she wished to do other than slip into an allotted place. The city she would live in, the biggest she could find, where nobody knew her, where she could make herself exactly as she would be and in the anonymity touch and let alone this or that as she wished, with neither history behind nor expectation before her.

At five-thirty there was an appointment at the dentist and she had two fillings. The high-speed drill burnt into her teeth so that the air around her mouth whiffed of the smoky smell of damp fire.

In her flat, at night, the curtains drawn, the essay a third done, she sat on the settee, one light only on, coffee and cigarettes to hand, a book, alone, peace. Such peace she would only have alone. The injection was wearing off and her cheek felt flabby and paunchy. She licked her tongue over the rough surface of the new filling. Then the soft tongue slid on to the enamel of her teeth, sliding, padded warm, across the hard enamel, hard, glossy; the tip of the tongue played on the teeth and then reached out to wet the dry lips. Soon made soft and pliant as the tongue itself. Too content even to sigh at the tranquillity of it. Perfectly balanced, she thought, being completely alone.

CHAPTER FORTY-TWO

The rain had stopped the work and the men sat on the floor of the shanty hut, waiting for the foreman to dismiss them. There would be no more done that day. There were eight of them in a hut less than ten feet square and the damp steamy sweat which had come off them mingled with burning cigarettes and the foamy air from the kettle spout to give a haze to the room which matched the haze caused by the rain, as the dribbling windows inside reflected the rain-run panes outside.

Richard was glad to be sitting with his back propped against the wall. He wore the jacket he had worn on his first arrival at Crossbridge – then a smartly cut article of fashion, now a dusty and torn flap of material – and through it he felt the hard wood press against the discs on his backbone. His feelings were almost all to do with his body. He had not the energy to ask for a part of one of the papers being read nor the will to pull out a cigarette. It was as if the terrible stiffness which had come to him after the first few days had been caught by the damp weather and locked into his joints, sealed by the drizzle which had come most days. His thighs slotted heavily into his hips and when he walked or sat or did anything he was conscious of this endless ache, as in his shoulders, his arms, his stomach, his calves, the work was wearing him down. He had caught a cold early on, and as colds had never seemed more than unfortunate, minor inconveniences which did not for a moment prevent you from doing what you were about, he had ignored it. But it had clung to him, now breaking out in wrenching coughing, now prickling his brow and chest to chill perspiration in the night, always muzzing his head, weighing on it, clamping him to put his entire concentration on what was at hand, for without his total effort it could not be done. Out of fear of staying at home and, in yielding to the cold, giving up his job even for a few days – the fear arising from his certainty that once relinquished he would never be able to take it up again, and then what? – he just went on. At first, it had seemed absurd that he should be so knocked up by such a job at his age; he remembered the way in which, not so long ago, he had pushed up Knockmirton and been unable to finish a day without pressing himself into yet more physical acitivity. Now that seemed not, as he had thought, a way of keeping himself fit, but the very least necessary to keep himself merely mobile. He felt no benefit from it when it came to labouring.

It was true that, once having given up teaching, and being determined to work around Crossbridge, there was little else he could do. To have become a farm labourer would have been too silly; he knew so little about farming, and, at his age, he could not be paid a boy's wages, while it would take training to make him able to do a man's work. He was not prepared to go through it. Similarly, he could have worked for the council on the roads, but that would have taken him all over the place and he wanted to stay at the cottage as his centre. Moreover, the work at the stone quarries had in it something fundamentally casual, which appealed to him. Underneath it all was the knowledge that when the quarries were done, work would be abandoned, the gutted crater left wild, and that would be that. And it was the place where most men who would always be falling out of permanent jobs and yet did not want the strain of piece-work on the roads would end up for a season. Only a few, the drillers, the foreman, the two men who did the dynamiting, only they had been long on the job. The others, like Richard, came and went, though he was the newest. He helped with the loading; all day shifting the lumps of stone from the ground into the lorries. His hands had blistered, skin had been chipped off, now they were harder but still they hurt, particularly two nails which had been torn across.

At first there had been some chaffing and testing, but that had developed into no drama. He was not ruffled by it, partly because he did not try, not once, to explain or justify his decision; partly because he had not much to say and did not show himself full of Everyman's interests; mostly because he himself felt no discomfort in the decision. He did not feel he had come down in the world, or was making a gesture (though that accusation could always be laid on him; there was nothing he could or wished to do to turn it; nevertheless it was *no* gesture), nor was he trying to prove anything. He wanted to stay on in the cottage, could not leave it with Agnes dead, someone had to stay, wanted to, now so vaguely and hopelessly, be reminded of, work into her way of action – and he needed the money from a job which would not, as teaching did, cause more trouble than it overcame.

But he had reckoned without this terrible soreness of every muscle and joint which made his body like some armour, ill-fit on him, which tugged and dragged at him wherever he turned and could not be removed.

"We'll knock off," said the foreman. "It won't ease up to-day."

The men rose from the floor, leaving their mugs and butts behind, all of them slouching into movement, not one brisk or snappy gesture among them, and the clothes so damp and impregnated with dust they might have belonged to prisoners condemned to hard labour. Richard liked their company, he told himself, but he could not shake off the feeling of being alone even among so many.

Outside he went across to get his bicycle. The rain began to come down more heavily.

"Hey!" Bob shouted, leaning out of the car – an unrelievedly battered Alvis which he had picked up for ten pounds from some college student. "Hey! Pile in here, Dick. We'll take you down to the church, anyway."

"I've got my bike."

"Chuck it in t'boot."

"Thanks."

The long, squat car set off down the track which led away from the quarries on to a small by-road. There were five of them in it and the joggling of the car shook the dampness out with quick sweat. It was a pleasant stench.

Outside, the land was banked with dampness. The track wound down through hills and their wet backs were morose, disturbed only by the shivering step of a sheep. What, in sun

285

and storm, was grand spaciousness or splendid desolation, was now, in the dampness, miserable acres of poor countryside. Under the patient drizzle, even the fells, even Knockmirton itself, lost majesty and mystery and became damp hills. No one was about as they bumped down the clay-coloured track and landed on the road, the road not glittering with swept rain but dully receiving the fine spread of drizzle, and the occasional farm and row of cottages passed, looking miserly. The slate-coloured stone without any painted relief, only dour, and that dour, uninviting. Nothing, as he looked through the window, nothing at all was there to be relished or explored, nor even had it the large oppressiveness which would make an act or feeling of rejection positive. It all seemed weary, toilsome, endless.

"Thought about playing yet, Dick?" Bob asked.

"Yes. I don't think I could do it," Richard replied. "I haven't played football for about ten years. I wasn't great shakes then, either."

"You've grown up a bit since then."

"He's been on t'nest. That's a help."

"How many times a week d'you get it, Dick?"

"She only comes back at weekends. He's crawlin' by Monday morning."

"You don't have to be great shakes in this team," Bob answered. "Anyway, we just do it for the sport, you know. Nothing serious. They're all friendly matches. Then the booze-up after."

"It's his Saturdays he's worried about, Bob. Don't press the lad. His Saturdays are rare."

"He'll have plenty of time after the pubs close."

"Now I've heard that she's one that goes to bed early."

"Getting ready, eh? Bloody marvellous. I wish mine would. She farts about downstairs, sometimes I'm asleep, waiting."

"Maybe that's what she wants, you nut."

"No thanks, Bob," Richard said. "Thanks for the offer."

"Well, keep thinking about it," Bob said, seriously. He was interested in Richard, protective towards him and a little piqued that, as protector, he found no real compliance in him who should have slipped into the attitude of protected. "A bit of sport would do *you* good, Dick. And there are nice fellas that play."

"Oh, we're all nice fellas."

"Going to Ennerdale to-night?"

"Who's there?"

"Johnnie Jackson, I think. Aye – him."

"Might."

So the weariness was in himself.

They let him out at the church and he began to cycle up to the cottages. A short distance. One side of the village triangle, and he remembered walking that stretch, following Janice after the bonfire. How long ago? He had walked then more quickly than he cycled now, for the cramped car sitting had stiffened him and he was disgusted with his feebleness. The front wheel trailed across the road and then drifted over to the verge. At the little slope, where Janice had slowed down for him, he almost dismounted, to push the thing. His grandfather had once been seen running through the town, pushing the bike, and in a hell of a hurry, couldn't stop, couldn't stop to get on it, take too much time.

When he arrived at the cottage, it was to see Mrs. Jackson coming out of it.

"I made your fire up," she said. "I thought you would be wet after today. There's a pot of tea just mashed. Would you like some?"

"No thanks. I think I'll change."

"You're welcome."

"Thank you."

He propped the bike against the wall.

"I saw Paula this morning," she said. "She's going to be a lovely little thing, you know. 'Hello lady,' she said. 'Hello lady.' I said 'I'm Mrs. Jackson.' 'Midde Axon,' she said. 'Hello Midde Axon.' She's a lovely little thing. Janice coming to-night?"

"I think so."

"I'll be glad to see her. They still can't get shut of that end cottage, you know. I get real lonely on my own here. I'm telling Mr. Jackson – if nobody moves in soon, I'm for a change. It's spooky being on your own. And, that place you used to have – that's never been taken since you left it. I said to Mr. Jackson, if somebody doesn't get in there quick, it'll be written off for dereliction. They've broken the windows already. I know who did it, mind. That youngest of Billy Munn's. He's a terror. They caught him wringing a chicken's neck the other day, 'And why did you do that?' they said. 'To see what it was like,' he says. To see what it was like! I would show him what it was like! Wring his neck for a bit so that he could see what it was like. Little beggar. Janice'll be finished after this year then, won't she?"

"Yes."

"Somebody told me she's going on to do more exams after that. I don't know what they're after with all their exams, do you? Well, you *do*, you've got them as well, haven't you? If you haven't got exams you can't do anything these days. Eh? I'm glad I missed all that. I would never have been able to catch them. Just an old dunce I am. I used to be t'school dunce, you know. With one of those hats you see, like ice-cream cornets, standing in a corner. Oh dear. I would have been out of everything now. You won't tell anybody I was t'school dunce, will you? It slipped out. It's with talking to myself all day.

"As I walked by myself
And talked to myself,
Myself said unto me:
'Look to thyself,
Take care of thyself
For nobody cares for thee.'

"I answered myself,
And said to myself
In the self-same repartee:
'Look to thyself
Or not look to thyself,
The self-same thing will be'. "

My mother used to sing that one. I can't remember the tune. Come in for a cup."

"All right. Thank you."

"Good. Your fire'll burn up without looking at it. And I banked it up nicely for you. Come in. Come in. Sit down. I've just baked some rock buns. Would you like some? Wif used to like my rock buns, you know. I could always get him with a rock bun. Is he still over with his brother? I never knew his brother. You know, I can't think of Wif Beattie living anywhere else but in that cottage. He was here when we came; you know, I think he should've stayed on. I would have done his cleaning. It would have been no bother. I would do yours if you would let me. It gives me something to do. I suppose you'll go when Janice is finished."

"Yes. I might."

"Aye well. And then there was one. Edwin's doing grand, isn't he? I always knew there was a lot in him. Have you – well you have because I know you two are quite friendly now and why shouldn't you be after all? – that garage place of his, and people swear by him, you know; they do. He's taken Mrs. Park's boy on as well. He'll be a rich man Edwin one day, but it hasn't changed him, has it? I mean, he was never an 'open' man, he would keep himself to himself, but he wasn't a 'cocky' man either. And he still isn't. He always waves if I go past. I thought he would come and take one of these cottages, but he will live in that one room that used to be the headmaster's study, you know. Oh, he is funny about it! 'I eat my fish and chips off a tomb of learning,' he says to me. Mind, he was bright himself, Edwin, and nobody made up better for missing his eleven plus. He should have got it, I think. Don't you think they give it to some funny people sometimes? I mean, Edwin should have got it. Still, he's done a lot better than many that has it." She threw her hand to her mouth. "Oh! I wasn't being personal mind, Richard. Everybody knows that you're up there just temporary. You're too soft, you know. You shouldn't let things get you down so much. What's done's done. You can't carry it around with you for evermore. It isn't fair on yourself. When will you start to think about going back to teaching again? – mind you, teaching isn't what it was – I think you should be in television again or in newspapers – be like your friend Mr. Hill, now he has a nice life, meeting interesting people all the time. You won't meet interesting people in a stone quarry – although I'm not saying anything against them but still, there's types and types, and you're not the type to be working up there. You've got brains all right. How many brains do you need to cart stones around? So what I say is – 'he's biding his time', 'he's had a terrible experience – in fact when you weigh it up, he's had a lot of terrible experiences – and he's trying to get over it.' But, good Lord, Richard, there's others been through worse. That's a comfort. A lot worse. There's help for you. Far worse. Think of that. Now I'll just put a fresh kettle on for Mr. Jackson – he looks a pit peeky these days, don't you think? Peeky. I'm worried about him, I tell you."

He went back more briskly into his own cottage. The fire had slumped into a small pyramid of coal which needed the very careful insertion of a poker to let air into it, and the clever stacking of new coal around it to let it catch again. He did it with care; saw it begin to build, and went to change, prompted to do this by some inflection in Mrs. Jackson's voice. He would have liked a bath, but with no fire all day the water was not even tepid.

289

Janice, as usual, was late, catching the last bus and walking the two miles that entailed, preferring that to the sacrifice of spending two unnecessary hours away from Carcaster and catching the late afternoon bus to the end of the lane. He did not want to eat, but, feeling restless, and moved by that feeling, since it was the first sparkle which had come out of the sodden earth of his mind, he began to search around the house, not for anything definite, merely for an accidental discovery which would help. He thought of going down to collect Paula, but Janice preferred to call for her on the Saturday morning, saying she was always too irritable to deal with her on arrival on Friday and anyway the child would be asleep at the time. Paula was already someone quite apart from him. In the few months since she had stopped living around his feet, she had grown more strange, it seemed, than other children he saw around the village. Not that she was an unusual child, just that he felt embarrassed before her as he would have done before an adult whom he had treated badly; and that embarrassment made his attitude towards her so formal that her reaction could not but be puzzled, restrained.

He regretted now that he had destroyed all his notes; at least they had provided someone for him to work against. But there was one pad, somewhere, which he had not burned, and in it he found a few pages. They were covered with lists. Things he wanted to do, things he wanted to be. From the very earliest days of his time in Crossbridge. A long reading list with six brisk ticks against the first six books and after that no more acknowledgments. A list of what he thought important in life. He looked at that as someone might stand before the recollection of a forgotten intention once intensely held, now alien. The simplest rules; no new ideas; a believing in the Sermon on the Mount; and, having reached the possibility of believing, an inability to find action which could realise it; so more words. Life so lovingly listed, even listing with weight of words was something; now, listless.

One entry was painful. He had written:

" 'Here I stand. I can do no other. God help me.'

"Luther. To be able to say that! I could say it only in inverted commas."

He threw that notebook in the fire, blank pages and all, and stirred it to brown-grey ashes with the poker. Janice was due any minute. He put the kettle on. The first time he had prepared for

her in that way for a long while. He opened a packet of biscuits
she had bought the previous week and arranged them on a plate.
He placed two cups and saucers on the table, sugar, milk, found
the remainder of a chocolate cake Mrs. Jackson had given him
and cut it into ready slices. That rhyme she had chanted?

"I answered myself,
And said to myself
In the self-same repartee:
'Look to thyself
Or not look to thyself,
The self-same thing will be.' "

CHAPTER FORTY-THREE

The first thing he had to do was to tell her – with no mumbling,
none of that embarrassment which conceals fear – the part he
thought he had played in her mother's death. This he had already
more than hinted at, but, as he was looking for reaction more
than absolution, it had to be done again, properly. For the
confession to Edwin, which had drawn him into such an unpleasant fraternity with Edwin who now greeted him as a con-
spirator, but he, Edwin, the old sweat, Richard the new 'lad' –
that had not achieved the purpose. He could not define the
purpose, feeling he would understand it when he saw it. Sometimes he thought that it was merely to do with relief – which was
fair enough, but nothing he could find the grit of expectation in;
and then he thought that it was more to do with truth, that there
were some things which *had* to be told and understood, otherwise
they could find no place, were merely settled on the mind like
squatters, had no rights.

So he was very careful to restrain the irritability which would
almost choke him whenever he saw Janice these days; cautious
about overdoing the consideration of her welcome; played a
game, in fact. Their meetings now were more a game than anything else, service and return, lines firmly drawn, the court set
in waste-land, and if the game spilled out of the court, they let it
go, retired, and then began again.

She told him about David's Love-In. He enquired unhurriedly
about David. She told him that David would soon be going back

to London. He thought it just as well. She told him that she had finished her essay for the prize. He asked her how it had gone.

He told her that Paula had a slight cold. She reacted appropriately. He told her that he was thinking of playing football. She encouraged him to do so. He told her a story that he had heard from Bob. She laughed.

He asked her what she would do in the holidays. She didn't know. He pressed her for an answer to help his plans. She lobbed back an equivocation. He demanded to know. She angled her reply harmlessly out of his reach. He said she ought to come home. She said she would do as she liked. It was typical. So it was. Disgusting. Perhaps. Paula? Yes. Well? Well!

Richard stopped. He still had to tell her. After that time which elapses in a married argument when each has drawn enough breath to be ready to move – in a state which each considers to be much more reasonable, even repentant, but is merely more dangerous, being primed with antagonistic silence – he began again.

And stopped almost immediately.

Then he plunged on.

"I must talk to you about your mother," he said, and as he said it, the confidence which her first appearance had given him – so that they were like and like, two young people fairly even – seemed to vanish, leaving her a cool, elegant young woman, himself a man losing his grip and sliding into beaten resignation. It was as if Agnes was resurrected and divided them, or her presence forced them to abandon pretence and be as the most true part of themselves, and all that useful fluff of mannerly affection was sliced away, Janice stripped to the hard phial of will she carried, Richard, sans hope, a tumbled-down man.

"Must you?"

"Yes."

"Why do you feel compelled? You – refer to her more than I do myself. As if she were, yes, your own mother. Sorry, I feel nervous when you look so – what is it? – fierce really. Yes. When you look so fierce."

"You thrash around so much. Why do you? Are you afraid of what I might tell you?"

"I know already. I know Mother saw you with another woman. Margaret, she was called, or is called – isn't she? I found her name and address on a piece of paper when I was tidying up. And you think that that killed her somehow. I prefer not to talk about it, you know. A confession needs a confessor and I'm no good at that I'm afraid."

"I'm sorry. I forget your feelings. I shouldn't raise it."

"You already have. And – though you did not imply it – I feel an accusation when you talk of 'my feelings'. I know everyone thinks I'm short on them. Father's so certain of it that he hasn't replied to my last three letters. I write twice a week. In his last letter he told me not to bother to come and see him. He knew it would be too much trouble. He sent you and Paula his 'best wishes', of course."

"I'm sorry."

"Don't be. It's a waste. Been said before but it's true. It is a waste."

"So you don't want to know. All right."

"You see, it doesn't matter, Richard. It just doesn't matter. Like most of the things you sit and brood over. It's all a waste. Why don't you face it? You'll never solve anything; there *are* no riddles; to think that somewhere is a secret to Life which you can uncover is blind, and stupid I'm afraid. Life isn't like that any more – if it ever was. You're what people would call 'old-fashioned' and rather pleased with yourself at being so; but you're not really old-fashioned. You undercut everything you turn to, just as we all do. Only you like to think that you're doing it because of the search for an absolute or a principle – in fact some relative of the holy grail. But I think that you do it from obstinacy. You don't like much of what you see around you – you think it corrupt, which it is, and see hardly at all past that because Corruption, to you, is all the Deadly Sins, although in fact it need not be more than the flaking on the gilt on the gingerbread – and so you look for something else, something which had to be old and tried because what is New is somehow Corrupt Altogether and you don't trust that at all. And when you've found the old song, you hear that it is out of tune but prefer to play away rather than be seduced by any new harmony. That is where you are obstinate. And none of it matters. You ought to decide to do something and just get on with it. The rest will fall into place. And if it doesn't, then, likely as not there's no place for it, and you haven't lost any time messing around."

"You think I'm 'messing around'?"

"What else could you call it?"

Richard nodded. He had not the energy to go on. Janice, by the laying on of light, dry hands, dismissed his agitations so that

293

he was silenced, sealed. That such a thing could be so easily done, or done at all, would previously have worried him. But it was as if his wind had been completely broken; he could not contradict her charges, knowing that it would set off an argument which might run for hours, and worse, tension between them, tension which made her only more poised, sharper, more lucid, and made him dizzy, frayed, disintegrate.

"I'll tell you what I *do* think," she said, unexpectedly, "I think you might have told me you were going around with another woman. I would have preferred that to finding out for myself."

"It was nothing. Nothing – happened."

"Don't make it worse by denying it."

"It's true. Nothing did. Nothing at all."

She looked at him, saw he was telling the truth, and laughed. It was a laugh which seemed to spring from nowhere, and kill all other sounds, standing alone, a hard cackle. Her eyes were not hard. Yet the teeth glinted and her face twisted with those contortions that could, with another sound, have represented pain. She was not meaning to hurt him.

Suddenly he thought it all a mistaken dream. That he should be there at all in muddy boots with aching shoulders. It should never have happened. There ought to be a pleasantly scruffy flat in London, with people dropping in, the latest film, the newest headlines, the state of liaisons, the cheap Indian restaurant, the replete fatigue at bistros and television programmes, the scattered weeklies and the half-secret 'projects'. Someone would have a grant from the BFI, did you see Ted's column? Just like his stuff at Oxford, did you know he was standing for Parliament? The pestering, jangled, puzzled, bitchy, restless, feckless, calculating, talented, blinkered, grudging, boasting, open society of those no longer fresh from University but thickened by a few years' work, building up behind the dam of their elders, pushing against the wall which they would, inevitably, trickle over, for the ruins were theirs for the taking. Now, too late, that appeared not unattractive. In it there was a certain gregarious exorcism, a seriousness which he had too easily dismissed. There were people like enough to himself for him to be untroubled by the superfluous strain of feeling singular, as he did in Crossbridge; it was, perhaps, not a good life, but not a bad one either. Such inevitability as his world had lay there.

So the image of what he had left, what he had abandoned, now, at the last, floated up before him, tempting because unobjectionable. Yet it was that image which had propelled him to Cross-bridge, he thought. All the more hopeless, then, if what he had so strongly rejected was no more than a pleasant pot-pourri.

Janice had cleared the cups and came back into the kitchen, her hands loosening her hair, getting ready for bed. She shook the hair so that it flew all over her face and shoulders. Then she stood in front of the mirror and peered at herself.

"I think I'll need glasses soon," she said.

Richard got up. He put his arms around her waist and drew her towards him, his head falling into her hair on the shoulder. She looked at their reflection in the mirror. Through her clothes, he felt the line and hardness of her body; his hands spread across her stomach reaching up to her breasts. The warmth that came from her lightened him at once. It was Janice he wanted. If they could share their love – for that, as he held her, was all that could occur to him, and the best that could – then there would be something; something into which all reaching and clutching could fall and be made livable. Not comfort – though there was that – nor sentimental mutual concern – though that, too, would be there – but with Janice, and only with her, he could have that passion which cannot be defined, only known through itself, which is the gift that obliterates need for explanations which cannot strike deep. In that, there would be real hope. He kissed her neck, weak as the strands of hair rubbed against his lips, hoping that the yielding skin would at last give him that, let his love for Janice spead and grow as it wanted to, as it ached to, as he now ached to make love to her. To make love for ever; to protect her, be patient, be her friend, be indulgent to her, gener-ous, helpful, loving, trusting – and there was no chance for that, not even for the beginnings of it while she would not kiss him without that tension, however restrained, which counted the action as superfluous, the seconds as wasted.

Now, pressed against her, he was hopeful, and from within him came a moan of expectation which he did not dare let pass his lips for fear of spoiling things. Silent seed. It now, at this moment, seemed imperative to make one disinterested move, do one action of selflessness, love, decency – the words moved in his head like the gavotte of sad Christmas ghosts. But there were no better.

He kissed her full on the lips, the soft flesh of that skin crushing tightly, and yet it was not savage, the kiss. Away from him fled and fell the marionettes of his life; the suspicions of affection, the sneers at good action, the cynicism of all motives but those most base, the weariness of anything save saliva-ed corruption twinkling like a fetish, the fratchiness of all friendships for fear that their foundation would confirm the worst suspicion, so sought always found – his way of living, that comfortless crucible he had made for himself and been unable to live without on leaving it – that fell away, and his mind and body were sweetened with silent nothingness in the kiss. He knew his love for her: he knew that he could love: and the knowledge came to him with exhausted exhilaration.

They stayed there, silently, neither wishing to move, to change, or to attempt more at that moment.

And yet it had to change. One of them had to move. Richard stood back, about to say something, checking himself and remaining as he was. He wanted to take her to bed but could not bear to fracture the fine web, newly spun between them, by one gesture which did not intuitively find an agreeing response in her. So they stood.

Then he laughed. Much as he tried to stifle the nerveless frivolity, the apparent discord of his action, there was nothing he could do to prevent it. Standing there so seriously face to face made him laugh. He was to wonder about that laugh for long afterwards, and finally he knew that it was the final echo from his previous life. And that tiny echo recoiled like a whiplash; its contempt for the present cut him from his past.

Janice, laughing with him, though perhaps the slightest fraction disappointed at the disruption of the tension, concluded that all was well, it would be a more pleasant weekend than most. She went to wash and then came to bed where they made love.

Richard could not sleep, and at about five he got up and went for a walk. It was still black and on the ground the blackness was so thick he seemed to wade through it. Not yet dawn and no bird sang. The cold swiftly pierced his careless clothing and he had to step out firmly so as not to shiver. On his face, the bristles of hair stood on end, feeling like so many thorns stabbed into the skin.

The cloud was dense, but still Knockmirton's cone shape and peak stood out, and it was up that fell he went, passing the seat on which he had once planned and hoped, without more than an instant's memory. The laugh had freed him.

CHAPTER FORTY-FOUR

The heather sank squelching under his feet, but instead of increasing his stiffness and emphasising it, the walk threw it off. Or rather, he himself threw if off by the vigour with which he walked. He was soon at the top, where the large and smaller cairns stood, and a few sheep huddled, starting, but not running away when he appeared. He lit a cigarette and waited.

Of Agnes, Janice had said: "It doesn't matter." Now, he thought as he stood there, she was right. It did not matter. She had died and it was useless to worry over his part in that death. But if that did not matter, what did, God, what did?

It mattered that Agnes had lived. However blurred and over-sympathetic his understanding of her had been, of her goodness there could be no question. That had mattered to him, and to everyone she had ever met. Such goodness may have been nurtured in soil that the greedy claws of his own generation had ripped off the top of all nature, but it had existed outside and beyond the area in which it had grown. It had been fought for by Agnes, her will making her carry on with what her sensibility crystallised into her duty. Had she been 'good because she could not help it', then surely she would not have made so many slips, had to persevere so often when she did not wish to go on, been often excesssive and sometimes a little vain about herself. No, it was no God-given thing. She had made it. She had put down her own roots, found, in some way, a contact with a Spirit, a Hope, a Religion, which had drawn from her all that was finest. He smiled as the thought rose to his mind that 'she should not die in vain', and this time the smile was neither nervous nor hopeless, but a smile at the long trail, dusty now, and worn, which had brought the phrase upon him.

If, then, she had made her own life – no matter that she might have had better tools, might have had conniving pressures which he lacked, traditional aspirations which he lacked, even super-stitious but aiding taboos, which he lacked – then it could be done. And it was on her ideal alone that he could want to base anything. To be successful was pleasant or not, to be rich also, to be a man of power or influence – all were the same external to that central certainty and capacity for truth which he now knew he valued more than anything. In love there was that, and he *was* in love; no more need to dissect it; it could be accepted. It had survived the convenience of that last sex with Janice, where it had again assumed the form of ejaculatory desire; and so it would survive other things.

For he could no longer be outside the life which he could go and pick up for himself. To withdraw for longer would prohibit entry to the point of his becoming a permanent self-exile, with the fear that he was so because he dare not test himself. Yet cheapest jibes are easiest appeals to vanity. He would move towards a return, but return at his own pace.

To be honest with himself, it seemed he had got nowhere in the time at Crossbridge. He had known what he now knew at the time he had arrived there. But, as never before, he realised the difference between mere knowing and knowing so firmly that you felt compelled and happy to act from that knowledge, prepared to do no other than what would be right for it.

What had he found? A commonplace. What did he want? Not little. There would be the danger of vanity, of carrying his new ambition around in him like a priceless phial, to be protected at all costs; of pomposity, of being in such grand relation to the world that the efforts of all others would seem fractious and mean; of over-worthiness, of thinking himself so very right that in time he would come to be unable to distinguish between that which disagreed with him and that which was wrong. It was dangerous and – again, but properly so this time – silly, to go around 'trying to be good'.

But Agnes's goodness had not carried itself around as its own banner. It had simply been the foundation on which she had tried to build and tried as hard as she could. He could not imitate her, though he wanted to follow her. And what he was looking for – an absolute sense of truth in his actions, something which satisfied all the feathered flutterings of his mind which rose on a hundred wings whenever direct proposal was made – maybe it was not in the word, the action, 'good'. No doubt he would never find it in that absolute sense, though he wanted to continue or rather commence to search; and if the word 'good' was not right for him, well then it was a pity; it would have to serve; at present he had no other.

Dawn. He turned and looked as it touched the tops of the fells – Starling Dodd, Great Bourne, Hen Comb, Black Crag,

Gavel Fell – like heavy beacons they were outlined, ready to be fired by the day. Awake, the birds thrust out their noises, at once filling the whole air so that he wondered what it had been like to be silent. And the sun seemed to send out its own wind, a sweet strand of warmth in the cool billows of air which rolled among the fells. He looked at the vast landscape, no cottage, no hut, no man, and felt neither the awe nor the intimidation he had once felt: for there were still the walls which, however broken or derelict, yet encircled the highest tops; and in the villages were houses and streams. The sun rose, and he could see in its enormous and stately heave the belief that it was drawn through the sky by a mighty chariot and celestial horses. Dew glistened with such ornament that it was difficult to believe that it was nothing but water; genii of diamond and emerald seemed to have crept over the grass at night and hardened it into precious minerals.

He turned and looked down on Crossbridge. Still dark, but beyond, clouds whitened out of the sea, like water turned by a blessing to milk and then to finest veils of air. The sun sent shudders of delight sparkling across the back of the Solway Firth and over the land beyond, a trembling, delicate stretching.

Alone, alone, Richard shouted aloud and his voice rang freely. Each way he turned the light was rolling away the shadows, the colours, unharmed by the night, revealed themselves again. His senses were sated and his breathing alone made him what he was: the thing he was which made him live. This breathing and standing, what was around him flicking his senses as a fish flicks its tail in the ocean, it was this that he had most forgotten and could now relish. Feel his own existence and let it trickle slowly through his silence.

The sun higher now, he could see the church without the steeple, see the houses where lived the people. See the reflections on the roof-tops of the cars outside Edwin's garage. There where he and Edwin had spent some evenings, half-enquiring, half-afraid that each might be opposite his own secret act – of murder. Yet the word was too big for them. Richard had gone to see Edwin on those nights wanting there to be earthquakes of doubt, remorse, protestations, leaving craters of guilt, a debris of all ambitions. There had been nothing but play, a meagre-hearted companionship and finally, abhorrence. In the act of talking to Edwin he had come to see how arrogant it was to impute the

299

worst without true cause; he was no murderer and it was his own despair alone which had persuaded him that he was.

He heard the clang of milk-cans and saw the smoke from chimney spouts chugging the minute houses to work. He lay down and looked at the sky and slept. He had a dream, but, on waking, could remember only the last flurry of it, an army of men suddenly gulped into slit trenches like those in the Great War. However hard he tried, he could not remember more. Their khaki uniforms had made them seem at once soldiers, destroyers of life and, on the brown, slit ground, so close in colour and movement to what sustained them that they disappeared as if they had been called to the earth rather than wiped from it.

He had slept for a few hours and the sun had long since become camouflaged by massive clouds which sped underneath it, every shape, every shade of grey, and here and there edges of lace as they broke and were struck through by a ray.

He set off down to Crossbridge. The land was ablaze with heather and bilberries. The steep gradient swung out his legs so that he felt himself loping down in magnetic boots which lifted and marched of their own accord.

In front of the cottage, Wif was crouched, playing with Paula. Richard stood still and watched for a minute. The old man was showing her how to make a cat's cradle and the concentration on the little girl's face was ecstatic. Coming out of the door with a mug of tea in her hand, Janice saw Richard and, as he motioned her not to reveal him, so she, by a quick glance at Wif, explained it all; that he had come to see them unexpectedly, that he was lonely, that in some way she and he were beginning, if not to make it up or forgive each other, at least to appreciate that there was something for them to enjoy and love in each other. And she was glad of it.

When Richard did come forward, Wif stood up, picking up Paula as he did so, and she held out her arms to him. He took her, joggled her up and down, letting her clasp her arms around his neck, her legs around his chest, and then swayed backwards and forwards so that she laughed – 'do it again, do it again'. It was not difficult to turn her from a stranger into an intimate; perhaps that seriousness which had grown on her would never go, but it could be overlaid with other things. Nothing need be banished, just covered with something else which, if strong enough, would only rarely break and show what had been abandoned.

Wif stood there, awkwardly, his very awkwardness the question. Suspecting Janice, and through that suspicion uneasy with Richard. Janice waited for a move to which she could respond. Richard longed for the exact words. And yet the exact words were not *so* important. He knew what he was going to do: if there were false starts, well then, there were.

"I think," said Janice, suddenly, "I'll go and do a bit more shopping. We'll need some more now. You'll stay over, won't you, Father?"

"If it's all right."

"It is all right."

"Then I will." He nodded and reached out for Paula who scrambled on to him most willingly. "What'll you be doing now, Richard?" he asked. "Finishing soon at them old quarries, I hope."

"Yes." Janice, who had gone for her basket, re-emerged from the cottage as he said that. He spoke to her. "Yes, I'll work out the month or two and then I think I'll join Janice at Carcaster. We can all be together then, with Paula. We'll still use the cottage for the weekends though.

Janice looked at him sharply. Her morning face belied the previous night's compliance. They were still far apart but she had sometimes known that she had loved him, and with no other, not even Paula, had she clearly known that. He saw her thoughts – both the defence and reconsideration – and smiled that he should so know her. Understanding his smile, she returned it, hesitantly.

"All at once," she said, softly. "Just like that."

"Yes."

She nodded and bent down to change Paula's shoes for wellingtons.

"And if she decides to do another degree," Richard continued, "I'll try to persuade her to do it in London. I wouldn't mind going back there. But there's no hurry."

As Janice stood up there was, again, a tightness about her eyes which both men recognised. But Richard was not troubled by it.

"Well," she said, "it's useful you're here, Father; I'm sure I would never even have been told if you hadn't been here. Come on, Paula."

"Why don't you move back into this cottage?" Richard asked Wif, as Janice began to go away. "Then we could be sure of seeing you when we came."

Janice stopped, turned, and now she fully understood. Richard would retreat no more. He might go back, but that would be a repulse, not a withdrawal. So. She could match him, whatever, she thought.

"No," replied Wif. "I think you'll have enough on your hands with one thing and another. And I'm very comfortable where I am. As long as I know I can come and see you of a Saturday."

"But of course you can," said Janice. "Now. 'Bye. I'll be about an hour."

Richard and Wif went into the garden and sat on the seat made for Agnes. For some time the memory of his wife was too strong in Wif's face to allow any words. So they sat, silent, smoking. Then Wif brushed his eyes with his sleeve, coughed, thoroughly, and began to roll himself a fresh cigarette, the fine strands of tobacco scattering at the touch of his thick fingers. "Dis thou know, Richard," he said, eventually, "there was a fella used to live ower in yon cottage – beyond yon top road. It's nivver lived in now. An' he was a fella wouldn't mix, thou knows; a terrible man for bein' on his own. You couldn't have dragged that fella intill a company. Couldn't have *dragged* him in. Lloyd, his name was. But he wasn't Welsh in his talkin', even wid' a name like Lloyd. Well," Wif pointed to his cigarette, straggly, botched with wet thumb-marks, smokable only with some will-power, "well he'd got this trick off of bein' able to roll a cigarette one-handed. Nivver met anybody else who could. Nivver one."

He nodded, struck a careful match, and sucked deeply at his handiwork. A few drops of rain fell. Mrs. Jackson came into the garden to bring in her washing. Above Knockmirton, the clouds spun up into the sky in boisterous whisking. Richard shivered slightly in the wind and then relaxed.

MELVYN BRAGG

THE HIRED MAN

Set in Cumberland and covering a period from 1898 to the early twenties, this is the powerful saga of John Tallentire, first farm labourer, then coal miner, and his wife Emily. John's struggle to break free from the humiliating status of a "hired man" is the theme of a novel which has been hailed as a classic of its kind – as meticulously detailed as a social document, as evocative as the writing of Thomas Hardy and D. H. Lawrence.

"An intensely moving, deeply worked book."

Sunday Telegraph

"A magnificently strong and sinewy novel."

Sunday Mirror

CORONET BOOKS

ALSO AVAILABLE IN CORONET

MELVYN BRAGG

☐	19852 4	Josh Lawton	95p
☐	19853 2	A Place In England	95p
☐	22314 6	Speak For England	£1.50
☐	19992 X	The Silken Net	£1.25
☐	21807 X	The Hired Man	85p

R. F. DELDERFIELD

☐	15623 6	God Is An Englishman	£1.50
☐	16225 2	Theirs Was The Kingdom	95p

JENNIFER JOHNSTON

☐	18815 4	The Gates	35p
☐	19950 4	How Many Miles To Babylon?	40p

ALEXANDER CORDELL

☐	20515 6	Rape of the Fair Country	85p
☐	15383 0	Race of the Tiger	45p
☐	17403 X	The Fire People	£1.00

All these books are available at your local bookshop or newsagent, or can be ordered direct from the publisher. Just tick the titles you want and fill in the form below.

Prices and availability subject to change without notice.

〰〰〰〰〰〰〰〰〰〰〰〰〰〰〰〰〰〰〰〰〰〰〰〰

CORONET BOOKS, P.O. Box 11, Falmouth, Cornwall.

Please send cheque or postal order, and allow the following for postage and packing:

U.K. – One book 22p plus 10p per copy for each additional book ordered, up to a maximum of 82p.

B.F.P.O. and EIRE – 22p for the first book plus 10p per copy for the next 6 books, thereafter 4p per book.

OTHER OVERSEAS CUSTOMERS – 30p for the first book and 10p per copy for each additional book.

Name ....

Address ....

....